The Cursed

PAYBACK'S A WITCH

L.A. KENNEDY

ENTWINED PUBLISHING

PAYBACK'S A WITCH

Dedication

For Dave

Chapter One

I fumbled in the dark, my hand clearing off the edge of my nightstand as I searched for my phone. The shrill ringtone made me hate the cursed thing even more than usual. It was becoming increasingly difficult to ignore the world when it sat in the palm of our hands. I inched my eyes open and had to blink several times before they'd focus on my clock. Three in the morning was not a favorable hour to call me, especially not when I had been awake until well after midnight, pacing, scared of my nightmares. I usually slept with the ringer off on my landline and cell phone, but lately, I had kept them on. I didn't like missing a call from Miguel. He and I talked every night, me when I was going to bed and him when he was getting up for the day. The time difference worked for us. It was the distance that killed me. Mexico was a five-hour flight from home, but it felt like a world away.

Thinking it could be Miguel on the other end of the line, I reached for my phone with a smile. The call display showed an unprogrammed number. The only people who called in the middle of the night were people who wanted help moving a body and strangers who needed worse things than an alibi. In my world, it was a coin toss. Would I be digging holes for a friend or finding myself in one? That was the question of the night. Hell, that was the question of my life on a daily basis.

"Who is dead or dying?" I asked, my voice still half-asleep. I envied people who could sound pleasant and professional no matter the day or time. My assistant, Philip, was like that. But, to the chagrin of everyone lucky enough to call in the middle of the night, I wasn't that person. I was a goblin when I woke up and sounded every bit the part.

"Dr. Kyteler?" a man asked.

"This is she," I replied. "And who am I speaking to?"

"This is Father Michael from the Holy Rosary Cathedral."

"What can I do for you, Father Michael?" I asked and sat up with a groan. Churches didn't ring anyone's bell in the wee hours without a hellish reason. My money was on a loose demon or a possessed person that the church had tried and failed to exorcise. I knew the route to most churches by heart for both reasons.

"We need you to come down here," he answered.

"Right now? Do you know what time it is?" I yawned around my words. "Unless someone is dying, call my office during business hours and schedule an appointment with my assistant, Philip. If it is demon-related, there are plenty of agencies with people on shift right now, just waiting for calls like this. Hell, call the cops. They have licensed witch practitioners currently on the clock and only five minutes from you."

"Ah, yes, your assistant, Philip. He is already here," he replied. "One of your students, Ruby, I believe her name is, is at our church. She called Philip when her circle was damaged. He told her to get onto holy ground. He's mentioned a demon may be near."

"Come again?" I jerked, a jolt of panic starting and pulled back my covers. "Where is Philip?"

"Talking to the police," Father Michael replied. "We contacted them when Philip became hostile."

"Hostile?" I questioned. Philip was the last person to become aggressive. He might be built like a brick house and could probably bench press one, but *hostile*? That would be the last word I would use to describe him. "What exactly did he say to you that made you feel like you needed police assistance?"

"He began yelling at us and manhandled several of my staff, attempting to pull people into the church," Father Michael replied. "He is locking people inside."

"Shit. He wasn't being hostile, Father. He's trying to save your life." I got out of bed, swallowing my urge to yell at the poor man. "I'm getting dressed. Tell me what happened and what's going on so I know how to prepare." I put my phone on speaker and changed out of my pajamas. I pulled on my usual black outfit. It hid the blood better. I didn't own a lot of color for that reason. Between my pitiful idea of fashion and being covered in blood at the end of most days, black was my go-to.

"Ruby summoned a demon and, from what I've overheard from your assistant, the demon was too strong for her. She contacted Philip for help. He told her to get to holy ground, and Holy Rosary was the nearest church. That is all I know."

"Fuck," I whispered, checking my phone and seeing three missed texts from Philip, telling me about Ruby. He'd call me if things went south. This had gone so far south that it scraped the gates of hell.

"Do you know where she summoned the demon?" I asked.

"Cathedral Square, across the road," he replied.

"Is that ground not consecrated?" I asked.

"We try, but no, not all of it," he answered. "The kids today make it difficult for us to maintain."

"Is the demon still there?" I asked as I put on my shoes.

"Excuse me?"

"Father Michael, is the demon loose, still held in the circle, or on the part of Cathedral Square that's blessed?" I sighed through my nose, trying to calm down. When he didn't answer, my temper flared. "Do you see the goddamn demon or not? He won't be hard to miss."

"Um, I don't know," he replied. "I can go find out."

"No, don't go looking for it," I replied and shook my head. Who in their right mind would go poking around with a demon potentially running around? "Did you listen to Philip? Are you inside the church or outside?"

"Outside."

"Idiot," I muttered. A man of the cloth should know better, but they rarely did. Until they came face-to-face with a demon, they never truly believed. But by then, it would be too late, and now his ignorance would make him a tasty snack for the cursed. "Get back inside and tell the others to do the same, including the police you called. You need to ask Philip if the demon is secure or…" I was cut off by screaming in the background. The sound raised goosebumps over my entire body and answered my question. The demon wasn't contained. "Get into the church. Get back on holy ground! Run, Father Michael!"

I bolted for my front door, grabbing my black duffle bag along the way. Inside was my usual gear for exorcisms, demon cleanup and witch gear. It was nothing more than a bag of hope and prayers that I wasn't too late. From the screaming on the phone, I'd be later than I'd want to be. When it came to demons and devils, I was always too late. People were always dead before I was called.

I jumped in my car and fired it to life. The moment it started, my Bluetooth connected. The screaming played from all speakers as I drove downtown. It would be a twenty-minute drive with my hazard lights on. Aside from emergency vehicles and the odd car from shift change, the roads were dead at this hour. It being the witching hour was the only saving grace. Fewer people on the sidewalks would mean fewer people would kiss death's lips this morning when the demon did as demons do — kill everything with a soul.

I hit the Number One and gunned it. I knew the highway like the back of my hand, having traveled it daily for years. I kept eyeballing my GPS to route around any overnight road construction and emergencies. When the phone disconnected, I called Philip. I hit redial twice before he picked up. Screaming ate up the start of the conversation, not his, but everyone else's. Philip was in the middle of chaos but maintained his cool. Not much scared the guy, which is probably why he was the only assistant I've had who hadn't quit within weeks. My last assistant had put in their notice before they'd even been in the system. She had said it was uncomfortable to be alone in the same room as me. My soul made her feel sick to her stomach. *Judgmental much?* To be fair, my soul made me sick, as well. Slicing it to bits in hell had left a few scars and tainted the air with the smell of brimstone and matchsticks.

"What the hell is going on, Philip?"

"Ailis!" Philip yelled into the phone and didn't bother with niceties. "There's a demon loose. I don't know where it is. There are people dead in the streets and screaming coming from everywhere. Dear God, it's bad. Father Michael is dead. He wouldn't come inside." More screams filled my ears. "Oh, Jesus. Where are you?"

I liked that he didn't bother with a long explanation. "Ten minutes out. What am I walking into?"

"I don't know. I'm in the church, and I'm not sticking my head outside to find out," he answered. "When I got the call, I came straight into the church. I only went outside to get everyone else to come in. They wouldn't believe me when I told them all hell was about to break loose. The church wouldn't send anyone to check the circle. They didn't believe me. They called the cops, thinking I was a nut job. Most of them are still outside, Ailis, along with a few squad cars of cops. They don't have a witch practitioner with them." Philip paused, screaming for someone to step away from the door and finally cursed when they left the church.

"No one will listen to me, Doc. People are coming and going as if they won't die out there. They think they can run faster than a fucking demon." Philip yelled again at someone else about it being their funeral. The phone rustled, screaming about lawyers and lawsuits, and a door slammed shut. "Get the fuck in the corner, you idiot. You can't sue me if you don't have a head in the morning. You can't outrun a demon, for Christ's sake. If you open that door again, I'll let you go." Philip pulled the phone back to his mouth. "I left Mannix a voicemail, hoping he was on duty and could help, but he hasn't called me back."

"Jesus. If they want to dig their own graves, it's on them. It's your job to keep yourself out of hell, not to make sure everyone else sees tomorrow," I replied and tried to think through the problem. "I'm almost there, Philip. I can see the police lights. Stay inside. Get to the head of the church and hunker down. Do not step outside until it's over. I don't care what you hear, if someone tries to leave or if the demon makes promises, do not inch a single toe out of that church."

"Same drill, different monster," he replied. "I'm sorry I didn't call you sooner. I didn't know Ruby actually summoned anything until I was already here."

"It's okay, Philip. Who would have known this would happen?" I replied. I would have known the minute she called me, but I assume the worst in people. People make bad decisions every day, including myself. But telling him he missed something wasn't going to help the situation. "Did Ruby tell you who she summoned? Higher level or lower? We may need backup."

"Yes, a lower-level demon, some murderer from a couple decades ago. She said she called him to ask questions for a paper she's writing for her sociology class."

"What?" I couldn't keep the surprise from my voice.

"She wanted a better grade, she said," he replied. "She thought if she had a few quotes from the main man, in his words, it would increase her grade percentage. She was showing off, and now we all get to hear and see the psycho firsthand."

"I hope it was worth it."

"She's dead, Ailis. The thing came up the church steps and took her. She thought she'd be safe as long as she was on the property. I tried to pull her inside, but the thing yanked her right out of my hands," Philip answered. "So, no, it wasn't worth it."

"She knew the rules, Philip. All my students do. This isn't your fault. She called on hell, and hell answered as it always does," I replied and slammed my brakes, squealing to a halt. "Do you have his name?"

"Theodor Black," Philip replied. "That is the name on the top of her notes."

"Fingers crossed, that's his real name. *Hey you*, doesn't have the same quelling power," I replied. "I'm here."

"I'm sorry, Doc. Be careful. I'll clean you off the road when it's over," he said, and I disconnected the call.

I parked a block from the church and grabbed my duffle from the backseat. I pulled out my bible, holy water and bags of herbs to have in my pocket for quick reach. I hung a hex bag around my neck and climbed out of my car on wobbly legs. Even if the demon was lower-level, I didn't like touching hell in any way. When you dipped your fingers into the pits, they always reached back. I cursed out loud. My aura had just fully healed from Mexico, and I was about to skin off a chunk because someone wanted a better grade. I once said mankind would be the doom of us all, and tonight was an excellent example of how quickly we were nose-diving into the end of days.

Up the road from my car bodies were sprawled on the ground, staining the slushy end of winter. The blood was brilliant under the street lights. It looked like the church had just gotten out with the number of people in the streets. People were strewn like trash, dead and twisted. I blinked away fresh tears and said a quick prayer for their souls. I scanned the area and cursed at how wide of an impact the demon had made so far. Demons were like bombs, killing everything for blocks wherever they first landed.

I pulled my bag on like a backpack and jogged up the road, feet already wet from melting snow, while I sliced the palm of my hand. It wouldn't take a lot of blood, just enough to drip a circle. At the intersection between the church and their small park, I stopped in my tracks. Ahead, in front of the church, stood the demon in question. I swallowed my scream. I might have the ability to send him back, but I was terrified.

The demon in question, Theodor Black, was somewhat clothed. Bits of old and stained fabric hung from his burned body. When he died, he had been burned, going into hell blistered and melted. He turned his scarred face to me and smiled. His nose was gone, leaving behind a raw hole. His lips, what remained of them, were thin and scorched. A shiver ran from my head to my toes. I swallowed my gag.

A thunder in the clouds rolled down the corridor, followed by a deafening silence. The nauseating stench of cooked flesh, decay and sin hung in the air like smog. The scent of burnt meat soured my stomach. With twenty feet between us, I was the only soul standing between his heaven and hell. His massive pupilless eyes stared at me with agonizing spite that made my throat flex, trapping a scream before it could break loose. I whispered a prayer that if I died in an intersection of downtown Vancouver, I'd take this beast of hatred and hell with me.

I dripped my circle of protection. *Tutela*, I thought, feeling my magic take root and flare my circle to life. I breathed in through my nose and out my mouth, clearing myself of the nausea that rolled through my gut when I pulled energy from my aura. My vision pulsed with my newfound headache. I wiped my sweaty palms on my pants, cleaning away the stickiness of blood and power that coated my hands.

The air in my circle carried the smell of my mother, ozone and matchsticks. The scent grounded me. I opened my bible to a random page and began to read out loud. It didn't really matter what I read as long as it came from the one book they hated the most. When I read from the bible, it caused the demon pain. When Miguel read from his worn bible, his absolute and unwavering faith could send a lower-level demon back to hell without the need for all the blood and pain I was soon to experience. I was a work in progress when it came to faith. Miguel was born into the arms of grace and had never once faltered from his beliefs.

My words carried on the breeze like whisps of a flame, starling the demon. A shriek escaped from his scarred mouth in unfathomable agony. Holy words were another fire for the creature to burn in. He turned his body fully toward me. His jerking steps gave me enough warning to know I'd be leaving pieces of my skin on the concrete. He wasn't just contained violence. He was hurried energy and death, waiting to pounce. He was on a clock, and he knew it. The demon became more and more menacing with every tick on that clock. He gave me his back and took two more steps toward me.

"Stop!" I screamed at the top of my lungs and held out my hand toward him.

The demon tried to move again and failed. I frowned. I should not have been able to control him without using his name unless I had been the one to summon it. I released tendrils of my aura, tasting the world around me. I could sense an imprint of myself in the air, following it back to a ruined blood circle in Cathedral Square. Someone had used something of mine to help invoke the summoning circle. I pulled my aura back in, along with the whisps of power rolling off the demon. Why borrow energy from hell when it was free for the taking?

I would have one chance at this, and it would be painful. I dripped more blood into the circle around me as the demon walked toward me. His hairless head jerked and twitched as if the movements had caused him pain. The skin on his neck stretched until even I winced at the strain. He tilted his head to the side as if surprised I wasn't running like the others had. My feet shuffled as I forced myself to remain in one place.

"Ailis Petronilla Kyteler." His words hurt my ears. It was like nails on a chalkboard and raked down my nerves. "There is a clock on your back. Tick-tock, bitch. We will never stop coming for you. You have something of ours, and we want it back."

"But *your* time is up today. Mine is not," I replied. "If you all didn't want me to learn the secrets of hell, you shouldn't have spoken them so loudly near a witch not fated to be caged just yet."

"Your time will come, and next time, you won't walk out," he answered.

"Same song you all sing," I answered. "Now, we can do this the easy way or the painful way. You can leave willingly or with force. You've had your fun, got your pound of flesh, and now it's time to go."

His laughter was all the answer I'd need.

"Theodor Black," I called his name, and the first flicker of fear flashed across his melted face. I braced myself for what would come next. "*Propello*, Theodor Black. I command you back to hell, to never return again."

Energy burst from my soul, and I was thrown across the pavement on my back. I was thankful I had left my duffle on, or I'd have left chunks of flesh on the road. The demon was on me before I had even seen him move. He was ready for the fight, but I was prepared for the attack. Demons did nothing the easy way, and the lower-level ones always kicked up a storm on their way home. His nails dug into my arms as we struggled. He sat up and raised both hands, bloody claws waiting to come back down, slashed through the air. I smashed the bottle of holy water into his side, the glass cutting us both. I flipped him off and watched him twist on the ground like an eel in a pan. The smell filled my nose, and I vomited on top of him. Burned flesh, demon or not, smelled the same to me—absolutely disgusting. With fresh blood dripping down my arms, I rolled to my feet and stepped around the screaming demon, dripping my blood on the ground. With a final drop of blood, I closed the circle, holding him inside.

"*Dominus reget me,*" I started my prayer in Latin. "The Lord is my shepherd."

"I will see you soon," he said, getting to his knees. "You're cursed, just like the rest of us."

"Until then, go to hell," I replied. I gave him the middle finger while I sent him back to hell. "Don't forget your party bag on your way out." I held a ball of taint in my hand and blew it over him, sending him away. "*Discedite!*"

"You bitch!" The demon screamed as my taint coated him.

"Just returning a gift," I said and closed my eyes for what was yet to come. I loved and hated this moment. Sending him home would kick my ass all over again.

The energy of sending a demon back to the pits hit me in the chest like an invisible punch. Blurring my vision, seeing through my aura, I watched the ground open up and dozens of hands pulling the demon back down to where he belonged. The earth closed up as if all was right in the world, with a burst of energy that sent me flying. I was tossed a few feet away as the circle holding him came down, and the air filled with the stench of hell. The moment my body hit the ground, I was thankful I couldn't breathe. I stared up at the morning sky with little sparkles dancing in my vision. The sounds of the surrounding screams finally faded, replaced with ringing.

Philip was the first to lean over me. "Relax, take a few breaths, and you'll be right as rain."

I closed my eyes and calmed my body. This wasn't my first rodeo, but I still fought the panic as if it were. Slowly, I breathed in a few gulps of air and rolled onto my side, groaning. Around me, paramedics were checking on the dead. The only wounded person was me. Anyone else stupid enough to be outside the church was meat for the critters. Philip helped me to my feet and to the first ambulance. I tried to wave them off when they began cleaning my wounds.

"Don't bother closing them up," I said to the woman looking over my hand. "I'm going to have to open the wounds to clean them with holy water when I get home."

"Holy water?" she asked.

"Demon blood mixed with mine," I answered. "Between his cursed scratches and the wound on my hand, I'm in for a special bath this morning."

"Does it work?"

I crossed my fingers. "Most times, yes. The odd time, the victim waits too long, and the curse takes hold. It opens a door between the victim and the demon who infected them. After that, they need a full exorcism and a few weeks living on holy ground, drinking holy water like Gatorade."

"I got you, Doc," Philip said, helping me off the rear bumper. "I'll give you a ride home for your special bath."

I took his arm, but before we were inside my car, my skin crawled like ants dancing across my flesh. I turned and scanned the crowd of onlookers who had arrived just in time to see the bodies but not become one of them. Most people were wearing work clothes and holding briefcases and handbags. Others were hitting the gym or heading to the seawall for their morning jog. But in the back, there were three people who stood out like sore thumbs. Two men and one woman, and they had my full attention. For one, their outfits said they didn't walk to work. For two, they didn't care about the bodies on the ground, like everyone else. Their eyes were on me and not the excitement of the morning. Before I could point them out to Philip, they walked to the black town car at the end of the block and pulled away. Something told me I'd hear from them again. They would either try to hire me or would ship me Bibles for my damned soul. I had received enough holy books in the mail that I could set up my own shop. Philip had used them to make a throne in the front room of my office and propped plants up with the rest. It gave our demon wing the kind of flare it needed.

Philip sat me in the passenger side while he took the driver's seat. He cranked my seat all the way back and pulled away from the nightmare that had been our early morning. Philip rambled about Ruby while I tuned him out. I cared about the reasons, but not while my body throbbed because of them. It bothered me that Ruby was dead, along with two dozen other people, but I wouldn't allow myself to think too long about it. This is what happened when inexperienced people dabbled in dark arts. Rule number one, when summoning demons, never call something you cannot put down on your own. If it takes more than you to call it, leave the cursed thing alone. And it was clear Ruby hadn't been able to summon on her own, given the carnage left on the streets. I was sad and angry. Ruby had paid for that lesson with her life and caused the deaths of innocents while making that choice. She would wake up in a cage for that. And as angry as I was with her, my heart hurt knowing exactly where she'd end up. I pushed the image of hell, the cages and the intersection on Richards Street from my mind and stared at my hands instead. The cuts weren't severe or life-threatening, but they did leave me with the risk of demon blood in my veins.

Chapter Two

My cat was waiting for me on the front steps when we pulled into my slushy driveway. I wondered how the blasted creature got in and out of the house. When I had left, she'd been inside, sitting on the back of my couch. Philip came around to my side of the car and helped me out. As much as I wanted to slap his hand away, I couldn't manage on my own. Between the slippery walk and my body already starting to stiffen up as the adrenaline wore off, I would have faceplanted had I tried it on my own. I slowly inched my way to my front porch, careful of my footing. One misstep, and I'd start bleeding all over again. Bleeding outside with the sun down made me nervous. Lord knows what would smell me a mile away. Although daylight was inching its way overhead, mid-February was a weird time in Vancouver. The sun still took its sweet time climbing out of her slumber while the rest of us woke in the dark.

I glanced down at my flowerbeds. The mix of snow and slush kept a death grip on my garden, half wanting to sprout and the other half already dead from the latest overnight frost. The bulbs I had purchased, spelled to live through winter, were the only things that held on. My first deep breath frosted my nose, melting as I sighed. *I miss Mexico.*

"Do you need a hand with the holy water?" Philip asked.

I nodded. "I don't think I can get all of the wounds on my upper arms, and I need someone to check my back."

"I'm on it," he replied. It wouldn't be the first time he had held me down to cleanse my demon wounds, but I prayed it would be the last. I snickered to myself at the thought. *Last time. My ass.* I should be so lucky.

Once inside, Philip started my kettle. I'd want a tea after this. It would feel like pouring acid on my skin while setting myself on fire and drinking boiling water. The last time I doused myself in holy water, I'd been alone in my shower at a resort in Mexico. Those wounds hadn't been demon-related, but they had hurt like Satan himself had given me a swat.

"I'll wash up down here when I'm done getting tea ready," Philip said from my kitchen.

"See you upstairs," I called back.

While Philip prepared for after my baptism of fire, I made my way upstairs to my bathroom. One look in the mirror told me why the paramedics hadn't wanted me to go home. I didn't look like I had sent a demon back. I looked like I had crawled out of hell. I was pale as a ghost, leaning toward gray and pasty. The kind of color reserved for dead people. My torn clothes hung off my body, parts stuck to my arms and back in blood-crusted clumps. Peeling them off was going to be a special treat.

I stared at the scars on my arms from meeting the Pack in Mexico and cringed at the memories they dredged up. I stripped down the best I could and climbed into the shower. I let the water soften the parts of my shirt that were stuck to my back before pulling it off and tossing it into my sink. The water burned as soon as it touched my wounds, but it wasn't as bad as what was coming. It stung as though I were already dipping myself in holy water. Carefully, I washed the blood and dirt off before turning off the taps. I had stalled for as long as I could. Patted dry, I stood in my tub in underwear and a loose camisole. I winced from the fabric on fresh cuts when I stepped into my soaker tub. I'd be hurting even more later today when my body gave me the bill for treating her like a sack of trash to be tossed around.

"Oh, damn, Ailis," Philip said as he walked into the bathroom, clean from the blood of victims and in a fresh set of joggers and a shirt. He kept a spare set of clothes in my trunk for moments like this. "You're pretty beaten up."

"I've had better days," I replied, then smiled. "I've had much worse, though."

"Let's get this night over with," he said and started checking me head to toe.

I had nail marks on my upper arms and one scratch on my left ribcage, whether from the demon or the glass on the road, I didn't know. We'd baste my body like a turkey, just to be on the safe side. Philip already knew where all my supplies were and had come with a dozen bottles of blessed water. From the sad look on his face, I knew he wasn't just my assistant, and I wasn't his boss. He was someone I considered a friend, and he felt the same for me. Up until gaining a few new furry friends in Mexico, I'd only had two to my name. Philip and Samuel. Both I cared deeply for. Both I'd do horrible things to protect. I squeezed his hand in silent reassurance.

"Ready?" Philip asked. His voice was soft and full of pity. Usually, I didn't like when someone felt sorry for me. It made me feel weak and pathetic. But tonight, I pitied myself along with him.

"Nope," I answered, and I wasn't. Nothing could prepare me for how badly this would hurt. "You may have to hold me down for this."

He glanced at the still-healing scars on my arms. "You didn't tell me you were clawed up in Mexico."

Smooth like butter came my lies. "You fight a demon back into hell and a coven of witches and see if you don't have a few flesh wounds."

He raised his brows but asked no more questions. "Take a deep breath, Ailis. This is going to hurt like a witch."

"I know."

I sat in my tub, put a cloth between my teeth and leaned back. Philip pushed some towels behind my head in case I jerked around and brained myself on the porcelain. I nodded once and immediately regretted it. The first drizzle of water felt like my arm was being sliced with a blistering hot knife. Before the bottle was poured, I was crying, gripping his arm and begging him to stop. The second made me vomit on myself. And the third ended with Philip sitting on my hips, inside the tub, with one hand behind my head to keep me from hitting it as I thrashed. He forced my mouth open and dumped in a bottle, sealing my lips with his hand after. I had two choices. I could swallow and hurt or choke on it and hurt just the same, but I would draw this out longer. I drank it down and screamed into his palm, jerking under him. I was glad his hand covered my mouth, or he'd have heard all the nasty things I called him. He was helping me, but pain changes a person while in the moment. I went from being grateful to being hateful in an instant.

My body felt heavier and heavier as each pulse of throbbing pain coursed through my soul, searing its way through my limbs. My head lulled to the side, weighed down from the pounding in my temples. I gripped my cross and prayed, desperate for relief, any respite I could find. I had tried to ignore it, grinning and bearing it, holding on for dear life, but nothing gave me what I needed to lie there and take it. Instead, I screamed and moaned when my breath was stolen. But with only two options—take it or leave it. I took it. Perhaps against my better judgment of doing this in my bathtub and not the hospital, where they could bring me back if I died, I swallowed the pain and continued onward. Two bottles on my back stung like hot nails ripping down my spine, but I was either used to the pain or had run out of screams for the night.

I had asked Samuel once why it still hurt even though I was cursed. He had said my soul was hanging on for dear life, and it was the parts of me that were still pure that screamed to the heavens. I was more of the opinion that I had been screwed over. I had one foot in heaven and one in hell, and I suffered for them both.

When there didn't seem to be an end in sight, it was over. The last bottle felt like warm water. The first nine had done their job. "All done, Ailis."

"Oh, thank God," I moaned.

"Welcome back, Doc. I think you passed out for a few minutes there," Philip said, climbing off me. "How you doing?"

I groaned and slowly sat up, Philip's arm doing most of the work for me. "I feel like a bag of smashed assholes."

"Shower, pajamas and tea?" he asked, and I nodded.

Philip helped me out of the tub and soaked clothes and into my shower. I sat on the floor and washed the vomit from my hair. When my tea was ready, Philip lifted me out of the shower and into fuzzy pajamas and a hair towel. The tea soothed my throat, and the cookies on my plate made the world feel a little brighter. I stayed leaning forward until the nausea and headache went away, and my eyelids got heavier. If I was lucky, I'd get a few hours of sleep before the police called for a statement, and I had to get ready for class.

"I need a vacation," I said to him as he tucked me into bed.

"Oh, you enjoyed your last one so much?" Philip's laughter made me smile. It was a familiar sound that chased away the knots in my stomach. "I'll call you later to make sure you're okay."

"Thanks, Philip," I answered.

"I'm the one who should be thanking you," he replied.

"Thank you for helping me, for staying and being a friend."

"Always," he said and released a long sigh. "I'm sorry this happened."

Before he stepped away, I grabbed his hand. I could have said a million things, scolded him for missing something important, for not calling me sooner, for going to see what was going on and trying to save the day on his own, but I didn't bother telling him what I knew he had already told himself. Instead, I told him the parts he really needed to hear tonight. I told him what would settle his soul. It was needed. He stared hell in the eyes and fought to save those he could. No one could ask for more.

"I should have called for help before I went there," he replied.

"You did what I would have done," I said, and it was true. I'd have gone to investigate, not wanting to waste police time on something that could have been contained. "You saved souls, Philip, in the face of terror. Most would have run and saved themselves, but you stayed and did what you could. I'm proud of you. It could have been so much worse if you hadn't gone."

"Thanks, Ailis. I appreciate that." He squeezed my hand before tucking it back under the covers. "I'll see you later today, unless you sprout horns and a tail. In that case, I'll see you tonight. Demons, from what I've noticed, are not morning people. Come to think of it, neither are you."

"You're a funny man." I rolled my eyes. "Thanks for your help."

"You too," he answered and left me to my sleep.

I sent a quick text to Mannix Ashford, a witch practitioner attached to city police.

Please call me tomorrow afternoon.
Information about the downtown demon: the summoning circle held the blood of a natural witch and the student. I could feel it. I don't know if it was my blood, but I was able to somewhat control the demon without using his name as if it were my circle. Check donation centers for missing blood. It could be nothing, or it could be everything. If it was my blood, you already know where it came from.

I felt better knowing I had given a heads-up. If it was a dead end, I'd have wasted thirty minutes of his time. If he struck gold, I'd have wasted nothing. I had told him a version of what had happened in Mexico, leaving out the hellhounds and Pack. He knew the witches had taken my blood and given it to the vampires. I'd had to file triplicate papers for missing hereditary witch blood with my insurance broker to cover my broomsticks if things went south. If my blood turned up at a crime scene, I needed the paperwork to protect myself.

My phone hummed not even a minute later with a message from Mannix.

Thanks, Ailis. I'm still down on the scene. I'll notify the on-duty practitioner to start calling around.

The summoning circle burned up the moment you sent the demon back. There is no trace left behind for us to test, but we'll look into it. I'm going through the security footage right now. I'll let you know if something pops up on it.

I'm glad you're OK.

I'll call you later.

I'd call Miguel later, likely after the police woke me up with questions. I pulled on my sleep mask, felt Cat jump onto the bed and perch above my head, and was out cold with my hand around her tail before I could even complain about my struggles to fall asleep.

Chapter Three

I hated Mondays almost as much as I hated hell. Both felt like torture, but this Monday felt sharper than usual. I had grazed evil over the weekend and was still moving slowly because of it. I had only just returned to work after my ordeal in Mexico and was feeling like the day I landed back in Vancouver—my soul was beaten to all hell. Fresh cuts and bruises, scabs and bandages, the trademark of a practicing witch, marred me from head to toe. My body was tight, and it felt like my entire back was one solid bruise with missing pieces of skin. My morning shower felt like another round of holy water, making me start my day screaming and crying.

Fuck demons. Fuck those who brought them to the surface.

Before class, I had spent an hour picking through my grandmother's spell book, looking for something to lessen the pain, and had come away with a tea that barely put a dent in it. I hadn't had time to make a salve. Tea was better than nothing, but I'd have been happy with painkillers and a full day of sleep. I'd stop for ointment on my way home from work. If I didn't have to suffer, I wasn't going to. Even if the cream smelled like it had been scraped off the bottom of a sewer.

Limping from the parking lot and into the school, I put my pity in my back pocket. The somber mood of the school this afternoon didn't make my mood any better. If sadness had a smell, it painted the walls of the university. Every breath I took while I walked to my office felt like breathing in soup, the air thick and heavy. No one made eye contact as they gave me a wide berth. It usually didn't hurt my feelings. From day one, people got out of my way, but today, it bothered me a little. Had I not just proved I was one of the good guys?

The rumor mill had spread the news of Ruby faster than a housefire. Her summoning had caused the death of fourteen innocent people and countless injuries. There were a dozen good folks in intensive care, having been dragged into the church by Philip. Had it not been for Philip, more would have died. Security footage had been leaked of Philip carrying two people over his shoulders, running up the steps of the church, taking three at a time, and a demon tearing his way up the stairs behind him. Philip did this over a dozen times, waiting for help to arrive.

I had watched each of the videos when the police came over for a statement in the early morning hours. It wasn't their first trip out to my house, and it likely wouldn't be their last. I cried the entire time the videos ran, listening to the carnage and Philip's prayer echoing through the streets. The look of fear on his face made me sick to my stomach. I've been in his shoes before. He was terrified but still doing what he could to save innocents. I had always respected Philip, but I had a whole new level of esteem for the man now. He had left my house this morning feeling guilty, but he had no reason to. He could have made different choices, but he'd done what he could with the situation and saved countless souls.

In class, Philip took a round of applause gracefully. But I knew him too well to know he wasn't happy or proud. The look behind Philip's eyes said he hadn't slept since the incident. He had seen his fair share of demons, but this had been his first fight to the death. I hoped it would be his last, but I knew it wouldn't be. People in my life stood close enough to hell to smell the oil on the gates. Anyone standing next to a witch or cursed tasted the brimstone in the air around us. Working in the demon department, as the students called it, didn't help the odds.

After the police had left this morning, I answered my missed texts and phone calls. The majority were from Philip and Miguel. Seeing Miguel's name on my screen twisted my stomach into a knot. I was homesick, not for a place, but for a person. I called him as soon as I was settled back in bed with my morning coffee and cried the moment he answered his phone. My tale of meeting a demon in an intersection fell on worried ears. But that was Miguel. A worrywart. An overthinker. A true friend. He was happy I made it out alive and cringed when I filled him in on all the gory details. He had the same suspicions I had about my blood being used.

I didn't have to tell Miguel how scared I had been. He would have known. Anyone who danced with a demon shook in their boots. If they weren't terrified, they'd either wind up dead or need to be hunted themselves, eventually. Miguel's concern shifted from my close call to the feeling I had of being watched. When I had described the three people I had seen, Miguel had said they didn't sound like the Vancouver Pack. Lycan blend they don't bring attention. Standing in the daylight in a few-thousand-dollar suit and driving away in a town car wasn't Lycan style. Gaining attention in such an arrogant way, with human witnesses, would break law. Now, had they cleared the scene, as Caser had done at my resort in Mexico, Miguel would have suspected the local Pack.

We ended the conversation with another warning for me to watch my back. It could be someone trying to hire me or someone who held a grudge when I wouldn't work for them. That happened more often than not. *Hell no. Full stop. Hard limit.* I don't meddle. Rule number one. I didn't care how much money someone waved in my face. It wasn't worth it. Money didn't spend in hell, and my soul wasn't for sale. In most cases, they found someone else who hadn't already spent a lifetime in hell to do whatever they wanted. That was usually where I came in — on cleanup duty when they failed, and some monster was rampaging through my city.

After my call with Miguel, I had sent a text to Cisco.

It worked, regifting my taint to a demon. It felt more like peeling my skin off than picking at a scab, but I gave away a whole tablespoon! Thank you.

Cisco replied with a series of witch-hat emojis, broomsticks, and a thumbs-up.

You can skin your soul off but can't take a tiny scrape?
I forgot how delicate you level-one witches are.
That Witch doesn't kill you, makes you stronger.

I sent him a middle finger emoji but smiled at his pun.

You're an ass.

Cisco's following texts involved him correcting my previous message to include the word 'fine' before 'ass'. I left him on read and walked to my lecture hall with a grin. Cisco had this way of making me smile, even when I was feeling like I had been beaten down with a baseball bat carved in hell.

After a series of texts with Mannix that brought no new information, no missing donations and an agreement to have all hereditary witch blood destroyed, I stood at the front of my class, discussing the three pillars of occultism — alchemy, astrology, and ritual magic. The better part of the class was focused on the basic rules of summoning after Ruby's name came up in conversation more times than could be ignored. I wanted to hammer it home, once again, that hell played games we could never win. Trading even one second of freedom for every wish granted wasn't worth it. Time moved differently there. It meant nothing to the cursed. One minute could stretch for eons to the soul. Nothing on this side of the gate was worth one second on that side of it. And as I said the words, I looked each of my students in the eyes to see who I'd have to ask to stay after class. Those who weren't scared, needed to be. Demons played for keeps. People died when they tried to best demons and devils.

"Alex Martins, you have a question?" I asked when his hand went up and back down. His teeth were back in place after he had summoned a tooth fairy and lost four to the little creature just a month ago.

"Rumor has it Ruby summoned a lower-level demon. How did she lose control of a lesser demon? Aren't they weaker? Didn't she have a circle set?"

"Much weaker, which should tell you how utterly strong a higher demon would be," I replied. "Just because they have their own power structure doesn't mean they are weaker than us, merely weaker than their brethren. Regardless of what was called forward, a circle doesn't guarantee safety. It helps, but there are things a circle can't keep out, powers that won't so much as pause at our circles. When someone untrained attempts to call forth a demon, they are tempting fate. In truth, whether you're trained or not, thinking a circle will save you will likely cost you your life. When quelling a demon, sending back what you've called, your circle may come down. Hell answers our call for their own, and most times, you break your own circle with the sheer force of hell claiming their demon back."

Alex frowned. "You used a circle in Mexico, and it worked. I watched the news reports."

I groaned internally. Last week, when I returned, I'd fielded dozens of questions from my class, who had heard about what happened to me on my vacation. I'd lied my way through the questions then, just like I would today.

"As I had mentioned, the cost to keep my circle standing was my aura. The aura of a full-blooded witch wasn't enough to keep safe," I answered. "I almost died that night, and I wasn't even the one who knocked on the gates to hell. Had it not been for the local authorities finding me bleeding out, I'd have died."

"If Ruby would have used more aura in her circle, could she have contained it?" he asked.

I shook my head. "No. Ruby was an earth witch, not hereditary. Her earth spells wouldn't have worked. It is why only certain types of witches are granted a license to summon and quell a demon. It takes years of study and approval from the Coven before you can even begin studying for licensing. Even with approval, Coven status, and a license, I will repeat my warning from the first day of class — do not summon for any reason."

"Why the hell are we here if we're not going to learn how to protect ourselves from hell?" His question triggered laughter throughout the room. It pissed me off.

"I am teaching you to protect yourself, not dig around in hell until something pops up."

"This class isn't teaching us anything we can't learn on the internet," he replied. "What am I learning here?"

"You tell me, Alex." I swallowed my urge to yell at him. "Did you enjoy your little taste of the weakest demon from hell when something smaller than your hand had the ability to hold you down and chew the teeth from your mouth? Had it not been for your mother, who learned the techniques I'm teaching you, the tooth fairy would have taken all of your teeth, and you wouldn't have survived the ordeal."

He glared. "How was I supposed to know?"

"By paying attention to the class you're bitching about," Philip said, leaning on my desk to my right. His eyes zeroed in on Alex, who shrunk in his seat. "Tooth fairies were covered on day two, Martins. Nothing down there can be called forward safely. That's the point Dr. K is trying to make. It doesn't matter how skilled you are, how much training you have, what blood runs in your veins, or what your intention was. When you fuck around, you find out, and the rest of us have to dig through dead bodies to get to you. When you poke at hell, you kill people with that curiosity." Philip visibly shivered. "If you're here to learn how to screw with hell and live, you know where the door is. Get the hell out. This class isn't for that shit. Dr. K teaches you how to survive, not be the reason others don't. Here, you learn how to sense the coming doom and what to do to keep your soul out of hell. You're here for decades of shared knowledge, to stay alive, not to use it for summoning. And when you stop paying attention to the warnings given, you die, and you take innocents with you. And I, for one, am tired of knocking on the doors of your loved ones to explain why you're dead. It's always the same reason — you didn't take this seriously enough."

"Sorry," Alex whispered. He had the decency to look ashamed.

I took over before Philip could keep browbeating my students. "To put it in a simple context, humans are nothing more than blood-filled piñatas when it comes to hell. A few good whacks, and we're done for it. No amount of training can prepare you for coming face-to-face with a demon. It is absolutely terrifying, even for me. I've been in plenty of situations where I forget what the hell to do. My fear takes over, and my brain checks out. A decade of muscle memory is the only thing that's saved my soul on many occasions."

"Not that I want to summon one, but I have a question," Sandra, to my right, piped up, looking at Philip, who nodded. "How can you control one, and she could not? Was it something specific, or did something go wrong?"

"Years of study and the sheer will of God helped me quell the demon," I replied. "Summoning one is what went wrong. Plain and simple, demons are stronger than we will ever be. It's why witch practitioners rarely work alone unless they are level-two or higher. It takes the ability to spool massive amounts of power to quell a demon and send one back. Unless you can hold that much energy, it fries your aura," I answered and added a caveat, "Just because we can summon doesn't mean we can control what comes up or have the power needed to send it home. We literally have no way of truly knowing what we're bringing up. What we think we're calling is never what crawls out of hell. Our mortal minds simply can't comprehend the horror of hell. Which is why I do not summon, not to mention the taint I'd earn. There is nothing I want bad enough to call a demon from hell."

"Not even your life?" Sandra asked.

"Not even that," I answered. "Summoning taints our auras. Spending eternity and a day in hell isn't worth the extra life we're given up here."

She leaned forward. "What did it cost to send back the demon Ruby called?"

"Bathing in holy water," I replied, and the room groaned. "I wish that was the worst part. That demon now knows my name, and if he ever pops back up and gets loose, he'll come knocking on my door. That is the price of hell. One touch is all it takes. They don't forget your name, and they hold grudges. Having your name on their mind is not a safe place to be."

"Why not wait for the police-issued witch practitioner if it puts you at risk?"

"People were dying, and I'm a licensed practitioner. The Good Samaritan law includes licensed witches helping at the scene of a demon attack. Part of a witch's licensing requirements states we must stop and assist until help arrives." I felt a lump start in my throat as flashes of memory flooded my rattled brain. "Regardless of the legalities or personal risk, had Philip or I waited, more would have died. It is one of the many downsides to becoming a licensed witch or practitioner. I've said this all before, but this isn't a field you go into without heavy thought and reflection. Your soul will be at risk every day. Do not take it for granted. If you're going to go for licensing, shadow someone attached to the police force. You'll get a front-row seat to what mankind calls up from the pits."

"Thank you for answering my questions," Sandra said, her face a little more haunted than at the start of class. "This really is the only class where we're told the truth. No one else takes it as seriously. Though, no other profs have spent time in hell."

"Sometimes even experience isn't enough. Going to hell didn't make me a better witch, but it did give me a good idea of what we're yanking out of the pits for foolish reasons." I shifted to an example to prove my point. "Do you all recall the incident in Venezuela last year, a demon killed two hundred people before he was quelled?" I got a few nods, but primarily blank faces. "Allow me to demonstrate what went wrong, what four powerful witches didn't know, even after decades of experience and training." I stepped to the middle of the room, between my desk and podium, where I had a circle etched into the floor. "Knowledge is power. Knowledge will keep you alive. Knowing you're at risk from *everything*, with and without a soul, the moment you need a circle could save your life. But sometimes, such as in Venezuela, a circle won't be enough," I said and glanced around the room. "Allow me to show you why Ruby died, how I could die, how four of the Coven's most powerful witches died, and how all of you in here could die. I need a volunteer. Nothing will happen. It's merely to show you what I mean."

Alex raised his hand, and with a nod, he moved to the middle of the room. "What do you need, Dr. K?"

I pulled off one of my bandages and brought a small swell of blood to the surface, setting the circle. It was weak, barely holding on. I used the same amount of power one of my students could muster. It was barely enough for my aura to notice. "Cross my circle, Alex."

He frowned and stepped forward. It took him a few moments and a shove of his aura for my circle to flare. With force and a few grunts, he finally crossed it. "Now what?"

"Exactly, now what? What do I do now? I would have to fistfight you to protect myself. And if there were four of you, I'd never be able to defend myself. I'd be bagged and tagged." I motioned for him to return to his seat. "In Venezuela, four highly powerful and fully trained witches, level-three Coven members, were killed when the demon sent dark art witches to bring down their circles. Sure, if I were to have fully set my circle of protection, you wouldn't have been able to cross it, Alex. But would my circle stand against four high-level dark witches? Those who sold parts of their souls to have powers the rest of us will never have? I have my doubts. And if I couldn't hold them back, how would I defend myself against dark witches and demons? I'd die. I'd never be able to protect myself against them. Or, in Hong Kong, a demon sent a child to take down the circle. The witch wasn't willing to kill the child and allowed their circle to drop just enough to pull the kid inside. That fraction of a second was enough for the demon to kill the witch and the child."

"What does this prove?" Alex questioned, his tone as irritating as his questions had been.

"That, in the end, keeping your fingers out of hell is the only way you can avoid having to deal with a demon. Hell is smarter, craftier, and so bloody ruthless. They don't care who they kill, and we simply do. What we have at our disposal to protect ourselves won't always work. It doesn't matter if we are level-three or kitchen witches. It won't always be enough," I answered. "Keep your nose out of demon business, save who you can, and pay attention. That is how you survive. That is the only way you can survive. When we go looking for trouble, we find it. But when it comes to hell, they find us."

The class sat in complete silence. When my words had failed to convey the message, my show had certainly hammered it home. Some would heed my warning. Some would be dead before they learned the lesson. I couldn't save them all, but I could give them the skills they needed to stay alive. The rest was up to them. Once the fear settled, I could pick out the students who would be dead before they earned their degrees. Those too curious would suffer the consequences. I made a few notes and passed them on to Philip. Four students to keep a close eye on and bump out of my class. Alex Martins was at the top of the page. I'd pass the same names on to Mannix for him to keep tabs on. I wouldn't give anyone the tools they needed to skip to the end of their story any faster than they were already heading, and Alex was a beacon for hell.

My desk timer went off, signaling the end of our class. I eyed the seating chart and glanced to the back right. "Noah Hudson, please stay after class. You just transferred in. I'd like to review upcoming assignments."

He stood and jogged down the stairs. The closer he got to me, the more I wanted to take a step back. The energy that poured off him reminded me of standing too close to Miguel when he was upset, only a watered-down version. Noah had been watching my every movement. He didn't ask questions, add to the conversation about Ruby, or bother to take notes. I knew what he was the moment he walked into my classroom.

"Thank you for accepting my transfer request, Dr. Kyteler," Noah said as soon as he got to my desk.

"I didn't," I replied and waited for the room to clear out. "Why would you drop your ethics class for this one?" I held his file and glanced over his papers. "All of your classes are pre-law. Why take this one?"

"With the way of the world, I thought this would give me a leg up."

"Uh-huh. Riiight." I drew out the word and rolled my eyes. "You and I both know why you're here, Noah. How about we skip the crap and get to the good part?"

"I'm sorry, I'm not sure what you mean?"

"Tell your head honcho that if he has questions, he can make an appointment to see me himself," I replied. "As for you, I'm denying your transfer. But since I feel bad for the situation you've been put in, I'll put in a request for you to get back to your original schedule."

"Please, Dr. Kyteler, I *need* to be in this class." Noah gripped the edge of my desk. The air around us prickled. He looked like a dog about to be hit by a car.

"I'm sorry, Noah." I shook my head. "You can tell your guy that I kicked you out. You're pre-law. You're taking up space for a class you don't need or even want."

"You don't understand," he stammered, as though he were trying to think of something he could say to convince me. "I spoke to your assistant, Philip, and he said all my papers were in order."

"I don't care what Philip told you. The last I looked, it was my name on the door, not his. This is my class, and I decide who takes it," I replied. "If you were here because you genuinely cared about taking my class, I'd be fine with it. But you don't want to be here anymore than I want you here. You added nothing to our group discussions. Hell, you looked bored more than once, during times we were talking about someone dying. If you're not going to pay attention to the actual class you've transferred into, why would I allow you to take up space?"

He leaned over my desk. "If you kick me out, I've failed. Please don't send me back to my...*honcho* as a failure. I'm begging you. Please. I'll keep my head down. I won't cause any problems for you. I won't fall asleep. I'll do whatever you need me to do. Just don't kick me out, please."

I thought about it for a moment. Being that low in the Pack must be damn scary. I wasn't even in the Pack, and I was terrified of pissing one off. "What happens if I kick you out? And skip the bullshit, please. We'll get to the end of this faster if we stop beating around the bush. We both know wolves are sitting in that bush, waiting to bite us."

"It'll hurt. I'll be hurt," he answered. "I'm only here for three years while I'm in school. I'm not a fighter, Dr. Kyteler. I don't have anyone to protect me here, and I'm not strong enough to protect myself. I'm already at the bottom. Any lower, and I'm in the ground. I just want to finish school and go the hell home, where they don't make me do this shit."

"What about the class you dropped?" I asked.

"I moved it to an evening class, rather than dropping it," he replied. "I don't want to spend another day in this city than I have to."

"Why were you sent to my class?"

"To keep an eye on you, that's all. I swear, nothing more. People are curious of the witch who has the..." He glanced over his shoulder. "Protection of Mexico. They've never given their protection to a human before. The local Pack is curious, that's all."

"Curiosity kills," I replied, but nodded. "If you cause me any grief, you're gone. If someone else needs your seat, you're out. Are we clear? I'll do what I can to help you out, but I can't screw over another student because your Lycaon is snooping around."

His body relaxed. "Yes, of course. Thank you, Dr. Kyteler."

"Oh, don't thank me yet. If I'm scratching your back, you're sure as hell scratching mine," I answered, and he blanched. "Information pays for your seat, Noah, not my good heart. Why has your Lycaon not approached me, if he's so damn curious?"

"You have the protection of Caser and Miguel. That alone keeps Pack at bay," he replied. "Everyone has heard of the Los Luna Pack and how absolutely ruthless they are when it comes to law. They don't bend, they don't negotiate, and the only payment they'll accept is death." H leaned in closely, his voice hushed. "We've all heard of Sofia challenging a hellhound and winning. No one is stupid enough to approach you directly, not when Sofia, the second of the Guardians, has given you, a human, her protection. I've met her. She's fucking terrifying. It took the threat of being sent home for me to even step into your class."

"She's not that bad," I replied, and he shook his head in disagreement. To be fair, Sofia *was* terrifying, but she'd grown on me, and she reminded me of myself. Crusty on the outside and soft on the inside. It was just hard to see beyond the razor wire and death threats. "All right, Noah, if anyone asks, I called you to the front to discuss the curriculum and upcoming assignments. We didn't have this conversation. You keep your mouth closed, and so will I." I passed him a course outline. "There's a paper due in two weeks. It's listed on the second page. Good luck. I feel like you'll be needing it."

"I hate this god-forsaken city," he replied, using his shirt to wipe the sweat from his brow. He had been sweating bullets since I had called his name.

"The city isn't forsaken, just those who gamble with their souls," I replied.

He grabbed the papers from my hand and scurried from my class. I packed up my books and headed through the side door into the hall. As with every other time I walked through the school, people avoided crossing my path. Most professors could have used a semester in my class. It would help dispel the notion that merely being polite to me would damn them to hell. To be fair, if a monster was working at the school, I'd probably give notice to the Dean, packing up altogether. Ignorance was alive and well in us all. Fear was a bitch to overcome.

Chapter Four

I pushed open the doors to my wing, which was a stretch of the word. There was a small office, taken up by Philip, with a short hall that led to my cramped office at the end. I didn't care how little room we had been given. I was just happy I had a space at all. If it wasn't for the donations my department brought in, I'd likely still be grading papers in the cafeteria. I glared at Philip as soon as I stepped into his office. I tried to keep the look from my face and failed. How was he to know.

"You know the rules, Philip, no transfers without my approval," I said as I closed his laptop.

"You've never enforced that rule, Doc," he said without looking up. He opened his laptop back up and went continued to work. "Professor Franklyn asked me for a favor, and I obliged. You never know when you'll need a lawyer in your back pocket. With the way you're always skinning your ass off on the cement, I'm sure you'll thank me later."

"I'm all in favor of a lawyer owing our department, but please run them past me from now on. I want to screen students before giving them the tools to kill a dozen people," I replied, my mind on Alaric Franklyn, one of the law professors. I wondered if he was part of Pack or if he was intertwined without even knowing it.

"Ruby wasn't your fault, Ailis." Philip stopped typing and finally lifted his head. He had this way of seeming sad without changing his expression. It was all in the eyes, and if you cared enough about a person, you noticed those subtle shifts. "You didn't teach her anything she couldn't learn with a few clicks on the net. Even Alex pointed that out. You're no more to blame for her summoning a demon as you would be if she had pulled a loaded gun in that church. She made deadly choices, and people paid for them. But it was Ruby who made those decisions, not you."

I sighed and finally nodded. "Thanks, Philip. I think I needed that. Class was rough today."

"I already passed the names on to Mannix, who said he'd input them into their system," Philip added. "He said the last three students I had mentioned to him were found trying to purchase summoning supplies and sentenced by the Coven."

I groaned but was thankful they'd been found before they'd been able to do any damage. "I think I need to call it a day and do my grading at home. It feels like I haven't slept in days."

"Sorry, Doc, but your next meeting is already waiting in your office," Philip called out as I poured a coffee. I lifted the pot in a silent offer, and he shook his head. He wasn't the coffee guzzler that I was. Philip flipped through my paper agenda. I liked a hard copy, while he always transferred the information back and forth from his online calendar. "A Mr....Conor Madden."

"What meeting?"

"It's been on your calendar for two weeks," he replied. "The upcoming charity event the university is hosting, you're meeting with a new benefactor. He's willing to donate to our department, but he won't donate until he meets you. Apparently, he wants to see where his money is going." He rolled his eyes. "As if we'll see a red penny."

"Shit, I forgot." I sighed. "Why is he donating to our department? Most sane people want to stay the hell away from, well, hell. Does he have a cursed sister? A demon banging on his door? A ghost?"

"From what he's said, his wife and two children had a brush with the cursed. Our work is close to his heart, or so he says. But if I'm going with my gut, I wouldn't be surprised if this didn't come with the same old strings, quid pro quo. He coughs up some cash, and you risk your life and soul in return."

"Sounds about right." I sipped my coffee. It tasted like a kiss from God himself. I glanced at Philip in his ridiculously expensive ergonomic chair. I had purchased it in hopes he'd never leave me. I was not above bribery. Philip was worth every penny. "How is it you can go through hell and bounce back like it didn't even happen? You look like how I wished I felt."

"If I lived off of coffee and cookies, I'm sure I'd look and feel like shit, too."

I frowned. "Did you just say I look like shit?"

"Yep," he answered with a grin. "I treat my body like the temple it is. Unlike you, who treats her body like a meth lab. When was the last time you had a glass of water or ate something not made of pure sugar?"

I lifted my mug. "Hot water, right here. And I have an apple in my bag."

He rolled his eyes. "Get moving, slowpoke. It's going to take you an hour to shuffle down your hall," he teased, and it was everything I needed to feel normal. "Also, they died. Both his wife and children. So don't bring it up unless you can get a few extra bucks out of him."

I chuckled at the comment and left Philip to his typing and checking whatever new dating app he had on his phone. His phone was constantly beeping with matches, likes, and connections. I couldn't keep up with the lingo he used. He had once tried to convince me to use an app to get over Miguel. Four conversations later and I'd deleted the app, cringing at how far we had fallen as a society and swearing I'd never date again. I had learned a new phrase from one unlucky fool—booty call. *As if.* I might treat my body like a meth lab, but it wasn't on fire yet.

As Philip had teased, it had taken me a few minutes to make it to my office. Every step felt like my cuts were reopening, making me pause, slow down and curse hell all over again. I kicked myself in the ass for not leaving home earlier this morning. I should have stopped in to buy some ointment from a local witch, a friend of Samuel's, before work. It stank to high heavens, but I'd rather smell like a public bathroom at Taco Fest than wince every time my shirt moved, or I breathed too suddenly.

At my door, my necklace pulsed, and I paused. Whoever sat on the other side was someone I didn't want to meet. I wasn't foolish enough to think I was safe in public, but monsters weren't as stupidly brave as I was. At worst, they'd threaten me. Death in broad daylight, in public, wasn't the usual way bad guys did business, and I hadn't done anything recently to have those types of bad guys at my door. On tired legs, I stepped into my office to find my appointment sitting across from my desk, seated nonchalantly, but with an air of authority that even I felt when I stepped into the room.

"Mr. Madden, sorry to keep you waiting," I said as I walked across my office to the other side of my desk.

I flopped my books and papers onto the growing stack, taking up a permanent place on the surface. I didn't need the pulse of my charm necklace to tell me trouble sat a few short feet away from me. My eyes scanned the room as I moved through it, taking in the energy I could feel. The hairs on the back of my neck stood. It felt like being watched a little too closely. It was a familiar feeling.

Conor Madden looked like he sweated dollar bills, but he was dressed casually. Yet something about him said he didn't tie his own shoes. He had one woman with him, who held a notebook and pen, poised and ready to jot down his commands. A man stood beside the door. Without a second glance, I knew he was the muscle. He looked like he was the doorman. No one gets in, and no one gets out unless he agreed. I gave him a once over, and in turn, he did the same. His lack of reaction said he hadn't dealt with a full-blooded witch before since he hadn't flinched even once.

"Ailis, thank you for seeing me." Conor stood and held out his hand.

"Dr. Kyteler," I corrected him. I shook Conor's hand and pulled mine away quickly, rubbing it on my pants. He grinned but said nothing. His aura felt awful, like too many evil deeds done, staining his soul.

"Dr. Kyteler, thank you for seeing me." He revised his introduction. Normally, that would have earned him brownie points, but not after feeling the taint on his soul.

He took a seat, and I sat at my desk. I didn't offer him a coffee. I spent thirty dollars on a truckload of beans. I doubted it would be to his taste. I glanced at his second and third bananas, each ready to do whatever it was they did when they were hauled out for action. I smiled. I had seen them all before, this morning, at the church. But I'd play their charade for as long as they wanted. I was curious as to why they had been watching me, but not enough to poke at it while I was shut in a room with them.

Most would give Conor the benefit of the doubt — he could have merely been seeing where his money would be going — but I wasn't most people. I gave no one the benefit of the doubt. Mankind really didn't deserve to be presumed innocent. We rarely were. And from the knot in my stomach, neither was Conor.

"You mentioned you wanted to meet before you donated?" I asked. "We could have met at the function and saved you the trip out to my office."

"I've come to the last four and have yet to see you," he answered. "Your seat is always taken up by your assistant. Had I wanted to meet your assistant, I'd be sitting across from his desk and not yours."

"Fair enough," I replied, internally wincing that I wasn't going to be able to shove this conversation onto Philip's lap as I had planned. I worked damn hard to get out of fundraisers. I wasn't a people person and definitely not a toy to pull out for functions. The school had learned the hard way, years ago, when they had tried to force me to dress up and dance for them like a puppet. It had gone badly enough for them to forward invitations straight to Philip, bypassing me entirely.

"Your donation is very generous and surprising. Not many make such a substantial contribution without strings attached. So, Mr. Madden, what are the strings attached? Will I be working in the Madden wing come next semester? Do you have a family member needing to cut the line for my class? What is it that you want, all wrapped up in a pretty expensive bow?"

"Straight to business, I appreciate that." He smiled.

"I'm not a fan of being out after dark. The sun will be setting in three hours, and I like to be home well before that." I glanced at my watch. Three hours until the creepy crawlies came out to play. That first hour, when the sun set, felt like waiting for something awful to happen.

"Some of my best deals have been made when the sun has gone down," he replied.

"What you do on your own time is none of my business, nor do I want it to be," I answered. "But just the same, if we could get *straight to business*, I would appreciate it."

"The donation is not from me, Dr. Kyteler," he replied. "We all have someone we answer to, and my boss would like a meeting with you. He is interested in having a conversation before handing over such a large amount of money."

I swallowed my urge to groan. "Can I ask why he would like a meeting, and why he sent you instead of coming himself?"

"Julian is…cursed, as you'd call it, and has issues with the sun," he answered. "But I don't presume to ask the Master of the City why he…"

"Get out." I stood and pointed to my door. *Vampires. You've got to be kidding me.* "You can tell Julian he can take his money and shove it where I wished the sun could shine."

Conor's laughter filled the room. "I see you've heard of him."

"Leave now," I replied and reached for my phone. "Or I call for security."

He reached for his inside jacket pocket, and I stepped back, eyeballing the door. I'd never get past the goon with all the muscles and menace. I took another step back and prepared to dig my nails into the palms of my hands. I stood on a circle of protection carved into the wood flooring. A force of habit. The circle wouldn't do me any good when a bullet came flying.

"Do you like having a soul, Mr. Conor?" I asked, coiling energy in my palms. His eyes went to my hands. "You're not going to enjoy what's coming next. I promise you that much."

"I'm not pulling a gun, Dr. Kyteler. I'm reaching for my checkbook," he said, moving slower.

"I don't care what you're grabbing. Get the hell out of my office before one of us starts screaming," I replied. "I don't meet with the cursed. Not now. Not ever. Not for any reason."

"Come now. You, yourself, are cursed," he replied. "Doesn't your own religion teach you not to cast stones?"

"Get out."

"Half the money now for this meeting and the other half, when and if you meet with Julian," he answered. "If anything, accept this money as an offering of his sympathies. He would like to extend his apologies for his child's behavior in Mexico, that is all."

One of Julian's children, one that he made with his very own fangs, had set up a blood den in Mexico and slaughtered countless underaged women. Before I'd left Mexico, two Pack members and I had stopped in for a visit. It had ended in ash and fire, and me with road rash on my back. Julian's child was my first vampire hunt and kill. Meeting with his maker was not high on my list. Vampire or not, killing someone's child tended to leave a sour taste in their mouth, and I wasn't about to risk finding out how forgiving Julian was.

"No, thank you," I replied and stepped away from my desk, as calm as I could be. I kept my eyes on the man who bench pressed more than my weight. He didn't so much as flinch, but his eyes tracked my movements as if he were waiting for a reason to grab me. Once my hand touched my office door and I pulled it open, I felt my chances of survival had increased ten-fold.

I walked out of my office and into the hall, in earshot of Philip. "Thank you for stopping by, Mr. Madden. I'm sure the university would be grateful for the donation, but I'm not able to assist you. I do hope you consider donating to another department should you change your mind."

Conor fought a snarl and stood. He didn't look like the type to be told 'no' all too often. His ego wasn't my problem. *Yet.* He stopped at my front and shook his head. "Don't be a fool, Ailis. Meet him on common ground or find yourself below it. He doesn't do well with rejection."

"Is that why you've been following me?" I asked.

He nodded. "Right now, you're being invited. The next time, it won't be as pleasant. It will end, as you say, with someone screaming. I'd wish for those screams not to be yours."

I gave him my best professional smile, devoid of all emotion. It was more than he deserved. I didn't like being threatened, however low-key it had been. "If Julian comes near me, Conor, with my pain on his mind, he will not enjoy what I'll do to stay alive. I don't bend for monsters, and I certainly won't be threatened by one."

"I said the same thing," Conor answered. "Yet, here I am."

"I'm sorry you're here, I really am, but I'll die before I'm in your shoes," I replied.

"Those are, in fact, the only options you'll have. When he comes for you, you'll regret not going willingly. It hurts much less if you agree, but one way or another, you'll do as you're told."

"If he comes for me, I'll kill him."

"I didn't say he'd harm *you*, Ailis. There are so many other creative ways to make you fall in line, and very few of them require his hands on *your* body," he answered, and I glared. I didn't like my friends threatened, either.

"Good day, Mr. Madden."

"Do not underestimate the severity of your situation or overestimate your ability to survive it," he replied. "The next time Julian sends someone for you, they'll not be nearly as polite as I have been."

"Nor will I." I closed him out in the hall, locking myself back in my office.

I double-checked the lock twice before I walked to my desk. I was well and truly scared. I didn't underestimate a thing when it came to monsters, and Conor, while still having a soul, was one of them. At first glance, a lot could be assumed when first seeing Conor Madden. He looked non-threatening, professional, dominant, and powerful. But there were two things I'd never forget, once I looked deep enough, and it was all I had needed to know. Julian had nearly lost all of his soul, and he'd take mine from my cold, dead fingers. I didn't want to be on his bad side. Conor didn't look like the type to have many enemies. He looked like the type to kill them before it escalated to an enemy.

With shaking hands, I called Miguel as soon as I sat back at my desk. My voice shook as hard as my hands. "Miguel?"

"Lish, I wasn't expecting your call for another few hours." Miguel answered. "Is everything okay?"

"Where do I even start?" I breathed out my tension and rubbed the center of my chest, willing my heart to slow down before I passed out. "The local Pack sent one of their members to spy on me, Noah Hudson. He's a visiting wolf, or whatever they're called. I found him in my class."

"Boot him out," Miguel replied as if the answer was so simple.

"I can't kick him to the curb. If he goes back to the local Pack, a failure, they'll hurt him. He's too weak to protect himself. Hell, even I think I could kick his furry tail if I needed to."

"First, where he stands in the Pack isn't your problem. He either earns his place or earns the right to step up." His answer was so pollical, it irritated me. "Second, it's not your job to protect him. If you try, you'll have every Pack member on your front step, challenging you."

"Why would they send someone?"

"We were expecting this, Lish. The moment Pack didn't take your life to keep our secret hidden, you knew your local Pack would hear of it," he answered, and I thought back to a conversation we had before I left. He had warned me that others would come sniffing around when they found out. I carried the smell of Miguel and his wolf, and that was bound to bring the wolves circling. "The Pack is curious about you. I wouldn't worry too much about it until it becomes a problem."

"And how will I know it's a problem before it's too late?" I asked.

"If another joins your class, let me know. If they start following you around, let me know. If they're somehow in your life more than this, then it's a problem waiting to happen," he replied.

"That's the least of my worries, unfortunately. Julian, the Master of the City, just sent one of his flunkies, Conor Madden, to bribe me into a meeting with him. Apparently, Julian wants to apologize for what one of his children did in Mexico. That vampire I killed the night of the full moon. But I don't buy it. He wants more than an apology. He wants a meeting."

"Did you accept the meeting or apology?"

"Jesus, no." I cringed at the question. "I kicked the guy out of my office."

"Don't accept either the meeting or the apology, not until I find out what's going on," he replied.

"Conor and his two cronies were the three people I saw at Ruby's crime scene this morning. They've been watching me. Why come see me at all?" I asked. "Since when does a Master vampire apologize for a damn thing?"

"He either knows about your link to Pack, or he wants something you won't want to give."

I groaned. "What the hell do I do?"

"I'll see what I can find out on my end," he answered. "He won't come for you, not yet. He'll likely call you or send you a gift to get your attention. Snagging the resident witch, especially one currently in the news, is bad for business. He won't do it until he has no choice, and right now, he still has choices."

"He's got my bloody attention, all right."

"If he wanted you dead, you'd be dead. Simple as that. He wants something from you, which is why he's not just snatched you out of your bed." He called out to Cisco and told him what was happening. Cisco's slew of cursing filled my ear, and I agreed with every word. *Fucking vampires.* "Don't accept the apology, Lish. That would be like telling him all is well. It's an invitation for future contact. He'll see it as an opening into your life."

"He can see the sun for all I care. What do I do if they come back?"

"If? There is no *if*, Lish. *When* they come back, you'll have to accept, or you'll be forced. Being forced is not a pleasant experience, especially when those doing the forcing have no souls. If you accept, at the second meeting, it may buy you some time," he answered. "I suggest you give Samuel a heads-up. He would know more about the inner workings of vampires and what steps to take. Pack kill them. We don't negotiate with them."

"Most still have souls, Miguel. They're lingering and following the vampire around like tattered ghosts," I replied. "When a vampire is near, it's not the vampire I feel. It's their tortured souls."

"I wouldn't mention that to anyone else. Imagine what the Elders would do to someone other than Pack could feel their souls. They'd fear you. Being feared by the Elders is not a good thing for solitary witches." He reminded me of a warning he had given me a decade ago. Keep my mouth shut about things people fear unless you have no choice but to cause the fear. "You need to keep that part of your power locked down tighter. You risk the rest of the world knowing the full extent of your magic."

"I try, Miguel, but I can't shut a door that isn't even there. I keep my shields tight, but tortured souls scream too loud, and it gets through," I replied. In the pit of my soul, I held power others would kill for. A parting gift when I walked out of hell, the door to my full powers had been ripped off its hinges.

"I know. Ask Samuel, when you see him, to help you build stronger shields."

"I will. I'm going to stop by his house on my way home," I answered, knowing Miguel was right. I didn't need a bigger target on my back than I already had. "I'll call you when I get home. I love you."

"I love you, too. If you feel something is off when you get home, leave. Don't take any chances. Make sure your cat stays close to home for now. Pay attention to her warnings."

"I know. She's a horrible creature but a trusty familiar," I replied.

"I'll call you tonight," he said and hung up, talking to Cisco in the background.

I stopped at Philip's desk on my way out. "Did you not know who that was?"

"Conor Madden," Philip replied.

"A flunky for the Master of the City," I answered, and Philip paled. "If you ever send someone like that into my office again, you're fired. Do I make myself clear?"

"Yes, I'm sorry. I thought you knew who he was," Philip replied. "I didn't know he was here for vampire business."

"What else would he be here for, Philip? That you knew and didn't give me a heads-up pisses me off. Risk my life like that again, and you can pack your shit and grab your final check on your way out." I left him sitting there, mouth wide, eyes wider. I won't be threatened, and I won't have those I trust sending me in blind as a bat.

Chapter Five

I made one stop along the way to buy the cream that would heal my wounds as fast as a few weeks of bedrest would. But it would feel like I was healing too quickly. All the pain I'd endure throughout those weeks, I'd feel at once. No magic was free. Everything had a cost. Mairi, Samuel's friend, lived in the historical neighborhood in West Point Grey. It was a hop, skip and a jump from the university. It was the neighborhood I had grown up in. When my parents died, I'd moved in with my grandmother, who never quite liked living so far from the largest ley lines in East Van.

Mairi's house was small compared to the sprawling mansions on either side of her. Her lot was massive, but all yard. For an earth witch, her gardens were heavenly. A gate with a keypad sat at the start of her drive, with six-foot fences and twenty-foot trees surrounding the property. Nothing about coming to her house looked inviting. But once I got beyond the gate, fence, wards, and sticky magic, it smelled like this was where I was meant to be. Well-tended gardens and rambling flower beds made me get out of my car once I pulled in. I loved the walk up her drive, even if it was more of a shuffle today. I had been coming here with Samuel for over a decade, and each time I arrived, it looked a little different, as though the gardens had a life of their own and shifted around according to the space they needed. Winter might still have had a hold on Van, but here, it didn't stand a chance. It stood in perpetual summer. Not too hot, not too cold, and changed depending on the needs of her guests.

Mairi came out of her front door with a smile that lit up her entire face, her arms wide open. Her wild black hair swirled in the breeze. It was as unmanageable as my own. Her mother was from Spain, her father from Scotland. It gave her interesting features, and I loved her all the more for her unusualness. Jet-black hair, like her mother, curled and frizzy like her father's. Her olive skin was covered in a smattering of dark-brown freckles. She was smaller than I was, but I could feel the power rolling off her in waves. She could have been a High Witch of the Coven had she thought they were worth keeping alive. She wasn't a fan of our Coven or any council for that matter. She and authority didn't mix well.

"My dear little witch, I've seen what that demon has done to you on the news. You skipped across the ground like a stone on the lake." Mairi pulled me into her arms. Her head came up to my chin. "I began making you a batch of salve at once. You should have called me last night. I would have come, you know that, right?"

"I do, and thank you." I lifted a white paper box from my shoulder bag. "Still the same price?"

"For you, yes," she answered and opened the box. Her eyebrows wiggled as she pulled out the mini cinnamon bun I'd bought at the bakery two blocks from the school.

"You know, if you didn't keep trying to burn down the university, you'd be allowed on the property," I said, taking a seat on her front porch. "Imagine how many sugar bombs you could buy if they didn't have a restraining order against you."

"Until they stop using live animals in their research, I'll keep breaking them out and setting as many fires as I can along the way. Animal testing is barbaric, and so shall I be until they stop."

"Fair point." I waited as she went inside with a cheek full of cinnamon bun.

"I made you four," she said, slipping them into my shoulder bag. "I doubt the expiration date will pass with you, but you have one month to use them up."

"I'll need them all in one go," I said. "My back and legs are hamburger." I extended my arms to her. "Do you have anything that'll get rid of these scars?"

She took my hands in hers to inspect the old claw marks from Mexico and hissed the moment she ran her fingers across them. "Not for those types of scars, Ailis. They went deep enough to touch your soul. Once your soul fully heals, your scars will begin to heal as well."

"Damn," I grumbled.

"They look an awful lot like Samuel's scars."

"Great. If he still has his, I'm not likely going to heal mine. I don't have centuries of healing to invest."

"Don't you worry about your soul, Ailis." She squeezed my hands. "Some souls take longer to heal than others, and Samuel has lived a great many lifetimes and has collected many wounds to his soul. His will heal, as will yours."

I nodded and pulled my hands back. Although her aura felt like a warm hug, I wasn't a fan of touching others stuffed to the brim with power. It crawled across my skin like spiders.

"You know the monsters of this city better than I do. Julian sent his people to my office today…"

"Stay away from him, Ailis, or scars like yours will look minor compared to what he is known to do."

"I don't plan on meeting up with him," I countered. "Do you know why he'd come knocking? Have you heard anything about him wanting a demon raised?"

"I've heard nothing like that, but Julian is known for his secrets. He is always a step ahead of the authorities and the Elders. I met him once, and that was enough for me to sense how purely evil he is." She shuddered. "His soul was impossible to silence. It hovered behind him, screaming so loud I had to leave. The cursed thing gave me nightmares for weeks."

"Bound souls suffer like no other." I shivered along with her. The breeze wrapped me in the calming smell of lavender. "Using your magic on your garden, aren't you scared of the taint?"

She shrugged. "A little taint to live in happiness is worth it. No God will shun me from their heavens for growing herbs I used to save lives."

I motioned to the ivy, moving along the ground. "This is a bit more than herbs, Mairi."

"That ivy is why I bought the property," she answered. "Most of what you see was already here and spelled long before me. The ivy is better than a guard dog."

"That's an uncomfortable thought," I said, keeping my eyes on the creeping plant.

"It's a curious thing," she said. "Likes to touch and feel those who bring me joy."

"I've had my fill of curiosity for the day, thank you," I replied and stood. "Thanks for the cream. Will you be at the Ostara event? Samuel has been planning since Winter Solstice."

"I wouldn't miss Spring Equinox for anything. I've offered my back garden for the party," she said, and one look from me made her laugh. "I'll put the plants to sleep for the night. Worry not. Will you be inviting Miguel? It's been so many years since I've last seen him. He's such a good boy. I was thrilled to hear of your rekindled romance."

I gulped. I had completely forgotten to invite him. I made a mental note to send him a text about it. "I have to run. I'll see you in a few weeks."

She gave me a light hug, kissed my cheek, and I hobbled back to my car. She pulled a fob from her pocket, and the gate swung open and let me out. I loved seeing her, but I was always happy to leave. The power that moved through her property nudged against my aura every time I came, as if trying to taste me or my intentions. I had never been injured, but I had always known the power was there, waiting for someone to do something foolish.

I headed away from Point Grey and made a straight shot into East Van. Samuel's place was on Main Street, over the bookstore he owned. I knew where the spare keys were, but unless I had a demon on my back and needed his spells of protection on his doorway, I didn't like going inside without him. The books in his living room whispered and made my skin crawl when Samuel wasn't there.

Samuel wasn't home when I got there. He didn't believe in owning a cell phone. He didn't like the idea of being hounded. If it were important enough to bother him while he was grocery shopping, it would still be important when he got home. I slipped a note under his door to call me when he got in, that it was, in fact, life or death. I added a drawing of fangs at the end as a warning. If I didn't hear from him in the next couple of hours, I'd call the police. The local cops owed me enough favors that they'd go over to Samuel's for a wellness check. Samuel was the closest friend I had. He was family, he was the closest thing I had to a grandfather, and would be the first the vampires would try to grab to force me into a meeting. I didn't doubt Samuel's ability to protect himself, but every additional minute of notice we were given would up our chances of walking away with all our souls intact. I didn't want to put him in the position of needing to skin his soul to survive. As I had always told my students, knowledge is power. I handed out a lot of advice I rarely took. Case in point — my battered body.

I made one more stop on my way home, the church that supplied me with holy water by the jars. Sister Ann met me out back and helped me load my trunk with eight massive recycled pickled egg jars. She said a quick prayer, as she always did, and ducked back inside. The church frowned on what I did, but Sister Ann had been helping me with holy water for years. Sure, we did it in the back alley, and neither of us spoke about it, but help was help, and I wasn't going to look a gift horse in the mouth. She had once said it was the lesser of evils, help me, a heathen as the church called me, or risk demons loose on mankind. I wouldn't argue the condition of my soul. Their opinion of me didn't change who I knew I was.

I pulled into my driveway and scrutinized every square inch of my yard and home. Even though it was still light out, I opened the smart-home app on my phone and turned on every switch inside. The place lit up like a dull Christmas tree, but it was enough for me to see into the dark center of each room. I waited to see if any shadows bounded across my windows but saw nothing. Cat strolled from a bench on my front patio to the top of the stairs. She gave one full body stretch and took a seat, waiting for me. If she was calm, I'd be calm.

I still walked through my house with a wooden stake, holy water and a bible, just in case. One could never be too sure. Being overly confident could kick my ass. With every single nook and cranny peered into, every closet opened, and the dark places I hated to venture into, ventured fully, I felt a little safer. Cat followed, purring and lounging where she could. I should take her word for it, but looking with my own eyes was a habit I never wanted to grow out of. Letting my guard all the way down was a slippery slope I wouldn't go down.

I stripped and pulled off two dozen bandages before climbing into the shower. I twitched as the water touched my wounds, and finally stood in front of my floor-to-ceiling mirror, eyeing up the cuts and bruises covering my body. I was already sweating and sore and hadn't even started the part I hated. I opened the first jar and was immediately sick in my sink. My cat left the bathroom, sounding like a hairball was caught in her throat. The smell was a kick to the senses. Breathing through my mouth so I'd only tasted it, I started the painful process of smearing the salve from Mairi over the worst of the wounds. I had about twenty minutes before the real pain began. Thankfully, it would come all at once, and if I was lucky, I'd pass out. I laughed at myself. It wasn't often I lost consciousness from pain. A few lifetimes in hell had done wonders for my pain tolerance. Naked and covered in cream, I leaned forward and put my elbows on my counter, waiting.

Little by little, my body absorbed the cream. As it soaked in, the pain started, finally buckling my knees. I opened my mouth to scream, but no sound came out. I closed my eyes and breathed through the pain. It was all I could do. If I wasn't on the radar of vampires, I would have pain-spelled myself after the cream and knocked myself out until morning. That would not be a luxury I'd gift myself for fear of being found by fangs while unconscious. Instead, because of monsters, I had to suffer. It took twenty minutes of panting, vomiting and crying for the pain to lessen enough for me to stand. I held onto the edge of the counter until the room stopped spinning before I got dressed. The pain wasn't gone but would fade over the next couple of hours. At least now, it was no worse than what I felt when I started. And people wondered why I didn't use magic idly. It hurt. It came with a cost.

Samuel called me thirty minutes after I had finished slathering my body. The smell lingered, but I wasn't willing to open a window. I was pouring holy water into smaller jars to go with the wooden stakes I had in every room in case I was chased into some random spot in my house. The thought of being stuck, unarmed, in my own home made my stomach turn. I'd learned some hard lessons over my twenty-six years, and that was one of them. Be prepared to fight, no matter if I was doing laundry or dishes. After tonight, if the bad guys wanted me badly enough to break into my house, they'd bleed for it. I was as ready as I'd ever be.

"Sam, thanks for calling," I said as soon as I answered.

"You know I dislike it when you call me that." He sounded winded, as though he had called me as soon as he had stepped in the door.

"Samuel," I corrected and grinned.

"What has happened?" he asked. "You said it was a matter of life or death."

"Yes, and the life I'm referring to is yours, well, and mine. Our resident Master, Julian, sent his cronies to my office. He asked for a meeting with me, offering a bribe to get me there. When I said no, Conor, one of Julian's day walkers, threatened to hurt me by hurting those I care about. You're closest, so I'm calling to let you know."

Samuel groaned as he took a seat. I could hear his favorite reading chair squeak under his frame. "Conor Madden is not just a day walker or errand boy. He is a familiar in training."

"Familiar in training?" I asked.

"Masters keep several day walkers, those to do his daylight errands, but only one or two familiars at a time. They are more important than a day walker but less than a full human servant," he replied. "Conor is Julian's muscle. He deals with the messier side of Julian's business. That Conor came and not someone weaker should tell you Julian sees you as a threat."

I swallowed hard enough for it to echo into the phone. "I'm not a threat."

"Whether you believe that or not doesn't mean a lick to anyone else."

"I sent Conor packing. He said Julian will be back, and next time, it won't be a friendly invitation."

"You need to call Miguel," Samuel replied. "He has a closer connection to vampires than I do."

"I already did, right after Conor left. He's going to poke around on his end. He told me to call you."

"You likely have a few days before Julian comes for you. If he extends another invitation, do not meet with them for any reason."

"Miguel said to accept the invitation to buy myself more time."

"If you're left without a choice, accept, with the caveat of a formal meeting. It'll buy you a day, maybe two. Come here or go to holy ground at once," Samuel replied. "But if they take you or try, kill them. Do not negotiate. They're better at riddles and lies held within truths. They are like dealing with demons. Do not trust a single one of them. You will die if they take you." Samuel echoed the same thing Miguel had.

"Would you accept? Even to buy a few days?" I asked.

"Never. I do not negotiate. But I have fewer issues with killing than you do. If you refuse, you're upping the risk of needing to kill to save yourself." Samuel's sigh made me feel like I had screwed up, even though, this time, I hadn't done anything.

"And what if I agree and they take me right away, anyway? I'll have bought nothing but a straight shot to Julian's bloody hellhouse and will have agreed to go."

"If Julian sends muscle, agree with the caveat. They'll leave you to prepare. If he sends his human servant, make a judgment call. Either way, like with any other monster, show no weakness and get ready to fight your way out. He'll take you regardless of your answer. He's known for cruelty and creativity that would make a demon blush."

"Great," I muttered. A pang of guilt sat in my stomach and soured. "I'm sorry you're at risk now, Samuel. Do you need me to help you get somewhere safe?"

Samuel's laugh made me smile. "They won't come here. Not even Julian is that brave. He has always given me a wide berth. I am far from a safe target." He paused for a moment, thinking. "He is aware you are my family. That he would be so bold to approach a family member of a guardian, retired or not, tells me you have what he cannot find elsewhere and is desperate enough to risk his life for it."

"Access to demons and hell?" I asked.

"I'd think so, but just in case it is something so far outside the box, do you need to stay here until Miguel finds out what's going on?"

"I'll come if the pot starts to boil," I answered. "If things go south, I know where your spare key is."

"I'll see what I can find out. I haven't heard of Julian's name coming up in conversation as of late, but he has always been a very secretive man. Most often, we don't hear about it until it's already been done, and we're cleaning up his messes," he replied. "Be safe, Ailis. Don't take any chances. Stop taking meetings for a little while until this blows over or comes to a head. Maybe give May a call and see if she's heard anything. Her fingers are on the very pulse of vampires. It's her job to know."

"Thanks, Samuel. I'll call you if things get heated over here," I replied and disconnected our call.

I scrolled through my contacts, looking for Dr. May Zhang, a semi-retired vampire hunter. Since she had come to town, we hadn't had much of a fang problem. She'd killed everyone who had stepped out of line within the first month of her arrival, and the rest were too bloody scared of her to tempt their fates. The most work she'd had since then was out of town. Other regions called her in where their own hunters had failed. Her day job was at the university, and it had little to do with her hunter abilities. She taught political sciences, and her classes were next to impossible to get into. Those who did get a seat either aced it or buckled under the pressure. She demanded excellence. Anything short of that was a ticket out and blacklisted from future classes. Wasting her time was taboo for current and prospective students. The only warning her students got was during the brief introduction on the first day.

Although we rarely crossed paths, teaching at opposite ends of the campus, she was one of the few people who gave me a nod and a courtesy wave, though I would have been fine if she didn't make eye contact with me at all. She scared the hell out of me. She was human, through and through, but there was something about her eyes that made me squirm and fight not to step back. She came from a long line of hunters, and I could only imagine how it would feel to stand in a room full of her family. But every time she nodded or waved, I would give her the same in return. I knew what it felt like to be ignored.

I found her number and called her. Her phone went to voicemail without even ringing. Her voice, even on the machine, felt like it could cut through rock. I hated leaving voice messages. They never sounded quite how I wanted them to. I was one of the youngest professors at the university, and recorded, my voice sounded like one of my students. It had always made me cringe. I worried my message wouldn't be taken seriously because I sounded like a teenager asking to stay out past curfew.

"Hello, Dr. Zhang. This is Ailis Kyteler. Would you be able to please call me back at your earliest convenience? I have a few questions about our local vampire population, and I was hoping you'd have the answers I needed. Thank you."

I hung up and sent her a follow-up text, just in case she was like me and rarely listened to her voicemail. Whether she called me back or not tonight, it didn't really matter. I was just as happy with leaving my name on the tip of everyone's tongue should something happen to me overnight. The more people looking for me, the better. I thought about calling Philip and telling him that if I went missing, to start looking for my body with the vampires. But thought twice about it. Philip would panic. I'd save that call for when I got really worried and needed someone to stay the night on my couch or give my eulogy. Philip would probably lie and tell everyone I was a lovely person or was loved by all. *As if.*

Philip had texted me half a dozen messages, apologizing, swearing he'd never screw me over again. I let him know we'd talk about it in the morning over the muffins he now owed me. Perhaps he thought I'd know who Conor was, or maybe, after running from a demon all night, it had slipped his mind. I'd cut Philip some slack. He, of anyone, deserved it. I followed up my message with a gif. If I was willing to send jokes, everything was fine once again.

Paranoid, I spent the rest of my evening rechecking I had holy water in every room and hiding spot. The doors and windows were locked and warded before I settled in for the night to consume hours of vampire research and how to kill human servants. I terrified myself into going to bed with holy water under my pillow and stakes spread throughout my bedroom. Up until recently, it had only been the cursed demons who bothered me. Sometimes, I'd get the odd ghost here and there, but they were harmless. Every now and again, I'd get a card-carrying nut job from a newly formed religious group, quickly dealt with by the police or me threatening to curse them. But vampires hadn't even been on my radar. I had a healthy fear of them, but they left me alone, and I didn't go looking for fanged trouble. I found enough of it without needling a species known for killing first and asking questions later. And now they had come knocking. They either knew about my association with those who hunted them, or they wanted something from me. I doubted it was my blood. I was cursed. Born witches weren't high on their list of food choices because we tasted like hell. Vampires drank the essence of their donor's soul, and mine wouldn't be a satisfying meal.

I thought of the usual reasons people came to my door. It could be a demon problem, but I'd have heard of it. It could be for *summoning* a demon, but it was odd they'd resort to such lengths to have me summon one for them. There were dozens of dark witches out there who would take cash on delivery, and I wasn't known for being one of them. There had been times when someone had tried to get me to raise their dead relative, thinking witches were the same as necromancers. Or asking me to clean out a haunted space, thinking I could convince a ghost to leave. Ghosts didn't listen to me any more than I listened to them. They were stuck here for reasons they didn't even know, and I was the last one to ask. When I'd exhausted all the reasons why a vampire would have my name on their lips, my stomach started to twist. It made me nervous, not knowing for sure the reason why. I could have asked, but I doubted I would have gotten an answer out of Mr. Thousand-Dollar Suit. Conor didn't look like the type to speak for his boss, and I wasn't willing to hear the words from the walking corpse himself—Julian.

Fucking monsters.

Chapter Six

I curled on my side in bed, my cat stretched out on my pillow, and stared at the wall. I tried to calm myself, but each time I closed my eyes, memories brought them back open. Although Cisco was alive, I could still hear him, in the back of my mind, dying. I could almost smell Sofia's cooked flesh from the silver chains the witches had used to bind her in a dungeon. The images of those who had been splayed for the birds, used to feed the Gods, made my eyes water. The bodies at the church, killed by the demon summoned by Ruby, and the feeling of holy water burning my skin all made my throat tighten. This was how I spent my nights since calling the hounds from hell — utterly heartbroken.

Conor's threat played over and over in my head, making me sit straight up in bed and turn on my bedside lamp. My pulse raced, thinking of what Julian would do if I avoided him. If he took me, I'd die. If he locked me in a dungeon, I'd tear my soul apart for my freedom. I couldn't go through it all again. Whatever he wanted from me was important enough for him to ask me nicely to meet with him. So far. The second time wouldn't go as smoothly, and it wouldn't be a question but a command. I was meeting with the leech, whether I went willingly or not. The question was, did I go freely to my death, or would I make my stand outside of the vampire's clutches?

Palpitations thumped in my chest until I pressed my hand into my heart, willing it to slow down. I could feel it move up my throat, speeding as it climbed. My vision became splotchy, and I tilted to the side, light-headed. Realizing I was holding in a scream and my breath, I finally relaxed, releasing a groan of fear. My cat stirred and jumped onto my lap, purring, trying to calm me. Trembling, I ran my hand down her back, holding onto her tail while I breathed in through my nose and out through my mouth. Slowly, I came back to myself, but the seed of panic sat in my stomach like soured milk.

I grabbed my phone and texted Miguel. I knew he'd be home, likely preparing for work at this hour. He was an early riser, work or day off.

Can you call me when you have time? I can't sleep.

A few minutes passed before he texted me back.

I'm in an early meeting and can't get away for another hour. Make yourself a tea. It'll help calm you down. I'll call you as soon as I'm through here.

I got out of bed, pulled on my housecoat and wandered to my kitchen with my cat in tow. I didn't bother turning on the lights. I knew my floor plan by heart. I never changed my living room. I liked everything where it was. If I ever had to run from the monsters, I wanted to be sure of where every obstacle was. The bad guys would trip where I jumped. And turning on lights would only ruin my night vision, which I wanted to hold onto should someone kick down my door tonight.

I laughed out loud at the thoughts I had. I'd rather walk around in complete darkness than risk my night vision. I turned on my stove light and flicked on the lamps in my living room. I poured treats onto the floor for my cat and started my kettle for tea. I dug out a few cookies while I waited for my water to boil. Cookies made everything better in the middle of the night. I leaned against my counter and flicked through social media for something to make me smile. Cats behaving like the little demons we all knew they were, were my go-to for a laugh. The idea that we'd invite little indifferent goblins into our lives and be snubbed by them on the regular was amusing to me. I glanced down at my cat when she sniffed her treats, groaned and walked away.

"Jerk," I whispered and went back to the video of a cat knocking over houseplants.

My phone vibrated, and a photo of Miguel swimming two days before I left Mexico popped up on my screen. That was when my real smile came, the one that settled me better than tea or cookies or cats misbehaving.

"Miguel, thanks for calling me. Sorry if I interrupted your meeting," I said, pouring my water into my black teacup, a gift from Philip. On the inside of the cup, it said, 'You've just been poisoned.'

"I need a favor, Lish," Miguel replied with a hint of amusement in his voice.

"Oh, do you now? The last time I helped you, I ended up in another Mexican prison," I answered.

"To be fair, you *did* owe me." A small chuckle followed. I could almost picture his smile.

"Every time you need a favor, I land in some hellhole needing bail money or someone to keep my heart beating," I replied.

"Not fair. I've always paid your bail, and I *did* keep your heart beating, didn't I?"

"Fair? If we're talking about being fair, you still owe me a five-star vacation with a spa, room service, and someone hand-feeding me grapes, which I've yet to get."

"Open your front door," he said as my doorbell rang. My heart jumped into my throat. "The best I can do is a foot rub, a movie, and take out. Cisco sent you homemade enchiladas."

I hurried through my living room to my front door, grinning. "How did you get enchiladas through customs?" I asked as I opened the door.

"I didn't. Cisco did. He can move weapons. Enchiladas were no big deal." He pocketed his cell phone. "Cisco got here before me to negotiate our entering a different territory. When you called about Julian, Cisco packed his things and jumped on the first plane out, just in case things went south before I could get here. Until we figure out a few things, you need someone from our Pack here with you, or you're a tempting little witch to snatch."

I jumped into his arms and wrapped my legs around his waist, catching him off guard. He fell to his knees, setting his bags and container of food on the floor. I pulled his mouth to mine, and as soon as our lips touched, I sighed into his mouth with relief. His arms around me felt like the world was right once more. He staggered forward and tried his best to kick the door closed. He put me on the floor and pulled my housecoat open, grinning, while spreading my thighs apart. He breathed me in, and every line on his face softened. He looked at me with heated regard. A need to mark me, taste me and love me flowed over his face. He gripped my thighs, pulling them wider and exposing me. He licked his lips and groaned at what he saw. It took all of a blink of an eye for his mouth to find my center and suck my pleasure into his mouth. His moans mixed with mine and filled my living room with a chorus of need and my building orgasm.

Miguel's tongue flicked back and forth against the tight bundle of nerves. He hungrily lapped at my bud before sucking it into his mouth once more, manipulating my orgasm with ease. His movements became more ardent with the quivering of my whimpers beneath him as I dipped deeper into bliss. He took his time tasting me, savoring every groan and call for more I made. Soon, everything culminated in a passion so raw I lost myself to the sensations. I heard nothing more than his encouragement. I felt nothing but his touch surging through every inch of my body.

I gripped his hair, pulling him into my hips while I ground myself against him. It had felt like eons had passed since I'd last felt his touch. Decades of waiting for this very moment. Miguel gripped my thighs and pulled me against his mouth, tight and secure. That was when I felt his energy shift. I could feel his wolf somewhere in the background, roaming, marking my home as his. I screamed out Miguel's name as soon as I felt his energy focus on me and my aura. He was home. He was safe. He would protect me. Knowing I could let go and he would catch me, my body came alive. I couldn't feel the floor under me. I couldn't see the room around me. With my eyes closed, a scream caught in my throat. I could smell the forest and hear claws gripping the ground. I could feel his wolf, his freedom and his happiness.

I held on to Miguel for dear life, my fingers entwined in his, as my climax reached its pinnacle and slammed down on me. Wave after wave, pleasure filled me to the brim and washed out of me in a pulse of raw energy. The pictures on my walls shook from the power that rolled through the room, slowly fading into the euphoria that tenderly ebbed and flowed, finally calming as I came back into reality, into the feel of Miguel's hands in mine. In this very moment, we were in complete sync. I felt all of who he was, his wolf, his heart, his soul. And in turn, I held nothing back from him. He could feel me right down to the hidden places within my soul.

I lazily slid back into reality, panting, my fingers still entwined in his. "Oh, dear God. It gets better and better each time."

"I wouldn't have been able to concentrate without tasting you first," he said, pulling himself up my body to my mouth.

I kissed him, tasting my orgasm on his lips. "I love you."

"I've been waiting to do that for weeks." He kissed me back. "I love you, too."

Miguel carefully moved to my side, holding me against him. He relaxed as soon as I turned to face him, putting my arm around him. Breathing him in flared my libido back to life with promises of lustful desires fulfilled and tantalizing temptations that made me want to ignore the world and drag him to my bed. He chuckled and kissed my forehead.

"Soon," he said. "I make you scream my name."

"I just did."

"Oh, love, that wasn't a scream," he replied.

Miguel ran his hand down my spine, then around my hip, pulling me closer. After weeks of feeling homesick and scared of shadows, I finally felt secure again, safe in his warm embrace, and responded instinctively, as if we were made to be together in all ways. Miguel, in turn, used his knee to push mine apart. He pulled my leg over his, grinding himself into my core. I reached between us and loosened his belt, tugging at his pants. With one hand, Miguel opened his pants and pulled himself loose. I shuddered as the heat of our bodies connected with each other. He guided himself inside, and I gasped as he filled me. In perfect harmony, we moved against each other.

"Deeper. More. I need more." I groaned. "Fuck me, Miguel."

"Oh, Jesus," he moaned, a hint of a growl edging his voice. "I love it when you talk dirty."

Miguel rolled on top of me and, in a swift motion, was on his knees, turning me to face the floor. He pulled my hips up and bent me over. Miguel pushed his legs between mine and, without warning, filled me fully from behind. I finally screamed out his name, how he had intended it. He held nothing back. His hips slapped my thighs and ass, his fingers dug into my hips, and he was lost to pleasure. He held me tight and no longer made love to me. He fucked me exactly how I had asked. Over and over, he hit my G-spot. My orgasm exploded suddenly while I demanded more.

Miguel pulled me up to his chest. His hands found my breasts while his hot breath covered my neck, as he fucked me. He bit down on my shoulder, and with a shuddering growl fit for the wolf within him, Miguel's orgasm spilled from him. He pushed himself as deep as he could go with each pulse until I fell forward, taking him with me, breathless and spent. Miguel collapsed on my back, kissing my shoulders, trying and failing to get his arms to work.

I pushed him to my side, rolling my back into his chest. His heart beat wildly at my back, mirroring my own. I closed my eyes and gave into the pure bliss that coated my body like sweat. My nose filled with Miguel's scent. The familiarity made my eyes water.

"I missed you. I missed your smell," I said, feeling the part of my soul that had been sitting on edge for weeks settle into the renewed comforts of home.

"I missed you, too," he said, pulling me tighter.

We stayed in the same position for ten minutes, relearning how to use our limbs, the silence between us only broken by our quiet breathing. After the intensity of seeing each other again and the powerful emotions we shared, there was something peaceful and calming found in the quiet hush following the screams. Entwined, our hearts and souls reconnected in ways we could only share with each other. We were destined for hell, had shaved off pieces of our souls for one another, and would do horrible things to really good people to protect the other. We were wrong for each other in so many ways, but we loved like it was the end of the world.

Eventually, I propped myself up on my elbow and nudged Miguel. He smiled without opening his eyes. He sighed and finally stretched, groaning at being forced to move. I leaned forward and gave him a small kiss, nudging him out of his afterglow.

"I want this moment to last forever," Miguel murmured, pulling my hand to his lips and kissing my palm before standing.

Once my heart stopped hammering in my chest, Miguel helped me back to my feet. "Aren't you a nice surprise?"

He smiled, putting his clothes back on. "I thought it would be."

"I can't tell you how happy I am to see you," I sighed as I breathed him in, tying my robe shut again. "Why did Cisco need to negotiate?"

"Anytime we want to come into a different Pack's territory, we need permission, or it's seen as an act of aggression," he replied. "I sent Cisco since he's not seen as a threat. Cisco could be Alpha if he wanted, but he's low enough in our Pack that others think he's weak."

"Fools. Cisco isn't weak. If anything, he's one of the stronger I've felt in your Pack." I pulled Miguel all the way into my house rather than have him stand at my front door like a guest.

"I agree. He's not weak. Not only is he physically strong, but he also has the soul of a warrior. It'll be their funeral if they push him too far. He hides his power better than any other Lycan I know." Miguel murmured as he leaned into my body, breathing me in. "I missed this."

"Me too," I replied with a deep sigh.

"So, is that a yes for the favor I have?" he asked. He lifted me into his arms, hugging me the way he always had, fully, completely. It felt like it had been years since I had last felt his touch. Our aura climbed over each other, and we both released heated breaths from deep inside. It felt good. It felt peaceful, even though, in the background, I could hear his wolf snarling and my power crackling like thunder. We were a match made in hell, right down to our souls.

"Depends on what the favor is," I replied. "Demons, yes. Anything worse, not a chance in hell. Get your ass back on the plane."

"Two things, actually. First, the local Pack has sent a formal request to meet you," he replied. "Second, Cisco needs somewhere to stay."

"Cisco is always welcome here. I'd have opened the door for him if he had come on his own," I answered with a smile. Cisco was welcome in my home, day or night. He had a special place in my heart and would remain there until my last breath. My smile soon faded, replaced with a groan. "Do I have to meet the local Pack?"

Miguel nodded. "Unfortunately. You have the protection of Caser, the Lycaon of the Los Luna Pack and his Pack. Word has spread that you've received our protection, little Grimmwolf. Most of Mexico has thrown in their protection for what you did for us. It is legend to do what you did. All of Mexico will follow you into hell. Your ties to them all bleed outward, and word travels fast. And now, the locals of the Noire Lune Pack want to meet the only human to have the protection of Lycan. Rumors have started about you calling the hounds. It's piqued the curiosity of many."

I cringed. "I can't really be the only one to have received protection?"

"The first human, yes."

"Is it going to be another shitshow?" I asked. "My first run-in with Pack didn't end well. I think I've had my fill of dead bodies and holy water baths for a while."

"That's why Cisco is here. He has eyes and ears everywhere. If there's a problem, we'll know about it before we get there. But truth be told, I don't know. There's been a lot of changes in this Pack since I was last here. There is a new Lycaon, and I don't know him well. All I really know is that Caser doesn't like him."

"Does Caser like anyone?" I joked.

"He likes you," he replied. "Caser doesn't trust the local Pack. There are rumors that Natt is a poor Lycaon."

"What's Cisco's take on him?" I asked. I trusted Caser's opinion, but I Trusted Cisco with a capital 'T.'

"He doesn't like him, never has. He says Nathaniel, the Pack Leader, has no honor," Miguel said, and I groaned. "He's heard that Natt doesn't protect the weaker members of his Pack. I don't know if it's because we run things differently in Mexico or if it's really just that bad here. Whatever the case, we go in expecting it to be a shitshow."

"When do we go?"

"Tonight." He ran his hands through his hair. He looked nervous. "Cisco jumped the first plane as soon as the invitation was sent. I came as soon as I was permitted. I didn't think you'd want to go alone."

"Why did you need permission but not Cisco? Is it because you're higher up in the Pack than Cisco?"

"Yes and no. Mostly it's because I'm stronger than the local Lycaon. He'd be crazy to allow me to come and go as I pleased. Caser would do the same. If someone was coming into Mexico who was stronger than him and the rest of his Pack," he replied, prompting more questions from me.

"Did you belong to this Pack when you lived here before?"

"No. The last Lycaon was good friends with Caser and made an agreement for me to be here to watch over you as long as I didn't challenge him. I didn't see any reason to challenge, though. He was a pretty good guy."

"And what about now? You said Cisco had to negotiate for you?"

"I had to make oaths. I wouldn't stand against him or his unless Lycan law demanded me to intervene or we deemed you were in immediate danger. You have our protection. I'm within my rights to protect you against all, including Natt, if he directly tries to harm you. Even if I didn't have permission, to protect you, they'd be fools not to expect me to intervene."

"Although I don't want to go at all, thank you for coming," I answered. "Whatever the reason, I'm glad you're here, Miguel. It's been…"

"I know." He kissed my forehead. "It's been hard for me, too. Half of my soul got on that plane when you left. Sofia has been watching me like a hawk, saying she gave you her word that she'd watch over me."

I huffed a laugh. "I may have asked her to make sure you didn't go off the deep end. But I had meant for her to watch you if I died."

"Being apart from a mate is a small death. I woke up yesterday morning with her sitting against my bedroom door, holding a gun, reminding me that she gave her word to you," he replied. "She takes her oaths pretty fucking seriously, Ailis. All of us do. In our word, an oath is life or death, honor and dishonor. We'd damn our offspring with shame if we broke it."

"Jesus." I winced. "Sorry. When I asked, I thought I was about to die."

"Don't be sorry. Sofia is one of the most loyal people I've met. That she's given her loyalty to you, be grateful. She'll come every time you call. Nothing and no one could stop her. She loves that deeply."

"I'll send her a basket of bullets and holy water as a thank you," I replied. "Let me get dressed, then let's go see what the big bad wolf wants."

"I wouldn't say that too loud. Cisco had a sign made for his house. It says 'Big Bad Wolf.' I don't think Cisco's ego would be able to take that slight if you called someone else that."

"What a dork." I laughed and led Miguel to my bedroom. *Our* bedroom, for now.

He put his bags down on the side of the bed I knew he favored. He eyed the photo on my nightstand of us from four years ago and smiled while I blushed. He kissed my forehead, knowing he wasn't the only one who couldn't let go of us then headed to the kitchen to make coffee. It was going to be a long night. I stood in front of my closet and wondered what one should wear when meeting a group of Lycans. The last time, I had just come from a crime scene where a body had been used as a human sacrifice. I went for something easy to move around in, such as running for my life or cowering in a corner. Comfort and function over style. That, and I didn't own anything other than comfortable clothes that hid blood stains. I pulled on black stretch jeans, a turtleneck sweater, and combat boots and twisted my hair into a top knot. I looked like I could kick some ass if needed. I also looked like I'd be presentable if the news showed up to report on a bloodbath.

My cat sat up out of deep sleep and meowed. I tilted my head and could hear Miguel's voice and... Cisco. I smiled. I turned off my bedroom lights and found Cisco standing in my living room with an army-sized duffle bag.

"Hotel Cauldrons and Broomsticks." Cisco glanced around. "I thought it would be more goth or…"

"Evil?" I asked, and he nodded with a laugh. I gave him one of those hugs that said I had missed the living hell out of him. "While I'm sorry for the reason you're here, I'm happy to see you."

"Oh, I saw a lot of you not but twenty minutes ago." He grinned. "I was on your front patio, right behind Miguel."

I blushed. "Oh, I didn't know you were out there."

Miguel chuckled. "I tried to kick the door closed."

"Sorry, Cisco," I said, feeling embarrassed.

"I'm not." He winked. "You witches are always trouble."

"You weren't complaining when I saved you."

"When I *let* you save me. I was five minutes away from breaking myself out," he replied with a mouth full of lies. It made us all laugh out the tension of the memories. "I'm glad to be back and to be standing inside your house rather than in the witchy woods outside. You wouldn't believe how many spirits follow you around. They're everywhere. It's like your own haunted forest out there."

"Yeah, it's one of the perks of being a witch that can see and hear souls." I tilted my head. "Wait, what? Why have you been sneaking around in the woods around my house?"

Miguel winced. "I'm sorry."

Cisco laughed. "Lovestruck Miguel here, sent me to check on you more times than I can count over the last two years. Usually, whenever I was in town for class at the university, or whenever there was a shifting power base or a largescale meeting. I'd come and hunker down in the bush to make sure your name wasn't on someone's list. Before me, he sent anyone else who was in town to make sure you were okay."

"Not gonna lie, that's pretty creepy," I replied.

"You're telling me. I tried to explain to Miguel that his request had major stalker vibes," Cisco said, shaking his head. "But after the first night, I didn't mind. You walk around a lot in your underpants and nothing else."

"Letch." I rolled my eyes and walked away.

With another all-nighter on my mind, I poured myself a cup of freshly brewed coffee. Cisco went straight for the fridge, pausing before he opened it. He fingered the note I had saved from a gift Sofia had sent me when I returned home from Mexico.

The monsters don't get to win this time, not when you have people who have your back.

Although this pot wasn't your mother's, I hope this brings you the same joy it brought her. You deserve to have happiness. You deserve to have good memories.

Cisco sends his love. He wants me to tell you that he chipped in twenty bucks and that you're welcome. What an ass.

Much love, Sofia.

He looked over his shoulder at the spelling pot they had sent me, sitting in the middle of my kitchen table. "Twenty bucks? I paid for half the damn pot and all the shipping."

I laughed when the cat jumped onto the table and climbed into the bowl. "She appreciates her new bed."

"Five grand for a cat bed. Your familiar lives in a lap of luxury while I still live in an apartment," he muttered.

"Do you want me pulling enough energy through your aura to cook your little wolf? Because that's what she does for me, while all you've done so far is complain," I asked, and he blanched. "I'd stop complaining about her luxury, then."

"Good point, although I've been told that my complaining is endearing. And, for the record, my wolf is massive," he replied, wiggling his eyebrows. Miguel snorted a laugh, earning a glare from Cisco. He reached into the pot and scratched my cat's head. The little beast lifted her chin and purred instantly.

"Traitor," I mumbled.

"I think not. Your cat attacked me a dozen times when I was camped out in your trees. It took the same number of fish to get her to calm down and stop making me bleed."

"When I told you the story of my cat, you played like you had no idea I even had one," I said.

He shrugged. "Yeah, because would have been the perfect time to tell you I had been watching you at night from your bushes?"

"That's fair," I answered.

He turned back to my fridge and groaned, poking through the lack of selection. I lived alone and ate out most days. Food in my fridge would have been a waste. I made a mental note to go grocery shopping for the hungry wolf who'd be living in my basement for the next little while. I offered him cookies, but he said he didn't eat anything that wasn't homemade.

"I wouldn't dare butcher my tastebuds or damage my wolf with packaged food," he replied, a look of revulsion on his face like I had offered him garbage, and put the cookies back on the counter. I made another mental note not to buy prepackaged food for the picky wolf. Though, if I was fueling a beast inside my soul, I'd probably opt for whole foods, too.

He pulled out a wooden stake from my crisper. "Don't tell me you have a beaver out back."

I smiled. "There another in the cheese drawer, and two bottles of holy water."

He made himself four peanut butter and jelly sandwiches and took the entire gallon of milk from the fridge. "What? I haven't eaten since landing. There's nothing open in the middle of the night but fast-food places. I'm still on Mexico time. My body is used to eating breakfast."

"Why didn't you eat the enchiladas?" I asked.

He shrugged. "I wanted you to have a piece of home from me."

I smiled at his comment. "I'll have them for my lunch. Thank you, Cisco."

Once Cisco had inhaled two sandwiches, Miguel got down to business. "What's your take on the local Pack, on Natt specifically?"

"The word around town is that Natt can't be trusted," Cisco said, around a mouthful of sandwich. I thought about pointing out that monsters, in general, couldn't be trusted, but I didn't want to go back down that road with them. "No one is talking too many specifics, but the weaker of his Pack are terrified of him. Not just the usual scared to step out of line, but utterly terrified to get on Natt's bad side. They don't look to him as their protector. He is their punisher."

Miguel's face filled with anger. "Despicable."

"No one is terrified of Caser?" I asked. "I hate to point it out, but Caser is scary as hell."

Cisco shook his head. "I love Caser with all my heart. He'd die for me, die for us all. I fear disappointing him. I'm scared to let him down. But terrified? Never. I would have had to do something horrendous for there to be a reason to be terrified of him. And even then, Caser would be the one to take my life and mourn the loss."

"Caser is our Lycaon," Miguel added. "He is our Leader. He doesn't demand our loyalty. He earns it through love, dedication, care, and trust. He protects the weaker until they can defend themselves. He is who a Lycaon is supposed to be."

"Is it different for shifters?" I asked. "I was trying to read up on them, and it sounds like their power structure is similar but much more brutal."

"Brutal is a good word to describe shifters," Cisco replied. "Their leadership is always in flux. They fight for power. We fight for mankind. We are happy to have the same Lycaon for decades, as long as they are doing what is right for Pack and humanity. Shifters, on the other hand, kill each other constantly."

"I'll add them to the list of groups to stay the hell away from."

Miguel laughed. "Good luck. There are more of them than any other spooky species in town. Hell, you have two wereleopards down the road from you."

"Mr. and Mrs. Haverland?" I asked, and both Miguel and Cisco nodded. "But they're so lovely."

"Being a shifter doesn't make you awful, just like being a witch doesn't make you evil. What you do with that power is what decides that," Miguel corrected my assumption.

"Okay, all right, enough small talk. Let's get to the good stuff," I said, finally done ignoring the elephant in the room. "When we go, do we tell them about Julian asking for a meeting with me? They're the local Pack. Shouldn't they have the vamps under their thumb?"

"Volunteer nothing. Let's see what they have to say first," Cisco answered before Miguel. "Something is up, and until we know what it is, we keep our cards close to our chests. Sofia is digging around on her end. She has a contact that's been feeding her intel. And until she gives the go-ahead, let's hold off making friends until we know if they're our enemies."

"Good to know," I replied. "What the hell do we do if they're our enemies?"

"Nothing you want to hear," Miguel said, his face a mix of 'don't ask' and 'you should know.'

"I may not want to hear it, but I need to know what the hell I do should things go down the drain," I countered.

"Do whatever it takes to get out of there, and I mean, whatever it takes. Do not let a single one of them approach you for any reason. It will come down to a kill or be killed," he answered. "I wouldn't worry about it too much yet. Natt won't want to piss off Caser or the entire Mexican Lycan community. We're tighter in Mexico than here. If he's a smart man, he will wait to see if me or Cisco leave before making a stupid move."

"Let's burn that bridge when we cross it," Cisco added. "In and out, keep the peace, and all should be well. And that means you, Ailis. Keep your temper in check. You have to live here, with them, I don't. You'll have to deal with the fallout of your attitude for a lot longer than I will. Don't piss off who you won't kill."

"I'll keep my attitude in check, but like the last time I stood in a room of you guys, I'm not shoveling Natt's shit any more than I was willing to take Caser's shit."

"I said keep your temper in check, not take his crap." Cisco's voice held an edge that grabbed my full attention. "If you take it, you'll look weak. You don't want to be the weakest in the room."

"And away we go," I mumbled. I looked at Cisco and grinned. "I feel like we've done this before, the big bad wolf dragging the little witch into the mouth of hell."

"Let's try to keep everyone's hearts in their chests this time," Cisco replied.

"I don't make promises I can't keep," I answered and grabbed my bag. Cisco passed me a gun on our way out to Miguel's rental Jeep. It felt a lot heavier than it should have. But bad decisions always weighed more.

Chapter Seven

Vancouver proper is known for being a busy and often traffic-jammed west coast seaport, hectic and rage-inducing on a good day, murderous on a bad day. Nothing makes a person lose their mind quite like bumper-to-bumper traffic, sprinkled with absent-minded texters and those who haven't paid attention since they pulled out of their driveways. But thankfully, we didn't see much of that in the middle of the night. We were one of the most diverse cities in Canada. Humans and monsters flocked to our shores in hopes of prospering in a region that accepted souled and soulless alike. There were still plenty of cities that wouldn't allow certain types of cursed, in both Canada and the States. It didn't stop the damned from buying houses, keeping their economy booming, but it was done under the radar. But not in Vancouver, where even the dead paid taxes.

I leaned against the back seat and stared out of the window. It wasn't often I was the passenger and I took full advantage of it. Van city was carved out of the mountains and sat on the edge of the ocean. The beauty was matched by the backdrop of hills and trails and some of the best ski slopes I had the pleasure of rolling down. And while I loved checking out and heading for the mountains, leaving Vancouver behind me, I lived here for the city herself. I loved the combination of historical buildings and architectural masterpieces taking up the skyline. Where some places were concrete jungles, Vancouver was green and lush. Gorilla gardens sprouted up on most corners, and cherry trees grew in most neighborhoods. The fusion of old and new, those with and without souls, the mundane and the magic, made our little chunk of the world a gorgeous, unpredictable mess of life and death. I morbidly loved that most about the place. That the winter couldn't grip the city for longer than a few months was reason number two.

Miguel turned onto East Hastings Street and headed west. He took two more turns then pulled up to the curb in front of the Chapel, an old church and funeral parlor. It's since been used for raves, fetish and kink events, art shows and everything less than holy. The first one-room Baptist chapel was built in the early seventeen hundreds and later knocked down and rebuilt without salting the earth in between. The original ghosts still haunted the place, which was one of the selling features for events. It's since collected more spirits and bad memories.

"A church?" I asked. "Do they know this place isn't sanctified anymore?"

"I was here when the Pack took it over, three years ago. Every room was fully blessed. They were supposed to keep it up weekly. Who knows, now," Miguel answered.

"I know," I replied, shivering at the thought of walking into another unsanctified church. Every time I had ever been in one, it had gone horribly wrong. Mexico being my most recent experience. "This place hasn't been blessed in a very long time, Miguel. I can feel it, like cobwebs."

"Ready or not, we're still going in," Cisco said, turning to face me in the backseat. "I feel it, too. A heads-up, it's much worse when you're inside. It feels like a disturbed graveyard in there. I can't see ghosts, but my wolf can feel them. There are too many for me to even count."

I groaned. "Great. Because I'm not scared enough."

"Ready?" Miguel asked, and I fought the urge to snap at him.

I breathed out my nervousness, unbuckled and gave him one nod. I wasn't ready. My stomach was gurgling, my chest felt tight, my heart pounded, and I was sweating like I had jogged all the way here. Cisco jumped out and pulled the seat forward for me to get out. Miguel came around the front and stood at my side. He squeezed my hand once, and all three of us stepped onto the sidewalk. The Chapel doors opened, and I stopped in my tracks.

"Philip?" I barely got his name out. I glanced at Miguel. "Did you know?"

"Yes," he replied.

"You didn't think to fucking tell me?" I asked. That I swore at him hammered home just how pissed off I was. "I can't believe you didn't tell me."

"Even with our secret out, it's not mine to tell," Miguel answered as if it were enough. It wasn't.

Miguel would have known from day one. I thought back to the weeks leading up to Philip's hire when I had been sitting at my kitchen table, reviewing resumes and cover letters. Miguel had picked Philip's out of the pile and said he sounded like the best candidate. He was smart, had a fitting background and had already graduated from my classes. I remembered Philip from my lectures. He took perfect notes, asked the right questions, challenged me professionally, and was a nice mixture of blunt and kind. But thinking of it now, I frowned. Miguel had leafed through over a hundred resumes and had only picked Philip. I had thought Miguel had an eye for talent. Turns out he simply had an eye for *Lycan*.

"Did you purposely have me hire someone so you could spy on me?" I asked, fuming.

"Spy is such a negative word," Miguel answered, and I raised my brow. "Yes, to keep an eye on you, protect you, call me if you were in trouble. Keep in mind, Lish, this was before we ended and well before you knew about Lycan. It's not like I could tell you, but I could take steps to make sure you were safe."

"You and I are going to have a little chat about this shit when we're home later. I want to know about any other little moles you have planted in my life," I said, and little lines around his eyes said I had caught him lying to me. "How many more, Miguel? I want the truth now. I'm not going in there with lies hanging over our heads. I won't be able to concentrate while I'm busy being angry with you."

"Three," he answered quickly. "Philip, your gardener, Hank, and the nurse at your doctor's office."

"Nurse? You have a goddamn nurse feeding you information?" I raised my voice. "My medical information is none of your damn business."

"That's the same thing she said. She doesn't tell me anything, Ailis. She called once when you had been clawed up by a demon and landed in the hospital. She told me you were fine, that she checked on you herself."

I nodded slowly. My face scrunched into a glare. "Philip and Hank are fine. My nurse, though, not cool, and it ends now, or I swear to God, I'll find ways to punish you that you won't like."

"Fair enough," Miguel replied and motioned toward the Chapel.

Philip stepped in front of us. "I can explain, Doc."

I released a long, shaking breath and tried to center myself. When I couldn't, I eyed Philip with the full force of my temper. My anger mixed with the winter chill, sending steam into the air around me. "What the fuck, Philip?"

"We can talk about it later, I promise," Philip replied. "But not here, not now, not with so many ears. I swear to you, the only information I fed Miguel was when your life was in danger."

"He called me half a dozen times," Miguel confirmed. "And each time, you were truly in danger of demons."

"I'm sorry I lied," Philip said, his voice smaller than it had been a moment ago. "I never wanted to lie to you. But to tell you the truth risked your life."

I let go of the anger. I was still ticked off, but I appreciated the position Philip had been in. I didn't understand their world, but I understood secrets and the need to protect them. My people survived because we were good at keeping secrets, and those who spilled them were burned or drowned. "You're lucky you're good at what you do."

"Or what, you'd fire me? Witch, please, you'd lose your broomsticks if I didn't tell you where they were." Philip leaned into my ear. "I wanted to tell you as soon as I knew the Mexico Pack outed us. My Lycaon forbade it. You have no friends in there."

"Why?" I asked. "If I already knew about you, why keep it a secret?"

"Games, power, greed, to show you who is in control here, pick one," Philip replied. "Keep your mouth shut, for the love of God. I won't be picking sides. I'm already on one. I can't protect you in there. I'd be just another body."

"You. Me. Tomorrow," I answered.

"I'll bring the muffins," he replied. "Let's get this over with. I still have papers to grade."

"You get all of them from now on," I teased.

"I already do." He laughed and walked ahead of us.

Cisco groaned and passed Miguel a twenty-dollar bill. "I had money on you punching him in the face."

"See, I have control over my temper," I said with a smile.

"Keep that in mind when we walk into a world that doesn't care about Philip in the same way that you do," Miguel said in a hushed voice. "Philip may be second from the top, an Alpha, but he can't help you in there. His job is to protect Natt and his Pack, not little witches."

"What a hairy position to be in," I whispered more to myself.

"Be smart with your care in these walls," Cisco added. "Your friend Philip has to live in this world. You don't. Do not get between him and anyone else, or he'll suffer later for it when you're not here to have his back. If you remember nothing else, remember that you're not part of the local Pack. You are barely a guest here. Focus on keeping yourself alive and let everyone else worry about themselves. This Pack is run more like the shifters' than ours in Mexico."

I glanced at Cisco. "What happened to you when you had my back in Mexico? The night you brought me to meet Caser and refused to leave me alone. Did you suffer for it?"

"Nothing happened," Miguel answered for Cisco. "For protecting you, he had my protection. No one is willing to challenge me to get to Cisco, not even Caser. When I'm not there, challengers have to get through those who are loyal to me. There's a long list of names, and the challenger would never survive them all."

"Sofia protected me." Cisco grinned. "When I went back after dropping you off, Sofia stood in front of me while Caser lost his temper. She held her ground until Miguel showed up."

"Does it bother you to have a woman protect you?" I asked. "I'm not saying Sofia can't kick some serious ass, but a lot of guys have egos so big, it causes their doom."

"Jesus, no. I have no problem bowing to Sofia. She's earned it and more," Cisco answered. "Her story is for her to tell, but she's one of the only Pack members who will go into hell for someone weaker and meaningless to a Pack. She's a true protector, and I'll always bow to someone who gives their life for Pack without expecting something in return. Bowing isn't always about physical strength, although she could beat the snot out of me. Her soul is stronger than mine, hands down. A pure soul is worth me crawling over glass for."

I smiled, thinking of Sofia and the night she came back for me. After releasing her from the dungeon, she carried Cisco to safety and returned for me as she had promised. She'd come with those whom Pack had considered weaker. Any monster who had stood in their way had been killed. When they'd gotten to the church and seen me in a circle, protecting one of their own from a hellhound, Sofia had challenged the hound. She'd still been bleeding from the wounds of torture but had stood firm. Holding a knife and a rock and a whole lot of faith, she'd driven the hound back to hell. Like Cisco, I'd crawl over glass for her. I added her to the list of people I'd do terrible things for.

My charm necklace vibrated against my chest as we inched closer to the building. I glanced at Miguel, who noticed. He leaned in with a warning. "Do not take their shit. Do not offer violence first, but by Christ, clean his fucking clock if you feel threatened."

With a nod of understanding, we stepped into the Chapel, and Miguel grabbed my hand. He, like me, could feel it. The Chapel was empty of blessing and full to the rafters of those who hadn't moved on. Some were older than sin, and some were here because of newer sins. Just standing there felt like I was stepping over graves. My skin prickled with static and goosebumps. At the edges of my vision, souls lingered. This building didn't just host ghosts — it was fully haunted. The mixture of evil, old and new, was an orchestra against my aura. Like a whisper, I could hear the moans of the freshly dead. I did my best to firm up my shields, but just knowing they were there broke my heart.

From the outside, the building looked like it would be cold and empty. It had been built to be a church and usher the dead into their next life. Since closing its holy doors, it had been turned into something less than religious, although a moment on the St. Andrew's cross at the front of the main room was a religious experience of its own. The only difference between what it had been and what it was, was the feeling you had when you stepped through the front doors. I shivered from the emotion staining the walls and wood floors. Sorrow, excitement and sexual energy filled the building and tainted the bones of the place. It reminded me of Mexico, the day I'd felt a group of them shifting, only tonight, it was missing something.

"There's no love here," I whispered around the urge to cry. It felt hopeless within these walls. I pushed myself into Miguel, breathing in his scent. If courage, duty and promise had a smell, it would be Miguel. "The energy hurts my soul. Such sadness."

"I feel it too," Miguel replied. "A wolf without a home. Pack without a cause."

"How long has Natt been using this place?" I asked.

"About two years," Cisco answered. "They started to rent it out when he took over the Pack."

I glanced at the windows, surprised to see them covered with thick, black curtains. The wood was off-color where the old holy symbols had once hung. I had been in the Chapel years ago when I'd been called for a summoned demon. At the time, the hanging crosses had still been fixed to the walls, decorated with fairy lights and fetish gear. I wasn't the first to notice the changes in décor. Miguel's eyes roamed the rooms we walked through, void of anything that would bother one of the cursed and damned.

When I opened my mouth to ask a question, Miguel shook his head. Now was not a time to point out the obvious or bring attention to what I was thinking. Why would the local Pack create a space comfortable for those they were supposed to be hunting? The building was empty of everything you'd want to have within reach, if killing vampires was their day job. Not a cross or bible or bottle of holy water. The only crosses in the entire place were hanging around our necks.

We stepped into the main room, where thousands of people had come and gone, mourning, marrying, and praying to their almighty. It felt dead. Aside from the energy of Pack, who were there in full force, the Chapel felt like an empty casket. Around the edges, men and women stood, their eyes fixed on Miguel. When I opened my shields just enough to sample the air, I grinned. Miguel was the strongest Lycan standing here. It rolled off him like waves crashing down on a stormy day. The others felt less in some way, muted in energy. Sure, the sheer number of them was terrifying, but I understood why they were staring at us like death had walked in the front door. The smell of his wolf filled my chest and firmed up my resolve. I could almost feel his fur rubbing along my aura, marking me as his. I was the Grimmwolf of the Los Luna Pack and the mate of one of their strongest. I wasn't feeling cocky, but I was feeling safer for it.

Cisco grabbed my other hand and let down the wall he used to hold in the energy of his wolf. It pulsed out of him as a warning, an utterly terrifying warning. Where Miguel was a thunderous storm of power, Cisco's energy was a calm before the storm. His wolf was a beast that stalked, striking when you least expect it. It was the first time I had felt all of Cisco's wolf, and it was beautiful and horrifying. When people stepped back, Cisco didn't smile, but I did. Death hadn't just walked through the door. He'd brought friends. Cisco's energy was only second to Miguel, and I felt a little safer because of it. I stood between hell and fury and relaxed just enough to release the tension building in my shoulders.

"Miguel Rodríguez, warrior of the Los Luna Pack, welcome to the Noire Lune Pack." The man at the front, to our right, spoke. Philip stood at his side. Another man I hadn't met stood on his other. He looked angry, but the anger had been there before we had arrived. The man talking, who I assumed was Natt, glanced at Cisco and scowled. "Cisco, how kind of you to show your true colors."

"Nathaniel," Miguel replied without a formal greeting. There was no emotion in Miguel's voice, not like when he was talking to Caser. If anything, I heard contempt. Like me, Miguel and Cisco would have felt the anger and sadness staining the air, already there before our arrival. It was the kind of hate that took years to build and had to be tended to like a prized garden.

Cisco tipped his head but didn't bow like I had seen Caser's people do to him when he entered the room. Not once had I seen Caser force his people to bow. They did it willingly for loyalty earned. I nodded my head once. I didn't bow to anyone for any reason. Lycaon or Alpha or demon, I'd never get on my knees willingly. Natt moved through his people to our front. He was arrogance, all ego and no honor. Natt felt like a fresh off the line lesser demon, weak and scared, and carried a similar smell. The evil he would have had to do to hold the scent of hell made me shiver. I let my eyes blur and looked at his aura through my own. *Brown and black. Insecure and tainted.* I didn't have to see his aura to have known that. The strips of red told me he only looked the part of a Lycaon, all muscle and fashion sense, but wasn't who he was supposed to be for his people. Warning flares went up in my soul. He was not a safe place for anyone, not even his own people. The rage stripped on his aura would almost be a match for my own.

He glanced at Cisco, then me, shaking his head. His blond hair, tied in the back, swung side to side. I smiled when I looked into his baby blues. He looked like he should be on a runway somewhere and not in a haunted church. His full, ruby-red lips scowled.

"Do we have a problem so soon?" I asked. "We just got here. It usually takes me talking to piss someone off, and I haven't even said a word."

"You, human, do not have a voice here," Natt answered. "You may be the Grimmwolf of the Los Luna Pack, but you carry no weight in these walls."

"Good, great. I'll be taking my leave then," I said and turned my back to him. I took two steps away when I felt a hand on my shoulder. I glanced at the hand and looked back at Natt. "You get one warning. Take your hand off me, or you and I are going to have a serious problem. You do not want to have a problem with me," I said and looked back at his hand in warning. "I don't like to be touched."

"You've heard the lady." Cisco pushed his body between us, shoving Natt's hand from my shoulder. "Is that the impression you want us to leave here with tonight? Putting your hands on someone who has the protection of the Los Luna Pack is a bold statement to make so early in the game. Touch her again, and you'll see why the Los Luna Pack is the most feared Pack on this continent."

I turned to face Natt and scanned the room for potential problems. No one had stepped forward to have their Lycaon's back. That was curious. Caser's people would have swarmed to protect him. But I suppose, in Natt's case, he couldn't scare people into being loyal or willing to accept death in his place. That was earned, and it was obvious he hadn't. Almost every eye was on us, waiting to see what would happen. The only person who didn't care was sitting in the middle of the room, leaning over a textbook and a pad of paper—Noah. He hadn't lied. He was here for school and wanted the hell out of dodge. I didn't blame him. And after mere minutes with Natt, I was glad I hadn't sent him packing. Natt didn't strike me as the type to be forgiving.

"You challenge me?" Natt asked Cisco.

"It's not much of a challenge if I know I'll win. Take it as a promise, Nathaniel. A warning, if you will, and the only one I will give you as a guest in your territory." Cisco grinned. "For my Grimmwolf, I will clean this fucking floor with the hide I will peel from your dead body. If you leave her be, we don't have a problem."

Natt looked around Cisco to Miguel, who was calm and smiling. "Does Francisco speak for you as well?"

"Oh, I think he's doing a fine job without my input," Miguel answered.

"You risk dying for this little wolf's words," Natt said and glared at Cisco, but Cisco stood his ground.

"Die?" Miguel laughed. "You will not be the one to take my life. Not now, not ever. But trust that if you move against me or mine, you will taste no mercy from my hands." Miguel's calm demeanor made me uncomfortable. He had gone to the place in his mind that I often went to before I did something horrible to survive. "We're here by your invite. You disrespect us by ignoring Cisco and Ailis, then you put your hands on one of us. If you did not want to deal with the fallout of your own actions, why did you start this night by dishonoring your guests and your Pack? Your behavior brings shame to your wolf, or what's left of it."

Natt took a step forward, an inch from Cisco's chest, but Cisco didn't move. Cisco's eyes narrowed on Natt. "You're not my Lycaon. If you think I'm going to take a step back from you, you've not been paying attention. The Los Luna Pack backs up for no one. You must earn that respect because I'll die before I give it under threat."

I cleared my throat. The tension in the air dried my mouth. "If you touch him, I'll end your cursed little life. I can smell the pits on you, and I know, without a doubt, the rest of the Pack smells it as well. You've touched hell one too many times, and sooner or later, they will collect. I wonder, little wolf, what you've been bargaining for? Power? Position? Money? Who has your ticket, Natt? Keep pushing, and I'll find out before your next finger touches any of us."

Natt's eyes landed on me. They carried a weight to his gaze that made me want to squirm under the pressure of it. But like Cisco and Miguel, I wouldn't back up for him. He could kill me faster than I could so much as harm a hair on his head, but I wouldn't go down without a fight. If he wanted to play games with our lives, I'd make him doubt his own safety. I wasn't exactly bluffing. I'd done so shady shit to save my life, but opening hell to shove him in was a very last resort. He didn't need to know that, though.

"I may have the protection of the Los Luna Pack, but they also have my protection in return," I said. The tension climbed, and I took a step forward. I lowered my voice, getting my point across. I wouldn't allow him to terrify me. I'd spent my entire life scared, and Natt was a drop in the bucket compared to the fear I faced on a daily basis. He had nothing on demons.

"I promise you, Natt, we won't be the ones to die tonight. I will open the pits of hell to save my friends, and you, wolf, would not be one of the people I saved tonight, but you'd surely be a meal for the Gods." I took another step forward. "One hair on our heads out of place, and I'll find you. I've already booked my trip to hell. Taking you with me would make the trip worthwhile."

"Back up, witch," Natt replied in a heated voice, but his eyes said differently. He was scared but wouldn't say it. I'd let him keep his position of the fearless top dog in front of his people, but both he and I knew I had rattled him.

"If you're waiting for me to cower, you'll be waiting all night. I play with demons and real Lycan. You, wolf, don't scare me." I let the amusement drain from my face. "Now, we can posture, fluff our tails and growl at each other until the sun rises, we can be civilized and get this over with, or we can keep jabbing at each other until someone bleeds. It's been weeks since I was covered in blood, but I'm fine if tonight ends my dry spell."

Natt smiled rather than continuing to needle me, turning the night into a crime scene. Though, I had never stood in the middle of a Lycan on Lycan fight for dominance. I doubted any of our bodies would be found. "You have guts. You may just live long enough for us to become friends."

"Don't hold your breath," I replied. "You wanted us here. Let's cut to the chase so we can go home. I'm tired, sore and starting to get grumpy."

Natt stepped to the side and invited us in. "Let's eat and discuss why I've invited you into the den of Noire Lune."

"That went better than I had expected," I said to Cisco and winked. It was the same thing I had said to him after I had met his Pack.

"No one died. It went better than the last time," he answered. "But the night is young."

"That it is," Natt called from a few feet away.

Miguel led the way, followed by me, then Cisco. I trusted Cisco to have my back, and Miguel had fewer scruples than I did, but we both saw eye to eye on me walking out of that Chapel in one piece. The crowd parted for us, eyes darting from their wolf in command to the small group of deadly visitors. Seeing their nervousness made me understand why Miguel and Cisco had needed permission. They were weak, watered-down and defeated. They reminded me of what failure looked like. My eyes found Philip's. He shrugged but motioned for me to keep walking.

Natt sat at the head table in front of an already-prepared plate of food. I don't know why, but it bothered me that Natt had someone dish up his food as if he were a king. Philip took a seat and pushed a chair out for me to take. We both sat out of arms reach of Natt. Miguel returned to the table with a plate of food. He had a mountain of food, as did Cisco. They both shrugged. Miguel and Cisco sat closer to the action, neither of them afraid. Cisco started shoveling in his food as soon as his rear touched his chair. That man could eat a meal while haggling for his soul with Satan. The rest of the room found seats, but their chatter was quiet enough to be able to hear whatever it was that brought us to the Chapel.

Philip and I were the only ones not eating. My nerves were shot, and I didn't trust Natt not to poison me. I didn't have the nose of a wolf and wouldn't smell it coming. I glanced at Philip again, surprised he was a second banana. He didn't look like he had the kind of clout it would take to hold that position. The moment I settled in beside him, he sighed, and his energy slowly started to roll off him. The energy pouring off Philip was pure, raw and staticky. It was warm but also told something deep inside my brain that it was time to run. He would never be as strong as Miguel or Cisco, but I was shocked Philip was a second and not the Lycaon. I shivered, and Philip snorted a laugh. I gave him a heated side-eye. I wasn't impressed with the secrets. It didn't matter the reason, not to my feelings. It still hurt like I had been lied to, even if Pack had sworn to always hide who they were from humans.

Philip leaned into my ear. "Muffins, tomorrow."

"I want a new car for this, Philip, not freaking muffins."

"Homemade with homegrown blueberries and crumble on top."

"That's more like it. Deal," I said with a smile.

Natt cleared his throat, and I glanced up at him, then around the room. Miguel and Cisco were discussing the odds of a Megalodon being real while watching a video on social media. Pack had started chatting amongst themselves. And not one of us paid much attention to the man in charge. He looked like his ego was bruised. He knocked on the table until all of us were staring at him. The kind of self-importance a person would need to have to believe they were deserving of attention for no other reason than a title was stunning. Sure, he'd had to kill for the title, but the rest of the world was pretty similar. Kill or be killed. Natt wasn't unique or special in that regard, although he thought differently.

"I asked you here for a few reasons," Natt said, louder than necessary. I fought not to roll my eyes. "One, I wanted to meet the woman who had the protection of the Mexico Packs and find out who could command that kind of attention. When you first walked in here, I didn't think you were worth the fuss, until you stepped up beside Cisco."

"I wasn't bluffing. If you touch my family, I'll kill you." The words came out of my mouth before I could think of what I was saying. "We're stronger because we have each others' backs, to the bitter end, Natt. Allowing your friends or your people to face danger on their own is a weakness, not a strength. And those who do, deserve to die in shame."

"And there you have it, the reason I turned my back and walked away. You have honor. You are Pack without an inner Lycan," Natt replied. "You are the mate of a wolf. You are one of us."

I smiled. "I'll be whatever you want me to be as long as it buys me freedom from being hunted by you all."

"We don't hunt our people unless we have no choice," he answered.

"So you say." I raised my eyebrows. He might not hunt them, but he didn't do a damn thing to protect them. I could see it written on the faces of the weaker Pack members. I kept my comments to myself, but it took effort.

"And the reason you called us here?" Miguel asked. "Your invitation said it was life or death."

I nudged Miguel. "Life or death?"

"Don't worry, little witch. Philip has been watching you since you returned from Mexico, and what an exciting time you've been having. We saw it on the news," Natt answered. "The local Nest has heard about Ailis and her Pack protection."

"And how would they know that?" Miguel asked, and Natt shrugged.

"Small world, Miguel." Natt's only answer.

"Fuck," Cisco groaned. "Your local fangs are a nightmare."

"Up until recently, I thought the local vampires were run by a woman, Elizabeth?" I asked. "When did Julian take over? Have things gotten worse since he set up shop?"

"Elizabet is her original name. She's gone by many names over the decades. Elizabeth is her current name," Natt answered. "She is Julian's human servant. Julian doesn't deal with humans. She does, or she sends one of Julian's familiars. I believe you've already met with Conor?" he asked, and I glanced at Philip. His face betrayed nothing. "Julian has always been the Master, and Elizabet has always been his awful puppet."

"Jesus, how old is she?" I asked. "How old is Julian?"

"No one knows for certain," Natt answered. "She's been with Julian for decades, and Julian is one of the oldest vampires I've ever met."

"If you've met the monster and his awful little creatures, why, pray tell, are they still alive?" I asked and felt Miguel still beside me. Ripping the scab off the truth was dangerous business. "I thought it was your job to take care of bad little monsters?"

"He's done nothing to warrant a death sentence that we can prove," Natt replied, and I rolled my eyes.

Miguel clearing his throat was the only thing that kept me from digging away at the horseshit coming out of Natt's mouth.

"If he's that old, why has he not moved on to the Elders?" Miguel asked.

"Tired of the shit, like the rest of us," Natt answered.

The answer made perfect sense to me, but Natt having those answers made my stomach flop. It sounded like he and the creatures he was supposed to be hunting were having some rather deep conversations. Why the hell would a Lycan, sworn to protect innocents, be socializing with the beasts who stole that innocence? Every time the man opened his mouth, more questions piled up in my mind. I glanced at Miguel, who had the same knowing look in his eyes but didn't let it fill his entire face.

"The local Nest has always known about me," I said, trying to pump out a few more answers from Natt. "Why does it matter who my friends are? Why would vampires care? I'm not a hunter. I don't have anything to do with them. I've never messed with the locals. Why now?"

"Who has your back is all that matters in this world, Ailis," Natt answered. "Who your friends are tells the rest of the powers that be, whether you stand higher or lower than they do. To have the ear of Pack means you have the protection of those who hunt *bad little monsters* like them."

I left his answer alone. It had holes big enough to drive my car into. Natt did nothing to protect mankind from Julian and his people. I knew the statistics. Although vampire attacks were rare in Van, they weren't zero. My mind turned with questions I'd never get to ask for fear of turning this polite bullshit into a bloodbath. I'd save my digging for later when we were safe and sound and away from someone I would now consider a bad guy. From the moment I'd met Natt, I'd known he would become an enemy, someone I couldn't trust.

"Are they going to try to kill me?" I asked.

"You're either being hunted or doing the hunting," Cisco answered for Natt. "It's the way of the world for us all."

"This is a warning to you, nothing more. If the vampires know, everyone else is soon to find out," Natt replied. "I'd watch your back. Word is, the bloodsucker you took out during your hunt was one of Julian's children. So far, there's no talk of retribution, given the sap was deserving of death, but that doesn't mean Julian is soon to forgive or forget. If I were you, the next time Conor Madden comes to your door, I'd tread carefully."

"Which is where I come in," Cisco added. "I believe you've received the request from Caser for me to remain in your territory until Miguel is able to move back?"

"You're moving back?" I asked Miguel, and felt my face flush.

He smiled. "I didn't have time to tell you."

"Cisco has my permission to remain. Miguel, you and I will need to discuss your permanent return to my territory. Until then, you have permission to be here for your vacation, as agreed upon. Anything more, we need to work out some ground rules." Natt turned to me. "Your oath to the Los Luna Pack extends to all Pack. Your silence keeps that heart of yours beating. But if it's all the same to you, I'd like to hear it from your lips."

"I'll keep your secret," I said.

"For as long as you keep your oath, you have the protection of the Noire Lune Pack," Natt said, and I believed exactly zero percent of his words. "Please don't make me or my people take your life."

"You'd have to get in line, it appears," I replied.

"Stay, go, but I'm late for another appointment," Natt said and stood. He didn't say another word.

My chair screeched on the floor when I stood. "Philip, would you be so kind as to walk me out?"

Cisco grabbed a handful of homemade cookies before he stood. Miguel was at my side, and Philip was at our front. Miguel squeezed my hand as we walked from the room, likely sensing my unease. As soon as we stepped outside, I let go of his hand and ran mine down my arms and neck. It felt like I had spiders crawling over my naked skin.

"You get used to it," Philip said, walking me to the Jeep.

"I don't want to get used to it," I replied. "I don't ever want to come back."

"None of us do," he muttered.

Before opening the car door, I give Philip a hug. "Did you tell Natt that Conor Madden was at my office?"

"No," Philip replied. "He brought it up. I didn't volunteer it."

"That's what I thought," I answered. "I wasn't called here to receive a warning, was I?"

"No, you're being sized up," he answered. "I'll come in the morning and fill you in. I can't be caught spilling secrets, or I'll be the next one *sized up*."

"Are you safe here tonight?"

"As safe as I am any other night," he replied. "I'll see you in the morning."

"You bet your furry ass you will," I answered and pulled him deeper into the hug. "If you need help, call me. I'll always come for you."

At first, he laughed. Once he realized I was serious, he relaxed. "Thanks, Doc."

I climbed into the Jeep and left my assistant at the Chapel with his people. All these years, I hadn't a clue what Philip was. I wouldn't be surprised if I found out the IT department was run by unicorns or the Dean was a bloody elf. The more I moved through this new world, the less I felt I knew. When it came to dancing with devils and taking meetings with monsters, the dark was a scary place to be.

Chapter Eight

After one stop at an all-night grocery, the three of us stood in my living room, none of us having said much on our drive home. The tension in the Jeep had been high enough for me to ask them to crack a window. The anger pouring off the two of them made me sweat buckets and squirm the entire way home. Once inside, after Miguel and Cisco had scouted the property and the house, I finally broke the silence, pointing out that my cat was calm and it wasn't needed if she wasn't going batshit crazy.

"When you said we'd take no shit going in there, I didn't think we'd do *that*," I said, shuddering. "That came pretty damn close to someone losing their heart again."

"He started it," Cisco said, a hint of amusement in his voice. "If he would have offered respect, it would have begun that way. Instead, he wanted to test how far he could push us, how much he could get away with when it came to you. He found out pretty quick that we pushed back and took your protection seriously. The show tonight is the only thing this Pack understands. Fighting is the only way to survive this Pack. The moment they smell weakness, they prey upon it, and I, for one, have had my fill of being someone's victim. I'll die first."

"Same," I answered, and I meant it. Until a person has been tortured for someone else's amusement, they'll never truly understand why death is a better option.

"I think it went okay," Miguel said. "Albeit tense, it could have been worse."

"Perhaps for you, but you have claws and fangs. I have a spell pot that my cat sleeps in and a broomstick," I replied. "I think Natt hates me. He hated me before I even stepped into the Chapel."

"He doesn't hate you, Lish," Miguel said. "Natt is threatened by you. At your weakest, you're still stronger than he is. He's scared of you, and that, little witch, is not a safe position for you to be in, with or without our protection. Being feared is worse than being loved."

"Speaking of, how the hell did Julian find out that I have Pack protection?" I asked. "Pack business isn't exactly common knowledge. Only Pack would know, and Caser would die before turning information over to walking tapeworms."

"Tapeworms," Cisco snickered. "I like that one."

Miguel grinned but soon sighed. "I was thinking the same thing. Someone from Pack would have had to open their mouths. Talking Pack business with anyone outside of our world is strictly forbidden."

"Yeah, so is consorting with monsters, yet he knew an awful lot about vampires for someone who gives a shit about Pack law," Cisco added, and the three of us nodded.

"How can you talk to me about it, and it's not breaking law? I mean, I'm human, minus the curse and familiar," I asked.

"You're not outside Pack. You are our Grimmwolf. And you're my chosen mate," he answered. "I think your claws are sharper than mine."

"Hmm, does being your mate come with any perks?" I questioned. His wiggling eyebrows were answer enough.

"If you were a Lycan, I'd call you my Luna," he replied. "Regardless of your personal ties to me, our Pack has adopted you as one of our *guardianas*. Spanish for Guardian. Someone who watches over the weaker Pack members. When you came to Mexico, you risked your life for our Pack. You called the hounds from hell to save the daughter of our Lycaon and to end the slaughtering of our people. It is a title of respect and honor."

"It doesn't come with any benefits I've enjoyed so far," I countered.

"You still have your head, don't you?" Cisco asked. "I'd say that's a pretty big perk of being part of Pack."

"I still have it for now," I corrected. It was currently one too many chopping blocks. I started to pace while Miguel and Cisco sat, watching me move from one side of my living room to the other. "How did Natt know that the flunky Julian had sent was Conor Madden? I asked Philip, he said Natt already knew about it and had asked him questions. He also said I wasn't called for this meeting out of the kindness of Natt's heart. It wasn't to warn me. It was to size me up. I think, like you said, Cisco, they were seeing how far your protection reached."

"I'm sure we'll find out sooner than later," Cisco answered. "Sofia is on the trail. Nothing gets by her. She's like a dog with a bone, no pun intended."

"Natt said Julian is one of the oldest vampires he's ever met," I said what I had been wondering during our meeting with Natt. "Why is he meeting with vampires and not killing them?"

"Good question," Miguel replied. "Like you both, I saw the missing holy objects at the Chapel. I also noticed that not a single Pack member was wearing a cross. This is the first Pack I've been to where there is a complete void of religion. Sure, hanging a ten-foot Jesus on a cross isn't needed, but our people are highly religious. We are some of the truest believers. Our entire existence is based on us guarding the very gates of hell, saving the souls of the innocent and ridding the world of evil. How could there be no evidence of this, with the very people sworn to do the duty of their Gods? I wasn't expecting the place to be a holy site, but I was expecting to feel it radiating from Pack. Belief, honor, obedience, trust, courage—something other than the emptiness I felt."

"That place is seriously haunted," I shivered. "Not old death, Miguel. There were so many new and tortured souls in there. They died horrific deaths, and soon enough, Natt would have had to be involved. I doubt a dozen people kicked the bucket, and he didn't know about it. He's a wolf, for fuck's sake, he would have smelled it."

"I felt them, too," he replied.

"Cisco, remember when I first met your Pack, and I told you I felt hate?" I asked, and he nodded. "I felt that tonight, fully focused on Natt. Along with fear so deep, it was like swimming in tears while we stood there. The auras of each member were milky with desperation and fear. Why were they so scared?"

"The hate was directed at Natt because he's a poor Lycaon," he answered. "The fear, though, it wasn't a fear of us or for us. They were scared we'd leave them behind. And we did. I hate that we did, but this soon in the game, we can't be challenging the local Pack without a damn good reason. Unlike them, we don't challenge for power and status. Sure, challenges are made, but only when someone can do a better job."

"It felt like walking on eggshells in there. I got the feeling that they were terrified to say something wrong. I wonder how they're being punished?" I asked but didn't really want to know. Monsters were creative, and Natt most certainly was a monster.

"I think they're being offered up as forbidden fruit." Cisco leaned forward. Miguel hissed, and I inched in, curious. "Sofia dug up a rumor about Natt. It's only a rumor for now, but she said it's from a credible source. She's heard Natt has allowed the bloodsuckers to drink from his people. She heard Natt has been offering up his Pack to Julian and his children since day one. To what end, Sofia didn't know."

Miguel's eyes widened, and he flew into a series of swearing and shouting in Spanish. He was too fast for me to follow, but the words I did pick up were in line with cursing a vampire into the pits of hell to burn for eternity. I wouldn't argue that.

"I didn't notice any bite marks on anyone tonight, but that's a pretty strong rumor to be circling about Pack. Rumors start somewhere, and Sofia didn't get the sense like it was idle gossip," Cisco added. "I'll stay on top of it, and if there's any truth to it, I'll let you know."

"Don't you guys have a council or governing body?" I asked. Cisco pointed to the floor, and Miguel pointed to the ceiling. "Heaven and hell? How do you bring a concern forward? It's not like you can send God an email."

"If laws are broken, the Pack member is challenged by whatever Pack found out. If the challenged Pack loses, the problem is dealt with. If they win, they keep going until someone bigger and better takes care of it," Miguel answered.

"Doesn't seem like a productive way of dealing with things," I replied.

"It can be dealt with in a matter of minutes rather than waiting on a tribunal of Lycan to decide someone's fate." Miguel finally stood. "I'm going to grab a shower and unpack. I'm still running on a different time zone and feeling the weight of it. Morning is a few hours away, and I have a feeling rest will be a thing of the past."

"Come on, Cisco, I'll show you to your room," I said and motioned for him to follow me. I opened my basement door, and he frowned.

"You're putting me in your basement?" he asked. "I thought we were friends? After all I've let you do for me, this is the thanks I get?"

"It's better than a dog house, wolf." I laughed. "Don't fret. It's fully renovated and furnished, has a full apartment, a gym, a four-person jacuzzi tub in the bathroom, and an entertainment room with a projection television. The last people who lived here left everything behind. It was all still wrapped in shipping crates. Trust me, you're not roughing it. It's nicer down there than up here. Also, the bar is fully stocked."

He smiled. "Well then, lead the way to my squalor."

We went down two sets of stairs into a part of the house I never needed to go but always kept spotless. I had this overwhelming fear that someone would come over, unannounced, see a little dust and tell everyone I lived like some big bad witch in a hovel. My grandmother had been almost compulsive with housework. Never once had a visitor seen a dirty dish or a used towel hanging on the rack. It had rubbed off on me, even though Samuel and Philip, and now Miguel and Cisco, were the only ones who came over, and neither of them had gone into the basement.

I showed Cisco around, ending at the entrance to the master bedroom. "Pick whichever bedroom you want, but this room is the one with a king-sized bed and the tub that'll beat the muscles right off your body. It's amazing."

"Do you have many guests?" he asked, dropping his bags in the master bedroom. "This looks pretty nice for a lone witch."

"Solitary witch," I corrected him. I fought not to blush. I didn't exactly have many friends. "You'd be my first actual guest."

Picking up on my awkwardness, Cisco squeezed my shoulder. "People don't know what they're missing out on, Ailis. You're worth knowing. Fuck everyone who doesn't realize that."

"Thanks, Cisco," I replied. "I love that you're here, but what about school?"

"You have me for seven months." He followed me into the living room. "I start next fall."

"What about work?"

"The Pack pays my wages while I'm here protecting the wicked witch of the North." He kicked back on the couch. "This vacation better not be as bad as yours just was, or I'm going back to Mexico."

"Does being here put you in danger?" I asked. "Is staying with me going to put you at risk?"

"No more risk than I am at home. I'm Lycan. Being what I am puts me at risk," he answered. "Don't worry about me. I can take a lot more than you can, and I'm not nearly as weak as this Pack is. It's like they're empty of everything that makes them Lycan. The youngest ones are terrified. Did you notice, when we walked in, their weakest were at the edge of the room, to be picked off as if they mattered not? Natt is pathetic."

"Yeah, I saw that. They didn't have the same energy as you guys. It was…unsettling. It was like their wolves were asleep."

"They've lost that spark, the part of our wolf that is always awake, always searching for a voice in need," he explained. "A gentle snort from my wolf would knock them on their asses. Don't worry about me."

"I'd be a crappy friend if I didn't worry about the very few friends I actually have."

"You're not going to be a lasting friend if you keep one foot in the damned and the other scrambling for a taste of heaven."

"How poetic." I rolled my eyes.

"What I'm saying is, be careful, Ailis. You have the protection of *my* Pack. You are loved by *my* Pack. You will never find that anywhere else. Natt will never protect you over his people. Hell, he won't even protect his own people, let alone a witch. He won't give his life for you like we will." He jumped up from the couch and gave me the kind of hug I'd have expected a brother to give me, had I had one. "Never stick your neck out for someone who is holding a hand behind their back. You never know what they're holding. And when it comes to Natt, he has fucking claws. Don't ever show him your throat."

On my way out of the living room, my cat strolled in and jumped onto the couch beside Cisco, purring. *What a traitor.* I left them both to the movie Cisco was picking out. It felt odd to hear the noise from others in my house. I had moved in a few months after I had left Miguel and hadn't had many people over besides Philip, demons, Samuel about demons, and the police about demons. Seeing Cisco talk to Cat as though she could understand him made me smile. Hearing Miguel speaking on the phone in Spanish made it feel like my house was perfectly full, like I had just eaten Christmas turkey and was slowly falling asleep on the couch. My eyes watered at the sensation. I've never had that full house feeling, and the instant I felt it, I understood why people gathered in groups and lived with every room full. Without them, my house would feel painfully empty.

When Miguel hung up, I wrapped my arms around his naked stomach from behind. His hair smelled like my lavender wash. "How's Caser?"

"Pissed off, scared, disgusted, wanting to jump on a plane." He turned to face me. "The more Sofia digs, the more I'd rather you come home to Mexico."

"I thought you were moving here?" I asked, kissing him softly.

"I'm having my doubts," he replied. He pulled me into his arms and kissed the top of my head. "This is going to get worse before it gets better. Worse means a lot of bodies on the ground."

"It always does," I replied. "When did you decide to move back here?"

"The moment you got on the plane to come home," he answered. "I went to Caser right after the airport and requested permission to leave Pack to come here. He had been expecting it and gave me his blessing. He said he'd help me negotiate my entry into this Pack, but now I'm thinking I'd rather be a rogue."

"Rogue?"

"A lone wolf. A Lycan without a Pack. Usually, it happens when a Lycan is kicked out of a Pack or has chosen the life of a solitary hunter. It's a hard life. We have a few in Mexico, all hunters. We're not meant to be solitary animals. We are very social and depend on our Packs for safety and care. But I don't think I'd be safe with this Pack, or cared for. I'd do better on my own."

"Can you start your own Pack?" I asked.

"It doesn't happen often in a territory this small," he replied. "It would be a constant war. I will speak to Caser. If I decide to remain rouge within this territory, I'd request the protection of his Pack while I'm here."

"Does that mean you're still part of the Los Luna Pack? Like when you were here before?"

"Yes, but unlike before, I wouldn't have the permission of the local Pack," he explained. "When I was here with you before, the Lycaon gave me permission. He invited me to Pack for celebrations, meals, hunts, and general closeness to Pack. He was a good man. I didn't like all of his practices, but he was a good Lycaon."

I pulled away and put my clothes in my hamper. I crawled into bed and patted the spot beside me. "Come to bed. The problems of today can wait until you have a clear mind tomorrow."

Miguel stripped off his gray joggers and climbed up the foot of the bed, his eyes brightening with each movement toward me. His deep growl made me squirm. He gripped my ankles and pulled my legs open, hard and fast. My breath caught in my throat as I looked down the line of my body to see him kneeling between my legs, his bright orange eyes roaming every inch of me. The air practically crackled with electricity, the energy of his wolf mixing with mine. Our shared excitement only grew with each touch of Miguel's hands. With every nerving sparking, I pulled Miguel up my body and to my lips, our passionate frenzy pushed beyond the limits of hunger for each other. I couldn't get enough. I gripped his hair and kissed him with force, bruising our lips together.

Our tongues danced in each other's mouths while our hands roamed freely. Miguel's arousal thursted between my thighs, hard and thick. With each press against me, my wetness coated him, inviting him to enter me. Miguel reached under my thigh, gripping my ass, locking me firmly in place. He leaned his body to the side, opening my thighs wide. He kissed his way down my jaw and shoulder, massaging my breast while teasing me by inching his tongue down my chest. Latching onto my nipple, I arched my back, moaning his name. Miguel's hands continued down my body, rubbing my stomach, my hip, and my outer thigh.

"Please," I groaned, lifting my hips toward his hand. "Touch me."

While still twirling my nipple in his mouth, Miguel ran his fingers down my core, settling on my clit. I jerked into his touch and released a long sigh as he increased the pressure, rubbing slowly in circles. I rotated my hips, increasing the intensity of pleasure. As soon as I pressed myself harder against him, our bodies finding the perfect rhythm, my need climbing, Miguel pushed two fingers inside, bringing a raspy moan from my throat.

"Right there. Don't stop," I begged.

At first, his motion was slow and deliberate. But as my breathing quickened, so did his speed and pressure. I let out a moan with each thrust he made, each sound a little more desperate than the last. I dug my nails in this arm as my orgasm built. Little by little, my grasp on reality faded, and I was lost to pure pleasure. I felt nothing but the pulse within. Gone was my bed, the room, my voice, my thoughts. Just pure ecstasy and the man I loved more than life, bringing it to the surface.

"Hold on, Lish," Miguel whispered.

Miguel held my squirming body tight against his as he continued to work my orgasm to the surface, letting down the walls to his energy. His aura mingled with mine, sending an entirely different sensation through my body. Finally, with expert precision, my orgasm rocked me from my core. My stomach warmed, my toes and fingers tingled, and energy coursed through my body like lightning, every nerve coming alive at once. My back arched, raising my middle off the bed, as the pleasure pulsed through my entire body. I moaned, swore and begged for more and less at once. I wanted it all but was on the verge of passing out from the energy. When I thought it was over, another wave would crash down, and my scream would be eaten by an intensity I hadn't felt before. When I reached the peak of sensation unlike anything I had ever experienced, where our energies met in the middle, I broke open like a geyser. With one final shudder, I fell back onto the bed. If Miguel hadn't been holding me, I swore I would have floated away. I groaned out his name in one long sigh, twitching as I came back to myself, back to the bed and his arms and my thoughts.

That had been the most intense orgasm I had ever had. It erased time and all other feelings but pleasure. It stilled my heart and sped my pulse. It felt like everything and nothing at once. Miguel rolled from my side, lifting my arms above my head and pushing himself inside while I still pulsed. I closed my eyes and groaned at the sheer size of him. Slowly, Miguel pulled himself from me, and I fought against his grip to draw him back inside.

"Open your eyes, Lish," Miguel said, inches from my face.

I glanced up at him and smiled. Bright orange with flecks of brown stared back at me. A shiver ran down my body as I held his dark, penetrating gaze. His aura flared with love and protection. His wolf, in the distance, ran through the forest of Miguel's mind. Pure joy and happiness poured from them both. Miguel let go of my arms and held my face, kissing me softly. From earth-shattering to something that felt even better. With each push of his hips, I felt loved.

"I love you, Miguel."

"I've loved no one but you," he replied and kissed me.

Our kiss felt like it had gone on forever, eating up the problems of today, taking away the fears and troubles and making promises to stand with me when I looked into the darkness tomorrow. I lifted my hips to meet his, thrust for thrust. I held onto his neck as his speed increased, finding the rhythm that would send us both over the edge. Tonight was not about rushing it. It was about enjoying more than the orgasms, more than simple pleasure. It was about us. I moaned into his mouth when he found the spot inside. Miguel's pace quickened as I demanded more. I was so close to the edge of oblivion. My eyes fluttered shut, and I rode out the pleasure with a scream of his name. As it rose, he was in the midst of his own orgasm. I dug my nails into his shoulder, and together, we brought the heavens into our grasp. Miguel drove himself in as far as my body would allow and growled my name into the night. As he spilled his pleasure into me, he kept his pace, willing the last of my orgasm to the surface.

Tears escaped the corners of my eyes. A cry of pure, raw, desperately craved pleasure ignited every fiber of my being. I tucked my face into Miguel's chest and let it wash out of me, leaving me feeling like a bowl of parts and pieces without a start or end. Miguel slowly settled on top of me, sliding to the side, his heart hammering and his legs still twitching. In the blur of my vision, I could see his wolf settling down at the foot of the bed, my cat coming in and stretching out beside him. All of my pieces now fit back together. Every part of my life now had a place, and I felt safe, cherished, blessed, and utterly exhausted.

"I guess that means you really missed me?" I whispered, rolling my back to Miguel and pulling his arm around me.

"It felt like I was holding my breath the entire time we were apart," he answered, kissing my shoulder. "I'll start looking for a place this week, so we can be closer. I know we agreed to take it slow this time, but I don't want to be apart like that again. Neither does my wolf. He's never been as settled as when we're together.

"Neither do I." I smiled and faded into oblivion with Miguel around me and his wolf at our feet, nuzzled into my cat.

Chapter Nine

I woke to the sound of my bedroom door creaking open. I slowly reached my hand to the head of the bed. Tucked between my headboard and mattress was a knife big enough to do a world of damage. Just as my fingers gripped the handle, my nose filled with the smell of cinnamon. Cisco always held a faint scent of cinnamon and coffee. I released the handle of the knife and calmed down. I should have known it was safe by Miguel remaining asleep. Had it been a threat, he would have woken long before me.

"It's me." Cisco's voice stilled my arm.

"I know. What do you want?" I groaned. "This better be good and better not be about a dead body or a demon."

He crouched beside my bed. "Sorry to wake you, but Philip is here."

"What time is it?" I whispered.

"Six a.m."

"Bloody hell, it feels like I just closed my eyes." I yawned around my words.

"Perhaps you should have gone straight to sleep instead of screaming Miguel's name out all bloody night," Cisco teased.

I rolled my eyes, knowing he'd see it, even in the pitch-blackness of my bedroom. "Philip better have muffins."

"He doesn't. I asked," Cisco replied. "He says he intercepted a group of witches on their way here on some sort of official business. He's been outside in the treeline for the last four hours."

"Creepy," I replied. When what Cisco said finally registered, I sat straight up, clutching the sheet over my chest. "The Coven."

Cisco turned on my lamp, and I winced as my eyes adjusted to the brilliance of my once-dark bedroom. He passed me an envelope. "They left a letter for you."

I eyed the envelope, torn open at the top. "Since you already read it, what does it say?"

He grinned. "Philip read it first to make sure it wasn't a threat. It's a notice that the Coven is establishing a council here. I don't remember the last time the Coven started a new Hive."

"About five hundred years ago," I replied. "They don't like to divvy up power the way other groups do."

"Why would they be doing it now?"

"Why does anyone do anything?" I shrugged. "There's been rumors for years, but there's always gossip. Some are saying there's a division among High Priests. Unless they come to an agreement, blood will spill, bonfires will be set."

"Sounds like a fun party to go to. The letter says you'll get a formal invite to their inaugural banquet," he said. "Doesn't make a lot of sense to set up here. There's nothing here. There is no huge power base for any species. Could they be coming because of you?"

I frowned. "I doubt it. I'm only one full-blooded hereditary witch here. The closest to my power is Mannix, but his mother wasn't full-blooded." I thought about what could have attracted them. "There are a dozen level-two witches here and dozens of elemental witches, but they fly under the radar until they do something stupid. I don't see why they'd come for me. I'm level-one and have made it perfectly clear that I'll pay my yearly dues to keep my membership and license, but I want nothing to do with them."

"Where do I start? Of course, you're attracting their attention." Miguel sat up in bed. "What happened in Mexico made the news. What happened at the church in Mexico made the news. What happened downtown the other night made the news and every social media platform."

"And? I've made the news countless times," I replied.

"But in the span of a couple months, you'd made the news with a Lycan at your side," he replied. "The Coven knows about Lycan, well, they suspect, but none of us have ever confirmed it. There's no medical test we can be given to prove one way or the other, so they've had their eye on a few of us, hoping we'd slip up. And here you are, working side by side with us. They're probably moving closer to you, either hoping you'll give them information or to keep an eye on a potential threat. A witch of your power, consorting with powers they know nothing about, even I'd keep a closer eye on you. Whether they actually start a new Coven here is up for debate. This may just be a cover to get closer."

"Great," I groaned and climbed out of bed. "Since we're up, we might as well have breakfast. Cisco, go tell Philip to come in for food."

"Philip is already in the house." Miguel rolled out of bed and breathed in the air. His head jerked toward the bedroom door. "Why do I smell vampire?"

Cisco grinned. "I saved the best for last and for the *lobito* to explain."

"Why do you call him little wolf?" I asked. Philip was six feet tall and built of solid muscle.

"He may be higher in his Pack than I am, but that says more about how weak his Pack is than of the members themselves. Philip is weaker, younger, inexperienced, and looks like he bites off more than he can chew," Cisco answered. "From the smell of him, he's choking on what he's bitten off...or allowed to have bitten off of him."

"Politics are going to be the death of me," I grumbled.

"Nah, my money is on a demon," Cisco said, and I gave him the finger on his way out the door.

"Asshole," I muttered.

Miguel left the room first, untrusting of the smell Philip had dragged into the house behind him. I couldn't smell a thing, but I also didn't have the nose of a wolf. I quickly pulled on some joggers and a hoodie then followed them into the kitchen. Philip already had a pot of coffee ready on the table and was pacing between my kitchen and breakfast nook. It wasn't often I saw him wound up like this. He dabbed his forehead with the sleeve of his sweater. The movement made him seem much younger today than it had any other day. His eyes darted from Miguel to Cisco and back to me. He took a few steps forward and dropped his hands and head.

"I think we're scaring him," Cisco said, taking a seat at the table. "You have nothing to fear from us, my new friend. Breathe, relax, and give Ailis a reason to beat the shit out of you."

"I'm not going to beat him up," I responded to Cisco's remark.

"Give it time, little red. The day has only just begun," he replied. "And this *lobito* has many secrets, don't you, Philip?"

Philip's eyes darted between Cisco and Miguel, and I turned to glare at them. I rubbed my hands over my arms. The tension in the air crawled over my skin. I couldn't smell fear, but I had been scared enough times to know what it looked like. It made me uncomfortable to see someone as afraid as Philip. I didn't know if he was scared of Miguel and Cisco or of me. I stood in front of Philip and touched his arm. He jerked as if he had been waiting for pain. His body heat poured off him in waves, like standing too close to a fire.

"It's okay, Philip. Calm down," I said, rubbing my hands up and down his arms. "You're safe here."

"No, Lish, I'm not safe anywhere," he replied. "I'm Lycan. This isn't like a club membership. I can't cancel it whenever I want. This shit will follow me to my grave."

"What shit?" I asked.

Philip looked around me to Miguel, who stood a few feet behind, leaning on the table. He looked casual, but I knew that position. His body was prepared. One wrong move and Miguel would be violence in motion. Cisco was busy pouring our coffees, but his attention was entirely on me and Philip. I'd have been as scared as Philip if I were in his shoes.

"Miguel, sit down, and both of you, stop freaking him out." I pointed at Miguel, then the table. "Plant your rear."

"It doesn't matter where they're standing," Philip said, moving so my body was between him and the others. "They are Alpha to me. If they lose it, I'm dead."

"They'll have to get through me," I replied.

"Don't die to protect me," he answered.

"You and I won't be the ones to die if they decide to harm one of my friends." I smiled as Cat strolled into the room, her deep meow the only warning given.

Cisco snickered from the table. Miguel finally took a seat and pushed a chair out for Philip with his foot. I pulled a chair to his side and made him a coffee, extra sweet, with a touch of cream. Philip drank the entire cup before he'd calmed down enough to talk.

"Philip, you're stronger than Natt. Why are you his second banana?" I asked. "I felt it the moment I walked into the room. Your Leader is weak."

"I don't want the bloody job," he replied. "I fought to get to where I am so I'd stop being everyone's meat. At least where I am, I can protect those who can't protect themselves."

"I won't pretend that I know what your world is about. I don't. But here, in my home, you're safe," I replied.

"While he's in this house," Cisco added. "Don't make promises none of us can keep. In your home, he's safe. Out there, he's on his own. We can't protect him, not without directly challenging his people, and I'm not risking my fur for him."

"That's a harsh way of putting it," I replied.

"But it's the truth," Philip said, running his hands through his hair. Usually his blond hair was tied back to make it look shorter. Tonight, strands of it had come loose and were tossed about like he had run here. "Where do I even begin?"

"From the start works," I answered.

"How about why you smell like a vampire?" Miguel asked. "I smelled them the moment I stepped into the Chapel."

"That answer would bring us to the start of this mess I'm in. We're all in," Philip replied. "Julian controls this city, always has, always will. He's stronger than any other Master I've ever met or heard of."

"Did he hurt you?" I asked, instantly appalled that Philip hadn't been protected by his people. I gripped the table and pursed my lips. I was moments away from a snarl.

"No more than usual," he answered. "Julian gets his mouthful of blood but doesn't do anything more than I've agreed to."

"You're feeding them?" The question fell from my lips before I could stop myself. Philip winced, his face blushing from my words.

"You have no choice, do you, Philip?" Miguel asked, and Philip shook his head. "He is an offering between powers. In Mexico, we call them the *dar sangre*, which literally means to be a blood donor. There are some Packs who send a *dar sangre* to a Master as payment for a life taken that should not have been taken. It's a punishment, and it's outlawed, but some still follow the old ways."

"Are you being punished?" I asked Philip.

"No. It's to keep the peace between vampires and Pack," Philip replied. "I volunteered. Those of us who are stronger than the other Pack members volunteer to feed them, so the vamps leave the weaker Pack alone."

"Does Caser do this, feed vampires his people?" I asked Miguel. I felt my stomach flop. Caser and I would have heated words if he did this to his Pack. If a single fang touched Sofia, I'd find a way to kill Caser for it.

"No," Miguel replied. "When Caser took over, he decreed the donation of blood to those we were sworn to protect innocents from was against all laws. He went as far as to speak to every other Lycaon in Mexico to ensure all others knew we would come if blood was shared. It stopped overnight throughout our entire country."

"The vampires slaughtered their way through Mexico in a revolt against us," Cisco added. "That was the first time your vampire hunter came to Mexico."

"May." Philip huffed a laugh. "I wouldn't count on her showing up any time soon. Her brother belongs to Julian. He was turned almost a decade ago. It's why she came here. She leaves them alone, and they don't force her brother to drink from innocents. They use him to control her. It's what they do, Ailis. Julian finds something or someone you're willing to die for and uses it against you."

"Oh Jesus, is it too early to start drinking?" I asked.

"Natt and Julian have an arrangement. If we feed Julian and his people, they'll leave the innocents alone, they'll leave the younger Pack members alone, and they'll keep the peace," Philip continued. "It's been going on since Natt took over. Literally, the next day, he had vampires drinking our blood. It's rumored he had their help when he challenged the old Lycaon. We can't prove it, but he's too weak to have won a fair fight."

"Oh, dear God." I clutched my throat.

"It's why I came here tonight. Natt was the one who told Julian about you and the Pack. He's been feeding Julian information only Lycan are to know."

Miguel's eyes grew wider, Cisco hissed, and I spat my coffee.

"Why would he do that?" I asked.

"At this point, I don't think Natt has a choice," Philip said. "He screwed us all the day he agreed to allow Julian to feed from us."

"We all have a choice," I answered.

"In a perfect world, perhaps," Cisco interrupted. "I'm guessing Julian is calling Natt?"

Philip nodded. "Julian can control almost all Lycans, including werewolves."

"Werewolves?" Miguel asked.

"It wasn't done by any of us," Philip said quickly. "Julian had some when he came here. He keeps a small Pack of them chained up on his property. When one dies, a new one is created. He keeps some in permanent wolf form, and some he allows to change back into their human form. It scares potential usurpers and challengers."

"They replace the dead with new?" Cisco asked. "And you say it wasn't done by any of you? The curse doesn't spread from werewolf to werewolf. It can only spread from Lycan to human."

Philip frowned and shook his head. He stared ahead at nothing with shoulders slumped. "I thought...but—"

"But nothing," Cisco cut in. "We are the only ones who can pass on the curse. It isn't the same as shifters and lycanthropy. Lycans are genetic. We share the curse when we are in Lycan form. Nothing else can do what we do, not even our cursed creations.

Werewolves aren't the same as the rest of the shifters, who have an actual virus. They can't pass it on."

"Natt had said Julian had found a way," Philip replied.

"Of that, I'm certain. Natt is probably the way," Cisco said, shaking his head. He looked sad, angry and disgusted. Everything I was currently feeling. "Those chained up with Julian are likely deranged demons by now. I've seen this before, in Gnaw Bone, Indiana. The werewolves were chained up, imprisoned, tortured, starved, kept in wolf form for too long and lost touch with their human side. The virus rotted their brains, and they were demons by the time we got there."

Philip leaned forward, putting his head between his legs, trying to slow his breathing. "I didn't know."

"You didn't want to know," Cisco added. "Any Lycan worth their fur would die before they let this shit happen."

"Stop poking at him." I glared at Cisco, who shook his head.

"No, he's right," Philip said, breathing into his cupped hands. "I was too scared to know."

I stood and grabbed a small paper bag from my cupboard. It already had crinkles at the top from my last panic attack in my kitchen. I passed it to Philip and paused, my mind finally catching up to the information dump.

"Wait, how the hell can a vampire call a Lycan?" I asked.

"They're too weak to fight the call. Their wolves aren't asleep. They're drained," Cisco replied. "They're feeding the vampires, weakening themselves and strengthening the very beasts they should be killing. Their Lycaon is weaker than those calling them. At home, if a vampire tried it, Caser would keep the weaker from going. Here, though, Natt is weaker than our youngest pup. Hell, Anna could probably clean his clock, and she hasn't even shifted yet."

"Could Julian call you two?" I asked Miguel and Cisco.

"Not us," Miguel answered. "We'd hear the call, feel it, but wouldn't be compelled to follow. If Julian is strong enough to call the entire local Pack, that poses an entirely different risk for you, Ailis."

"Natt is hoping to befriend Ailis, so you two leave," Philip said, sitting up, a few shades paler.

"Ah, yes, the reason you're here. Let's skip to the good parts, shall we?" Cisco said, still smiling. "Where Ailis beats the shit out of you."

Philip's swallow was audible. "Natt sent me here to tell you a load of bullshit, to get you on our side. He wants you to think the vampires are threatening us and are too powerful for us to stop. I suspect he only wants to keep you closer and offer you over to Julian as soon as Miguel and Cisco leave."

"If you're not spreading his shit, why are you here?" I asked.

"I came to tell you what was really happening in hopes you could help me...help us."

"Help you do what?" I asked. "How?"

"Kill Julian," he replied. "Once we stop him, we can stop Nathaniel. I can't ask Cisco or Miguel. Law prevents me from seeking help from another Pack to help me remove Natt from power. I have to challenge him myself, but I'll never win with Julian still alive. And if I lose, there will be no one strong enough to protect the weaker of my Pack. We're fucked without your help. Things are heating up to the point where I don't think my Pack will survive."

I started to laugh. But I was alone with my laughter. "Look at me, Philip. I'm scabbed, bruised, and healing from quelling a demon. I can't kill a fly, let alone a vampire as powerful as Julian. Hell, I barely killed one vampire, who was missing an arm, clinging to life, and lived to tell about it."

"Couldn't you curse him?" Philip asked, and I stared at him for a moment, trying to decide if he was being serious or not.

"And damn my soul to hell? No way. I'm on a fast track to the pits as it is. I don't need to get there any faster and for reasons that will keep me there," I answered. Philip sighed, his eyes down on his lap. "Drop the other shoe. You're holding back, I can tell."

"If you don't help me, Julian will eventually come for you."

"What the hell did I do to earn Julian's attention?"

"I'm sorry, Ailis, but you're the one who bit off more than they can chew with Pack, and now you're going to choke on it. Whether Natt told Julian or not, the vamps would have found out eventually. You reek like wolves." He breathed me in and shuddered. "He wants you for something, and he isn't going to stop until he gets it. There's no one here that will stop him."

"Did you come here to threaten me?" I asked, standing up and stepping back. I wasn't scared of him. I was afraid of getting hurt when Miguel launched himself over the table at him.

Philip eyed Miguel and Cisco. Both were smiling, though they weren't friendly expressions. He put up his hands in an immediate surrender. "No. I'm not the one who is threatening anyone. I'm here with the truth. You just don't like it."

"It sounds like a threat," Cisco replied.

"It sounds like an ultimatum," Miguel added.

"Lish, you know me." Philip turned back to me. He tried to make himself look smaller, less threatening, which was impossible when he was built like a tank. "Well, most of me. You know I'd never do anything to hurt you or intentionally bring you harm. If you're not going to help, you need to leave, or this problem will knock on your door eventually."

"It's not my problem," I replied.

"Yes, it very much is," Philip countered. "What did you think was going to happen when you tossed your towel in with Pack? You got Pack's protection, but I'm sorry to say it comes with claws. The devil is in the details, as you always say. If you want protection, you have to give it. That's how things work. I wish it wasn't true, but in this world, you get nothing for free."

"I agree, nothing is free, but I'm not paying a bill my ass didn't create," I countered.

"This is me, your friend, asking. Not Pack. Not Natt's second. Just me." Philip groaned. "Please. Help me. I can't protect everyone from Natt and Julian."

Before I could open my mouth to argue, Miguel leaned forward. "What are you asking of her?"

"Find a way to stop Julian," Philip answered. "The rest, Pack can deal with."

"And if she says no?" Miguel asked.

"Natt sent me here to earn her trust, to invite her into our Pack. If I go back to Natt with a refusal, he's going pull local Pack protection from Ailis," Philip replied. "I'm not strong enough, with Julian alive, to challenge him or go against his rule." He turned to me, his eyes pleading. "I'm sorry, Doc. I never wanted you in our world. I swear to the Gods, I have done everything I can to protect you, but I'm not strong enough for what's coming. I need your help. If Natt pulls your protection, everything this side of hell is coming your way. I won't leave your side. I'll keep protecting you, but I will certainly die for it. The entire local Pack and Nest will knock on your door. Four of us against dozens. I don't think we're walking away."

I sat hard in my chair. "Fuck."

"Cisco, get on the horn," Miguel said, and Cisco pulled his phone from his pocket. "Let Caser know what's up. I want Sofia and Diego on the next flight. Also, call Ben."

"Ben?" Cisco asked, eyes wide. "Shit will hit the fan if we bring him in."

"Who's Ben?" I asked.

"Benedicto Martínez," Cisco answered. "My blooded cousin. He's a hunter from Mexico. He is a lone wolf, a hunter like May, only hairier. He and May have worked together a few times."

"Julian and Natt aren't going to allow a random hunter into the city," Philip said.

"Which is why we're calling him in. Someone Julian can't control," Miguel answered. "Natt sent you here to help him get closer to Ailis. Let him believe she's accepted his protection and friendship. Spin whatever lie that's believable. It'll buy us time. Tell Natt that me and Cisco will remain in the city for the next week or two to ensure this Julian business is put to rest. Natt will expect us to make a move against Julian for his aggression toward Ailis. To do nothing at all or fly under the radar would raise suspicion."

"If you want our help, we do it our way," Cisco added. "The vampires made the first move by showing up at Ailis' office and threatening her, knowing full well she had Pack protection. If they're going to come for her, we're going to be ready. The Los Luna Pack will not be intimidated."

"Natt isn't going to like this," Philip said.

"You can tell him the show of force is to send a message to Julian." Miguel's calm tone reappeared. The one that said he was thinking of horrible things he'd do if he were baked into a corner. "If Julian didn't want her to protect herself, he shouldn't have forced her hand. Julian hasn't lived this long without being two steps ahead. He's likely already planning for our response with his own. And I'm not going to be outmanned or out-fanged. The Los Luna Pack is known for being utterly relentless and brutal, and now we will show this Nest why Mexico is feared."

"Thank you," Philip sighed, his body finally relaxing. "Do you mind if I head back? I have to give Natt an update. I'm supposed to check-in. There's a pool going to see how long it'll take for one of you to kill me."

"I'll call you later," I said as I gave Philip a hug. "If things go south, come back. You have a key for a reason."

"If things take a turn for the worse, Ailis, being near me isn't going to keep your ass above the dirt."

"Then we all die together, like one big happy family," I replied and waved Philip off. I went to the fridge, my stomach growling and mind racing. "Pack needs to update their membership contract. Nowhere did I read that I'd be hunted by association. Keep a secret, you said. Defend the Pack, you said."

"This was a lot to take in," Miguel said, standing from the table. "This city has always been a nightmare of power and death."

"Did you know the Van Pack kills for every challenge?" Cisco said, cringing. "The only position you need to kill for is Lycaon unless he retires and appoints. These beasts fight to the death for every single position. How utterly shifter of them."

"Jesus," I groaned. "Why is it so different between Natt and Caser?"

Miguel shrugged. "Power and greed turn most good men bad. We follow the older traditions of Lycan, the original writings, the laws of old. There is no power for Caser to hoard. Although he is Lycaon, he is also a warrior and a hunter. There is no position within Pack he doesn't stand with. He fights alongside us. He carries his weight, if not more. He is of the belief that he will never ask someone to do what he won't. If a ditch needs to be dug, he's already started before the rest of us show up. When we're done, he thanks and feeds his people for their help. It isn't an expectation of his. He is genuinely thankful for the help. Caser is a true leader, whereas Natt barks orders."

"Caser is a bit of an asshole, though," I added, making them both laugh.

"Caser is a complete asshole. He wasn't always that way, though. When he had Anna, he got pretty protective and forceful of that protection," Miguel agreed. "But as our Lycaon, I couldn't ask for a better one. Those of us who leave his Pack to head our own follow in his footsteps. It's part of the reason all of Mexico tossed their hat in with you. Most of them were once under Caser or his father and greats. Their respect for Caser's line runs deep, and when Caser gave you, a human, his protection, the others never doubted how deserving you'd be. They simply gave their oaths to the Gods and your soul."

I smiled and, for the first time, felt loved by Caser. "I suppose he grows on you."

"Like mold," Cisco answered, opening my fridge. "Do you have any bacon?" He grabbed a package of meatless sausage and cringed. "You have no meat? Who doesn't have meat?"

"I don't eat meat," I replied. "I'll go shopping again later. Just cook it downstairs. I don't like the smell. It reminds me of...hell."

"I'm sorry, I forgot." He squeezed my shoulder, his eyes carrying sadness. "I'll eat out. I don't need to bring it here, but my wolf can't live off a vegetarian diet."

"You get used to it," Miguel said, digging through my cupboards.

"I have a barbeque out back," I said. "I'm okay if you cook outside. I even have a covered area with a nice little setup for outdoor dinners. Samuel installed four heat lamps. So we can have dinner out there on nights you want to eat chunks of hell."

Cisco kissed the top of my head. "I love you, little witch."

I froze in place. Cisco was the second person to say those words to me, outside of blooded family and Miguel. My eyes watered, and my pulse thumped in my neck. I warmed from head to toe. Miguel smiled from across the room, looking up from his cell phone.

"I love you, too, Cisco," I squeaked out.

Cisco stepped away to make his calls. His voice was low, but I could feel the pressure in the air rise. Cisco and Miguel were pissed off, and Philip had been terrified as he bolted from my house. Cat was roaming around everyone's legs, and I was beginning to feel jittery from frayed nerves. I busied myself in the kitchen, trying to think of solutions, but could only think of how I'd want my funeral to happen. *Would an open casket be too tacky if my throat was torn out by a vampire?* I leaned against the counter and shoved cookie after cookie into my mouth, thinking of Philip's comment about treating my body like a meth lab. With a shrug, I ate two more. As the kids say nowadays, *yolo*. Unless you were a witch going to hell, but from what I remember, cookies had never once been on the menu between torture and horror.

I picked up the notice from the Coven and eyeballed it. I took a photo and texted it to Mannix, asking him if he had heard about their coming. He skipped the texting and called me.

"I just got my notice," Mannix said as soon as he answered.

"What the hell, Mannix, no heads-up?" I asked. "Your father sits in second seat of the council. You could have warned me when you found out. I almost had a heart attack when I got my notice. It's the same way they summon us before the Coven for wrongdoing."

"A warning, what a novel idea. As if my dad would tell me a damn thing. I didn't know until I got back to my desk thirty minutes ago and saw my notice sitting on the top of my paperwork. I had no idea. I've been fielding calls since I got in."

"Why are they setting up shop in our neck of the woods? It isn't central to any other power base."

Mannix sighed. "God knows why they do anything, Ailis. I'll dig around, but I doubt I'll find out any sooner than you. If you hear anything, let me know? I'll do the same."

"Besides there being a major ley line running through East Van, I've only heard mumbles," I replied. "Before I left for Mexico, I heard rumors of a Hive split. Half of the Coven wants to move away from the old and stale way of doing things, while the rest are still holding firm to the ancient ways."

"The Coven has always been on the verge of civil war, but they fear it bleeding out and innocents dying."

"If they split into a new Coven, we've got bigger problems, Mannix. We'll be forced to choose a side, and they'll come for us full-bloods first."

Mannix groaned. "If you can't beat them, you join them, or you die trying to stay impartial."

"Keep me in the loop. I have enough problems without the Coven making more." I mirrored his frustrated groan. "How many Coven members are in town?"

"Two Higher Witches. The rest will be here in a couple weeks for the banquet. I'll give you a heads-up if it changes. Keep your spells in check. You don't need them personally knocking on your door."

"I have a sneaky suspicion I'm the reason they're here."

"I've got your back. You won't be a lone witch, I promise you."

"Thanks, Mannix. The same to you," I replied and ended my call.

Although Pack and Nest were new problems on my plate, I was a witch with my very own witchy problems. Just because someone new wanted me dead didn't mean everything else took a backseat. I didn't fully buy that the Coven's arrival was a coincidence.

They had eyes and ears in places the rest of us didn't want to think of. It wasn't beneath them to consort with demons for information. We had a few dozen walking above the crust, under the protection of the Coven, in exchange for information. I didn't want to think of what else they had crawling in the shadows.

"Sofia and Diego are packing," Cisco interrupted my morbid thoughts. "They'll be here later tonight. Heads up, I told Sofia about Natt feeding his people to Julian, confirming what she's already heard. She's coming like a bat out of hell."

"Oh, Jesus, have mercy on that fool," I answered. Sofia had a special kind of hate for vampires who fed from the forbidden fruit. She had spent time as one of their victims before. I pitied Natt and Julian.

"And Ben?" Miguel asked.

"I left a message for him to call me back. The last I heard, he was in Costa Rica, hunting a rogue vamp on the run from Cancun." Cisco took a seat and pulled out his phone, punching a number. "Caser wants me to call back and put it on speaker. He's pissed off."

"At us?" I asked, my stomach sinking.

"No. Caser has never liked Natt," Cisco replied. "No one really likes the guy, from what I can tell. Natt isn't strong enough to hold his Pack, and I've been wondering why the hell someone else hasn't taken it from him. Tonight, we found out. Natt isn't holding this territory. Julian is."

"A vampire ruling Pack," Miguel muttered, his face twisted into disgust. "There is a special place in hell for Pack members who break our sacred oaths."

"If there's a cage for me, there had better be one for Natt," I grumbled.

Cisco shook his head. "No cage for bad little wolves. They aren't treated nearly as nice as having a place to escape the torment. Their torture doesn't end, no need for a cage."

"Finally, something I see eye to eye on with the demons."

Chapter Ten

Miguel called Caser while Cisco portioned out a small chunk of raw tuna for my cat, purchased as a 'necessity' when we stopped for groceries. The little beast purred as she wove in and out from his ankles, meowing delicately as if she weren't a tiny monster that had spent years terrorizing me. *Traitor*. I had agreed to the fish but drew the line when Cisco had wanted to buy her a roast. Watching him slice up the tuna and whisper to my cat made both me and Miguel grin. For a big bad wolf, he certainly was easily won over by a furry little house goblin.

"I don't care if God himself knocked on our front door and gave you those cursed leather pants, Anna. You will take them off and put on something presentable. You are not coming with me to the senior's center dressed like that." Caser was yelling at his daughter as he answered his phone. "Jesus, save me now. Is that a belly button ring? That was not there yesterday afternoon." Anna's voice called from the background, as light and fluffy as I remembered, and Caser's return growl made me flinch, and Miguel laugh. "You put silver in your body? You can't...sweet mercy, you're killing me, child." My snickering caught Caser's attention. "Hello, Ailis. Is my suffering funny to you?"

"Good morning, Caser," I answered. "Trouble in teenage paradise?"

Caser sighed, and I could almost picture him rubbing his temples. "She pierced her flesh. She snuck out last night and met some of the younger pups in the back caves."

"The haunted caves." Cisco said. "Growing up, all of us had to spend a night in there to prove we were brave. It scared the shit out of me."

"Teenagers will be teenagers," I replied. "Caser, let her be foolish while she's young and has you to help her clean up her messes. The world is a scary place to make mistakes and be alone with them. She's finding her own place in the world. Stepping out from behind a mighty big shadow cast by her father is bound to be scratchy. Not just for you, but for her."

"Sofia said the same thing. I worry, that's all. Maybe if I had a dozen, I wouldn't mind one of them risking their life every time I closed my damn eyes," Caser yelled out the last of his comment to Anna, her laughter filling the background. After a series of curses, his door clicked shut. "Enough about the plight of a father. Let's get down to business. What the hell is going on? Sofia left here like her fur was on fire, grabbing Deigo on her way out the door."

"Where do we even start." Cisco slid into his chair. He leaned back, and the cat jumped onto his lap. I glared. "We met with Natt's Pack, and it went as good as I thought it would. But the good stuff happened when we got home. Ailis' *lobito* came knocking and asked us for protection."

"He didn't ask *you* for protection. He asked *me* to help him," I corrected.

"Lish." Miguel's voice felt like a warm touch. "You are Grimmwolf of the Los Luna Pack. To ask you to help with Pack matters is to ask all of us."

"Did you offer your aid?" Caser asked.

"Yes," Miguel answered for us all. "Nathaniel is feeding his Pack to the Nest. He is allowing Julian to drink from the vein of Lycan, a trade for peace and power." Caser switched over to Spanish, cursing the souls of the damned. "Natt has been feeding more than blood to the vampires. He has been spilling the secrets of Lycan, giving information to protect the vampires."

"If you don't kill him when this is over, Miguel, I will," Caser replied, and Miguel stilled under the threat. "Our secrets are worth killing for, but to offer up the vein of a Lycan, that is worth a smokeless death. He will not see his next life with honor."

"Why is the one worse than the other?" I asked. "I mean, I understand why spilling the goods about Pack is wrong and why forcing your people to become blood bags is wrong, but why is one worse than the other? You'd think keeping Pack a secret would be more important."

"Vampires have known about us since they were spat onto the earth," Caser replied. "But to willingly allow a demon to feed from us is sacrilege. Outside of harming an innocent, aiding a demon is the worst thing we can do."

"Perhaps I misunderstood then," I said. I felt like the more I was told, the less I knew. "I thought other Packs did this as a punishment, or to keep peace between Pack and Nest?"

"Just because it is done doesn't make it right," Cisco answered.

"It is outlawed in Mexico," Caser added. "Some of the weaker Packs have ignored the original law of Lycan. They're too weak to fight, so they buy their peace through blood. I'd see us all dead before I'd willingly let one fang sink into me or my people."

"If it is against the law, how are they still in power?" I asked.

"They don't remain in power for long once we find out," Miguel answered. "Those who break our laws are dealt with swiftly. Those who drank from the cup of Lycan are killed."

I cringed. "Tight ship you're running here."

"To protect mankind, we do a great many of things I wish not to speak of," Caser said, a sad sigh filling the speaker.

"When it is time, Natt will be dealt with," Miguel finally answered.

"You'll probably have to arm wrestle Sofia for the honor," Caser said. "She beat me the best out of three this week and almost tore my arm off the last time. I now have to wash her car for a month."

I grinned. Pack or not, they were the typical family. "Teach you for underestimating her."

"I won't make that mistake a hundred and one times." He muttered. "What's the plan?"

"Dig up answers, see what's really going on in this city, protect Ailis from vamps and Pack, take out the trash, but first find May," Cisco said, as if ticking off a to-do list in his head.

"Philip said May wouldn't be that big of a help," I added. "Apparently, her brother is one of Julian's children."

"Explains how your local Nest has turned into a problem," Caser said. "Having loved ones complicates things and makes for easy targets when the bad guys come knocking."

"I'm still going to try and talk to her when I go to work today," I said, to the surprise of all three of them. "What? I need to check on Philip, talk to May, and grab a few supplies for if demons are going to be knocking next. Not to mention the Coven."

"What's going on with the Coven?" Caser asked.

"I received a notice from them a few hours ago. They've notified the local witches of their plan to create a new Hive, a new Coven," I answered. "Here, of all places."

"Why there?" Caser asked the question but answered it himself. "My guess is to get closer to the resident witch who has the protection of Pack. They've always poked around but never gotten close enough to us for answers. We can smell them coming from miles away."

"Do they dig around often?" I asked.

Cisco nodded. "Oh, yeah. A year ago, their Grand Inquisitor snatched a Lycan down in Ecuador."

"The Hammer?" I whispered his name as if saying it too loud would summon him to my front door.

"That's the one," Caser added. "He tortured the wolf for weeks, but the wolf wouldn't talk. He sat there and took it."

"How'd he escape the Hammer?" I asked. "No one lives through an inquisition."

"We brought him home," Miguel answered. "No one lives through a Pack hunt."

"But the Hammer is still alive," I pointed out.

"Had he been there, he'd be as dead as the rest," Cisco said while petting my cat as though talking about killing people wasn't a big deal.

"I suspect the Coven is coming to be closer to you, Ailis." Caser parroted the same thing Miguel and Cisco said. "I don't think I need to remind you of your vow."

It didn't sound like a reminder, more of a threat. I rolled my eyes. "I'll take it to my grave."

"I certainly hope so, for all our sakes," he replied. "People are mighty creative when they want information."

A laugh burst from my mouth, and I felt my face heat. "No one is as creative as hell, and not even demons managed to break me. Unless the Coven is planning to hold me in the pits of hell for decades, I can hold out. I have a happy place to go to and can endure like a demon."

"That you can," Caser said, and I could almost hear the smile in his voice. "Keep me posted, and I'll make some calls on my end and see what I can find about Coven, Pack and Nest. Jesus, when it rains, it pours. Let's try not to piss off the shifters while you're there. We don't need another group chopping on our asses."

"Sorry?" I said to them all.

"You are our family," Caser answered before anyone else could. "We don't leave our hairless pups to fend for themselves."

"Hairless pup?" I asked.

"Humans," Cisco answered with a grin. "I'll call you later, Caser, with an update."

"Keep safe, keep strong, keep your faith," Caser said and ended the call when Anna walked in wearing an outfit that made Caser's head damn near explode. It was the perfect way for the line to go dead. From plotting murder to Caser asking the heavens what he had done to deserve a daughter who wanted his heart to stop.

My phone started to ping with messages from local witches. Cisco stood and began preparing a vegetarian breakfast without a single complaint, and Miguel made a few phone calls. The world around us was crashing down, and we were calm and collected. When a person could go about their business while the world burned, it was a pretty good sign of living a life too close to the edge.

I answered texts to worried witches. Every flavor of witch teetered between irritation and complete terror. From kitchen witches to your average green witch to the more powerful elemental, all had been notified. Eventually, we would all come together under one roof for the banquet, and we'd have no choice but to face the Coven. Those of us who valued our lives and power avoided the Coven like the plague they were. Most witches in town had never even met a Coven member, let alone attended a Convenire or official gathering. The smart ones did all they could to stay under the radar. I wasn't smart, and I pinged their radar far too often as of late.

The one and only banquet I had attended in Europe had been grand and opulent and had scared the hell out of me. The power had prickled my skin and kept my legs tense and ready to bolt at a pin-drop. Every Priest and High Witch had been a little too curious about me and my round trip to hell. They'd asked too many questions laced with power to compel answers. Had it not been for my shields and the spells woven into my soul, thank you, mom, I'd have bent to their will. That I hadn't made them all the more curious. The Coven was the last people I wanted to see or have living in my little slice of hell.

Cisco set out pancakes, eggs, vegan bacon and sausage, toast, French toast, fruit salad, and juice. "Breakfast is ready."

"Did you invite an army?" I asked.

Miguel slid into the seat across from me. "Grab what you want before this dumpster takes his fill. There won't be anything left when he'd done."

I grabbed a bowl of fruit salad and a slice of toast. Miguel took a plateful, and Cisco took the rest. It was enough to feed five or six people. "How can you eat so much?"

"My wolf is a hungry beast," he answered. "I burn too many calories not to replenish them. I eat three large meals and three or four smaller meals every day. It's worse when I'm healing. I need to eat every hour or two, or I don't heal as quickly as I should. But when I'm away from home, from the energy of Pack, I use food as my fuel."

"Miguel is right here. Doesn't that count?" I asked.

"No, he won't spoon me like Sofia will," Cisco laughed.

I glanced at Miguel, a lone wolf for so many years while he was with me. "How come it doesn't affect you like it does Cisco?"

"I have a mate," Miguel answered as if I'd understand. He smiled and set down his fork. "As I mentioned, Lycan are not solitary creatures. We need our people to feel secure and safe. Our energies intertwine, feeding our souls, our wolves. When I'm with you, our auras mix, our energies mix, my wolf roams freely with you. Being mated feels like I have an entire Pack with me, as long as you're close."

"It's better than spooning," Cisco added and sighed with a smile. "To have someone we love so deeply that the spirit of our wolves will roam freely, there is no better feeling in this world. It is the only time we can let go and become all of what we are—man and wolf. When we mate, it is for life, and it is a tiny little Pack within our souls. We do not need to look outside our home for the comfort of Pack. We already carry it with us."

I smiled at the thought. "That sounds like heaven."

"It is why Miguel doesn't load up like I do," Cisco said. "He's already full."

I reached across the table and squeezed Cisco's hand. "I hope, one day, when you sit down for a meal, you find yourself already full."

"I have my eye on someone. I'm playing the long game. Soon," he answered.

"Sofia?" I asked, the question falling from my mouth before I could stop myself.

"Gross. She's like my sister." His face scrunched. "No, not my sister. A wolf from a neighboring Pack. A friend of Sofia's, so don't mention it around her. I don't think she'd appreciate me flirting with her friend."

"I bet she'd be happy," Miguel said. "You're a man of honor. Sofia can see through your bullshit."

"Enough about my love life." Cisco waved him off. "If you're going to the university, you're not going alone."

"Agreed," Miguel added. "We're coming."

"I'm not having two bodyguards in my office," I replied. "I have a hard enough time with the other teachers and students without dragging around two wolves."

"We're coming, so figure out a way to make that happen, witchy woman." Cisco leaned back and crossed his arms.

"You both can come and wander about, but you're not following me around. Stay out of sight and stay out of my office. If Philip is there, I don't want you two scaring the shit out of him. He's scared enough as it is."

"Philip isn't my concern. You are," Miguel replied, but one glare from me made him soften his approach. "Keeping you alive *is* more important, but I understand why you're protective of Philip. He's your friend and has had your back for years. We'll hang out and sniff out trouble."

"Sniff out trouble." I laughed. "Deal. If you hear me screaming bloody murder, you can scare whoever you want."

I left them both to clean the mess of the kitchen, since they were the reason every dish I owned was dirty, and I headed for the shower. Miguel came and went from the bathroom while I prepared for work. We fell into the same rhythm we'd once had all those years ago, making small talk about the coming day while we each got ready for the day ahead. It felt right, and like Miguel, I felt full. I dressed in my best professional 'this won't stain if I'm attacked and bleed out' outfit, and Miguel dressed in his 'this will hide a gun' outfit, and away we all went. A witch and her two mythical creatures.

Chapter Eleven

The drive back into the city was a clusterfuck of traffic, construction and vehicles taking up more than just the shoulder, slowing vehicles to a crawl. I drove my car while Miguel tailgated me the entire way, not wanting to risk someone else getting between us. *And people say I have trust issues?* Both Cisco and Miguel scrutinized every passing vehicle, ready and willing to slam the Jeep into anyone who blinked the wrong way. I offered to drive us all, but Miguel didn't want anyone to see us arrive together, since they planned to be nothing more than shadows. I didn't bother reminding him that most monsters could smell other monsters *and* the guns they were packing. Miguel said to ignore them and act as though this was just another typical day. I didn't feel it was necessary to tell him that this was, in fact, just another ordinary day for me. Being under threat wasn't new. Looking over my shoulder wasn't new. Thinking today would be the day I died certainly wasn't new to me.

I parked in my stall and grabbed my bag and coffee. I weaved my way through the students rushing to beat the door for their next class. Most professors locked their doors when their classes started. I wasn't so cruel. Life got in the way of learning most days. If they could make it on time or had a damn good reason they didn't, I marked them as in attendance. Sometimes, we all needed a little help.

I walked to the sciences wing, where May's office sat. It was larger than mine and filled floor to ceiling with books. She had taken the one massive room and divided it in half, one for her assistant and in the rear, her office. I tapped on the door and poked my head in. Her assistant, Morgan, sat at a large circular table in the middle of the room, typing furiously on her bright orange laptop. Her equally bright-haired head bobbed up. She lifted her finger once, asking for a moment, and finished typing.

I had a long list of questions for May, and none of them could wait for her to answer any of the dozen messages I had sent her. May had never been known for answering her phone, a text, or an email that didn't pertain to her students, class, or school. But since my questions weren't related, I didn't expect her to reply. Instead, I came knocking with my inquiries. Cornering her may be the only way I'd get answers. I wanted to know what the hell was going on in my city and why the monsters were allowed to run the show. Since when did vampires have this kind of power in a city overseen by one of the best Hunters alive today?

"Dr. Kyteler," Morgan's voice was a pitch that attracted hummingbirds. She was always cheerful and colorful, and had the kind of manners I knew May appreciated, even though she backed up whenever I was near. Morgan was human, but even humans could sense hell on someone. "What can I do for you this sunny morning?"

Her smile made me smile in return. Scared of me or not, she was always polite to me. "I'm wondering if I could snag a few minutes of May's time? Is she in her office or in class?"

"I'm sorry, but Dr. Zhang is on leave," Morgan said.

"Leave?" I was surprised. May didn't take holidays and only left town for vampire hunts. Even then, a lot of people needed to be dead before May closed her classroom door. When one of the labs blew up, and the school was evacuating, they'd had to force her to stop grading papers. "What kind of leave?"

"All I am permitted to say is that she is on family leave until further notice. Classes are currently on hold," Morgan answered. She looked as surprised to be telling me the news as I was at hearing it. "As you well know, she doesn't allow coverage."

I leaned against the closed door. "Family leave? Since when?" I asked. Aside from a brother, she had no other living family. They were long dead at the hands of vampires.

"I really don't know much, Dr. Kyteler. May is a very private woman," she answered. "A couple days ago, May called and asked me to clear her calendar for the next month. The Dean was as surprised as I was. May doesn't take extended personal time off."

"I know," I replied, worried. "If you hear from her, could you let her know I'm looking for her?"

"If you hear from her before me, can you let me know if she's okay? I've tried calling her, but she's not answered my calls. That's not like her," Morgan asked, and I nodded. I left her to a stack of papers seven inches thick.

The walk from May's office to mine was far enough that I drank my entire coffee, ignoring the stares and murmurs from others. I picked up bits and pieces here and there and was glad I hadn't heard all of it. Apparently, I was a demon-loving witch who was going to burn for all eternity. It was close enough to the truth, minus the demon love parts. When I got to my office, the front door was still locked, which meant Philip hadn't been in yet.

I sent him a text as soon as I sat at my desk.

Are you okay? I came in today to check on you.

The little icon at the bottom of the screen came to life with Philip texting back.

Hey Doc, I'm okay. I'm just leaving my apartment. Want me to pick you up a coffee along the way?

Tension I didn't even know I had, released from my shoulders.

That would be great. I'll see you in a bit.

I picked through the stack of papers on my desk, freshly graded by Philip. He was harder on the students than I was and graded them as firmly as a devil. I had never argued a grade he gave but pitied those who would read Philip's remarks: *I think you're in the wrong class. Reread the chapter. Have you been sleeping this entire semester? Perhaps you should take an intro class before Dr. K's.* And the dreaded *'Make an appointment to see me.'* Pour souls. Philip went for blood, but I agreed. When they graduated, they'd have the power to kill through demons and magic. Someone half-assing it needed to understand that more than just their degree was at stake.

My smile fell as soon as my charm necklace flared to life. I dropped the papers as my office door opened, and in walked a corpse puppet. I knew Elizabet from anywhere. She was on every talk show, in every newspaper and had her own social media pages. Although she worked her fingers to the bone to make vampires look sorely misunderstood, the look on her face today said they were underestimated. Elizabet was human-ish. She was a human servant. She could still die like a human, but it would take the strength of someone much bigger and badder than me to make her taste a coffin. She walked right in as though she paid my bills, closing the door behind her. It wasn't lost on me, her intentions, when the door lock clicked. I could feel the chaos of her aura. It filled the room and stuck to my skin like cobwebs. I had two choices — try to get around her or buy as much time as I could until Philip got here, or I missed a check-in call from Miguel. I wasn't going to make it out of the door alone. I could feel it. I was leaving with her or dying where I sat.

"Elizabet." I glanced at her, cleaning the pages from my lap and setting them neatly on my desk. I didn't want my hands full when I found out why she, the servant of a vampire, had come unannounced.

"Elizabeth," she corrected me.

"I'd invite you in, *Elizabet*, but it seems you have no manners."

"Nor do you, it seems," she replied.

Elizabet was tall and lean, but muscular as hell, and walked as though she were a cat in a previous life. Her charcoal pantsuit was painted on like a second skin, and the heels she wore said she didn't care much for her ankles. Her glossy, jet-black hair was pulled tight in a high bun. For an aged hag, withered away inside, she certainly kept up with the fashion trends. Her ear-to-ear smile said she ate something I loved. It was the same pleasant look she gave to the reporters and cameras. It didn't fill her face the way genuine happiness did. Her soul was empty, leaving nothing but a vacant grin. It was the same smile I had when the Dean tried to force me to attend fundraisers and social events, void of everything but warning.

"What can I do for you?" I asked, glancing at my watch. "I have a busy schedule today and do not have an open-door policy for dirty needles or their little pin cushions."

"Conor did not exaggerate. You're a rude little lady," she said.

"Lady? I've been called worse." I huffed a laugh. "And this is where you tell me why you've crawled out of your swamp and into my office."

"You have not accepted Julian's invite? I have come to ask why." She took a seat and crossed her legs. With her hands clasped on her thighs, her brilliant red nails polished, she looked ready for a board meeting. And like any other meeting I had ever attended, I didn't like this one any more than the rest.

"I thought I made myself perfectly clear to flunky one. I have no desire to meet with your people and don't care for the reasons why the invite was extended," I answered point-blankly. I knew I should have made the agreement to meet, to buy myself a little more time, but hated bullies as much as being threatened by them. The day I started backing down to them was the day they'd be measuring me for a casket. "Perhaps if you had been polite and made an appointment, I'd be in a more giving mode. Instead, you show no regard for me, my schedule, or etiquette. I'm inclined to do the same."

There was no reason to lie. She'd have felt it the moment it slid off my tongue. Though not a vampire herself, human servants held gifts from their Master, skills that kept them alive and at the beck and call of vampires. Some saw it as a reward. I saw it as slavery. Of all the cursed out there, vampires were at the top of the list of those I hated being in the same room with. They had centuries to perfect their predatory games and just as long to grow in power.

"You clearly know where my door is. Please see yourself out."

"Come now, there's no reason for such hostilities. Let us be friends," she replied, her voice silky smooth. "Enemies would not be as enjoyable. For you, that is."

I fought not to roll my eyes. "Can one truly be friends with a leech? I've watched enough movies and attended enough crime scenes to know what friendship with a vampire looks like, *Betsy*."

She flinched, the first sliver of emotion finally breaking through her well-worn public persona. "Do not call me that."

"Sore spot? Miss being fully human?" I asked, but didn't wait for her answer. "Listen, *Betsy*, I'm busy, and I've asked for you to leave, yet here you sit. Now I'm telling you, get the fuck out of my office before I call security."

"You're an interesting little creature, aren't you?" Her award-winning smile and friendly voice had returned. "Since you prefer straight and blunt over polite and cordial conversation, allow me to respond with the same sharpness. Whether you wish it or not, you will meet with Julian. You can meet willingly or have him attend the next time. You will not appreciate him clearing his schedule for you. But it is your decision. I thought giving you one, a decision that is, would extend a warm welcome and show you we are here for business and not pleasure."

"Do not threaten me," I replied. My charm necklace heated against my chest in a warning. My stomach flopped as it spoiled energy getting ready for the potential violence hanging in the air like rotting fruit.

"That is not a threat. It's simply a fact. Julian does not do well with disappointment." She reached into her pocket, her eyes never leaving mine. She pulled out the same checkbook I had seen before, the first time the vampires had sent someone. "And as a show of faith, we would permit you to bring one of your dogs. Philip, perhaps? I do like him much more than the rest. He can take so much more pain."

I swallowed my urge to vomit. I stood from my desk, shoving my chair back and out of the way. The air around me charged with static. The loose whisps of my hair began to lift. "Touch him, Elizabet, and I'll fucking kill you. He is not your toy, victim, friend, or animal."

Her laughter was genuine. A mixture of surprise and amusement. "Perhaps you'd like to inform Julian that Philip has your protection? Please do make sure I am there to watch the show when Julian tests the limits of that protection."

"Touch any of them, and I'll burn you all alive. I will eat every drop of your souls," I replied. "You prey on the weak. You are pathetic."

"We all prey on the weak, little witch. It is how we all survive, including you." She tapped her long, manicured nail on the arm of the chair. "This grows old, and, like yourself, I have other business to attend. Julian expects you in three days. That should give you the time you need to prepare."

"Prepare for what?"

"Why, to raise a demon, of course. Why else would I be in the office of a demon expert?"

My eyes narrowed. "I don't know who the hell told you I could do that, but I can't raise a demon."

"Can't or won't?" she asked.

"Both."

"We're most certain you can," she answered, a knowing smile formed over her perfect teeth and expensive lipstick. "We know of your work. We were there in Mexico, watching. After the sinful seven failed to do what we hired them to do, we turned our focus to you."

My jaw dropped. "You hired them to raise that demon?"

"Not that one specifically, no. They found him all on their own," she replied. "A year ago, we hired them to raise a demon here in Vancouver. When they failed, your name came up on our radar. It took a great deal of planning and that unfortunate event in Mexico to convince us of your abilities."

"Unfortunate event?" I barely got the words out. I blinked as rapidly as my pulse thudded in my throat. "You watched as they brutalized countless women? You watched as they took a child to kill?"

"As I said, it was unfortunate," she said, as if it wasn't a big deal. "Since seeing your work, we have learned you can summon and quell demons on a whim. The seven couldn't even raise more than irritants from hell. Even with the help of their demon in Mexico, they were no stronger than when they last were in Gastown...Vancouver."

Jesus, how old is she if she was still calling Van Gastown? It hasn't been called that since the mid-1800s. I shook my head. "You want Chac raised?"

"Goodness, no, not him. But we would like a demon raised, and you will summon him."

"No, the fuck I won't. I can't."

She gave me a look that said she thought I was lying and doing a poor job at it. "Come now, I've not lied to you once. We witnessed your time in Mexico, and watched you banish the demon Ruby called." Elizabet spoke about Mexico and demons and death like she was ordering her lunch. I hated to think what would actually rattle her if this conversation stirred nothing in her warped heart. "You can summon one small demon for us. If it helps, it is not the demon the witches had attempted. One should never reach for more than they should."

"If you wanted my help today, you could have helped me in Mexico. Even if it wasn't out of the goodness of your heart, I would have owed you. Instead, you watched, just like I will watch and do nothing to help you here." I wondered how the hell she knew about Ruby but wasn't about to start questioning her. I didn't care enough to keep this conversation going. "As for the demon downtown, I don't know what you're talking about. A lower-level demon got loose, and I was called in to help."

"Ruby was a sad little accident. I'm so very sorry for your loss," she replied, ignoring my answer altogether. "We thought she was stronger than that, but she did say she could do it and more. When she raised the lower demon, as you call him, a sample of her skill, she lost control of it and consequently died for her mistakes. But that is the way with such things. When you speak before you think of the consequences of those words, you pay with your life. It is the cruel way of the world."

"Such is life," I said, rather than fly off into the cursing I wanted to say. Elizabet had answered a question nagging at the back of my mind since Ruby had died. Why the hell she would risk her life for a better grade. Ruby wouldn't. And she hadn't. Worse, she had done it for money, to help the monsters we were supposed to protect the rest of the world from. "You've wasted your time. The answer is a firm and resounding *no fucking way*. I'm not meeting with Julian. Try to take me against my will, and you and your people will suffer for it. I don't work for monsters. I don't raise demons for anyone. And, just because I don't fucking like you, Elizabet, if any of you come back, I will press charges for threatening me and attempted bribery of a practitioner. Further, I will file a harassment complaint with the Coven, and you can explain to them why you want a demon raised."

"That's absolutely adorable." She laughed at my threat as though she had heard them all before, and obviously, none of them had panned out, given the freedom of her and Julian. "I thought you'd rather get paid for your work, rather than do it for free. Alas, I was wrong."

It was my turn to laugh. It burst from my lips before I could stop it. "I'm not doing it for money, for free, or for all the tea in China."

"There are other witches out there. Much darker and willing to work for a fraction of what we are offering you." She smiled. This time, it was empty and menacing. She pulled a small glass vial from her pocket, filled with blood. Without having to ask, the look on her face said it was mine. I had wondered where that blood had gone, taken off the knife that stabbed me in Mexico. I knew I would see it again one day, but I was a little surprised it would be the local vampires bringing it back to me. "Say, we were to give your blood for them to use. I wonder what would happen? It certainly helped Ruby call forth the demon." She grinned when saying Ruby's name. "Having your blood tied to a circle that was not yours to control? Having your blood used to summon would certainly anger the demon. I wonder who he would take his anger out on? Perhaps we'll loose it on the city when we're done with it, with your blood on his lips."

"I doubt it helped Ruby at all, given she wasn't able to keep her circle closed. The blood was dying when it was used. Though, I could feel it in the air when I approached the demon," I replied with a half-truth.

I had more than just felt it. I had been able to command the demon because of it. I fully lied now, knowing she wouldn't be able to smell it like a Lycan could. Perhaps if she was a vampire and not just a finger-puppet, she'd be able to call me out on my bullshit. But I had a firm rule about not helping monsters, which included not giving them more information than I absolutely had to. I mixed truth in with my story to make it more believable. That was the trick to being believed. Make most of it true.

"As you probably know, since you collected my blood, yourself, in Mexico, blood is dead after thirty minutes outside the body and uninvoked. It's good for about a month, a month and a half if stored properly. Hereditary witches, as you've probably been told, vary from witch to witch and die at different rates depending on how powerful the witch is," I said, and her left eye twitched at the news. "That vial, I'm afraid, is not transfusion grade, and it's been weeks since it was taken. Ask any blood bank in town, and they'll tell you that you're carrying around the memory of leverage. You may be able to get some small magics out of it, but nothing more than an irritant from hell if you're lucky." I sat silently as she struggled to come up with something to say. "I think you already knew that, or why bother coming to the source? I'm sorry to say, but you're barking up the wrong tree. I can't be bought or threatened. But I can be pissed off, and you've really pissed me off now. If you come back, you bring your fate on yourself. There is nothing I'm not willing to do to stay alive."

She chuckled, amused by my bravery. She obviously had no idea how utterly serious I was about survival. "Oh, silly witch. Do not make threats you cannot follow through with. It makes you look weak and pathetic. That is not a good position to be in when standing toe-to-toe with those who can kill you in the blink of an eye."

"You should take your own advice, Betsy." I lowered my shields just enough to let her feel a sliver of what hell had done to my soul. She jerked as the room filled with the stench of brimstone. "I won't be the only one to die, and that's about as good as it gets when it comes to digging my own grave," I answered and motioned to my door. "I hope there won't be a next time for us, you day-walking hag, because the next time we meet, I won't be alone, and you won't walk away. Do not make me hunt you to the ends of the earth to prove my point."

"We've been tracking you, and you certainly have been a busy witch. Do you really think that little vampire hunter can help you?"

"You know as well as I do, May is not who I'd be calling to run you to the ground." I let all the emotion leak from my face and gave her the same stare I would if I were standing over her with a gun. "But since I'm pissed off and not in a live-and-let-live mood, I hope, little puppet, for your sake, you've not touched a hair on her head."

"Worry not, I haven't been the one to touch her," she answered. "Agree to meet Julian, and I will ensure she is safe."

I shook my head.

"Are you so willing to let others die in your place?"

I nodded. "Yep. It's worked out for me so far. Why mess with a good thing?"

"If I didn't dislike you, witch, I think we'd make good friends."

I stepped around my desk. "Get the fuck out of my office."

Elizabet reached for me, and I jumped back. She moved with the kind of speed I had only seen in monsters. As if her body were made of liquid lightning. She swung faster than my eyes could track. I fell into a defensive position quickly, protecting my face and vitals, blocking what I could. She was fast and unrelenting, but I hadn't had someone I could unleash on in a long time. I let my anger boil to the surface. The years of being tormented by the monsters, being seen as easy prey, the attempts on my life and times I've cried myself to sleep in fear of not waking up the next day. I coiled energy in my hands, and each swing connected with a force that staggered her.

She tossed me across my desk, sending my careful disorder to the floor. I watched my enchiladas hit the floor and spill. Now, I was enraged. I kept the momentum and rolled to my feet, fists up, and swung as soon as she jumped to my front. She was ready and pulled my arm into her, wrapping her arms around my throat. She was busy threatening to pull off my head when my office door splintered and skidded across the floor.

"Get the fuck off her!" Philip's scream vibrated down my spine. He grabbed Elizabet and threw her across the room into my bookshelves.

Elizabet stood, smoothed down her pantsuit and laughed. "If it isn't my favorite dog."

"Run!" Philip screamed at me.

"Where?" I asked. Elizabet was standing in front of the door. I scanned the room for my phone. Philip shoved me back, and I crawled under my desk. I found my desk phone and scrambled to grab it, dialing Miguel's number. The room erupted in screams, the sound of bones breaking and Philip soaring through the air, down the hall like a skipping stone. Elizabet grabbed my ankles and tried to pull me out from under my desk.

"Miguel!" I screamed his name when Elizabet lifted my desk as if it were a book.

"You're wasting my time, witch!" She screamed and pulled me, kicking, to my feet. She yanked me against her body, her forearm tight against my throat. "I offered you the easy way. Now, we're going to walk out of here like civilized ladies, or I'll fucking kill you where you stand."

I leaned forward then slammed my head back with every drop of force I could muster, her nose crunching against my skull. Her arms loosened, and I made it two steps from her grasp before I heard the telltale click of a gun safety clicking. I stopped and raised my arms, looking out of my office window. Everything slowed down and came into perfect focus. Elizabet's shoes clicked against my hardwood floors toward me, campus security yelling at her to drop her gun, her gun pressing into my back, my phone ringing with the Mexican anthem, Philip telling me to kill her, and Elizabet growling in my ear. I could see Miguel and Cisco running across campus, but they'd never get here in time. One of us was not leaving this office alive, and the decision was simple. Elizabet would die at my feet.

I closed my eyes and breathed out, pulling the spoiled energy from my aura, hearing the faint purr from my cat, giving me what she had, knowing I'd need it to come home to her. Hot tears rolled down my cheeks. I hated Elizabet, but I hated taking a life even more, regardless of the reason. It always hurt. Later, I'd replay the events of today and would be able to point out how I could have avoided this, what I could have said or done that ended with them staying alive. She deserved death. I'd felt feel it the moment her aura touched mine. But I wasn't her judge or jury.

In the blink of an eye, I twisted away from her, and her gun fired into the window in front of me. My energy flared, and I pushed enough power into her aura that I could smell her skin cook. I swallowed my gag, the reminder of hell, and tossed her over my shoulder into the window. The frame broke apart from the force, the wood splintering, piercing her at every angle. Her eyes focused on me, and a smile filled her face the moment a chunk of wood pierced her heart. For the briefest of moments, I could feel her joy. She was finally free from Julian, free to die. Elizabet closed her eyes and fell to the ground, landing between Cisco and Miguel.

Philip limped to my side, looked out once, and wrapped his arms around me. I shook until I dropped to my knees and vomited in my wastebasket. I screamed as I was sick. Hate for her and disgust in myself for taking her life. It didn't matter how hard I tried. I swore the end of every monster's road was my front door. Part of me wished I could be as brutal as they were. Maybe then they'd leave me the fuck alone.

Miguel slid into the room and pulled me into his arms. The police and Mannix got there moments later. A dead body on the ground usually brought the cops. The body being that of a human servant brought Mannix. Philip led the officers to his desk and pulled up the security camera from the front room and hallway. It had no sound but showed Elizabet arriving, snooping through Philip's desk, double-checking her gun, then entering my office. Thirty minutes later, Philip came in with coffee and tried to open my office. He said he could hear a commotion, me screaming for help and kicked down my door. The video feed caught her attacking me and Philip defending me. The rest was captured perfectly in the frame of the camera.

I zoned out, sitting in my office chair, watching people filling in and out, snapping photos, poking around, whispering about the shell-shocked witch. Miguel and Cisco stood at my desk, eyeballing everyone who tried to come too close to me. Once I was allowed, after photos had been taken, I used my office bathroom to clean myself up. I washed the blood from my face and was surprised at how few punches had landed on my face. My arms hadn't faired as well. I had new bruises starting over top of already healing bruises. I brushed out my hair and braided the mass of kinks and frizzy curls. I changed into the spare set of clothes I kept in the locker of my bathroom. With the type of labs I had in class, I often needed a change of clothes. I placed my ruined clothes into a paper bag given to me before coming into the bathroom. I felt a little better, smelling and looking like I hadn't just killed someone. I handed over my clothes to the officer outside the bathroom as evidence.

Philip was standing beside Cisco, smiling. Cisco was patting Philip's back, saying thank you for helping me. Miguel wrapped his arm around me and walked me to Philip's desk. The police had a few questions for me, but Mannix was closing the case. I wouldn't be charged. The evidence showed perfectly what had happened, and a witch was allowed to use deadly force when their life was at risk. It was the *only* time we could kill with magic. Had it not been for Philip or the cameras, I'd have been escorted to the police station and held, waiting for the Coven to come for questioning. Their brand of investigation hurt more than death. They dug the information out of your head with a metaphysical spoon. For me, warded from prying minds, I'd end up locked away in the Vanishing Towers. They'd see it as me hiding something rather than me not being able to allow them in. The Vanishing Towers were where witches went and never heard from again. The Coven called them the Towers of Justice, but the rest of us knew damn well what they were.

Philip passed me the coffee he had brought for me, rewarmed in his microwave. One sip and I flinched. The inside of my cheek was hamburger from biting down when Elizabet punched me. I still took another drink. The heat of it calmed my trembling hands. Miguel sat beside me, pulling me under his arm. His body heat seeped into me and stilled the panic floating on my aura.

"Dr. Kyteler, my name is Detective Calvin Raynott, I work with your colleague, Mr. Ashford." Calvin's voice was pleasant. It was the kind of calm that put you at ease. I opened my shields a little, feeling too relaxed by his voice. I slammed them shut and gave Calvin a knowing look. Somewhere in his family line lived a nymph. And like their fairy cousins, they could lure you off the beaten path and into their bellies, all while you smiled.

I leaned forward. "Since when is the monster squad hiring irregulars?"

"Irregulars?" He huffed a laugh. It was the polite way of saying someone wasn't human. "Since every scene we go to is because of irregulars."

"Fair enough," I replied. "Pull your power in, Detective. I can feel it pouring out of you."

"Couldn't I just be a nice guy?" He smiled when I shook my head. "It is, I'm afraid. This is as tight as I can hold it back. You feel it more because your aura is raw, and you've been through a troubling time. I swear to you, I am doing nothing more than asking you a few questions."

Miguel's scent filled my nose and Calvin's lure faded. Miguel's aura patched up what I'd shredded to kill Elizabet. I glanced up at him and mouthed, *thank you*. "All right, Calvin, what questions do you have?"

"Can you provide any information as to why you were attacked by Miss Priestly?"

"A few days ago, her colleague, Conor Madden, came to my office, offering a donation if I met with his boss," I answered. "I, of course, said no. Today, Elizabet returned. She said her boss, Julian, wanted to hire me for a job. I said no again. When I asked her to leave, she attacked me. She said I'd meet with Julian whether I wanted to or not."

"Why would Julian wish to meet with you?"

"To raise a demon, I believe. I don't know what demon or why, or any details surrounding it. I said no and threatened to file a complaint with the police and Coven if they continued to harass me." I gave him enough truth to leave me alone but left out the parts about Mexico, my blood, Ruby, and everything that potentially could land me in the Tower or was attached to Pack.

"That fits into why she was looking at your demon books on the wall," Calvin added. "I don't think I need to ask, but I need you to stay in the city until this wraps up in case we have more questions."

I nodded. "You know where I live."

"Indeed, we do," he replied and left us at the table.

Miguel helped me stand on trembling legs. I grabbed onto Philip as soon as I was within reach. "Thank you. Dear God, Philip, thank you for what you did for me."

"This is going to have horrible consequences," he replied. "I attacked the human servant of Julian. He's going to peel the fur from my back."

Cisco gripped his shoulder. "You have my protection. Give my name to any challengers, fang or fur."

Philip visibly relaxed. "Thank you."

"You risked your life for Ailis, we won't forget it," Miguel added. "You have my protection. We protect our own, and you, Philip, are very much ours."

"Oh, thank God. I don't like the idea of being beaten to death with my own limbs," Philip replied. "I'll catch you at home later. I'm going to finish up here and lock up."

"If you run into any trouble," I started, and he smiled. "You're always safe at my house. I've got your back."

We left Philip barking orders at the campus security. He had given them a list of names, along with photos, of who was not allowed on campus property. He wanted answers, and they had none to give. I pitied them. The university was a literal city of its own, wrapped in two thousand acres of dense forest. Campus proper was over four hundred acres, with countless miles of public realm. Although we had our own police force, playfully called Uni-Cops, and campus security, it was next to impossible to police every mile. Unless you were going into restricted areas, no one cared who came and went. Folks came to our little metropolis for the beaches, pubs, shopping, and to check out the open-access museums and art installations.

"Ailis," Mannix called out from behind me as soon as we hit the front walk. I waited for his notebook to come out and the questions to start flying. Instead, he pulled me into a shaking hug. "Jesus Christ, witch, you scared the shit out of me. When I got the call that a body was thrown out of a window from the demon den, I thought it was you."

"Demon den?" I pulled back. "That's a new one."

"I've confirmed the incident was self-defense only. My report has already been signed and handed over to the campus, and my captain," Mannix said and leaned into my ear. "That bitch got what she deserved. I've been to dozens of scenes after she's been there. I hope she rots in hell."

I nodded. "The weirdest thing happened when she knew she was going to die. She smiled. I could feel her aura. She wanted to die, as though she had never wanted this for herself."

"Would you want that life?" he asked, and I shook my head.

"Why wouldn't she just kill herself?" I asked.

"They can't," Mannix answered. "They are bound to their Masters, compelled through ties, not to harm themselves or their Master."

"Dear God, they can't end it even if they wanted to."

"She's gone now," Mannix said. There was no sympathy for the wicked woman from him. Though, if I was shoveling bodies because of her, I'd step over her dead body without batting an eye. "What the hell happened?"

"On the record or off?"

"Off."

"This is the second time Julian sent one of his flunkies," I answered. "Both times, they tried to buy me off, then threatened me. She said she saw what happened to me in Mexico. They were who hired the

185

witches who took me. She had my blood, Mannix. She went ballistic when I said no and kicked her out of my office. I either walked out of here willingly, or I could die in my office."

"Elizabet wasn't just a flunky. She was his human servant. She's been with him for almost a century," he corrected me. "He likely felt the entire death as if it were his own. This isn't going to sit well with the bloodsucking corpse. He's killed people for slights so small most others wouldn't notice it. For this, though?"

"Oh, fuck," I groaned.

"You can say that again." Mannix mirrored my groan with his own. "What does Julian want?"

"For me to raise a demon," I answered, and he cringed. "If I were you, I'd warn any witch powerful enough to summon. If Julian can't get to me, he'll take one of them."

"Holy hell. I'll warn the Coven. Vampires messing with hell isn't a new thing, but it always goes horribly south when they do."

I nodded. "They don't have the same fear of death as the rest of us with souls."

Mannix leaned in. He was on duty and couldn't be seen as picking sides, but his loyalty wasn't something a paycheck could buy. "You need to get underground. Julian is going to go berserk. Our little city will bleed red before this is over. Julian isn't going to stop until he takes it out on you, personally. We're calling in every hunter who will answer our calls. Julian on a rampage is all kinds of red flags and body bags, Ailis. Find a safe place and keep your head down."

"Sorry, Mannix. This time, I didn't go looking for trouble."

"Get to safety until this either blows over or Julian is killed by his own people. This last time someone managed to kill a human servant, the Master went on a killing spree. Remember, in Vegas, Horatio went ballistic and killed eighty-seven people before he was stopped."

Cursed and damned fucking monsters.

Chapter Twelve

"Cisco, you take my car, we'll drop it off at my place," I said, sliding into the front seat of the Jeep.

"What do you mean, drop it off?" Miguel asked.

"We're burning daylight here. Elizabet mentioned May. I want to see if she's okay before I duck and cover for the night."

Cisco whistled, long and surprised. "You just killed a human servant and you want to head back out?"

"You need rest," Miguel said.

"When the sun sets, I'm on the chopping block. Rest will come, but the sun won't stay up forever," I answered. "I'm not sitting back and watching my options melt away with the day. You can either come with me or go home and wait for me to get back from May's. Your choice."

We buckled in and hit the road. Miguel gripped his steering wheel until it groaned under the force. I tried to lighten the mood by reminding him it was a rental, but the joke fell to the floor. He weaved in and out of traffic, Cisco hot on our tail, as if he willed the people to get out of his way. With the tension rising in the cab of the Jeep, I, too, wanted to get the hell out of his way.

"I'm sorry," I finally said. "I know you want me to go home and lock the door, waiting this out until it's over, but I can't."

"You can. The issue is that you won't," he corrected me. "Twice now, Julian has sent people for you. You killed his human servant, Lish. The next time he comes for you, he's coming for your death, not your help. You could have agreed and bought yourself some time. Instead, you hung a noose around your neck and the necks of everyone near you."

"You're right, I can, but I won't," I answered. "And no, I couldn't have just said yes, and this problem would have magically disappeared. She would have taken me right then and there. I could feel it. She offered me three days, but she wasn't leaving without me."

"We were there. We could have stopped her," he countered.

"And she'd still be dead, along with innocents she would have shot. Did you forget she had a gun?"

"You didn't know that until she pulled it out. You decided to tell her off before things even got heated."

I paused, staring at him. I nodded once and turned in my seat, facing forward. "I didn't want to kill her, Miguel."

He reached over the middle console and squeezed my hand. "I'm sorry. I didn't mean for it to come out that way."

"Yes, you did. Just because I'm not one of your people doesn't mean I can't tell when things are going to turn out badly for me. I may not be Lycan, but I can feel intention. I can feel evil," I answered. "The moment she walked into my office, I felt her aura. If I didn't leave with her, she was going to kill me. I tried to buy as much time as I could until you called, and I didn't answer. I tried to keep her talking until Philip showed up with coffee. I let her beat the shit out of me until help came. I did everything I could to keep her alive. Even when I knew I was going to kill her to save myself, I cried. Don't you dare suggest I created a situation that ended her life. I didn't. I didn't invite her into my office. She came in, locked the door and took a seat. She's the reason she's dead. When she pushed a gun into my back, she ended her own life."

"Julian will come for you, Lish."

"I know. Between now and then, I'm going to check on May. They took her because of me, to keep her from helping me."

"And what do we do when Julian sends his goons for you during the daylight hours?"

I glanced over once, and he grinned.

"I'm not leaving your side this time. I don't care how many people we terrify or what it does to your reputation. Alive with a bad rap is better than dead."

My phone vibrated. Samuel's name popped up on the screen. "That didn't take long."

"Ailis," Samuel said before I could answer. "Are you okay? Is what they're saying true?"

"Hi, Sam," I said and this time, he didn't correct me. I knew then he was scared. I gave him the condensed version of what had happened in my office.

"And you're doing what now? Going for tea with the local hunter?"

"No. I'm stopping to see if she's home or taken. If she's taken, I'll notify Mannix."

"Girl, I wish you'd go home and stay put," Samuel said. "I'm glad you're okay. You need to start calling me after incidents. I hate finding out a woman was tossed out the window down hell hall."

"Hell hall?" I laughed. "I'll make sure to call you the next time someone tries to kill me."

"Which should be any minute," he added, a layer of reality that made me squirm. "Home before the sun sets or you may not make it home at all."

I glanced out of the window. "I have five-ish hours before I need to hunker down."

"Put me on speaker. I need to speak to Miguel."

I pulled my phone away and hit the speaker. "You're on the air."

"Philip has risked more than his fur with the local Nest." Samuel didn't tiptoe around the secrets Pack killed for. "Nathaniel is going to kill him for attacking Elizabet. I've heard rumors of the alliance between Natt and Julian. If they are true, we both know the younger pups are at risk of being called to aid Julian in his hunt for Ailis if Natt doesn't outright order them to kill her to protect his position within the Nest."

"Shit," I grumbled.

"If Philip can get the pups to me, I will house them until this is over."

My throat went dry. Miguel gripped the wheel lighter. "You risk your life, Samuel. The local Pack is weak in Lycan standards, but…"

"Don't you worry about me, wolf. This is not my first cull. Tell Philip to meet me at Mairi's. Julian's call and Natt's commands will never reach your people through the power of her property. It is where I have housed the possessed, being called by the pits. Demons and devils can't touch a soul in Mairi's grounds, and neither will these beasts."

"Thank you, Samuel. We will not forget this," Miguel finally replied.

"Oh, you most certainly will not. You will get the food bill, and Mairi will probably want a favor."

I rolled my eyes. "Tell her I'll smuggle her onto university property, where she can free some animals and start some fires."

Samuel's laughter told me everything was right in the world again, minus the Master of the City wanting me dead, which could happen at any minute. Between the vampires and Miguel driving as though we were being chased, my life was on a stopwatch.

"I'll call Philip and will keep you posted," I said and ended the call, punching Philip's number.

"Don't tell me there's another body on the ground," Philip answered. "No, wait, if there is, that means you're still kicking."

"Samuel said for you to get the weaker of Pack to Mairi's. Apparently, the spells on her property will stop Julian's and Natt's calls to them," I said, wasting no time for small talk. "If they're stuffed away from their call, they won't be commanded to hunt me down."

"On it," he replied, without question. "Mairi's yard is haunted. Between the living vines and actual ghosts, it's going to freak them the fuck out, but they'll go just to get away from Natt and Julian."

"Nothing in her yard will harm you, as long as you've been invited in. I wouldn't suggest storming the gates, though. Those vines will tear you to pieces."

"Do not risk yourself," Miguel called from the driver's seat. I put the phone back on speaker. "Get who you can without raising too much suspicion.

Come nightfall, get your ass to Mairi's house. Skip coming to Ailis' house."

"I'd never hurt Ailis, Miguel," Philip's voice was sad.

"Philip, I have no doubts of what you will do to protect her. I'm not sending you to Mairi's because I'm scared of what you'd do to Ailis," Miguel replied, smoothing his message out. "You are an Alpha, Philip. You need to stay with the younger Pack in case something goes sideways, and they need someone stronger than Natt to control or protect them. Julian is angry, likely unhinged. Combine that with the force of your Lycaon. I don't know what'll happen. If you're there, you can keep them calm, keep them from shifting, keep them from leaving."

"Okay, I can do that," Philip answered, his voice back to the Philip I knew. Hopeful. "Keep me in the loop?"

"Will do. Call me if anything nefarious happens," I replied. Philip laughed as he hung up. We pulled into my drive to grab our gear before heading to May's. I wasn't going to poke around without the ability to kill whatever else was going the same. I hopped out of the car. Miguel noticed I was no longer sluggish and limping. I smiled and shrugged. "I couldn't have the po-po thinking I wasn't a poor, defenseless little witch attacked in my office, could I? I'd have never gotten away without an interrogation, and the threat of Coven, had they known I was fine."

Cisco skidded into the drive behind us and jumped from my car. "Let's gear up. I'm not going out there without being strapped to the teeth."

Cat lounged on my front stoop. Miguel and Cisco smelled the air and nodded before I opened my front door. I'd have hated to make it all the way home and be killed before I even stepped inside. Cisco headed straight for his bedroom, Miguel went upstairs, and I pulled out my bag from the closet. I slipped a thigh holster on, two knives, four stakes, and enough holy water that I sounded like a box of beer bottles clinking around. I wrapped my braid into a bun at the base of my neck, removing the temptation of being swung around by my hair. I yanked on my black hat and black sunglasses. This was as disguised as I would get.

Cisco and Miguel hit the living room at the same time. Neither of them looked armed, but I knew Miguel would have enough firepower to take out a few dozen people. Cisco wiggled his eyes, patting a few locations on his body. He was as ready as Miguel. We were back on the road within ten minutes. May lived twenty minutes away. I hadn't been to her house, but Philip had, once, years ago. He had helped grade a few papers that had included demonology. Philip had never gone inside, but she had gifted him a basket for his help. He still had the coffee mug that said *Teacher's Pet* stamped to the front. Whenever they crossed paths, and he was drinking from it, he lifted it with a smile.

Miguel circled the block twice before parking a few houses down. "In and out, Lish. If she's here, great, give her a heads up. If she's not, there's nothing we can do right now. We need to wait for our backup to arrive and come up with a plan."

"Got it," I answered and was thankful he didn't try to make me wait in the Jeep.

I followed behind Miguel, Cisco in the lead. May's house was a one-story, hedges and a white picket fence. I grinned. It looked nothing like how I'd thought it would. For starters, it looked pleasant, which she was not. It looked quaint, which she was not. Then again, I had no idea who she was away from work and the rumor mill. Cisco was over the tiny fence and beyond the hedges in an instant. Miguel held me back until Cisco returned with a nod. I wasn't as graceful as two Lycans, but I climbed the fence without faceplanting on the other side and pushed through the hedges with relative ease.

"Do you want to order a marching band while we're at it?" Cisco asked. "You sound like an angry elephant."

I shrugged. "I thought I did pretty good, considering I'm a cursed human."

"Cursed, yes. Human, the jury is still out on that one, witch," Cisco teased.

"Do I need to turn this break-and-enter around and bring you two back home?" Miguel asked, bringing his finger to his lips and glaring at us both.

I got back into position behind him, Cisco in the front. Cisco knocked on May's door while Miguel and I looked in the side windows. Her house was completely trashed. Furniture was flipped, drywall dented, plants, books and art were strewn about, broken on the floor, and blood soaked her light gray carpet. I pulled back and motioned to Miguel.

"She's gone." Cisco came from the front of the house. "Her door was unlocked. I took a quick look inside. It stinks of vampires."

"Damn it." Anger coursed through my system. "One more stop, and I promise I'll go home and won't leave until we have a concrete plan."

"Where?" Miguel asked.

"I need to talk to a demon about a hunter," I answered.

"Fuck," Miguel cursed back.

"Who, what?" Cisco asked.

We walked back to the Jeep as Miguel explained. "A topside demon cursed into the meat suit of a once witch practitioner."

"Does the Coven know about this?" Cisco asked. "Shit, how did *I* not know about this?"

"He has a working visa from the Coven, or that's what they call it. It's a spell to remain above," I answered. "He's the Coven's token demon, their confidential informant."

"I didn't even know they did this," Cisco said, leaning back in his seat. "I learn something new every day, and each day, I don't like what I learn."

"He's basically harmless," I replied. "He's muted because of that spell."

"But not completely harmless," Miguel added. "I've met him before. He's no more powerful than a level-three witch, but level-three will still fry your ass."

"And why are we going to meet with him?" Cisco turned in his seat. The look on his face made me laugh.

"*We* are not, I am. I have a few questions."

"And what does that cost you? Demons don't give up anything without something in return."

"He'll want information. He trades straight across. If I wanted something crazy, though, he'd ask for the same in return."

We headed to Blood Square, down in what used to be called Gastown. The steam clock was still there, but it had received a makeover a few years back. It now looked like one of the pillars the gates of hell were attached to, with steam pouring from the top every hour. It was all screaming and melted souls. I preferred the old clock to the current reminder. At one time,

Blood Square had been a single alley but now it had overtaken three straight blocks of Water Street. Prime real estate was eaten up as soon as the vampires moved in. It was a popular hangout for the cursed and the damned. It was also a tourist hotspot in the summer, which was why they had their own police unit that patrolled around the clock. Missing tourists were terrible for business.

Miguel parked and grumbled at how little things had changed, and Cisco jumped out immediately, turning in circles. Music poured from cafés and dark places those with pulses shouldn't venture into. We walked from the only stalls that were ever open in front of a pop-up church in an old restaurant, toward the heart of Blood Square. Cisco looked in every window and even made us wait while he ran into a little art shop to buy a pair of socks with fangs and crosses on them for Sofia. He wanted her to be able to walk all over the bloodsuckers whenever she wanted.

We stopped on the corner of heaven and hell, literally, under the Coffin Club sign. It would open at sunset and close at sunrise. This was not be a place I'd like to be standing during nightfall, especially in my current situation. But during the day, when I didn't have a price tag on my back, I could refill my spelling supplies, buy some new shoes, and grab a coffee while looking at artwork. The area had been gentrified a decade ago and monster-ified soon thereafter, pushing out everyone but the artists and those unwilling to pay three grand for an apartment elsewhere in the city. Rent down here was cheap, but you also couldn't get life insurance if your home address was in the Blood Square district.

"Cisco, you stay on Ailis' six. I'm going to take a look in Bone Alley and ask a few questions about Pack," Miguel said, his eyes fixed on the crowds.

"What's Bone Alley?" Cisco asked, not dropping his gaze from the shoppers.

"Shifter territory," Miguel answered, surprising me. "I'm still owed a few favors, and I'm going to start collecting. Meet back here in thirty, not a minute longer. I want to get home with time to spare."

I wrapped my arm in Cisco's and pulled him toward Alchemy Co., in the center of Blood Square. It had everything from baby shower gifts to summoning supplies to the darker and more arcane. Although it was run by a demon, I still shopped there. This was one of the few witchcraft shops that didn't turn their sign to closed when I came around. They thought since I smelled like hell, I must dabble in the dark arts. I didn't. But no amount of trying to convince them was going to get me anywhere.

"Wait outside," I said, standing under an old-fashioned broomstick. "There is an exit in the rear which leads down an alley and pops out half a block down, red door. You can't miss it. There's a broomstick painted on the door, with Alchemy Co. written in bold. You can hold up there."

"Twenty-nine minutes," Cisco said, pointing to his watch. "Please don't make me come in and get you. It'll be embarrassing for us all."

I rolled my eyes and left him leaning against the brick wall. As soon as I stepped through the doors, I could feel the taint hanging in the air. It was painted onto the artifacts and sculptures on every shelf. The spelling supplies, however, were clean as a whistle. Still, I'd be talking to a demon and firmed up my shields and aura. The store stretched back fifty feet from the front with breakables and collectibles in the middle and spelling supplies around the edges. From the ceiling, clusters of bones and flowers and furs hung to dry. I glanced at the twisted herbs and was tempted to browse, but I wasn't going to waste any of my twenty-nine minutes buying what I probably already had or didn't need. Most of my herbs and roots came from Mairi, anyway. And she wasn't a demon.

"Hello, Ziggy," I said as I stepped up to his counter.

"I do wish you'd stop calling me that," he said and pointed to his name tag. *Witch Practitioner Ziggtmoy* was stamped onto a witch-hat pin.

Ziggtmoy wore the body of a man who had summoned him decades ago, but when I blurred my vision, I could see the demon for who he really was, and he was scary as hell. In his possessed body, he stood a few inches taller than me, and was thin, attractive, with baby blues that made you feel right at ease. His smile and voice told the kind of lies that made him safe and harmless, just a simple shop owner trying to make ends meet. But the demon within stood eight feet tall, built like an ox, both in size and features. His horns always looked bloody to me, and the ring in his nose was made of flame. Both made me shiver until I cleared my eyes back to the man who looked like a schoolteacher.

I rolled my eyes. "Just because you're wearing the meat suit of a practitioner doesn't make you one."

"The Coven sees it differently," he replied, smug as every demon who sold secrets to the Coven could be.

"For now," I answered. I ran my finger down the side of a wooden carving on his counter. "So, this is how you all offload your taint, binding it to objects, then selling it to unsuspecting tourists?"

"It is covered in the disclosure on the bottom, just like the labels you humans need on candles," he replied.

"Insurance for when you dump it on someone unsuspecting," I added, and he smiled. I eyed the too-small-to-read printing on the bottom of a cross. If nothing else, demons were infamous for their fine print. I laughed at the warning. "This relic may or may not contain aura." I put the statue down. It contained a hell of a lot more than simple aura. I looked at a cross and chuckled. "A demon selling religious pieces?"

"Even demons pray to Gods. Now, what can I do for you, witch?" He smiled. The tourists would have been settled by the kindness on his face but I couldn't feel a soul behind his grin and wasn't settled in the least.

"The Master of the City is looking to raise a demon. Who is the demon?"

"I don't know nothing about nothing," he replied.

"That's a load of crap if I've ever heard one. You have your finger to every pulse in this city."

"I don't know nothing about nothing without a payment to jog my memory," he replied.

"How about I don't tell the Coven about your side hustle?" I asked, glancing around his little shop. "You've put your taint on everything in here."

He shrugged. "It is not illegal to cover relics with aura."

"It most certainly is when that aura is taint straight from hell. It's in the latest Coven manuscript, which I know you have if you have a current cursed license to sell."

"I do love our song and dance, Ailis Petronilla Kyteler, but I have appointments to keep and taint to offload." His smile was gone, replaced with a look in his eyes that I trusted — all fire and brimstone. Sure, I didn't trust a demon in the way I'd trust a witch, but the guise was gone.

"It's Dr. Kyteler or Ailis, unless you want me to go back to calling you Ziggy." I didn't really care about the taint. It was so minor that your aura would heal before the end of the day, no more than the taint you'd pick up from touching a stranger. I motioned with my hand to keep talking.

"There's not a lot of talk about Julian on the street. The little blood clot is secretive as hell, but I've heard for months now that he's looking for a witch or an off-the-book practitioner."

"Who gave them my name?" I asked.

The demon laughed. "Pack. Who else?"

"Who, exactly, gave them my name?" I asked again. I wanted to know for sure, away from Pack, who I could trust. I eyed a piece on the shelf. "That looks mighty expensive and covered in several years of taint. It would be a shame for it to break. All that nasty taint going back to its owner."

"Bitch," he muttered, and I smiled. "Nathaniel gave your name to Julian. Conor Madden was in here months ago. He asked what supplies a hereditary witch would use for summoning."

"You sold him summoning supplies?" I asked.

"No. Not even I want to piss off the Coven like that. Those supplies are so heavily regulated, I only sell to those with a practitioner's license."

"Any practitioners come in lately?" I asked.

He pulled a massive leather-bound book from under the counter. "Mannix was here a month ago and purchased lavender and a small herb mixture for sleep. He put in an order for a new spelling pot from India.

It's on backorder. An out-of-town witch by the name of Liliah Temps purchased spelled ink for her Grimoire. I remember her. She was here for a class at the university, a creative writing class, I believe. And you. You were here around the same time as Liliah and purchased winter bulbs for your garden."

"That's it?"

"There aren't many practitioners in our little city. Most of my orders are from out of country, and none of them are for summoning supplies. As you well know, I can't ship those items without physically viewing their licenses." He motioned to the far wall. "Most witches prefer to make their own summoning mixtures."

"What was Conor looking for, specifically?"

"Nothing, specifically. He asked what would be needed, and I said I needed to see his practitioner's license before I could assist him. He gave me a list of items to purchase, and I was only able to fill three things. A ceremonial knife, a copper bowl and worm silk cloth. But his list was pretty spot on for summoning a demon, albeit dated."

I frowned. "No one uses worm silk anymore."

"You catch on quick," he said with a smug lilt. "The spell he has is at least thirty years old. That's the last I heard of worm silk being used. Spells of that age, my guess is he is looking for a pretty big demon. No one tries to raise those nowadays. There hasn't been a new spell for them in a few decades."

I raised my brow. "People do stupid stuff every day."

"If it weren't for fools, we'd both be out of a job," he replied. "You, for instance, are one of the biggest fools I know. You killed Elizabet, and here you are, standing in my shop as if the entire city isn't going to come for you the moment the sun sets."

I shrugged. "I've been in worse situations."

"Speaking of. I just got some new hex bags in. Would you like to restock? I heard your latest vacation was a fool's errand."

"I make my own," I replied. "One can never trust a demon, after all."

"I doubt there are many you can trust, caller of hounds." He raised his eyebrows.

"I don't know what you're talking about. And, if you want to keep your above-ground permit active, I'd not be saying that too loud."

"Since the last we spoke, you've made enemies of the local Pack and Nest, as well as new creatures from hell. Sooner or later, budding demon, you're going to find yourself in the pits faster than planned."

"Why the sudden concern for my mortal soul?" I asked.

"No concern for your soul. With you topside and your enemies around every corner, it's bad for business," he answered, and I smirked. "Demons in my neighborhood are never a good thing."

"Always looking out for number one."

"You should take lessons and start looking out for yourself rather than these meat suits, as you call them. You'll live longer."

I headed for the door, giving him a one-finger wave. "Thanks for the information, Ziggy."

"Ziggtmoy," he called out to me as I reached for the exit.

I turned. "Do you know why the vampires would take May? I mean, I get why they'd want a hunter gone, but they've left her alone all this time, and only now they take her? I know about her brother, but why now?"

"Control and power, the same reason any cursed takes anyone of importance," he replied. "If guesses were gold, I'd say Julian has bigger plans than you think, and he's taking out those who would stand with you to stop him. It's what I would do."

"Where would he hold her?"

"Where else would he hold a victim?"

"Hotel Hostage," I grumbled.

"His basement is not a place even I would wish to venture."

"You scratch my back, and I'll scratch yours," I said, more of a question.

"What do you have?"

"You'll have to trust me," I said, and it was his turn to give me the same look I had always given him. *Trust a witch? When hell freezes over.* "Take it or leave it."

"What do you need?"

"Information," I answered, and he motioned for me to ask. "Julian's day-walking puppet mentioned a few things about my time in Mexico. She said they hired the witches to raise a demon, and when they failed, my name came up on their radar."

"If that is what she said, why are you wasting a question on it? Even I know she was there and why."

"I want the entire reason of why, from start to finish," I answered.

"If what you give in return is not worth the information I'm about to give you, you will be sorry."

I shrugged. "I'm already sorry, but what I have will help you more than the help you'll be giving me."

"This is rumor only. I've not verified it, as I do not care about Pack or Nest. The Lycaon, Nathaniel, has hated Miguel from the first day Miguel came to our city. Whenever Miguel was around, Nathaniel was pushed to the side. When Miguel left, Nathaniel feared his return and became quite close to Julian. When he heard that Julian was trying to raise a demon, he sold you out to the vampires in hopes they'd kill you when they were done with you, or kill Miguel while he tried to save you. Nathaniel is not picky on which of you dies first, or how."

I ground my teeth together. "Bastard."

"The local Nest had a good thing going here. Attracting true Lycan would bring it to a halt. But when the seven failed, they had no choice but to turn their attention to you," he continued. "Unfortunately, you're not easily motivated. Death threats don't work on a hell-bound soul. They needed to motivate you the good ol' fashioned way, by putting those you love at risk. If you were not so weak, you'd be above such things, and they'd have nothing to control you with." The demon shook his head, disappointed. "Nathaniel went to Mexico to sniff around and found Evette, who was more than happy to help. Elizabet put the seven witches in contact with Evette, and you were there for the rest."

"And now we're back at square one. Them threatening me."

"Worse. Those you love are right here with you. If they can't force you with the threat of death, they'll kill those here to protect you," he answered. "You should have stayed in Mexico, where your Pack could protect you. You won't find safety within these forests."

"It doesn't make any sense. If they wanted me to raise a demon, why didn't they intervene in Mexico?

Why did they let me damn near die? A dead witch isn't that useful."

"Must I do all your thinking for you?" Ziggy placed his hands on his hips and stared down his nose at me, like a teacher scolding a slow student. "Your survival is why they are now at your door. That you lived through that ordeal has proven to them that you are the witch they're looking for."

"Speaking of Mexico, I tried calling you a dozen times while I was there. Why the hell didn't you call me back?"

"Hell, that is why." His answer made perfect sense to me. Not even demons wanted to mess with where they came from. "To be honest, I thought you'd die, and I wanted nothing to do with a dead witch."

"Plausible deniability," I replied, and he nodded. I glanced at the bookshelf ahead of me and cringed. "Bottom shelf, left side, the two-headed goat sculpture has a leak. Taint is slowly slipping off and making its way back to you."

"Ah ha! That's where it's coming from." Ziggtmoy jumped over his counter. "That was not worth the information I've provided."

"And that was not the information I had for you, but it is part of it," I replied as he grabbed the statue and bagged it. "There is a raid scheduled in two nights, starting in Blood Square. Your shop is on the list for three in the morning, depending on how the other sites go. You and I both know you have relics and spelling equipment outlawed in the back rooms. If you're caught with it, you will lose your topside permit. And before you think of bringing it home, like last time, your house is also on the list."

"What areas are they not hitting?"

I gave him a look that said I wasn't going to do the thinking for him.

"May is being held in the lower-level of the basement, fourth room. Word is, she's in bad condition. She was bitten when she tried to save the life of one of the younger Lycans."

"He has Lycan prisoners?"

"Indeed. He delights in their blood now that he's gotten a taste for it. How many, I don't know. The numbers change on the daily."

"You can dump your crap on Deadman's Island. The last time they did a walk-through, two didn't make it back out. There's a pack of ghouls living behind the Naval Museum, and no extermination team is willing to tempt fate to move them out. They offered me a lot of money to try, but I told them to find a necromancer. They've found one willing to do it, but she's away for another week. You'll need to find a new hiding spot next time."

"The clock is ticking for you to get to May before the virus sets in," he added for free. "And you have a day, maybe two, before Julian's people grab you right out of your bed. If you're going to act, I suggest you stop wasting your time on questions you already have the answers to. The moment you met Nathaniel, you knew who sold you to the blood devils."

"We never had this conversation." I pulled open the door.

"What conversation?" His voice followed me out and into the chilled air.

I cleared the smell of incense and candles and set my feet in motion, pulling Cisco with me. Miguel was right where he said he'd be, tapping his watch. I was lost in my thoughts as we walked back to the Jeep. I did my best to keep my eyes scanning for danger, but I kept getting sucked down into my thoughts. Once inside the Jeep, the chattering began. I spilled everything Ziggtmoy had said while they both scrutinized every detail. Miguel confirmed Julian had May taken, but added the bonus of Nathaniel knowing it would happen and doing nothing to stop it.

"Natt has been gunning for you and me since day one," I said, leaning back in my seat. "That son of a bitch has been playing a long game from the moment you left for Mexico."

"Let's not jump to conclusions," Miguel said in an attempt to keep my temper in check. "You have to take what a demon says with a grain of salt."

"Julian doesn't just have May. He has Pack, Miguel. Ziggtmoy doesn't know how many but knows Julian has them in his basement, feeding on them." The Jeep swerved, and the steering wheel whined under the grip of an angry Lycan. The heat in the cab soared until I needed to take my hat and sweater off. "Oh, now it's okay to listen to a demon?"

Cisco turned his full gaze to me, and I fought not to squirm. His eyes were bright orange, yet dark, and they promised things I didn't want to experience. "Do you believe him, Ailis? This is a life-or-death question. Do you believe the demon?"

I nodded. "He's never lied to me. Sure, he plays games, but he's never lied. He calls me his buddy demon. I think he helps me because he thinks I'm almost one of them."

Cisco nodded. "If you believe him, so do I. I don't trust him, but I trust you."

"May was bitten trying to save one," I said, feeling my blood boil for what I knew they'd be doing to her.

"We won't leave her there," Miguel finally answered. "We go home, wait for backup, and burn that fucking Nest to the ground."

Finally, a suggestion I could live with or die for.

Chapter Thirteen

I texted Samuel as soon as I got in the door to let him know I was still alive. While Miguel and Cisco made dinner, I showered, washing off a day that hurt my soul, watching it swirl down the drain. I tried to compartmentalize, stuffing the fear and hurt down to deal with later, but it came out hard and painfully. I sat on the floor, knees to my chest and cried into my hands. I replayed every minute of my morning, looking for ways I could have walked out of my office with Elizabet still alive. I could have simply stayed home, I could have let Miguel and Cisco follow me around as they had suggested, I could have locked my office doors as a warning, I could have called Miguel the moment she walked in. Instead, I had done what Miguel accused me of. I'd let the pot boil. I'd decided to tell her off before things had even gotten heated.

Miguel opened my shower door and picked me off the floor. "I could smell your tears from the kitchen."

"My heart hurts," I said as he sat with me in his arms on the edge of my tub.

He wrapped a towel around my hair and dried me off, saying nothing while I cried. He helped me get dressed, knowing I wouldn't feel comfortable in pajamas with people gunning for me. He brushed out my tangled hair and twisted it into a braid, then carried me to the couch. Before I could tuck myself into bed, Cisco set down a tray with mushroom soup, a sandwich and crackers.

"I know you're tired, but you need to eat," he said, eyeing me until I picked up half a sandwich.

Not tasting a single bite, I finished dinner then curled onto my couch with a black knitted blanket, a winter solstice gift from Philip. I closed my eyes, needing sleep more than anything else. I knew the night would be brutally long, and fading wasn't an option. In the background, like soft music, Miguel and Cisco made calls non-stop. Cat propped herself up on my hip, purring until I was sound asleep, healing under her touch, holding her tail.

"Lish," Miguel's whisper pulled me from a dream about walking through the bodies at the church in Mexico. "Your texts are buzzing, it's Philip. Do you want me to answer him?"

"I'm awake." I pulled myself seated, wrapping the blanket around my shoulder and blessed Miguel when he set a coffee and cookies on the coffee table for me. I scrolled through my missed calls and text messages. Philip gave me a play-by-play of his day, saying he was calling Miguel when if didn't respond. I missed a call from several unknown numbers, none of which left a voicemail. I could only imagine who was calling me. I sent a text to Philip right away.

Is it safe to talk?

A moment later, Philip's face popped up on my screen as he called me.

"Oh, thank God, are you okay?" I answered my phone, my cheek full of cookies.

"I'm okay," he said, and I blew out a sigh of relief. "I'm at Mairi's. I managed to get three dozen of the lower Pack together. I told them it was a training exercise since shit was hitting the fan."

"How'd they take the news of being hidden away?"

"Relieved, to be honest. None of them want to deal with what's coming next. They're terrified of Natt and Julian."

"Are they okay?" I asked.

He chuckled. "They were nervous as hell coming to Mairi's. They've heard of her, but none of them have ever met her or stepped foot on her grounds."

"Yeah, her place is a little weird." I laughed.

"Samuel was already here, which calmed everyone down right away. You know how Samuel is. He may be a retired guardian, but he still has that magical touch. When we got here, the younger ones were on the verge of a shift, too scared to control themselves. Between me and Samuel, they swallowed their wolf," Philip replied, and I smiled. Samuel had calmed me down while I had two demons literally hanging off my back. "Mairi has been so welcoming. She already had a feast ready for when we arrived. She's roasting a pig on a spit as we speak. She has music going, magic and ghost stories that have been acted out by that creepy ivy. If the world wasn't about to burn down, I'd swear this was nothing more than a camping trip. What's up on your end? I spoke to Miguel an hour ago, and he mentioned what Ziggy and the shifters in Bone Alley said."

"That's pretty much it," I answered. "Thankfully, nothing new to report. Stay put for now, please."

"No problem, I'm not missing one of Mairi's pig roasts. Be safe, Doc," he said, and we ended our call.

I finished my coffee and did a few stretches. My body felt like I had been stuffed into a tiny box and made to stay that way for years. My joints popped, and my muscles protested against the force. Cisco came out of the kitchen, eyes focused on the door. I ducked low and reached under my coffee table, pulling out a gun and taking a half-kneeling position, my aim at the door.

"What are you doing?" Miguel asked from the kitchen. "Sofia and Deigo just pulled up."

I lowered my gun. "How the hell would I know that? I can't smell people in my driveway."

"Sorry, little red." Cisco laughed. "You smell like Pack. I forget your nose is so…*basic*."

I gave him the finger but put my gun back in its holster under my table. If he wasn't pulling one out, I didn't need mine. Or maybe he'd forgotten I couldn't grow claws, either. I stood, shaking out my arms and legs. In the blink of an eye, my body had prepared for a fight and now felt like jelly. Cisco opened the front door with a grin and arms wide open. I wished I could open a door with the same confidence and not fear who was standing on the other side. It was usually someone wanting to hire me, steal me, torture me, or kill me. Or all of the above, in that order.

Sofia hugged Cisco on her way in, finally shoving him out of the way when he tried to dip her into a romantic pose. Deigo came in next, offering his hand to Cisco. Cisco pulled him into his arms, hugging him.

When Deigo didn't protest, Cisco dipped him and planted a kiss on a squirming Deigo's lips. Sofia shook her head and rolled her eyes, but the look on her face said she missed Cisco. Her face filled with an ear-to-ear smile when she saw me and Miguel.

"You can cut the tension out there with a knife," Sofia said, setting her bags to the side of the room and pulling off her fur-lined jacket and army boots. "Dear God, it's cold here."

"We're a rainforest, if you can believe it," I replied. Sofia hugged me suddenly, catching me off guard. Her warmth filled me, and I breathed in her scent. "Thank you for coming, Sofia."

"I wouldn't miss this for the world," she replied, pulling back. "I will always come. Remember that."

My eyes prickled with the threat of tears. "As will I."

"We are Pack, Ailis. You are family…" She paused, holding her hand under her nose. "What the hell is that smell?"

"Me," I answered. "Well, the healing salve I'm painted with. It's been a rough few days."

"Sweet Jesus," she replied. She knelt and dug a jar of cream from her bag. "Anna makes this. It speeds healing and smells better than whatever you've slathered yourself with. Hell, Cisco's boots smell better than you do."

I opened the jar and breathed in the scent of Anna, Pack and secrets. "Lavender."

"I had to smuggle it across Caser's property for her. She gives me a jar a week for risking my life and limb for those flowers."

Deigo held out his hand to me once I'd dabbed a little of Anna's cream on my neck, hoping it overpowered the smell of the septic stench I knew poured from me. "Dr. Kyteler, I'm sorry we're seeing each other under such circumstances."

I skipped the handshake and gave him a hug, just as Cisco had done, minus the flare and kiss. He went stiff as a board. "Don't tell me you're still scared of the witch."

Cisco's laughter filled the room. "He's scared of Miguel. It's not proper to touch the Luna of a Pack member without permission."

"Sorry, I didn't know." I stepped back. "Wait a minute, permission? Who do you need to ask? It better not be Miguel. No one makes my decisions for me."

Deigo's eyes darted between me and Miguel. He was nervous. I wasn't a wolf, but even I picked up on his lowkey anxiety. "Custom says only those within your closest circle, those you would refer to as a family, are free to touch you if you permit. Those outside, such as myself, require the permission of your mate," Deigo answered. "To be clear, Miguel has not enforced such rules with you. But it is unnerving for those of us who follow our laws and customs to the letter to be pulled in a different direction. Dishonoring you would bring shame to me and my position within Pack and would end in a long conversation with Caser, right after Miguel, Sofia and Cisco were done with me. I'm sorry, but those are not conversations I want to have, just to greet you as you greet me."

"You have my permission. Come in peace, and I'll give no war," Miguel said, then looked at me and my hands on my hips. I was a solitary witch. I did whatever the hell I wanted, with or without a mate. The very pits of hell would freeze over, and all demons would die before I let anyone own me or my body. "I say it purely out of custom. Do you want him to be on edge the entire time he's here? Scared to be near you without me in the room?"

"As long as everyone knows I'm an independent witch and answer to no man," I said.

"No one is stupid enough to think you're anything but an independent witch, but it's a sign of respect," Cisco said, grabbing Deigo's bags and leading him into the kitchen, mentioning meatless snacks.

"Why is there no meat?" Deigo asked. "Did you eat it all?"

"No. Ailis is sensitive to the smells. It reminds her of hell," Cisco answered quietly, but I could still hear him. "Don't bring it inside, and if you eat it, wash up after so the smell doesn't linger. It really bothers her."

"What a horrible memory. I can go without red meat for a few days," Deigo replied. My fridge was opened, and jars were moved around. "What about this fish?"

"Drop the fish, you beast," Cisco's voice carried through the room. "It's for our cat, not wolves."

Our. I smiled. Miguel stepped to the door although there hadn't been a knock. I froze, but Cisco came around the corner with a smile. Miguel opened the door to one of the scariest men I've ever seen. His very presence made me take several steps back.

"Benedicto, welcome," Miguel said, stepping out of the doorway.

Benedicto made Miguel look like a small man. He ducked coming into my house. He carried four large duffle bags like they were filled with air. His jacket was thrown over his shoulder, and his long-sleeved shirt was pushed up as if it was summer and he was hot. Tattoos covered the skin I could see, and I knew he'd there'd be more under his clothes. Scars around his wrists and neck told me that he had the same experience as Sofia — silver chains holding him down — and from the look of it, he had been in captivity more than once.

"Ben!" Cisco grabbed his cousin, hugging him tightly. Cisco beamed with happiness. "It's been too long."

Benedicto set his bags down and hugged Cisco just as tightly. "Cisco, I am honored you called for me. It has been many years since we hunted together."

Cisco pulled back and extended his arm toward me. "And this is our *independent witch who answers to no man.*"

Benedicto quickly removed his hat and shoes before stepping forward. He bowed his head. "*Médico*...Dr. Kyteler, I am honored to meet the Luna of warrior, Miguel, and the Grimmwolf of the Los Luna Pack. Thank you for inviting me into your home."

"Please don't bow, Benedicto," I said as I stepped forward and tried to force his shoulders back up. "And please, call me Ailis."

He stood and towered over me. I had to step back or crane my neck. I stepped back. "*Gracias.* Please, my friends call me Ben, *por favor.*" He breathed in the air around me, and I felt my face heat. "Señorita Mairi was sent from the heavens to help heal the guardians of the gate." He sighed. "And lavender. You smell like home."

I glanced at Cisco, who was sticking an entire sandwich into his mouth at once. "Did he get all the manners in your family?"

Cisco swallowed his food without chewing. "I got the charm and good looks. He has the manners. It was a good trade, in my opinion."

"I think he got a better deal," Sofia said, leaning her shoulder into Cisco. "I'm glad you called me. I was getting worried, with what I had been hearing about this sorry sack of pups. This city has gone to hell since the last time I was here."

"Worse," Miguel said. "Hell is easier to deal with. A power-thirsty Lycaon and a Master gone unchecked, is what we're up against."

"We have overcome worse," Ben replied. "Together, a strong Pack is unstoppable. We will make our stand and drive the evil back to the pits, where they belong."

"That we shall, my friend," Miguel answered, shaking Ben's hand, his face filled with pride. It wasn't lost on me how strong Miguel's Pack had been in Mexico. But I hadn't realized how utterly devoted they were to their calling until I'd seen Natt's Pack.

"Please, come in, Ben. There's food in the kitchen." I motioned to Deigo, standing between the kitchen and living room with a large mixing bowl of cut-up fruit. "Sorry, there's no meat here. And with how things are going, I wouldn't recommend getting delivery."

"Only the weak require flesh to sustain their wolf," Ben said, looking at Cisco teasingly, who barked a laugh in return that warmed my soul. "Cisco informed me of your food restrictions, Ailis. I ate before I came here. But I'd never turn down sharing a meal with family. A hunter rarely has these opportunities. Thank you."

"Don't touch the fish," Deigo said as Ben walked by him. "It's for their cat. Cisco said he'll skin us and feed it to the beast if the fish goes missing."

"Oh, I love cats."

"We're not allowed to eat the cat, either," Deigo said, gaining a laugh from Ben.

I stood in the living room, hugging myself. Miguel wrapped his arm around me. "Are you okay?"

"I've never had this many people in my house at once."

"It takes some getting used to."

I smiled. "It feels full, but in a good way. I think I'll be sad when everyone leaves."

"I'm not going anywhere." He kissed my temple. "Once this settles, we'll find a way to live peacefully but keep the full home feeling."

"I'm looking forward to vacations in Mexico," I added as we followed the others into the kitchen. The table was already full of food and drinks. "How any of you can afford your grocery bills is beyond me."

"Potluck. We gather together, and everyone brings one or two things to share," Sofia said at my side. "We may live on our own, but we're rarely alone."

"That must be really nice," I said, imagining how it would feel to have that for myself.

"You'll never be alone again, Ailis," she said. Everyone ignored the tears I tried to hide. She passed me a plate with a piece of pumpkin pie. "I had to threaten to stab Cisco for the last piece, so enjoy it. It came with death threats."

"Mmm, death threats, my favorite." I took a bite and grinned at Cisco.

I sat and ate my pie while Miguel and Cisco filled them all in on what had happened over the last twenty-four hours, focusing on the intel we'd gotten today. The three new ones bristled at the mention of Natt and raged when they heard of wolves being handed over to Julian for food. I added my two cents here and there, but Miguel didn't miss much. Listening to Miguel reminded me of years ago when we'd hunted down bad little monsters together. He was straight to the point and held nothing back.

"So, let me get this straight," Caser's voice caught me off guard. Cisco put his phone on the table and grinned. I hadn't even known Caser was listening in. "This all started because Natt had a hard-on for Miguel?"

"Good thing I didn't start talking shit about you," I said, then snickered at Caser's choice of words, thinking of how to answer his question without making reference to Natt's erection. "Yes, Natt has had an issue with Miguel from day one. His ego took a hit every time Miguel came around."

"He couldn't challenge Miguel and hope to keep his life," Cisco added. "The Noire Lune Pack has always fought to the death. Miguel would have killed him instantly. Natt wouldn't have stood a chance against even the weakest of our Pack."

I raised my brows.

"Truly, Ailis. Anna could clean the floor with him. She has enough power and faith in her still-human body that she'd kill him before he even shifted."

"During training a few days ago, she beat the shit out of Caser," Sofia said. "Got on his back and got him into a chokehold he couldn't get out of. She held on until he went down and beat the crap out of him with his own boot. He tapped out."

"Why do these conversations always circle back to me and my shame?" Caser said, and the rest of us smiled. The jokes kept us all level-headed and not running into the dark with guns and claws. "Back on the problem. Natt's been gunning for an awfully long time. Miguel, did anything happen between you two for him to be carrying a grudge this long?"

"No," Miguel answered. "I don't even remember interacting with him. He smells familiar, but it's more that my wolf remembers the smell of this Pack."

"Slighted," Caser said.

"Natt was jealous," I said, cringing that Miguel was blaming himself. "Offering me up to Julian solved everything for him."

"He underestimated your will to survive and Miguel's drive to ensure your survival. Getting between a mated couple is a death sentence," Caser said, and the rest of the group nodded. "And now they pay for it. You can't wait on this too long, Miguel. The hunt begins on their end, any minute."

"It began the moment the sun sunk below the trees," Deigo said from the edge of the group. He had spent the conversation listening more than contributing. "Every power will have felt us enter the territory. The Los Luna Pack is not a group that can be ignored. One of us, maybe, but seven of our Pack's most powerful?" He grinned, including me in the count. "It'll help bring down the number of folks willing to risk their lives for the cash reward on the head of one of our people, but we're pretty much a lighthouse for those willing to chance it."

"Julian isn't stupid. He will know Ailis' Pack has come to help her," Ben added. "But if vampires were smart, there would be more of them and less of us."

"Fucking and feeding, that's all they think of," Caser said. "Everything else is secondary, except when it comes to Julian. God knows how old that prick is, but he hasn't met the sun for a reason. He's not a fool. Remember that when you go for his heart. Many have tried before, and all have failed."

"The Los Luna Pack hasn't tried, and we will not fail," Ben countered.

"Anything from your source?" Cisco asked Sofia.

"Our communication is patchy, at best. When things heated up in Van, his communications slowed down." She pulled out her phone, her fingers sliding around on the screen. "The last I heard from him was minutes after Elizabet was chucked out a window. He said, 'The witch killed J's puppet. If you don't have her out of the city by sundown, she's as good as dead.' And that was the last I heard. He hasn't responded to any of my nudges."

"I'm not getting run out of my own city." I crossed my arms. It was my final answer. "Fuck that. I'll burn it to the ground first."

Sofia grinned. "And I'm not here to drag you out. We're here to hunt vampires."

"*Eat them!*" Cisco mimicked my screaming during the first and only vampire hunt I had been on. It earned him a brand-new middle finger. Really, how was I supposed to know they'd taste like a rotting body? I played with hell, not walking corpses.

"We have no choice but to move on him tonight," Miguel said. "Julian will be hunting Ailis for the death of Elizabet. Word down in Bone Alley is that whoever sees her first and presents her to Julian will be awarded cash, no questions asked. Each hour that passes, the amount goes up. Come sunrise, if Julian isn't dead, there's no safe place for Ailis in this city."

"Another day, and there's no safe place in this country," Deigo added, looking up from his phone. "Word travels fast. My contact just over the border, in Washington, has heard of Julian's offer. It's not high enough to gain much attention, but soon it will be."

"Christ," Caser growled. "Chitchat time is over, kids. The time to plan is now."

Ben, who hadn't said much during the replay, pulled a large blueprint from his bag. "I am here to hunt, but May is sitting in a hole in the ground, bitten. I cannot leave a hunter to that fate. She must be saved or killed and sent off, with honor, to her next life. Her people have customs I must carry out."

I raised my brow. "Honor? Did you miss the part where she hasn't done anything to keep the monsters in line? I mean, of course, we won't leave her to the mercy of fangs, but honor is a bit of a stretch, isn't it? Perhaps if she were doing her job, Julian wouldn't be standing on a mountain of innocent bones."

"I miss nothing, Ailis. But you have," Ben replied, turning his focus solely on me. I squirmed under his stare. "How many drained humans do you find in your territory? Very few. I have come to May's city, at her request, when wrongs needed to be righted. She never told me the reason she was unable to carry out her duty in this territory, but I have done it for her. It is common for hunters to help each other in these ways. In turn, she has hunted for me in Mexico when the problem was too close to my own door," he explained, and I felt about an inch tall. His face softened slightly when he saw the shame I felt roll across my face. I groaned and felt like a complete tool. "It is okay. You are new to this world. As long as you are willing to learn, I harbor no ill feelings toward you or your lacking knowledge."

I nodded, thankful I hadn't made a complete fool of myself.

"Hunters do not involve themselves in the squabbles between powers, such as Nest and Pack. She could only carry out a death sentence when humans are involved, and Julian is smart enough to leave you fine folks, alone. The odd time one of his children stepped out of line, May called me. More times than not, Julian killed his creature before I even got here. What he is doing to Pack, she could not interfere with."

"Until now," I added, motioning at myself. "He's been pretty direct in his wish for me to help him or die refusing."

"When Julian targeted you, I'm certain she would have hunted him. It is why they took her. To keep her from her duties," Ben answered. "It is why I will not leave her there."

"He doesn't see you as human," Sofia said, moving the spelling pot from my table, Cat going along for the ride. "You're a witch, and now, Pack. You're fair game to Julian."

"A month ago, May emailed me the blueprints to Julian's known hide outs and meeting places. She said something was brewing but didn't know what it was. At the time, we thought it had something to do with Coven being spotted in town. She wanted me to have these in case something happened to her." Benedicto unrolled the blueprints. "Julian's fortress."

"You knew something was up, and you didn't say anything?" Miguel accused.

Ben swallowed the insult. Rather than lash out, his face softened, understanding Miguel's frustration and anger. "Miguel, if I thought it had anything to do with your mate, I would have come to you at once. My brother, I would never risk your Luna. Until we found out what was going on, we kept a close eye on those we thought could be targeted, including Ailis. May added Ailis to her nightly scouts. I called in a few favors with the local shifters to scout when May could not. It was not until Cisco contacted me that I learned of Julian's intent toward Ailis."

"I'm sorry, Ben, that was out of line." Miguel unclenched his fists. "Thank you for the protection you offered from afar. I will not forget this and will come when you call."

"So, now that the tension has risen high enough to pop my ears, what's the plan?" Cisco asked, his eyes darting between his cousin and Miguel.

"There is no tension, Cisco. Miguel is a mated wolf, and his Luna has been threatened. We, as his family, must understand the grief of his wolf. We, as his Pack, must eat the pain for him, so his wolf gathers strength to defend her honor. It is not just Miguel who needs us. If we cannot share in his pain, we are useless to his wolf and, therefore, useless in this hunt." Ben turned his attention back to the blueprints.

The energy in the air turned heavy but not uncomfortable. It felt like they had all taken a step closer, sharing their warmth with Miguel's wolf. My cat lifted her head from the spelling pot, meowed once, then hunkered back down, a show of solidarity. The heavy blanket that now wrapped around us steadied my courage. I had no doubt that Ben was as ruthless as he was kind and generous, but in this moment, he was everything I needed him to be. With the tension finally gone, worked into something pleasant and needed, Ben pointed out every way into Julian's lair. And from the look of it, there weren't many ways back out. If things went into the tank, we were screwed.

"North Van is simple enough to get to, but there are many narrow passages where we could be cut off." Ben pulled back from the blueprint. "I recommend we split up. Group one goes for May and Pack. They're being held in the basement. Group two kills Julian, his children, and those who get in your way. We will regroup, and together, we will put the werewolves out of their misery."

"Ailis is with me," Miguel said right away.

I shook my head. "No, Julian will expect us to be together. If he takes us both, the plan goes bust. If only one of us goes down, we still have a chance of rescuing the others."

"She's right," Ben said. "Me, Sofia, and Ailis will go for May and our people. Once we free them, we will make our way to the rest of you."

"I don't like this," Miguel said, his voice holding a hint of fear I didn't often hear. "I don't like the idea of entrusting her life to just anyone."

"I am not anyone, Miguel," Sofia said, reaching around me to grab his hand. "You can trust me with her life. You know you can. I'll die before I allow harm to come to our Grimmwolf." She glanced down at me. "I stared down a hellhound for her. How badass would I look now if a vampire got her?"

"All right," he finally answered. "I don't need to stress the importance of only killing those we must. Just because they are with Julian doesn't mean they want to be. We kill when we must, not because we can. Let us not forfeit our place at the gates for the taste of revenge tonight. We are the deliverers of justice, not retribution."

I rolled my eyes. Optimism was not a shoe I wore. "You do you, Miguel. See how far your fluffy morals get you. As for me, I'm strangling the life out of that piece of shit the moment I see him."

"Match made in hell," Caser said and breathed a long sigh. "Keep safe, keep strong, keep your faith. And, Ailis, sharpen those teeth. Tonight, you hunt alongside Pack. Show them how it's done."

I grinned. It had taken my entire life, but I finally fit in somewhere. With the monsters. The good kind, if that was even a thing.

Chapter Fourteen

I handed everyone a spell bag that rattled with bones and stones. "Don't ask where these came from or what's inside. They're not exactly legal to have or make. The Coven has a bit of an issue with creating spells that alter auras."

Deigo sniffed his and cringed. "What the hell are these made of?"

"Did she not just tell you not to ask?" Sofia said, smelling her own and turning to stare at me. "Who died to make these?"

I shrugged. "I don't know, someone important and innocent, I suspect. All that juicy soul is pretty tempting, even for a witch." They all eyeballed me a little closer, and I laughed. "It's chickens. Bloody hell, like I'd have bags of human sacrifice kicking around? They're still not legal, but they're not evil. I got them from a demon. I traded brownies for them."

"Jesus, I can smell human hair in the bags," Deigo muttered, but pulled the bag over his head. "What does it do?"

"It's my hair and soon to be my blood. It's a small sacrifice to invoke the spells within," I answered. "It alters your aura, sort of. It is more like hiding it from those who can smell or feel them. It'll act as my aura would, shielding you. Although you all can keep the power of your wolves inside, you can't hide the fact that you will smell like wolves. Natt and those Philip couldn't hide are probably here, scouting or whatever bad little wolves do for evil maniacs. These hex bags will hide your smell and energy from them."

"Will it hurt?" Deigo asked.

"Only if your soul is evil or badly tainted, I suppose," I answered. "These bags have been blessed. It only hurts if your aura is tainted. The spell has a hard time grabbing onto too much taint."

"*Muchas gracias,*" Ben said, putting his over his head with a smile. "I love working with witches. They're much more creative than wolves."

"*De nada.*" I smiled, giving him my thanks, and pulled out my trusty pocket knife. With a small poke in my spelling finger, I touched the front of each hex bag and tucked them under their shirts.

"No fancy spell?" Cisco asked. "I've yet to see you pull out your witch guns."

"Not for this, I'm afraid," I replied. "My magic is in my blood. I don't use a lot of earth magics or elemental, where I'd need the words to back up the ask. Usually, my blood is more than enough to kick the spell in the ass. And, this way, I'm not taking on any taint by willing something that is not meant to be, into reality, like a circle of protection or quelling a demon."

"Mind if I ask you a question? I couldn't find the answer online." Deigo moved up to my side as we began the one-hour hike into Julian's property. We would split up halfway there. I motioned to go ahead. "This may be a stupid question, but why do witches call it quelling? The church calls it vanquishing."

"Quell, to bring an end to something with force," Ben answered for me. "The term was coined by the original three, long before the church was willing to admit demons were real."

"Who are the original three?" he asked.

"The original Coven," Ben and I answered at the same time.

"I tried to take an occult class last year. They wouldn't let me enroll," Deigo said, a look of question on his face. "I was hoping to learn a little more about witchcraft and magic. Anna gave me a list of studies to take, you know, to help me become more valuable to Pack."

"You're not a witch, that's why," I answered. "At the risk of sounding rude, it's not for the layman. It's difficult to learn without a knowledge foundation in place, such as growing up with magic or having it run through your veins. Though, if you were to imagine them speaking about your wolf rather than your inner energy, I'm sure you'd catch on in no time."

"You are of value to Pack, Deigo, but I get what you're saying." Miguel inched up to my side, quiet as a mouse. "As the world changes and different powers come and go, we need to be ready. When you get home, ask Anna to introduce you to Maggie. But let this be your only warning. Maggie may look like a sweet little old lady, but it's for appearance only. She'll clean the floor with you if you step out of line. She's who taught me most of what I knew before meeting Ailis."

"I'd recommend the same thing," I added. "You should take a look at my bookshelves when we get home and make a list. I have a few extras that I save for my students that you can have. Start reading all you can and speak to those willing to share knowledge. There are hundreds of free online seminars. I'll send you a link to the ones I have for my intro classes."

"Thank you, I appreciate that," he replied, then glanced around me to Miguel. "You're not coming home with us, when we leave, are you?"

"No. My home is with Ailis. We will come and visit, but my wolf has made a home here, as have I."

"It is an honor to be called to protect your new home, Miguel," Deigo said and walked off, likely to gossip.

Miguel grabbed my hand, his aura pouring over mine. The jungle of trees and shrubs around us brightened. It felt like every tree had stepped to the side for me to pass. The others moved with ease as if they were made of shadows and forest and light as air. Miguel pulled me with him a little faster. Finally, we were all running through the woods, not a branch snapped or rock clinked. In the back of my mind, I could smell Miguel's wolf. I could see him out of the corner of my eye, running beside us. The wave of Sofia's hand brought my attention to the clearing we'd branch apart at. Sitting on a fallen log, my cat.

"Is that your cat?" Sofia asked.

Cisco jogged up to our sides. "I let her out before we left, just in case you needed her. Philip texted me this afternoon. Samuel suggested we allow the cat to roam when we leave. She would know where she was needed."

I took a seat beside her and rubbed her cheek, right where her whiskers started, bringing out a calming purr. Ben went over the plan once more and answered every question that came up. I had the most questions, and all of them involved what I would do if I was trapped, about to die, taken. The answer was always the same—kill them all. Ben, Sofia, and I would be heading down to the second level of the basement and would work our way back up, checking each room along the way. No one, regardless of their species, would be left behind. Anyone found would be brought back to the window we would use to get in and ushered out into the night. Deigo would be standing by to bring them to safety, using the extra hex bags to shelter their scents. The plan was solid, except for all the parts where we could die, but no one spoke of what could happen. Before everyone moved out, they each touched my cat as if she were good luck. I wasn't going to jinx myself, so did the same. I didn't see where the cat ran off to, but I knew she was close by. Miguel kissed me once then was gone in a blink, blending into the night.

I followed behind Ben, with Sofia at my back. The rest of the way was flat and easy to maneuver. Every so often, Ben would hold his arm back, catching me from moving forward. Both he and Sofia had the noses of bloodhounds. I wasn't about to question each time we switched directions or circled back. As Julian's estate came into view, my stomach clenched. It was massive. A three-story sprawling mansion sat in the middle of nowhere, gated, treed, and lit up like the fourth of July. From our vantage point, I counted over a dozen fully armed men and women.

Ben held out four fingers to our right and three to our left. He motioned for me to lie on the ground. Sofia would go to the left, and he would go to the right. The plan, if it went accordingly, was that they would take out those who stood in our way while I hunkered down and prayed not to get caught. If it went south, I was to run back to one of our vehicles. Get the hell out of dodge and call Samuel along the way. So, I got down on my stomach and waited, praying this was not the end of our rescue mission.

Sofia clicked her tongue at my left. I waited until she gave me a thumbs-up and got up. Ben returned seconds later and gave a thumbs-up. I didn't ask what had happened or how they had pulled it off without so much as a splash of blood on their clothes. They were expert hunters, and I was a witch with a knife. I'd be covered head to toe if it were left up to me.

Back in our line, we made it to the fence line and walked the edge to where the fence met the trees. Ben went first, clicked his tongue, and I went next. Sofia didn't wait for any signal and came straight in behind me. We stood at the rear of the yard, waiting. Sofia motioned for me to slow my breathing. In and out, she mimicked with her hands. I hadn't realized I was panting until she pointed it out. My heart was pounding in my chest and ears. I closed my eyes, grounded myself, and when I opened them, it was time to move. A small flash of light signaled from the house. Deigo stood at the window we were heading into, his flashlight blinking that the coast was clear. Not a word was exchanged.

Ben grabbed my hand and ran, my feet barely touching the ground. It reminded me of flying, the one and only time I had tried and failed, landing on the ground outside a blood den and leaving chunks of skin on the rocks. With any luck, I'd not lose too much skin tonight. Without saying a word, Ben went through the only window into the basement. He turned and reached for me, yanking me through and dropping me to the floor. I think he had expected I'd have the same agility as everyone else and land on my feet. I didn't, and landed on my hands and knees. Sofia was next, closing the gate to the window behind her. Ben picked me up and winced. He shrugged, and I smiled.

At the door, Ben paused, listening for any hint of life. He counted down with his fingers, and on three, we were in the hall of Julian's million-dollar blood den. Fresh blood and old death filled my nose, and I swallowed the urge to vomit. It smelled like the bathroom of a dirty butcher's shop on a blistering hot day. My eyes watered from the stench. I glanced at Sofia. She was scrunching her nose to the smell. I mouthed *Mexico*, and she nodded. It stank like the stone prisons we had been chained up in. A wave of dread washed over me. I didn't want to see what was down there.

At the stairs, Ben went first. At the bottom, he clicked his tongue for only Sofia to hear. She nudged me, and we both descended, quiet as snow falling. I followed Ben to the end, and we started our room-to-room search. The first two rooms were empty, the third held bodies long dead, and I couldn't bring myself to look. I had enough nightmares. In the fourth room, as Ziggy had said, was May. Ben motioned to Sofia, who was keeping watch at the stairs, and we all went in. The door held back the odor, and I released an audible sigh that May had not been in the third room.

May was chained to the wall, her arms over her head. Her clothes were torn and bloody. Ben got to her first, lifting her head to check her pulse. Her eyes flew open, and in the kind of grace you only saw on the stage, she lifted her legs from the floor and wrapped them around Ben's throat, pulling him back and slamming him into the stone. He tapped on her thighs repeatedly.

"It's Ben, it's Ben," he kept repeating.

Her almost feral eyes blinked, scanning the room and finally the wolf she had in the death grip. "Benedicto?" Her face softened in an instant, releasing him.

"I knew you'd still be alive," he said, inching up to her side. He snapped the chains as though they were raw spaghetti noodles.

"Not for a lack of their trying." She rubbed her wrists, shaking out her arms. She glanced up at me and tipped her head once, a silent thank you. "Ailis, do you have holy water? I was bitten earlier this morning."

Benedicto pulled May's torn jacket form her neck. The wound was purple, and it looked like whoever had bitten her had shaken her like a ragdoll. Sofia, an ER nurse, jumped into action. She hissed the moment she smelled the wound. I pulled out two bottles of holy water and handed them over. Ben gave one to May and uncapped one of his own. May drank the bottle in her hand, and Sofia poured the other onto her neck. May closed her eyes but didn't make a sound.

"You're made of tougher things than I," Sofia said, cauterizing the wound with a little pen and placing a clean bandage over May's neck.

"It's not my first time," May replied with a shaking voice. "I'll need a full bath, perhaps a night or two on holy ground, but this should help slow it down."

"Jesus," I muttered. "I screamed like a baby when it was my turn for that."

"You were bitten by something more powerful than a vampire." May touched her nose but didn't name the truth that would take her life. "Those bites burn the soul. Thankfully, vampire bites do not reach nearly as deep, or I'd be unconscious now. I'd risk the moon before I passed out here. Later, when I bathe in holy water, I'll scream like everyone else with a soul worth keeping."

"We need to move," Sofia said, ignoring that May knew about Lycan. Or maybe now was just not the time to tie her back up and beat the information out of her, how she knew and who'd spilled the beans. I was spending too much time with bad guys if that was what I was thinking about at a time like this.

"Can you walk?" Ben asked her.

May stood and rolled her shoulders, wincing a little at the wound on her neck, and stretched out her body. "Give me a moment for the headrush to settle, and I'm good to go." She gripped Ben's hand. She looked sad for someone who had just been rescued. "Why have you come? You shouldn't have risked yourself."

He smiled. "Because you came for me when I was taken. Twice. I owe you."

"Fool," she said. "What's the play?" May asked, smoothing away the care and bringing forth her hunter.

"We have a small team upstairs," Ben replied, mirroring May's get-down-to-business attitude. "We're going room to room and grabbing who we can before the shit hits the fan above. You in or out?"

"My brother is chained up somewhere in this hellhole. I'm in, but I won't leave him here."

My eyes popped wide open. "And…we're adding a vampire to the list of people we're saving tonight?"

"Saving, yes. Rescuing, no. If I can find him, I will take his life, end his suffering," she answered. "Ming did not choose this life. He was taken from me and turned, Julian's way of trying to control me. If I can find my brother, I will end his suffering."

"If things take a turn, we're out of here. If we don't find him before we leave, we're out of here emptyhanded. We're going to bring the attention of everyone who owes a vampire a favor," Ben said. "Once we regroup, we will come back for your brother."

May's face fell. "If we leave, they're going to torture him."

"I'm sorry, May, but if we don't, they're going to torture all of us," I replied.

She nodded and turned to Ben. "Swear you'll come back with me."

"I swear," he said.

"Your word is gold, Benedicto," she answered, and released the desperation that lined her eyes. I knew that look from anywhere. I saw it in the mirror enough times to remember what May was feeling. No options, no way out and the people I cared about were at risk. I hated myself for wanting to leave without making sure she found her brother. "There were three younger" — she searched for the word with her hands and finally gave up — "pups down here in the basement. I tried to get them out, but they were too far gone to blood loss. I tried to patch them up the best I could, but I regret to tell you that I failed you, Benedicto. They didn't make it, and as you can see, I didn't make it out of here, either."

I watched Benedicto's throat bob. He nodded once. "Thank you for trying, Meiling. We will bring their bodies home when we return."

Until now, I hadn't known her full name was Meiling. I could tell by how he touched her, with such reverence, he cared deeply for her.

She pulled a scrap of paper from her jacket. "I got their names for you. In case their bodies went missing. So that you'd have their names to give to your Gods."

He put the page in his pocket. "Thank you for this."

"Nathaniel knows they were here," she said. "Matt, the youngest one, those were his last words. Natt sent them here."

"We know," I answered.

"When they took me, I broke out twice," she said, and I stared at her in question. She shrugged. "I tried to save who I could. I wasn't leaving here without help, and I knew it. I got one out of the window a floor above, when I was caught and bitten."

"One escaped?" I asked.

She nodded. "He could hear the call of his Alpha, Philip. I don't know if he made it or not."

Philip hadn't mentioned it, so I doubted he'd made it. Ben opened his bag and strapped May with new weapons, exactly her size. She gripped the cross he put around her neck and double-checked her supplies. From the look of how she handled her guns, they were hers. I wondered when he had stopped there, but it wasn't important enough to eat up time with questions.

Ben turned, and Sofia pushed me behind her. I didn't have to ask why as the door opened. Conor Madden, Julian's flunky, strolled in, wearing his usual thousand-dollar suit. The energy that filled the room made my stomach flop. He had received a promotion. I could feel it. I could taste it. He was Julian's new servant. A brutal servant, just like Elizabet.

"You shouldn't have come here." Conor shook his head and peered around Sofia, making eye contact. "I tried to warn you. Both Elizabet and I warned you. You should have accepted the invite. This will be most unpleasant for you now."

"My, my, haven't we moved down in the world," I replied. "From a blood bag to a puppet. I bet your parents are proud."

"Like yours, they're dead," he answered. "Place your holy objects on the floor."

"I'll keep mine, thank you."

Conor lifted his hand and pointed a gun at Sofia's head. "You can take them off, or I will shoot my way to you and do it myself. Your choice."

"Asshole," I said and took off my cross like everyone else.

"Wonderful." He extended his arm to the door. "Shall we?"

I laughed. "That's the problem with monsters today. They can't accept no as an answer."

"I'm certain you'll scream 'no' enough times tonight for the word to carry the same meaning to you as it does to Julian." He stepped to the side for his creatures to come in.

There were so many vampires in the room that it felt like the walls were closing in on us. I counted two dozen before I gave up and settled on the number of *too fucking many*. The one to my right put his hand under my arm, digging it into my armpit. I pulled back once, and his grip tightened.

I looked down at his hand. "That won't regrow, you know. Remove it, or I'll make sure you lose it."

"Come now, Brandon. Let's not manhandle our guests," Conor said and shook his head. "You just can't find good help nowadays."

"Pot calling the kettle black," I retorted.

I followed Conor. May, Benedicto and Sofia followed behind like a nice little line of lambs being led to the slaughter. Up the stairs we went and down the hall into another stone room. The smell had improved slightly, but now it mingled with the scent of my fear. The crew fanned out as if we were waiting for the star of the show, or for one of us to do something stupid. I didn't have to see Sofia's face to know she'd die before letting one of them touch a hair on her head. She moved up to my side and grabbed my hand. I gave her a sympathetic squeeze in return. I watched her look at Conor, nodding her head. In return, he gave her one nod back. I frowned.

The energy in the room popped my ears. Sofia burst into a rage that echoed into my stomach. Ben followed her lead, and May had two down before I realized what was happening. Sofia shoved me out of the door and shut it behind her. I didn't need her to tell me to run. My feet were already moving. The window we had crawled into was out of the question. It was on the other side of the room, now erupting. I pulled my shields up as tight as they could go and ran back down the stairs.

From the blueprint, there were a dozen places I could probably squeeze into to hide until I figured out how the hell I'd get out of this maze of horror. I ducked in and out of rooms with alcoves and gaps in the walls. The alcoves did nothing to hide me and the holes were useless unless I was willing to cut off limbs to fit. The room filled with two layers of dead had a hole in the wall big enough for me to climb into. Holding my breath, I shimmied in and wiggled myself between the walls. I inched my way as deep as I could go and tried to calm my pounding heart. I breathed in through my nose, turning my stomach from the stench, and out through my mouth, wanting to scream.

With my heart at a pace that wouldn't knock me out, I pushed my aura out around me, blocking my scent and energy. Calmed, I crept a little farther. The wall wasn't closing in on me as I had felt just moments ago. I inched into the underground until I was far enough away to think. In the distance, I could hear voices, and they weren't people I wanted to reach out to.

"We have her wolves. She'll come out eventually," one said. "One by one, Julian will kill them until she does."

I wiggled my arm down to my pocket and pulled out my cell phone. *Zero bars, no signal.* As if anything would be so simple. I continued down the gap between the stones, following the slight wind and smells of earth. Nails on rock and squeaks made me squirm. If rats were close, a way in—and out—was near. I followed the sound of scurrying rats. One crawled over my foot and I paused, scanning the floor. A small vent in the rock held the outside world at my feet.

I opened my legs and cramped down to the floor, skinning my knees and lower back on the rock. I was now thankful for Miguel forcing me to do yoga for years. *You never know what skill you'll need,* he'd say. I'd say thank you when and if we lived through the night. I penned a text to Ziggy, the only one I knew would have information on Julian's lair. I inched my hand out of the small hole in the stone and damn near cheered as one bar popped up on my signal.

Ziggy, I'm stuck in the basement of Julian's. How the hell do I get out?

He replied with one word — *Ziggtmoy.*

I rolled my eyes at having to repeat myself.

Ziggtmoy, how do I get out?

He replied — *I'm busy.*

Give me a fucking break. I've warned you countless times of raids. I've even stored haunted relics for you. You damn well owe me, and I'm calling in my favors right this minute. How the hell do I get out of the basement?

A moment later, as if he had to think about it, I watched the icon bounce on the screen as he typed.

You can't. The only way out is up unless you can magically turn yourself into a rat and crawl through the sewer lines.

I didn't have a spell for shifting. I didn't even know if that was possible. *Shit.* I pressed my forehead into the stone and wanted to scream. I thought back to when I had asked what to do if I got trapped and couldn't get out. Everyone had said to kill my way out. I couldn't kill any entire Nest of vampires alone. Hell, I'd barely killed one armless vampire in Mexico. I still had a scar on my chest from when my cross had flared to life and blinded us all. I wasn't exactly who you'd call when it came to hunting vampires. I wasn't really someone you'd call to chase down anything outside of hell, and even then, I ended up looking like a demon took me from a ride before I could send him back.

Ziggy sent another text.

You have choices, witch. You just don't like them. You could summon a demon and get a ride out of there, lickety-split, but that ride comes at a steep price, and you seem particularly attached to that tattered soul of yours. Or you can show the Nest why hell wants you dead so badly, why every loose demon eventually finds its way to your door. But leave no one alive. That is not a secret you want the world to know, lest you wish to be hunted by all.

I groaned internally at my options.

I can't. If the Elders find out what I can do, they'll kill me.

Death today or death tomorrow. Your choice.

Ziggy typed another message. *There are Lycan in that basement. Not all are dead. I heard Natt has delivered a new batch in exchange for the death of Miguel before sunrise. If you're going to run, free them first. They'll take most of the heat while you run for cover.*

I ignored him and sent one final message to Samuel.

Julian has the others. I'm stuck in the basement. I'm going to look for Pack and hopefully find a way out of here. If I don't make it, I love you.

I put my phone back in my pocket and waited until I heard not another whisper of a vampire before I moved. When the coast was clear, I inched my way out of my hiding place with legs of pins and needles from crouching between the stone. As quietly as possible, shields up at maximum, holding my breath as the stench returned, I made my way back to the room where we had found May. Inside, I found our bags and strapped myself down with more weapons, along with the crosses still lying on the floor. If I was going to die today, I'd do as much damage as I could on my way out. I leaned forward, hands on my knees, and steadied my pounding heart. *What the hell are you doing, Ailis?* My doubt crept in. I wasn't a hunter. I wasn't even that good of a fighter for someone my size and strength. Vampires were far beyond my size, strength, or speed. I stood, shook out my hands and stepped out of the room. I'd find those trapped, but not to take the heat off me, to give them a chance if what I did next went south. Which it would. I could feel it in my soul. I wasn't walking out of here without tearing my soul into pieces — the trademark of any witch, a soul dragging on the ground behind her.

Chapter Fifteen

I followed the lingering energy of Pack, I was so weak I had a headache from concentrating so hard on it. To my right were the stairs up to the monsters. I steadied my breathing and prepared myself for what would come next. When I reached the stairs, my charm necklace pulsed. It wasn't a warning—it had given up on those as soon as I'd landed on the floor of this hellhole. The necklace was warning me that there was more down here. Up ahead, beyond the stairs, were three doors. I inched toward them, my aura pushing out to sense what my brain wouldn't register. I could feel vampires and Lycan, but I didn't know which lucky door held either from a distance. I wasn't calm enough to sort through what my aura was picking up.

I stepped to the first door and pressed my hand against the rotting wood. Tortured souls sat on the other side. *Vampires.* The second room held the same, along with an almost dead Lycan. When I leaned into the last, I could feel Pack, and my heart broke completely. Five living Pack members, and from the smell, they sat with their death brethren. I paused before opening the door. They could be working for Julian, and I could be heading straight into a trap. It didn't matter in the end. I'd be meeting Julian face-to-face tonight, no matter what I did. I wouldn't be walking out of here without a handshake and a beating, if at all.

I inched into the room and held my finger to my mouth. A silent plea to keep quiet. I scanned the room while my aura pushed to its limits, wrapping the space in my shields. I had been practicing with Samuel, but the pull staggered me for a moment. I grabbed the wall to steady myself. My stomach twisted with familiarity. My head jerked to the right. Philip was leaning against the wall, bleeding at the neck, eyes closed. I quickly made my way through the dead and knelt at his side. Wrapped around his wrists and legs was a silver rope. It reminded me of when I'd found Sofia in the cell beside me in Mexico. It was cooked into his skin. He felt clammy but still had a pulse.

"Philip, it's me, Ailis," I whispered, pushing my arm to his nose in the same way Sofia had when we'd found Cisco broken and bruised in Mexico. I took one of the crosses out of my pocket and put it around his head.

His eyes jerked open as he breathed me in. "Doc?"

"Shh, not so loud. I'm going to take the silver off you," I said and cringed. "This is going to hurt like a bitch, it's cooked right in. I need you to not make a sound."

He nodded, and I began pulling the silver from his flesh. And, like the first time I had done it, I gagged. The chain had sunk into his flesh and muscle. Blisters popped as I pulled it off. My entire body flushed with heat as I fought not to vomit. The sound of it made it so much worse. When it was off, I pulled him into my arms, hugging him as tight as I could. My heart was absolutely shattered to see him here.

"Do you trust everyone in this room?" I asked, my mouth pressed to his ear.

Philip nodded. "We're the ones who wouldn't help Natt. I got the weakest members to safety, but the rest of Pack was called here. I tried to save who I could but ran out of time. Natt and Julian called the others when they realized what I had done."

"It's okay," I said, although it was far from okay. "I get why they're here, but how the hell did you end up here?"

"Travis," he answered, and I frowned. "A pup escaped with the help of May. I heard his call and came. I did what I could to buy him time. Travis got to my car and sped away. I sent him to Mairi's house."

"Oh, Philip, I wish you weren't here," I said, touching his cheek.

"Where are Miguel and Cisco?" Philip asked, and we both started moving from one person to the next, pulling the silver from their bodies. Not even one of them made so much as a groan. I hated to think of what had been done to them for them to sit through this.

"Julian has them," I answered. "Are you strong enough to kill the vampires in the rooms beside us? I counted three in one and four in the other. They're feeding, I think, on your people."

"Give me a few minutes, and yes, we can." Philip stood on shaking legs. "They're coming in here and taking us one at a time to feed on. But they're taking too much."

I glanced at the bodies on the floor. A whole new resolve set in. "When you kill them for this, save who you can and get the hell out of here."

"What about you?"

"I'm going to kill Julian," I answered. "It's the only way we win tonight."

"Come with me."

"He has Miguel. He has my friends. I won't leave without them." I offloaded my weapons and the three extra crosses. "They'll take them from me anyway. Might as well put them to good use. Standard vampire kit. Stakes, guns, holy water, and a few extra crosses."

"I hope I see you tomorrow," he replied, sorting through the goods and stuffing what he could into his pockets. "God speed."

"Do as much damage as you can before you leave, but for the love of God, don't die on me," I said then ducked back out of the room.

Once I was at the top of the stairs, I followed the scent of Miguel. It was a smell I'd never forget. I breathed in and released a long sigh, pulling my aura back in and tossing my hex bag to the side. It took three blinks before two doors opened, and the hallway filled with the damned.

"Hello, fellas." I smiled. "Aren't you going to invite me in?" The closest one grabbed me under my arm and hauled me forward. "You don't have to be so rude."

He pulled me through the doorway and into the room I had been pushed out of. The energy prickled my skin, making the hairs on my arms and neck stand on end. The power in the air made the room feel smaller than it was. It felt like the moments before lightning struck, how the air held a charge waiting for release. I was yanked to the front of the room, through vampires, and shoved to the floor, skinning my knee on the uneven stones.

"Asshole," I muttered as I pulled myself to my feet. I spun to face where the power was coming from and froze. I had never met Julian, had never once seen him on the news or in the paper. He was a recluse. Seeing him now, I understood why. It took me several tries to get my words out. "You're...oh God, you're a child."

Julian looked like his last living breath had been taken before puberty could finish its job. His shoulder-length blond hair was still that of a child, wispy and wavy. He was uncomfortably pale and looked fifteen at most, and that was giving him credit. I stepped back until I hit someone. I turned to see Sofia. I said a quick apology out of habit but didn't take my eyes off Julian. Sofia's eyes were bruised.

"Do not allow his looks to deceive you. He is very much not a child," Benedicto was the only one to speak. He was standing to my right, bloodied and bruised, but arms crossed like he had felt none of it. Behind him, an untouched and unconscious May. It looked like he had defended her and suffered all the more for it.

One scan around the room, and my panic set in. Where was Miguel? Where was Cisco? I looked back at Sofia, who gave a slight shrug.

"You are most correct," Julian said, smiling. His fangs were hidden, but I knew they were there. His voice was soft, almost childlike, and kind. It creeped me the hell out, but it didn't matter how he sounded. I knew better. The older vampires could blend in near perfectly compared to the newer ones, given they had been hunted to near extinction a few decades ago.

"Why the hell did we decide to let them live?" I asked, more to myself.

"Bleeding hearts were writing laws at the time," Sofia answered, and I fought the urge to laugh. "Men and their live and let live. If they could only see the shit we have to put up with now because of it."

"I have a feeling this is going to be a long night." I turned back to Julian, keeping my eyes averted from his gaze. I didn't know if he could trap me, but I didn't want to find out.

"Welcome, Ailis," Julian said, and I cleared my throat. "Ah, yes, Dr. Kyteler. Welcome to my home. Can I offer you anything? Drink? Food?"

"A gun would be nice," I answered. "Maybe some holy water?"

"Interesting you'd come in unarmed. I thought for sure you'd kill your way to me."

I huffed a laugh at his comment. "I am not unarmed."

His smile widened, showing his fangs. "Nor am I."

"I can smell your breath from here, Julian. Haven't you heard of brushing your teeth after eating people?" I asked.

"Jokes to the very end." He shook his head. "Let us waste no more time and get to the point of this cat-and-mouse game."

"To the point," I snickered.

"I was disheartened to learn of my Elizabet's death, but she was a jealous and hateful creature, killing anyone that gained my notice."

"Probably the only mercy she had in her," I said. "I wouldn't have killed her if you would have accepted my refusal."

"I am willing to forgive and forget. I was growing tired of her and her constant complaints about her soul. But my forgiveness comes at a cost." He stepped toward me, and I stepped back. "Look me in the eyes, witch."

His energy rolled over me, tempting me, convincing me. He was safe. He would care for me. I glanced up and met his eyes. I could feel the influence, like a lousy friend whispering in my ear to do something I definitely shouldn't do, but he didn't have enough juice to make me bend. He barely had enough for me to feel uncomfortable. He lacked a soul, the very thing needed for mine to listen. Even then, my soul wouldn't even cower for a demon.

"You will raise a demon for me, Ailis Kyteler." Julian's whisper crawled up my legs.

I shook my head and decided to dig for answers before showing him his failures. "I don't understand. Why?"

"Raise the demon, Ailis, and I will take away all of your troubles. The demon will allow me the power I need to remove the Elders once and for all. Vampires will return to the ways of old, removed from society, back into the darkness, and not flaunted in public, feeding on your children."

I cracked open an eye. "That's the stupidest idea I've ever heard. Nope, not helping you with this one."

Julian was at my front in an instant. He gripped me by the jaw and pulled me into his chest. "You will do this, or you will watch your people die."

"No, I won't. You've been watching me for years, Julian. When have I ever given in to a threat?" I asked, and he shoved me back. Sofia's hands kept me standing.

"Hearing a threat and seeing it carried out are two very different things," he answered, snapping his fingers. The only door out of here opened. Cisco and

Miguel were led through, already bloodied and held in silver chains.

From my head to my toes, I filled with rage. Julian's people took a collective step back. "I wouldn't do that if I were you," I said as Julian took a step toward Miguel and Cisco.

"You will do as I've asked, or you will watch the consequences of your choices take a life," Julian replied.

"Have you ever wondered why sane people leave full-blooded witches alone?" I asked. "Pissing one of us off leaves a trail of bodies for miles, although I'd settle for just this room. Revenge is in our blood. You don't want me hunting you for payback, Julian. I'm warning you, let them go, or you're going to piss me off, and that's not a safe place to be."

"You silly little witch. Who do you think led us to you?" Julian asked. "The local Pack gave us your name because of Miguel. You'd risk your life for the man who is the very reason you're standing here?"

I smiled. "I'd do worse things to better people than you, for them."

"Raise the demon, or I will kill them one at a time until you finally do it, and you *will* do it. There are a lot of souls in the city for me to bleed dry."

"Do you want to learn firsthand what hell taught me? What parting gift I left with? Why hell hunts me day and night?" Every inch of my body stilled. Every emotion drained from my face.

"You won't save them with a history lesson," he replied, cocky.

"It isn't a lesson, it's a warning." I finally smiled, but it wasn't friendly. "You see, Julian, like any curse, there are things we can't account for that change the course of that curse, such as fate and death. The day I died, and they dragged me into hell, where I was fated to go, the curse died. The door between my soul and the perks of the curse swung wide open, and when I was spat from hell, the door remained open." My smile faded, leaving behind the hell that was the middle of my soul. The pieces were still stained and crying. "But while I sat down there, I paid attention. I watched, I learned, and I listened. They speak so freely when they don't think you'll leave. They answer questions in exchange for years of torture per answer. But I was already down there for eternity. What was another few years?" Like presents on Christmas morning, I saved the best one for last. "Born the only surviving twin, I have the power of two hereditary witches inside my soul. I am a witch without limits, holding the secrets of hell."

His response was laughter. Like those who had come before him, he didn't believe me.

"You've lived too long, Julian. You have no fear of death," I replied. "The problem with your kind is that you think you'll live forever. You won't." I looked into Miguel's eyes. He shook his head. He knew what I was about to do. He had been the one who'd helped me build a wall around the curse. "For you, Miguel, some secrets are worth showing. I love you."

"I'll enjoy those secrets when we are finished," Julian said, laughter thick in his voice, as if he had already won.

"Oh, Julian, you silly little corpse, you're not going to walk out of this room. You and your people will die with this secret." I laughed with him. "Have you ever wondered what can kill a demon? And you, Julian, are just a weaker version of a demon." He didn't answer with more than a twitch of hesitation around his eyes. "I am the witch the demons couldn't kill."

I let go of my control, the mental webs I kept wrapped around my full abilities. In the very center of my soul, I held a ball of cursed power. The kind that peeled flesh from bones with a simple thought. To touch it would bring buckets of taint and send up signal flares to every demon walking on this side of the gates. But if we were all going to die, we might as well go down in a ball of flames. Little by little, my energy flowed out of my soul and filled the room with the smell of home and my cat. The power I had used to push and pull Sofia's wolf, I would use against the vampires ten-fold.

"Do you remember what it feels like to have a soul?" I asked Julian. I could now feel his soul hovering. It was almost sunrise. When the vampire sleeps, his soul hovers an inch over his chest, unable to let go, unable to move on. I reached for his soul and squeezed him. Julian flinched, feeling his soul for the first time in centuries, and I smiled. He spun in a circle, looking for it.

"Kill them all," Cisco whispered. "He will never stop…"

Julian slapped Cisco, and I looked at Miguel, begging him with my eyes. Miguel didn't want them all to die unless there was a reason. Cisco, on the other hand, was much more pragmatic. *Take them out now so you don't have to come back later to finish the job.* Miguel finally nodded. On the other side of the room, my cat sat in the doorway.

"Do it," Conor's lips moved, but not a word was spoken. His eyes nearly begged for help. Had he sold out his Master? It wasn't unheard of, just rare. "Please."

Everything slowed to a crawl. I had all the time in the world. The house filled with the sounds of growls and screams. With my aura pulsing through the room, I knew Philip was clearing the house. I reached for Julian's soul once more, only this time, the aura of my cat blended with my own. Behind him, it drifted, terrified, tortured. I grabbed onto his soul with my mind, wrapping fingers around his throat and leached his energy out, draining him. I screamed as my core burned with the knowledge of killing a soul. Only monsters ate souls. Only the cursed took away the chance of moving on to the next life.

I could feel the horror Julian's soul felt. The pain and fear poured into me, along with his energy. My scream echoed that of Julian's soul and my own, tormented and broken. Looking Julian in the eyes while he died was a different kind of hell. It hurt, and it should. I kept staring at him, my punishment for taking his life. Whether he deserved it or not, taking a life should bother me. It should stain me, or I'd be just another monster. I'd be happy he was gone, but I shouldn't revel in my ability to be the one to do it.

Julian didn't scream. He dropped to the floor, shriveled up, while the room erupted in screams. Conor stood there, staring down at him, his shoulders sagging. A look of relief filled his eyes. I wondered how long he had been planning for this death. But I also wondered how long it would take before he sold the rest of us out. If nothing else, vampires were opportunistic. Survival of the fittest, and those willing to serve up others as sacrifice.

Some of his creatures died the moment Julian did, others turned animalistic at the sudden cut between them and their Master. The room was a tornado of screaming and breaking bones. My body jerked from behind, and I went forward, covering my face as I hit the floor. My shoulder burst with blistering pain as fangs sunk into me. I tried to roll him off and failed. Conor reached through the fight and yanked the vampire off my back, staking him in the heart and moving on to the next fight. On the floor, watching us outnumbered, I searched through the room for cursed souls, draining those I could while the others killed the rest.

"This is so like you, sleeping on the job." May grabbed me by the scruff of my sweater and pulled me to my feet. "Your secret dies with me."

I closed my eyes and searched for any soul close enough to have heard what we had done in here but found none not belonging to Pack. My secret would die here. I stared down at Julian's body. "Payback's a witch."

"Isn't it?" May said, driving a stake through Julian's heart.

I stood, hugging myself, as May and Benedicto, along with Conor, staked the other vampires. "Where is Miguel and Cisco?"

"Hunting down the Pack who helped Natt. I gave him a list," Conor answered.

I approached Conor, calm and smiling, and punched him square in the jaw. "You piece of shit!"

"Wait, Ailis, Conor is my source!" Sofia slid into the room and got between us. "Conor has been feeding me information."

"I pieced that together on my own. I don't care who he is to you. He's a fucking monster!" I screamed around Sofia's arms. "You deserve the same fate as the rest of Julian's people."

"Sometimes, Ailis, we have no choice," Sofia said. "Julian took Conor's family. Don't tell me you wouldn't do monstrous things for your family. I've seen what you're willing to do for those you don't even love, let alone what you just did for Miguel."

I pulled back, pushing Sofia's hands from me. "I'd never hand over an innocent. Not for any of you. Not even for Miguel." I pointed at Conor. "But you did."

"I'm glad you've never had to make that choice," Conor said, spitting blood.

"Fuck you!" I lunged again. Sofia caught me mid-air and stepped a few feet away from Conor. I wasn't angry at *him*. I was just angry. I wanted someone to blame, someone to answer for what happened. But the one truly responsible, the one who decided who lived and died, was dead on the floor.

"He has one daughter left. Every time Conor refused Julian, he would torture his wife and children. Only one survived. That's how many times he said no. That's how many innocent people he wouldn't hand over. All but one daughter of four is alive," Sofia explained. "I know what you're feeling. I know you want him to pay, but he has, in spades."

"What will happen to him now?" I asked.

"They'll be flying to Caser tonight and will be housed at Caser's church until they can be transported to the convent a few hours away. That is punishment enough, Ailis. He will never leave holy ground again. He will never be free. But he will have his last child, and they will go into protection."

"It's not enough," I answered and turned my back on him.

"It's never enough," she replied.

I walked away with Sofia, reminding her my secret was as deadly as her secret. She would make it perfectly clear to the rest that the consequence would be death. Miguel got to the room as I was walking out. I pushed my face into his chest, wrapped my arms around him, and cried. He led me from the hell house and into a waiting vehicle. Samuel had come, and he had brought his calvary. The grounds were crawling with witches, shifters, Pack who had been at Mairi's, and those who owed Samuel favors. I caught sight of Noah Hudson, the visiting Pack member who had been forced into my class. I smiled, thanking the Gods for sparing him.

"You came for me," I cried as soon as Samuel lifted me into his arms. "Did you get my message?"

"I got your message about ten minutes ago," he replied. "The damnedest thing happened. We were having dinner, and Mairi had a panic attack, saying she could hear your cat. Pack started to get restless, saying they could hear Philip calling for help."

"I didn't think Pack or Nest could get through Mairi's spells?" I asked.

"Philip's call was a Lycan call to hunt. Nothing stops that call," Miguel answered. "The true call to arms can be heard all the way into the pits of hell."

"I don't feel very good," I whispered. My head swam. My aura felt patchy, but more than that, I felt like I was being sucked into a deep sleep against my will. "I'm tired."

"She's been bitten," Miguel said. "She's bleeding pretty bad."

Before Miguel could close the door, Cisco grabbed the handle and climbed inside with my cat, setting her down on my chest. Cat didn't curl up like she usually did. Instead, she sat on my chest, kneading my shoulder. It hurt like pushing on a bruise but stopped the burning that had started to spread. I reached for her tail, and the world went dark while Cisco told Miguel they had found the werewolves. They were warped and twisted creatures. There would be no saving a soul. Benedicto and Sofia were putting them down, then bringing May to her church for a holy water bath. My last thought was of the bath I'd soon be taking.

I hated holy water for the same reasons monsters did. It hurt like hell.

Fucking monsters.

Chapter Sixteen

Pain. So much pain that it went well beyond the definition. The world came into hyperfocus and faded as soon as the searing agony became more than I could stand. My aura was spent, leaving me raw and experiencing the delight of every sting. Although I was in a tub of warm water, it felt like I had been set on fire with no way to put out the flames. Inside and out, I burned like the witches who never made it out of the hunts. The room was too bright. I couldn't focus on an object to center myself.

"Though I walk...through the valley...of the shadow of death..." I prayed, teeth chattering, words hitching in my throat. "I will fear no evil."

This was how I'd die. Crying and vomiting in a tub of water, in the only safe place I knew, Samuel's house. Cat's purr brought my eyes to the chair beside the tub. My vision was too blurred to see her, but I could sense her. Each time I screamed, she meowed in solidarity.

Her tail dipped into the water, and I grabbed on as though it were a lifeline.

"Hold on, Ailis, I know it hurts." Samuel leaned over me, his hands on my shoulders. He pushed my upper body back down, and the burning started all over again as soon as the water touched my shoulder.

"Please, stop," I cried. "Please."

"I'm sorry, but to stop would mean to lose you," he whispered. "I can't lose you, Ailis. Life would be boring without you stirring hell with your bare hands."

"I fucking hate vampires," I said, tears streaming down my cheeks, and with one nod, he pushed me back under.

"Miguel!" Samuel shouted when I started to thrash. "Help me hold her down. This will go a lot faster for her if we can keep her under."

Miguel's scent filled my nose, and the pain started all over again. I got sick, and the world darkened, only to come screaming back in fiery brilliance. In and out, crying and begging, being force-fed holy water and getting sick all over again. One after the other, until they fought to keep my jaw open to dump the holy water down my throat. It poured from my nose while Miguel held his hand over my mouth.

"She didn't react this way when one of my people scratched her," Miguel said.

"Her aura wasn't spent when she cleaned those wounds. She had a layer of protection over her soul. Tonight, she used it all to kill Julian and his people. Her soul is in pain, and she won't share it with her familiar."

"Cat." I finally opened my eyes, shaking like a leaf. I rolled my head to the side to see her still sitting in her chair. My hand was wrapped around her tail. Her purrs calmed my pounding heart. The burn had finally stopped.

"Try another bottle," Samuel said, lifting me to sit up.

I drank it down without vomiting. Samuel passed me one more for good measure. "I'm never hunting vampires again."

"You did good, little red," Cisco said from the door.

I lifted my bottle in a salute and downed it. "I need a shower and a change of clothes. I'm covered in blood and vomit."

"Let me help you," Miguel said.

"Oh, no, wolf, you and I are going to have a little chat," Samuel interrupted. "What Ailis had to do to save you is going to have severe consequences for her." Samuel pointed at Cisco. "Get your ass in here and make yourself useful."

Cisco shook his head. "I don't think so, guardian. I'm not taking her clothes off."

"Scared of a little puke?" I joked.

Cisco nudged his head to Miguel. "I'd rather drink that bath water than deal with Miguel after I've touched your naked body. A wolf will not understand."

Miguel smiled. "It's okay, Cisco."

"Like hell it is," he replied but still came forward. Miguel and Samuel left Cisco to help me. Cisco stood at the side of the tub and closed his eyes, lifting me into his arms. He walked to the standup shower as though he had memorized every inch of the room. He likely had.

"I can stand, Cisco. I just need help getting out of my wet clothes."

"Fuck," he groaned out the word. "I don't like the idea of touching your naked body. Even my own wolf is telling me to keep my paws off. I'll do it, but if Miguel gets all weird, you're standing between us."

"How about we leave my bra and panties on? I'll take them off once I'm in the shower?" I asked. I didn't bother poking fun at him. I didn't understand Pack, but I understood love.

"Okay, I can do that."

Cisco helped me undress, keeping his eyes on the floor. He stepped forward with me, setting me on the floor and turned on the water. His attempt to hand me soap and shampoo resulted in every bottle landing on top of me. He closed the glass door and put his back to me. I leaned against the wall and closed my eyes. At Cisco's feet, my cat sat, purring. I could feel her.

He dropped a small towel over the top. "Can you cover yourself?"

"Thanks, sissy," I whispered. My throat was raw. I wet the towel and covered my chest with it.

"I wish Sofia was here. I'd have made her do this."

"You wouldn't have had to ask her. She'd have volunteered," I replied. "Why is it a big deal to see me naked?"

"Seeing you naked isn't what the big deal is. I've seen you naked plenty of times over the years," he said, turning to face me. He sat on the floor, opened the door a little, and grabbed my hand, giving it a squeeze. I don't know how he knew I needed to touch something other than hell, but his hand felt like it kept my mind out of the dark pits of regret and sadness. "Touching your undressed body is a sign of disrespect."

"I doubt Miguel would see it that way."

He chuckled. "It's disrespectful to *you*, Ailis. I'd do anything for you, but dishonoring you is not one of those things."

"What if I needed help and you were the only one?"

"I'd do what was needed, but I'd feel guilty for it," he answered. "I don't think you understand what you mean to Miguel or my people...or me. You are our Grimmwolf, Miguel's Luna, and my sister. I don't want to do anything that would make you think less of me."

I smiled and squeezed his hand. "I love you."

He sighed. His energy filled the room, making Cat purr even louder. "I love you, too, little red."

"I feel like a drowned rat," I groaned, running my hands through the tangled mess on top of my head.

"I once saw a rat floating down in the cenotes. It looked a little boiled and half-eaten. You look like him."

"Dickhead," I replied.

"I told you, I got all the charm in my family."

I washed my hair and body in the soaps Samuel kept here just for me. Lavender, rosemary and lemongrass all made by Mairi to calm my soul and heal my aura. Cisco spoke about nonsense until we heard Samuel's voice echo into the bathroom. Cisco leaned forward and repeated back to me what he could hear between Miguel and Samuel and, apparently, what was yet to come. The Elders and demons and Coven and everything in between.

"Story of my life," I sighed. "We better get out there. Samuel is only going to get angrier."

"Miguel still seems pretty calm. I'd rather stay in here than face a pissed-off guardian."

"Be thankful it isn't directed at you or me. I've been on the receiving end of his temper, and it wasn't pleasant."

I inched my way back up the wall and washed off, somewhat steadier than when I'd first climbed in. Cisco turned his back, handing me a towel. I dried and wrapped the towel around my hair while Cisco snooped through the dresser for clothes I kept at Samuel's.

"Stop playing with my panties and give me a change of clothes," I scolded when he held up a red thong.

I didn't need Cisco to help me dress, but I did need help slathering salve on my wounds. Cisco, like me, almost vomited as he put it on. I held onto the edge of the tub, gritting my teeth and groaning as it absorbed. I breathed in and out, fast at first, until the initial shock of rapid healing set it. He bandaged the wound and helped me brush out my rat's nest. I pulled it to the side and braided it. If I let it dry without doing something to it, it would be a tumbleweed of wild and frizzy curls within an hour.

Cisco waited in the hall while I changed. I limped out of the bathroom and into the living room with Cisco following. Miguel and Samuel both stood when I came into the room. Miguel looked relieved, and Samuel looked angry. I took my usual seat in a leather wingback close to a brick fireplace, already lit, and pulled the knitted blanket off the back. The chills had begun the moment I got out of the shower. Cat jumped onto my lap and curled into a little ball. With my fingers in her fur, Samuel passed me a cup of tea and a plate of cookies. I smiled, thinking back to Philip's comment about treating my body like a drug den.

"Has anyone heard from Philip?" I asked. Miguel passed me my bag and I rummaged through it for my phone. There were dozens of missed calls and messages from dozens of people.

"He's okay, a little banged up, but healing. He's at your house with the others," Miguel replied. "Sofia has an eye on him."

"What's all the screaming about?" I looked over my teacup at Samuel.

"I was filling Miguel in on what I've learned about Nathaniel," he replied. "He's been feeding lower Pack to Julian and his people since day one. When Miguel returned to Mexico, the power base throughout Van shifted. I believe the old Lycan and Miguel were the only ones keeping the Nest at bay."

I looked at Miguel, then Samuel. "How can you talk about them, but everyone else who knows, kicks the bucket?"

"As a guardian, Samuel has a free pass," Miguel replied. "He knows more secrets than anyone else on this side of heaven and hell. Just because he's retired doesn't mean he doesn't have the almighty grace behind him. Guardians, active or not, are doing God's work, and Pack would never come for him."

I rolled my eyes. "God's work."

"Don't you use his name in vain, child. I will get the soap." Samuel scolded me, and I smiled. He'd once tried to make me eat a bar of soap for cursing his God.

"Sorry," I replied, and he nodded.

I sat and listened, with tea and desserts, while they talked about that which we humans shouldn't talk about. I played with my cat's fur, tuning most of the conversation out. I flicked through my missed calls and texts. I half expected Natt to have sent a few threats, but not a peep from him. I sent one to Philip and Sofia, telling them I was okay. I texted Ziggy and thanked him, telling him I survived. His only reply: *Ziggtmoy*. May sent me a text to thank me and to ask me for tea when the world settled. I accepted. I put my phone back in my pocket when Cisco tapped my shoulder, motioning back to Samuel and Miguel. Samuel was getting heated again.

"Change, in any direction, is painful, Miguel," Samuel said. "And great change within your world only comes with great death. There is no other way for Lycan. Your very law demands blood be spilled for what has been done."

"I'm not here to kill Natt out of vengeance," Miguel replied.

"Then do not complain about that which you're unwilling to change," Samuel countered. "You have the power to force change, to bring this Pack back in line, but will not do what needs to be done. Do not complain about something you have the power to fix but lack the backbone to do."

"I'm not complaining," Miguel responded with the same calm he had at the start of the conversation. "I'm trying to understand your point."

"He handed over Pack in exchange for your life, Miguel," I said. "He gave me to monsters. What part of that don't you understand?"

"You're not Pack, Lish," he said, and the words hurt. "It is much more complicated…"

"But I'm good enough to shave off my soul for them?" I asked.

"That's not what I mean. It's not as cut and dry in my world…" Miguel started, but Samuel finally lost his cool altogether. I knew it was coming. Even Cisco pulled himself back a few inches. Miguel didn't seem to notice the pressure in the room building. But he saw it now.

"Damn you, wolf! You're blind, and it will cost Ailis her life!" Samuel banged his fist on the table, and I jerked in my seat. I've seen Samuel worried, irritated, scared for me, mad, but never had I seen him this level angry. He never lashed out when I was in the room. He always asked me to leave before losing it. "If you're not here to fix what your people are doing to my family, why are you here, Miguel? Nathaniel sold her out to the Master, and you won't deal with it? You put Ailis at risk again. The first time you involved yourself with my granddaughter, your Pack sniffed around like dogs. By the grace of God, they left her alone. Then you called her into your lands and into your Pack, and she almost died for your people. And now this one, Nathaniel, wants a piece of her to punish you. You did this, Miguel, by not handling Pack as Pack demands." Samuel stared down his nose at Miguel, the full force of his energy directed at Miguel. Miguel didn't so much as squirm. "Favor or not, you caused her to tip perilously close to the gates of hell. And once more, she's touched hell. Now, you will bloody well fix it, or I will. You will do what the almighty tasks you with, or I will, and there will be no survivors. Unlike you, I do not care about your people. I only care if Ailis lives or dies. And I will open the gates of hell for her."

Both Cisco and I backed away from the table.

"Samuel," Miguel's calming voice filled the room. The static in faded as if Miguel was eating it up.

"Bad idea," I whispered. Samuel wouldn't appreciate the show of power.

"Don't give me your shit, wolf! You weren't even a glint in your momma's eye when I was slaying beasts worse than your greatest nightmare," Samuel replied. "Do not make me put my shoes on, boy. I'll kick your ass all the way back to Mexico. You have young pups being bled for blood and power. The cursed were drinking the essence of Pack, and you want to understand *what*, exactly? They put a price tag on my granddaughter's head, and you say you are trying to understand? Understand this, do your job or get the fuck out of the way of those who will."

"It's okay, Samuel," I whispered. "Please, let's calm down. Miguel will…"

"Not this time, Ailis. You used great magic to save yourself and his people," Samuel replied and turned back to Miguel. "You don't understand, Miguel, what she's done for you. The Elders can never find out. Leaving Nathaniel alive leaves Ailis at risk. What she did to the vampires, pulling their souls, no one can even know she is able to do that. If the Elders were to find out, they would kill her for it. It's fair game if she can best one, but with powers like that, they'll outright kill her. If not them, the Coven will come for her. They'll shove her into the towers, and we'll never see her again. Not even I have the power to get her out of there." Samuel's voice hitched. Raw emotion poured from him. "You will control Natt, or you will kill him to protect Ailis. If you can't, I will. To keep her from the tower and hell, I will slaughter all your people. Not a soul will live. I am willing to carry that taint for her. What are you willing to do for her?"

"I agree." Miguel nodded. "I will do terrible things for Ailis, but I will not do them simply because you command it, Samuel. Law demands I speak to Nathaniel. I cannot kill him because I'm scared for Ailis. If I take the law into my own hands, I'm no better than Natt. I must talk to him, get him to admit what he's done, and only then can I carry out his sentence."

"Challenge him," Cisco spoke up. "Challenge him, and it doesn't matter the reason why."

"It matters to me," Miguel answered.

Cisco shook his head. "I'll do it, Miguel, if you don't."

Miguel stared at Cisco as if seeing him for the Lycan he really was.

"I'm sorry, but on this matter, I don't support your choices. I'll do it for Pack to protect the weaker. You didn't see the bodies in the basement. I did. Natt sent his people to the slaughter. They were bound with silver and drained, not for food or survival, but simply because they could. Our people, Miguel, died terror-filled deaths. My conscience won't allow me to walk away this time. And my wolf will not let me remain at your side if you do nothing."

"I respect that, Cisco, but I will not go around Pack law for retribution," Miguel said. "I will contact Nathaniel and will give him the option to step down or be taken down. I cannot kill a man if he's willing to walk away. I'm not built that way. Pack is not built like that. We will follow law, all of us, Cisco. It is the way of Pack. It is the law of Pack," he softened his voice and looked at Cisco. "I know you want vengeance, and so do I. I know your wolf is calling for the blood of your enemy, so is mine. But we will follow law. It is the only way we separate ourselves from the monsters. Do not risk your wolf to see Nathaniel bleed. You are better than that. Once law and judgment have been passed, whatever happens to Natt, after, he will have earned."

"I can live with that," Cisco replied. "But Natt will not leave this territory alive."

"If Natt admits to what he's done, I will challenge him and carry out his sentence," Miguel said, looking sick as he said the words.

Samuel closed his eyes and shivered. "The Elders are here."

"That didn't take long," I answered, my stomach flopping.

"They will see nothing more than Pack delivering justice," Samuel said. "Not even the Elders liked Julian, that will work in your favor. But just in case, you will remain here until the sun shines in the heavens."

"What do I do if the Elders come for me?" I asked.

"Whatever you can to survive," Samuel replied.

I huffed. "I'm sitting here because I did what I could to survive."

"No, you're sitting here because you won't," Samuel replied. "You could have solved many problems if you weren't so squeamish."

"I like my soul right where it is, thank you, outside of hell."

"That is not a luxury you will have for much longer if you don't start dealing with those who stand against you immediately. You give enemies the time to gather support time to gain power. A good enemy is a dead one." Samuel left me to stew and started breakfast. He, like me, didn't eat meat, to the chagrin of two hungry wolves. For some reason, it made me smile. If my life was one massive ball of shit and grief, a minor inconvenience for someone else made me feel a little better about it.

Cisco and Miguel each pulled out their phones and started speed-testing their people about the Elders in town. I sent a text to Mannix, warning him of potential fallout. Mannix's only reply was a string of cursing and skull emojis. *It's just another day in the life of a cursed witch.* We'd stay at Samuel's until the sun came up, and it was safe to leave. The darkness was not a safe place for witches.

* * * *

Samuel spent the early hours of the morning on the phone with his contacts, gathering information about the Elders. So far as Samuel could tell, they believed Julian had gained the attention of a neighboring Pack and had earned his death sentence. At Julian's house, they found evidence of Pack's blood and death in the basement, along with several humans who had been brutalized. I breathed a sigh of relief. The Elders had come to town, and my name had been kept off their list. Before they left, they hunted several other vampires down, those higher up on the food chain than simply lackeys, and killed them for drawing the attention of a neighboring Pack. One message from Mannix and the rest of the city was under the impression the Elders had killed Julian. Two hours later, I was safe at home.

Sofia was the first to pull me into a hug, her eyes red from tears, but I said nothing about it. Mine were puffy and red for the same reason. Hugs were given, tears ignored, and I closed myself up in my bedroom with my cat. Although I had made it, the fight wasn't over, and I knew it. I changed into something I'd rather be wearing if I had to run for my life again. Yoga pants didn't hold up to concrete and rocks the way jeans did. That I lived a life where I decided my outfit based on how many death threats I had received pissed me off.

Miguel poked his head into the room. "Are you okay?"

I turned from my closet, holding two sweaters. "Which one do you think will hide blood better?"

"The right one," he answered without pause.

"But I do like it more, and it'll probably get trashed the moment I step out the door," I said, stuffing it back into my closet. "What do you need, Miguel? Did the gates of fucking hell open up with a formal invite for me? Is Coven at my door? Is your goddamn Pack demanding another pound of my flesh?"

He stepped in and closed the door. "No. I just came to check on you. You've been up here for three hours."

I frowned. I felt like I had just stepped into my room. "I'm fine. I'll be right down."

"You're not fine," he said and tried to pull me in for a hug.

I pushed his arms away. "I'm not in the mood, Miguel. I don't need a hug."

"Maybe I do?"

I huffed a laugh. "Go get one downstairs."

"You're mad because I won't just kill him, aren't you?" he asked, and I glared. "If not that, then why are you angry with me?"

"Can't I just be angry?"

"Yes, but it's directed at me."

I paced, trying to find words to explain why I was upset, and finally, when I decided to keep it to myself, not wanting to hurt him, I waved him off. "Don't worry about it. It's been a long night. I'm tired, I'm cranky, I'm sore, I'm scared. I'll be fine. Go be with your people."

He jerked. "*My* people?"

"Oh, yes, *your* people. I'm not Pack, Miguel. I wouldn't understand. It's *complicated*."

"I didn't mean how you took that."

I smiled. It was weak and irritated. "You know what? I don't care what you meant by it, Miguel. I don't care that I'm not furry enough to understand. I don't care that I'm not one of you. I just don't fucking care."

Miguel stood in my path, stopping my pace. "I'm sorry, Ailis. I meant that Pack isn't as simple as you think. I was trying to explain it, but I wasn't given the chance. I wanted you to understand that this isn't as simple as killing a man."

I pushed his hands away from me. "You weren't given the chance? Fuck you, Miguel. No one has given me a chance. No one. I have fought tooth and nail to survive. Every single day, I could die. I am a fucking beacon for death. Don't talk to me about not getting the chance." The energy in the room climbed until he stepped back. The hair on my arms and neck stood. My cat howled at the threat my rage posed. "*Your* people, Miguel, are trying to kill me! *Your* people sold me out to goddamn bloodsuckers. You want a chance? What the hell are you doing to make sure I have a chance? You have to be browbeaten into saving me, for Christ's sake. I would do anything, *anything*, for you. And you spout law and wanting to understand. Well, understand this— Get the fuck out! I don't give a shit where you go. Just get the fuck away from me. Run along and negotiate for Natt's surrender. I'll be here planning how the hell I'm going to survive when he walks away unscathed."

Miguel took a seat on the bed. "No. I'm not leaving this hanging in the air. If you want to be angry with me, go ahead, but you will understand why I won't outright kill him for you."

I clenched my fists. "I don't care that you don't want to kill someone who has tried, for two bloody years, to take my life."

"If I challenge him for revenge and I lose, you are dead, Ailis. Nathaniel will kill you and suffer nothing for it. There will be no one to stop him. If you are my reason, you could die."

"As if you'd lose," I answered.

"Everyone gets lucky once, Lish," he answered. "Don't think for one minute I don't want to tear him apart for what he's done to you. My wolf is pacing with the need to tear Natt apart. But say I don't win, you are dead. You die, and those who stand with you will die. My need for vengeance isn't blind. I will cause the death of you, Sofia, Cisco, Deigo, and Benidicto. If I don't use law to corner him, you all die. My want for his blood isn't so strong that I'd risk the blood of those I love."

I slumped on the bed beside him. "And through Pack law?"

"I will get my revenge without risking everyone I love," Miguel replied. "If I challenge him and lose, he is within his rights to remove my supporters. It is an old law that no one follows, but no one could stop him if I lost. Those who try will die."

"I'm angry, Miguel," I finally said. "I'm so bloody tired of running for my life. I'm tired of being a broken mess. My soul hurts for what I keep having to do to stay alive."

Miguel slowly, as if still scared, put his arm around me. "I'm so sorry, Lish. I'm sorry this is your life. I'm sorry your soul calls to evil. If I could carry it for you, I would."

My tears fell silently. "I'm tired of being scared."

"One day at a time," he replied. "When this is over, we'll take that vacation I promised you."

"It better not be to hell," I joked. "Unless it's to poke sticks into Natt's cage."

"Philip is making breakfast. Let's go be with Pack. You'll feel better, trust me." He nudged me to stand. "Then we'll call Natt and make death threats. Those always make you feel better."

"They do, don't they." I laughed. "I'm sorry, Miguel. Thank you for not getting the fuck out."

He chuckled. "It's not the first time you've kicked me out. Remember when you locked me out of my own house and threw two bags out the window, telling me to get a hotel room?"

"You broke in that night. I almost stabbed you when you crawled into bed."

"I think my favorite fight was when we were killing that ghoul, and you leaned against the car, telling me to do it my way since I was so smart. The damn thing dislocated my shoulder before you'd help me."

"It got my point across, didn't it?" I grinned. "You stopped being so pigheaded after that."

With a smile, my rage back under control, and Cat following us, we hit the living room and everyone scattered, pretending they hadn't all just been listening to me having a meltdown. I followed Miguel into the kitchen, and the moment I sat and breathed in the scent of home, the last dregs of temper flowed out of me. Oh, I still wanted Natt's head on a platter, but I was willing to do it Miguel's way for now. If Pack way didn't do the job, we'd do it the witch way. I'd pry the gates of hell open and shove that bastard in. Because Natt could get the fuck out, too.

Chapter Seventeen

I shimmied into the corner, between Miguel and Sofia, and picked at a blueberry muffin with crumble topping. It wasn't the homemade ones I extorted from Philip every chance I got, but the bakery near his apartment was a close second to my heart. The others found their places, sitting or standing, and the conversation flowed like it only could within a family. Unlike the last time we had gathered, no one held back. We talked about what happened. Although it made me wince, I knew they all had gone to the brink of survival and stained their souls. They needed closure. They needed to be told it was okay. I hated to admit it, but I needed the same. It was hard to stare our inner monster in the eyes and walk away feeling like it was worth it. Sometimes, we needed someone else to say it for us.

Miguel didn't flinch when the others spoke about killing Natt. I squeezed his thigh as a show of support, but Miguel simply agreed and ignored the rest. Being at the top was a lonely place—he was the only one in the room who had to answer to the decisions made. It would be his blood, his life, his soul, that would be at risk. For that, hate-filled or not, I'd support him until my way was the only option left. None of us could argue against the growing opinion that Natt had to die for what he had done. Not even Miguel, who had agreed, selling out Pack was worth a death sentence. Selling out me was worth even worse.

"How was your bath?" Sofia asked. "I heard Benedicto had to sit on May and hold her under the water."

"Awful. It felt like hell," I answered.

"She took it like a champ," Cisco added.

I laughed. "No, I didn't. It took Samuel and Miguel to hold me in that tub. It literally felt like hell. Like the pits of hell were painted over my entire body, head to toe. Even my hair hurt. Was anyone else bit?"

"Vampires do not affect us in the same way," Miguel answered. "We still clean the wounds with holy water, but it isn't as painful as when a full demon bites us."

"Lucky you," I replied. "I need a holiday."

"Mexico is nice this time of year," Miguel said.

"It better be nicer than last time." I laughed.

"May will be coming to Mexico. Perhaps we all could rent a boat?" Ben spoke up. "She is taking a few more weeks off. I'm going to take her snorkeling in Cozumel."

"Solid choice," Cisco added. "There's a sweet spot in Playa Las Gatas if you want to see some amazing marine life. The water is calm, there are lots of caves to explore, beautiful coral reefs, and the fish will be everywhere. Let me know. I have a diving buddy there that can take you all out."

"I may just take you up on that," Ben replied.

"I hate to break up the smiles," Philip said, looking up from his phone. "Natt has been contacted by the new Master of the City. They're looking to make a deal for peace between Nest and Pack."

"What?" I blurted out.

"Who is it?" Miguel asked.

"A fang by the name of Demetrius," Philip answered, and Miguel stiffened. "Know him?"

"I do. He's better and worse than Julian. He's as ruthless, but I'm surprised he'd be reaching out to Natt," Miguel answered.

"In three days, Demetrius will be coming, along with his ilk," Philip said, putting his phone away. "I don't know if that means they want the same deal as Julian had, but it's never a good sign when a vampire wants to make a deal."

"My guess is Demetrius will kill Natt and his Pack," Ben said. "He won't be making any deals. He never has and never will. He hates Pack with the same viciousness that we hate vampires with."

"If you could all excuse me for a moment." Miguel smiled and wiped his mouth with his napkin. He looked calm, but all of us felt the shift in energy. Miguel ducked around the corner.

"What's going on?" I asked. They all shushed me and pointed toward the living room.

"Miguel," Nathaniel's voice came over Miguel's speakerphone.

"Nathaniel," Miguel spoke, his voice calm but edged in anger. "If you meet with the Master of the City, you are damning your people."

"The rumor mill spins quickly."

"If you survive a meeting with Demetrius and manage to work the same deal with him, feeding your

Pack to vampires, you are breaking law," Miguel said, Natt laughing on the other end. "This ends now."

"Aww, are you still angry about your Luna's unfortunate run-in with Julian?" he asked. "You have three days to be out of my territory, Miguel, or you and your people will face the consequences. And take your little witch with you. I will not honor the protection of Los Luna Pack. I have pulled the protection of my Pack. Any caught consorting with the witch will be challenged and sentenced accordingly. You can inform Philip of this, since he's currently with you."

"If you throw your support in with the new Master, offering up a single drop of your Pack's blood, you will be found guilty of breaking Lycan law."

"And what, Miguel? What will you do about it? I am not scared of you or your Pack."

"You gave the name of my mate to the Master of the City. She is the Grimmwolf of the Los Luna Pack. She is human," Miguel accused. "For that, I will take your life."

"If you lose, she'll be the next on my list," Natt said.

"I will not lose, and you will not touch my mate. I will see you at nightfall, where you will draw your last breath."

"If you come, I will not grant you a transition. You will die here tonight."

"To the death. I will see you on the rock when the moon is high." He hung up and made a call. "Tonight, Caser."

He didn't return to the kitchen. I waited a few minutes before following him to my bedroom. I curled around him on the bed, holding him tight as he cried into my arms. I didn't have to be Pack to know what he felt. Every life I'd ever taken cut me up. My soul didn't care if they were monsters. It bled for everyone just the same.

"I'm sorry," I whispered to Miguel. "I know you don't want to kill him."

"This is about innocents, Lish, not what I want or what anyone else wants. Law demands I act. Innocent people have died and will continue to die if Natt isn't stopped. You will never be safe with him alive."

"Sometimes we have no choice," I muttered.

"You finally understand." Miguel tucked himself into my arms. "This moment reminds me so much of when I was forced to take Izzy's life. Not only was she a Pack member, but she was my friend. Isabell was a woman of God, a true believer. Her heart and soul were purer than anyone I had ever met. She would quite literally give you the only food she had, the only dollar to her name, anything you needed. While Nathaniel isn't worth his own fur, and it shouldn't bother me in the same way, it does. Taking a life, no matter the reasons, should be weighed heavily, should stain us, and should never be done hastily. And sometimes, it doesn't matter. Sometimes, we have no choice but to do a task that hurts our souls."

"I'm sorry, Miguel. I truly am. If I could do it for you, I would," I said, and he huffed a laugh.

"Because it's that easy for you?" he asked but didn't wait for an answer. "I've seen you take a life, Lish. It kills you inside. What you did last night tore your soul in half."

"I'd do it for you, though. I'd do it so you wouldn't have to carry this on your heart."

"I love you." He kissed me, long and warm and wet with tears. "I don't think I could face Natt without you, without knowing for sure you'd still love me after."

"It's the same reason I hesitated with Julian and waited for you to nod. I'd rather be dead than have you think I am a monster."

Miguel jabbed his finger into my ribs until I laughed. "Oh, I've no illusion of your wicked ways, little witch, but I'd love you no matter what."

I pushed myself into his chest until I was sitting on his lap, holding him down on the bed. "I'll do wicked things for you."

Miguel grabbed my sweater and pulled it over my head. "You can start by taking your clothes off."

* * * *

Caser arrived sometime after dinner to support his friend in his first challenge for the position of Lycaon, while Miguel and I were in my bedroom. He had told the others to leave us be, not wanting to be the reason either of us had to get dressed. On the night of a challenge, a wolf seeks out only their mate and fills their energy with love. That Miguel spent those hours in my arms told Caser that Miguel was worthy of winning. Had he been gloating, Caser would have doubted Miguel's right to challenge and would have withdrawn his support. Caser saw challenges in the same way Miguel — that they should not be done out of vengeance or the need to restore a mate's honor. You beat the shit out of each other for that. Death should never be reduced to such trivial reasons as ego. Cisco and I thought differently, but as Caser pointed out, that was why we sat on the side of warriors and protectors. We were far too ruthless to be given power. Both Cisco and I agreed. We'd have been drunk on it, killing everyone who crossed us, including that hag who had yelled '*burn the witch*' the last time I spoke in public. *Me, petty and vengeful? Never.*

An hour before midnight, Miguel showered and changed into lose fitting clothes, ready to face a fate he didn't want. His shoulders hung, and I knew the feeling of being faced with choices we didn't want to make. I had been there. I had *just* been there, at Julian's.

"You will win if you stop being squeamish. Go for a quick kill. Do not wait for him to attack. This is a kill-or-be-killed fight," Caser said. "You are stronger than you think. You could have taken my place several times over."

"I don't like killing," Miguel said.

"Then why did you challenge a Pack leader? You knew you'd have to end his life to win," Caser answered. "If you don't do it, he'll kill you. Do not make us watch you die when we all know you can win."

"Just because I don't like doing it doesn't mean I won't," Miguel replied. "I will do what is necessary."

Sofia grabbed Miguel's shoulders. Her arms were shaking. "Natt will shift before fighting. Use it to your advantage. Also, Philip said Natt has a bummed knee from an injury that didn't heal right. It's weak. A kick and…"

"Sofia," Miguel's voice was soft, loving. "It's okay to be scared, but remember, I know how to fight, and I know how to win."

She nodded. "Your Pack is with you. Fenrir is with you."

"If it doesn't go down like I planned, get Ailis out of here. Get her to her people. Only Coven will be able to protect her."

One by one, Miguel hugged and touched his Pack before we all split up and took vehicles to the old meeting grounds. Miguel didn't say much as we drove to Stanely Park, to the original meeting place of Pack, a large stone deep in the middle of the park. I held his hand as we drove and told him stories that I knew would warm his soul and give him reasons to come home.

"Do Pack marry?" I asked.

"Are you planning on making an honest man out of me?"

My laughter was sharp and loud. "If you play your cards right."

"Some have a human ceremony and make it legal for the country they reside, but for Pack to recognize it, two Pack members would need to ask their Lycaon for a blessing and complete a Lycan ceremony."

"Oh." I scrunched my face. "I suppose that rules me out."

He squeezed my hand. "You misunderstand. I'm not saying you're not Pack. As Grimmwolf, you are seen as one of us. What I meant was, we'd have to have two ceremonies for us to be considered married by human law and Pack law."

"Two parties, two heaping piles of presents, I could live with that."

"Are you asking me to marry you?"

"I'm just seeing what my options are."

His laugh settled the knots in my stomach. He pulled into a parking lot. We'd have to walk the rest of the way. Sofia and Cisco had already given me the very condensed version of what would happen tonight, what could and couldn't happen, and the only grounds we could jump in to save Miguel, which was if

Nathaniel brought in a weapon or had someone step on the rock on his side. This was to the death. Short of cheating, someone was going to die tonight.

The others had already arrived and were taking the lead, fanning out around us. The energy in the air staggered me as soon as I got out of the Jeep. It was a mix of excitement and nervousness. It tasted like tears. Miguel held out his hand, his aura blanketing me as soon as we touched, stilling the bluntness of Pack. I followed him through the lot and into the trees, touching the bark as we walked. Up until learning Pack had a special little place smackdab in the middle, I had loved coming here. It felt like the city was a world away, and every problem was dropped in the parking lot.

One of the university environmental studies classes had had a week-long installation at Science World. I'd attended with Philip and was enamored by the history and roots of the place. May had held an unpopular lecture soon thereafter, about the missed history of the park's true purpose as an indigenous ceremonial site and the political implications of whitewashing history. The university had asked her never to do it again and threatened her job, since it had resulted in a month-long picketing of the park and threats of donations withdrawn. She'd done it twice more, and had her paper published. May didn't kowtow to anyone. The rest of us at the school stood behind her and threatened resignation if they removed her.

Miguel pulled me through the younger trees and brush and into the forest I loved. The woods were vast and luminous under the touch of Miguel's wolf. Young saplings and old-growth trees. Hemlock, cedar, fir and spruce towered over me, making the newer pine trees look like dwarfs. Shrubs sprouted out of every opening between branches and stumps, night-blooming flowers reached for the stars. The canopy above swayed in the night breeze, letting drops of moonlight pass down to the sprouts ruling the flat and fertile ground. Vines and flowers clung to the occasional tree, making the perfect homes for spiders and mice.

The tension slowly built as we grew closer to the Pack. Howls screamed for the moon, and growls mixed in with the cacophony of the dark. Critters and creatures abandoned their nocturnal hunting, scurrying out of the paths of Pack. Sounds from every direction filled the air and almost completely muffled the pounding in my chest and ears. In the distance, under the energy of Pack, the flow of the forest, I could feel it. *Hell.* It felt like a decision not yet made, hanging in the air. It felt like the moment between jumping off a board and waiting to hit the water. Uncertainty, regret, pride, terror.

I squeezed Miguel's hand. "Can you feel that?"

Miguel nodded. "I can smell it."

"Natt has bargained with a demon tonight," I said. "I can feel the taint in the air. It's following him around, a bargain not yet completed. Isn't that cheating?"

"Yes," he answered. "But he will pay that price when he is in a cage, and the hellhounds smell it on him."

"I love you," I said as we stepped through the treeline and into a tight clearing.

Three dozen Pack, all that remained after last night, stood around the rock. As soon as we arrived, the majority of Pack moved with Philip to step closer to us. Natt didn't miss the movement and snarled at Philip. If Miguel didn't win tonight, Natt would skin Philip alive. Natt stood in jeans, no shirt, no shoes, his hair wild and free. He looked like a fighter but didn't feel like one. His soul felt old and faded, torn at the edges, burned in the middle. He stank like the pits — one sniff, and I had to swallow the urge to be sick. I hated that smell more than anything else. It was worse than Mairi's salve.

Miguel stopped next to Cisco. "My whole world is in your hands."

Cisco took my hand from Miguel's. "I will give my life for her, Miguel."

Miguel kissed me once, breathed me in then stepped onto the rock. I gripped Cisco's hand and blinked rapidly, trying to will my tears to stay inside. My pulse ate up my hearing. I watched but heard nothing more than my inner panic as Natt welcomed Miguel to Pack and accepted the challenge. Sofia motioned for me to slow my breathing. She then mimicked my pounding heart. I nodded rapidly, not knowing how I'd calm down when I was about to see something I had only read about in horror novels.

"Last chance, Nathaniel. Step down, and I won't take your life or the lives of those deserving within your Pack. Or, you will die on this rock tonight," Miguel said, and I cringed. Bleeding heart to the bitter end.

"This is my Pack, and I will run it as I see fit," Natt replied.

"No. You won't," Miguel said. His face was a mix of emotions. Disappointment, anger, sadness and, finally, resolve. "You will die here tonight. You are a disgrace."

Cisco leaned into my ear. "Miguel's wolf is angry. This will be over soon."

My nose tickled with the smell of fresh brimstone. I glanced around the crowd couldn't see anyone from the pits waiting around to collect on a debt. Hell tickled the back of my neck, and I looked up to the rock and prayed Miguel could sense what I could. If Natt shifted, it was over for Miguel. As Natt came closer and closer to the moment he'd fight, the smell of hell grew with him. The bargain was attached to his wolf.

The tension exploded on the rock, and I covered my mouth with my hands, catching my scream where it started. Natt began to shift, taking up precious moments. He wasn't as fluid as Cisco or Sophia. Miguel shifted his hand, claws like butcher knives sliding from his fingertips. And in the blink of an eye, Miguel tore Natt's throat out. His other hand ripped Natt's beating heart from his chest. Natt's eyes flew wide as he realized he had lost. His face was frozen in time, half man, half beast. He looked surprised, as if this was not what he had bargained for. He fell to his knees, grabbing at his throat, his jaws snapping at the air. Miguel stepped out of his way, and Natt fell face-first to the ground.

I stood at the edge of the crowd, palming the gun Sofia had said I wasn't allowed to bring. But I didn't have claws like the rest of them, and if a single one of these bastards went for Miguel, I'd shoot them. When it came to making sure my family came home with me, all of them, I'd break every fucking Lycan law there was. Future laws would be written because of me.

Caser leaned in from behind, putting his hand over mine, keeping my gun in my pocket. "Watch. The fight is over."

Sofia stepped up to the rock and knelt on one knee, dropping her head. "Miguel Álvaro Cruz, Lycaon of the Noire Lune Pack."

Caser was next, followed by Ben, Deigo and Philip. Cisco stayed at my side but bowed to Miguel. The others knelt where they were, some still limping and bruised. Miguel looked my way, and my heart broke for the pain I saw in his eyes. His hands were fully back to the ones I had felt caress my body time and time again, but tonight, he held them behind him.

"I love you," I whispered, but I knew he'd hear me. "I will still love you tomorrow."

Cisco grabbed my hand. "It's time for little witches to leave."

"Will he be okay?" I asked, not wanting to be pulled away.

"He's fine," Cisco said and turned me around, nearly dragging me into the forest. When I tried to look back, Cisco turned my head and shook his. "Things are about to get extra gross now, little red. He won't want you to see what he does to the body."

I felt my face scrunch and, in the background, heard bones crushing. "Oh, Jesus, are they eating him?"

Cisco laughed. "No. Nathaniel died in disgrace. He will not be granted a transition service. He will be dismembered and tossed in the dump, where he belongs."

Chapter Eighteen

I waited on my front steps, wrapped in a blanket, for Miguel to come home. My cat sat at my side, ever vigilant, my warning of pending doom. Every rustle in the bush brought our focus to a raccoon or squirrel. Cisco was inside, making breakfast, wanting everything Miguel would need ready. Sofia was the first to return, saying all was well in the land of Lycan. But until I saw with my own eyes, I wouldn't believe her. Caser and Benedicto came next.

"Good evening, Dr. Kyteler." Benedicto tipped his head.

"Ailis is fine," I replied.

"Oh, it's fine for him, but you rode my ass for weeks to call you by your last name," Caser teased.

"You threatened to kill me when we first met," I answered.

"So did you."

"True. But I have the feeling everyone introduces themselves to you with a death threat." I smiled. "Where is Miguel?"

"He's coming, ma'am," Benedicto said, motioning to the forest surrounding my house. "He's running out his wolf's adrenaline. Do you mind if I start making breakfast? He'll be hungry when he gets home."

"Cisco has already started it. But, by all means, go and give him a hand. I'm letting him cook meat for Miguel."

Benedicto sniffed the air and smiled, touching his hand to his heart. "Cisco would never do such a thing to you. I smell beef jerky. That is the only meat."

I smiled right down to my soul. "Tell Cisco I'll take him to an all-you-can-eat buffet at the Casino. There's more meat in that buffet than a butcher shop."

Caser took a seat beside me, his body heat warming the chill that had been setting in for the last two hours. "Things are going to be pretty tense here for the next few months while people find where they belong and years for them to learn the true ways of Pack. Cisco and Sofia are going to remain here for that."

"Cisco can't. He has school coming up. I can't ask that of him, and neither can you. He's given enough," I replied. "But Sofia is welcome to stay for as long as she wants."

"Cisco is going to apply to the local program. Philip, your assistant, has a favor owed to him and is going to pull some strings. Cisco can study here and travel as needed," Caser replied. In a matter of minutes, it felt like Cisco's life had been planned out. The irritated look on my face made Caser smile. "Don't say no. He's finally found where he wants to be. This wasn't my idea or Miguel's. It was Cisco's. He approached Philip on his own."

"His home is Mexico," I said, feeling guilty.

"His home is with his family. He's been standing on the outside since the passing of his mother, biding his time until he found the one place he wanted to settle into. Let him have the only family he knows. Miguel is like a brother. He wants to be here to support him. And you, Ailis, are his family." Caser smiled as if remembering something fond. "The day you saw beyond his wolf, you brought down the wall he has around his heart. But the day you opened that door and killed a vampire for him, risking your life to save him and his people, he tied himself to you like you are his blooded sister. He's attached himself to your soul like a loyal hound would. If you ask him to leave, he'll take it as the worst kind of rejection. You and Miguel are his Pack now, the Pack he wants. I've never seen his wolf so calm or him so happy. I'm asking, not as Lycaon, but as his friend. Please do not take this from him."

"What does this mean for you and him? Can he ever go home if he stays here?"

"I'd always welcome him back. I love Cisco as I would a son," Caser answered. "But right now, Cisco is needed here and wants to stay. Miguel will need all the help he can get. To go from my second to a Pack Leader will be a difficult transition."

"If anyone can do it, it'll be Miguel," I replied. "What happens to Miguel, though? He doesn't want to be a Pack Leader. Could he ever come home after this?"

"He's on the fence about remaining Lycaon. I suspect he will abdicate to Philip once Philip has proven himself, but his home is no longer Mexico. He won't come back if you're here, Ailis. *You* are home to him."

"How do you feel about him leaving you to run their own Pack? Is this like a gang, being jumped in and body bagged out?"

"It's much easier to get out of a gang." Caser laughed. "It's common, within my Pack, to raise up Alphas who are strong enough to have their own territory. After learning the true ways of Lycan, they move on. It's part of the original tasks of a Lycaon to teach the ways of Lycan, to ensure those ruling over territories are doing so with honor and grace. My people stay until they have a calling elsewhere, and they leave with my blessing, and some, on occasion, return to our open arms. We are not like shifters, Ailis. We are all family, all connected, all welcome. Or, that's how it should be."

"Grace," I snickered. "You're the least graceful person I know."

"We have that in common, witch." He laughed with me.

"Caser, how do I secure our permission to enter into your territory to visit?"

"You ask," he replied, and I smirked. "For you, I'd skip the formalities. You and Miguel are welcome anytime. Just let someone know ahead of time, or you'll scare the pups when they feel your arrival."

"Come fall, I will no longer teach a full-time schedule. I have promoted Philip, from an assistant, who really was a lecturer, to be honest, to a full-time instructor. The Dean had no choice but to accept, given my resignation was attached to my request, and there are literally zero others who can do my job." I grinned at my conniving ways. "That'll free up my schedule to be able to go with Miguel to Mexico. We could live there for almost half the year. Would we need different permission for that?"

"You, Grimmwolf, never need my permission to come and go. Whether Miguel starts his own Pack or not, you will always have the protection of *our* people." Caser put his arm around my shoulder. "I'm so glad I didn't kill you."

"Ditto," I answered. "I don't think Miguel would have approved of me slaughtering his Lycaon. He's pretty squeamish about murder."

Caser's laughter barked into the night. "You've got guts and fangs, witch. You're going to be just fine."

My stomach jerked, and I stood. "Miguel is coming."

"You felt him before me," Caser said with a smile. "A mated pair is stronger together, Ailis. Love him fierce tonight. He will need it."

"I will love him like hell every day," I answered.

Miguel tore through the trees, sweat covering him. When I met his eyes, my nervous laughter bubbled out of my throat. Caser ducked inside as Miguel jogged up the drive, his eyes only for me. I dove from the stairs and jumped into his arms as soon as I could. I wrapped my legs around his waist, grabbed his hair and kissed him as thought my very heart would stop beating without him. He held me in his arms and dropped to the ground, whispering his love for me between kisses. I pulled back and hugged him, trying to squeeze his brokenness back together with love.

"I'm okay, Lish," he finally said.

"I'm so sorry, Miguel. I'm sorry," I cried into his neck. "I can feel your wolf, he's hurting. I'm so sorry."

Miguel breathed me in. "We will heal. That is why Pack is here. We will heal together."

"Let's get you cleaned up for breakfast, you really stink." I laughed, pulling back and kissing him again. "You smell like you jogged through the sewer."

"I fell into a gutter on my way home. I forgot about the natural coyotes here."

I helped him to his feet. "Did a little coyote scare the big bad wolf?"

"You bet your ass. One bit my leg when I was trying to get away."

With his arm around me, we stepped inside. His people waited for him. As he went by, he was given hugs and nods. Philip came in behind us with trays of food and muffins, pushing his way through to my kitchen, complaining about the mess and yelling out that breakfast would be ready in thirty. I pulled Miguel through the house and into the bathroom, stripping him out of his blood and sweat-soaked clothes. I didn't mention the blood or bits of fur. I got undressed, ran the water and held him as he silently cried. I washed him and hugged him. There wasn't anything I could say. A broken heart is a broken heart. In our world, more times than not, we had to do things we didn't want to do because to do nothing would hurt more.

Miguel lifted my chin and kissed me. He was gentle at first. But once I gripped his hair, his tongue exploded into my mouth until his teeth nipped at my lip. I encouraged him with the press of my hips into his. Without pause or hesitation, he spun me around and placed my hands on the wall, positioning himself between my thighs. He nuzzled into the back of my neck, dragging his teeth across my shoulder and biting down just enough for me to moan. Miguel pushed my thighs open wider, pressing his length against me.

"So wet already? I haven't even touched you." Miguel groaned as I wiggled my hips.

"Please, fuck me," I said, a hint of desperation in my voice. I needed to feel him, all of him.

He pulled his hips back, and at a pace almost painful, he pressed forward, filling me. I groaned into the crook of my arm. He pulled back out and slammed back in, knowing this position was perfect for the kind of rough and dirty we all needed once in a while. There was nothing slow or gentle about his needs tonight. Miguel gripped my hips and fucked me, as I had asked, as we both needed. I bit down on my arm to keep myself from screaming. He repositioned himself to get the angle I liked and rolled his hips as he pushed and pulled from my body. I squeezed my eyes shut and groaned his name through my clenched teeth. Working his body faster, falling into a rhythm, his hips slapping against me, he built up my orgasm. Each stroke brought a wave of pleasure until my entire body began to twitch and vibrate.

I reached behind and dug my nails into his thigh, finally releasing my scream along with an orgasm that weakened my legs. Miguel grabbed me before I could fall and held me standing while his release built. He covered my mouth with one hand and worked my clit with the other, keeping me riding the knife's edge of pure ecstasy. A growl tore from his throat, followed by a shout that bounced off the walls and felt like a cannon going off. Miguel staggered forward, putting one hand on the wall, pumping against me until ever drop of orgasm was wrung from us both. He pressed his head into my back, panting. I slowly moved forward, testing the strength of my legs. I turned into his chest and hugged him until we both floated back down into reality, pulses steady, and our balance returned.

"I'll never grow tired of this," Miguel said, helping me out of the shower.

"We need a bigger shower. We barely fit in there together," I replied.

"Our next house, we'll make sure it has a locker room shower." He laughed while I smiled.

"Our," I whispered. "I like that you've always planned for me in your life. You've always made room for me."

He kissed my nose. "I've never seen my life without you in it."

After we toweled off, I cleaned his wound, and he squirmed as though I was burning him with a hot poker. "You're such a baby."

"It stings. Fucking coyotes," he complained. He hissed when I cleaned the cuts on his knees. "I fell into a gutter. It was filled with sticks, rocks and trash. Thank God I can't catch human disease, or I'd be in for a few needles at the hospital."

"Yeah, I get that. I just think it's funny that I've seen you go toe-to-toe with a demon, and here you're damn near panting over some minor abrasions."

"Keep laughing, witch. I've seen you cry over less."

"I'm not a big bad wolf. I'm just a wee little defenseless witch."

"Defenseless, as if," he countered, and I flicked his raw kneecap. "Witch."

With cuts bandaged and Anna's ointment healing the coyote wound, Miguel and I joined the others for breakfast. My table was filled with food, the counters as well. We all had to hold our plates, but it only made the morning better. Philip handed out fresh rolls and butter biscuits while Cisco placed a package of beef jerky on everyone's plate and vegan jerky on mine. He gave me a wink, no one complained, and no one spoke of what happened last night. Slowly, more Pack showed up, asking if they could join. Miguel rose to each knock and invited them all inside. This morning was a time for closeness, and they all searched for a place to heal and belong.

Cisco and Philip spoke about the biology program at the university. Cisco was excited. Philip would bring him to meet the Dean, who was part of the local leopard population. It was more information than I wanted to have. I showed Sofia to the basement, where she kicked Cisco out of the master bedroom. She took it and the master bath with the whirlpool tub. Cisco didn't care. He'd slept on the ground many nights. The second bedroom was a luxury to him. Caser would leave in a few days with Diego, who was about to take over Miguel's old job. Benedicto would stay until May was healed and could come back out of retirement, but first, a vacation to Mexico. Philip was scared. Natt had protected him since he was a blood donor. He had always given his protection to the younger, but now didn't know who would protect him.

"Natt" — Sofia spat his name on the floor as if it were a curse — "did not protect you, Philip. But I've got your back. I know what it's like to be anyone's meat." Sofia cleared her throat. "Before Cisco found me and brought me to Caser, I was in your very shoes. Like you, I took a lot of pain and torment to protect those weaker than me. For that, if you need help, I will stand with you. But if you open your mouth to the wrong person, you're on your own."

Philip physically eased. "Thank you. And if you need my help, trust that I'll run and find someone to help you."

"That's the right answer. Find Cisco or Miguel. If I need help, I'm going to need one of them." She laughed, but when it died down, her eyes zeroed in on him. "Fuck me over and I'll wear your fur next winter."

"I'm mangy. You wouldn't stay warm," Philip replied.

"With your hide, I'll fair just fine," she added. "Air out the smell of bachelor, and you'd make a lovely pair of gloves."

That everyone laughed made me a little uncomfortable, but it eased the tension, and there was enough of that to have all the windows open. Small talk and laughter filled my kitchen and heart. It felt right. It felt like my entire life had built up to this moment. A full house. My cat sat on Caser's plate and scratched him every time he tried to move her.

"What did I do in this life to get this kind of treatment from a cat?"

"Where do I start?" Samuel's voice called from the front door.

And now, the morning was perfect. Samuel came in with Mairi and two bags of food. Mairi pulled a small wagon behind, filled with Tupperware containers from the feast she'd held while housing the Pack. I snuggled into Miguel until my eyes drooped, and my head kept jerking forward.

"Let's go to bed," Miguel said, picking me up into his arms.

"I don't want to miss the party," I answered. "I don't want everyone to leave while I'm sleeping."

"There will be more parties, more meals," he said, already walking up the stairs with me. "You're not going to have an empty house again, Lish."

"I hate being alone," I answered. "Make sure you ask them to come back. Make sure they know they're welcome here. Tell Philip…"

"He knows, Lish. I will tell them all, I promise."

* * * *

"You two clean up nicely," Philip said to Miguel and Cisco, handing me a glass of champagne. "I can't believe the Coven let you R.S.V.P. three people."

"They didn't." I grinned. "Mannix has you down as his plus one."

"I hope he knows I don't put out on the first date," Philip replied, catching Mannix's eye from across the room. Philip's wave was enough for Mannix to finish up his conversation and head over. "This shindig is ritzy as hell."

"I didn't think you'd show up." Mannix leaned into me for a casual hug. "I had a good alibi ready for you."

"Demons?" I asked.

"Not that big of a stretch. I've been running my ass off for days," he replied. "There's been a massive influx of demons popping up. Do you think it has something to do with why the Elders came and went? Or the new Master's arrival tonight?"

I shrugged. "It could be because spring is in the air, Coven is in town, it could be vampires, or it could be that someone lost a bet on the horses. Your guess is as good as mine."

He stared at me long and hard but dropped it. "My father has his eye on you tonight. Heads up."

"Thank you," I said, and found Torin Ashford shaking hands with a couple that looked like they paid for this entire thing. "I'm not looking forward to that chat."

Mannix left us to find a hiding spot before his father could loop him into another chat with another eligible lady. Cisco stood a good ten feet to my left, power-eating a plate of meat with Philip. I leaned into Miguel, swaying to the music. Caser and Deigo had left early this morning, Deigo with two suitcases of books from me and Caser with an urge to rescue a cat. Ben had gone to May's house to make sure she was protected when the new Master arrived. Demetrius wasn't happy to learn of Natt's demise and called Miguel the next sunset. Miguel had very few words to say to him but got his point across. The Pack doesn't negotiate with vampires. If Demetrius stepped out of line, Pack would send him on to his next life. That the entire city knew May was out of retirement sent a strong message. *Our city. Our rules.*

I tensed as Torin made his way through the crowd, dressed in a suit that cost enough to feed a family for months. He was handsome the way Mannix was. Only his son held compassion and love in his eyes, where Torin's eyes were deep pits of unrelenting power. The kind of power that broke people to his will.

"Dr. Kyteler." Torin extended his hand, and I smiled. I had always enforced he addressed me professionally. "What a pleasure it is to see you again."

"Miguel, this is High Priest Torin Ashford," I said, pulling my hand back and wiping it on my black dress. "Mannix's father."

Miguel held out his hand and smiled. "Pleasure."

Whatever Torin felt, he didn't like and pulled his hand back quickly. "Could I borrow your dear for a dance?"

"You would need to ask her for yourself," Miguel replied.

I groaned. "One."

I followed Torin to the dancefloor and let him pull me into his body for a formal dance. Torin danced like he was made of air while I stumbled about like a newborn calf. I'm sure if I had let him lead, I'd have looked graceful. But Torin had always rubbed me the wrong way. He was power-hungry and a bully. It was a losing combination if he was trying to win me over. I hated both qualities in a person. He made small talk about Mannix and his prospects as though his son hadn't a will of his own. I feigned interest. Torin didn't see his son the way I did. Mannix could be a High Priest one day, and a damn good one at that. His power was just that great, and his soul just that pure. But because of his father, he'd never reach for greatness. He'd keep running from Torin because his life very much depended on it.

"I've heard everyone else's thoughts of the Coven starting a new Hive on the West Coast, but you've yet to offer yours," Torin said, dropping the topic of his son since I had nothing I was willing to add out loud. "We're splitting from the old ways, entering into the world with a fresh view of a world we've shied away from."

I nodded. "That's what I hear."

"Since you do not attend the Convenire, I'm here to answer any questions you may have."

"Who will be seat one? You?" I asked, and he nodded. I groaned internally. Torin was a third-level, third-degree ordination. There was no higher he could go unless they created a new Hive on this continent.

"That troubles you," he said. My face betrayed me.

"I worry about what that means for the rest of us. The last time Coven branched out and created a new Hive, a new council, a war between us started. Your council, Torin, came for the full-bloods and gave them an ultimatum—join or die trying to remain impartial. Those who didn't throw their hats in with the current Coven were put to death," I regurgitated our history to the man who'd helped write it. "There will be two councils. Will the expectation be that we decide which council to support?"

"Not at all. There will only ever be one council. Only now, there will be three Covens. One in the Americas, one in Europe, and one in Asia. All Covens will answer to one council," he answered, and I paused. I hadn't heard of a third taking form in Asia. "As our lines grow, so do the needs of our people."

"Let me get this straight. You will hold seat one in our Coven and a chair at the council? How is that impartial?"

"It wouldn't be. I do not get a vote in matters for my region," he answered.

"I'm sure you've thought of everything," I said, trying to keep my suspicions to myself.

Torin spun me around, and my eyes landed on Miguel. He looked like he felt sorry for me. I know I did. Mannix stood on the edge of the room, eyeballing the exit. Torin caught his son trying to inch his way out of the room and shook his head. Mannix's shoulders fell, and he shuffled back over to Cisco and his date for the night, Philip. I felt more sorry for Mannix than I did for myself.

"Did you know, at one time, the Coven used to enforce the breeding of hereditary witches to ensure a pure line remained in control?" Torin asked out of the blue.

"No, I didn't know that."

"Your parent's marriage was arranged for that very reason."

That was news to me. I shrugged. "They loved each other dearly."

"They grew to love, but it wasn't like that in the beginning. Your mother was very much a child of magic, wild and free. She had to be tamed, much like I believe you would be."

I laughed at the thought. My mother had stayed wild until the end, and my father had never once tried to hold her back. He would sit for hours, watching her craft spells, set fire to the yard, blow up the basement, smash out every window in the house. He loved her as a wild child of magic and encouraged her when her magic failed or went sideways. And like my mother, I'd never be tamed either. That Torin spoke about them so personally, irritated me.

"Good thing that's a thing of the past," I replied.

"Perhaps not a thing of the past," he said. "It is our old ways that have kept us safe and our power strong, or so say those in this room, those who fear change."

I eyed him. "I'd pity the man who tries to enforce it once again. Some may want the old ways to return, but those of us who would suffer under them would rather die than be forced to do a damn thing."

"Mannix would be a good match for you. You and he are much the same. You are both wild and untamable. Together, you would be one of the most powerful couples to walk the earth."

I smiled. I wasn't insulted. Mannix truly was a good man, and any parent would want him to be matched with someone deserving of his devotion. "Thank you, Torin, really. Mannix is one hell of a catch, and any woman would be lucky to have him. But I'm already involved with someone."

"Speaking of," He motioned to Miguel. "I'd like to discuss what happened in Mexico and how a room full of vampires suddenly died. I appreciate the reports you gave and your willingness to admit you were there." Torin clicked his tongue. "Julian was strong enough to sit on the council of Elders. The Coven has questions about how the vampires died. Your recollection is very spotty."

I shrugged. "As I mentioned before, it's all very foggy. Both times, I was bitten and suffering from the curse. In Mexico, a demon bit me, and I don't remember much of the event or the days leading up to it. As you well know, it's a side effect of demon venom. The same for vampire bites."

"We could compel you to remember," he said, and I knew what that meant. A spell and a bloody painful one.

"You could try. I'm even willing to come to Council and allow it. But, as you found out when you tried to dig the information out of my head after my parents died, it would be a harrowing experience for those of you who survived it," I answered. My parents had woven spells of protection over me when I was born, as all hereditary witches did for their children. It kept us from being taken and used. To try removing or circumventing them would cost someone their life. It already had, once.

"That's fine for now, but eventually the truth comes out."

"Yes, it certainly does," I replied. My lies slid off my tongue like butter, as they always had.

He glanced at Miguel, standing with Cisco. They were in deep conversation, but I knew both of them had their full attention on me. "I see you have Mexico with you tonight."

"My partner, Miguel, who you just met, and his cousin, who will be attending school here in the fall," I answered. It was all truth, sort of.

"I've heard of Miguel. He was once a priest and is now a demon hunter. I've seen his cousin before. Is he a demon hunter as well?"

"He dabbles, but his focus is on his studies." From the look on Torin's face, I shrugged. "We all need hobbies."

"Interesting choice of friends, Ailis."

"I'll take whatever friends I can get. You never know when you'll need one."

He leaned his mouth to my ear. "I could be a very good friend to have. Step in line, once and for all, and you would benefit from a mutual friendship with me. To do otherwise would not be prudent."

I smiled at his threat. I had been threatened by better over less. "And I can be an awful enemy to have knocking on your door if you threaten me again."

"Come now, I haven't begun to threaten you."

I laughed, playing up to those watching us standing at a complete still in the middle of a moving dancefloor. "Neither have I. Stay away from me and mine, and I won't be the biggest nightmare you've ever seen."

"I can see why Mannix cares for you. You're a beast, just like his mother."

"Thank you," I replied and stepped away from him. "Compliments like that can make a gal blush."

I left him on the dancefloor and made my way back to Miguel and Cisco, my stomach twisting in knots. I pushed myself into the warmth of Miguel's arms. I had always kept the Coven on my radar, but tonight, I moved them up to first place. They'd be watching me closer than the pits. I grabbed Mannix's hand and pulled him out with us as we left. I wasn't leaving him to the mercy of Torin, even if that bastard was his father. Blood didn't make a family. Love did. And Torin only loved himself and power.

With a thank you, Mannix bolted from the banquet hall. He would be hiding out until his father left. Me and Miguel went home while Philip and Cisco headed to the university to look around. Philip had an all-access pass to every inch of the place, and Cisco was itching to see where he'd be spending the next five years of his life. Miguel listened to me vent about Torin and witches and Coven and cursed bloodlines and *the fucking nerve of some men*. But once we got home, the worries of today were left at the door. Home was safe. It could be invaded by assholes who spraypainted my walls or delivered baskets of threatening promises on the front stoop, but together, it was our fortress. A place of solace and peace.

"We have the house to ourselves until Sofia gets back from Pack," Miguel said, nuzzling my neck. "She almost dropped dead when she went into the Chapel today. She's having all of the religious artwork brought in from storage. A priest has been there all day, with his team, trying to get rid of the ghosts and blessing every square inch of the place."

"How long do we have?" I asked.

"An hour, tops." He glanced at his watch. "Barely enough time for me to do what I want with your body."

I bolted from the front door with Miguel hot on my trail. He scooped me up and tossed me over his shoulder, taking two steps at a time. He dropped me to my feet and kicked the bedroom door closed. I prepared myself to be taken wildly, using up every minute of the hour we had. Instead, he reached behind my back and unzipped my dress. Letting it fall to the floor, he stepped back, nodding at what he saw. Under my dress, I wore a black lace bra, stockings, and lace booty shorts. All his favorite pieces. He unclipped my hair and let it fall around my face and shoulders.

"I've always loved your hair when it's wild and untamed," he said, leaning into my ear. "Just like you, wild and untamed."

He backed me into the foot of the bed, lifting me up and laying me down. He opened my legs and took his time crawling up to my lips. He kissed each leg, slowly, so painfully slow. I squirmed, reaching for him to pull him up, but he batted my hands away. At my thighs, he breathed me and pressed a soft skin at the apex of my thighs, only to pull away. In a graceful move, he stood at the foot of the bed and removed his clothes, piece by piece, while I watched, chewing my bottom lip. Miguel was muscular but not hard. He had the kind of body that felt good to snuggle into and the strength to make me feel safe while doing it. Nude, Miguel was breathtaking. His sun-kissed skin and wavey hair made me lick the drool from my lips.

He slid onto the bed, on his stomach and pressed his lips over my panties. I closed my eyes, gripped his hair and didn't let go when he tried to control my hips. I tugged him against me and ground myself into his mouth. Before my pleasure built to a place of no return, he pulled back, thumbing my panties and pulling them down. I knew I'd get the release I needed the moment a groan escaped his lips. But it wouldn't be his mouth bringing me tonight. Miguel climbed up my body, nipping at my skin until he kissed me. I could taste the promise of my orgasm on his lips. He positioned himself perfectly, jerking his hips back and forth, teasing me. I dug my nails into his ass and pulled him toward me.

"No torture tonight," I said, trying to pull him against me. "Please."

"I love it when you beg," he said, finally plunging himself inside.

"Fuck," I moaned long and hot.

There was no gentle start. I didn't want it. Not tonight. I wanted release. I needed to feel his heart pounding against mine. Miguel gripped my thigh and lifted my leg for a better angle. I panted as he drove himself as deep as my body would let him and pull back out until I squirmed for more. I closed my eyes and let my aura crawl over his, filling him with my need. Miguel dropped my leg and pulled me into a kneel, holding my thighs and pumping against me. He rolled my clit under his thumb.

"Come for me, Lish," Miguel said, working my body to the point of almost too much, an overload of sensation.

But with that simple request igniting a fire inside me, I groaned out his name, dug my nails into his thighs, and let the pleasure wash over me. Gone was the rest of the world, leaving only me and Miguel and love so great, my eyes watered. With my orgasm on the brink, Miguel was a force of desire and hunger and bliss. I called out his name, and my body felt like it had fractured, crumbling into a million pieces. Nothing mattered but the crashing wave. Miguel pushed himself in as deep as he could go, gripping my thighs and echoing my scream with his own. I arched my back, lifting off the bed. He lifted me to his lap, where I took control, dragging his orgasm out of him with my nails down his back and my teeth in his shoulder. He held onto my back and bucked under the mix of pleasure and pain.

"I'm going to... Fuck!" Miguel's scream turned into a growl, twisting into a shuttering moan.

I rocked my hips until he tapped my legs and fell to the side, dragging me with him. We stayed twisted around each other until my foot went numb. Lazily, Miguel shifted on the bed, pulling my leg out from under him with weak arms. I rolled onto my back and stretched, glancing at the clock.

"We still have five minutes left," I said, nudging Miguel and wiggling my eyebrows.

"I distinctly remember you telling me that witches did not have time to laze about all day, having sex," he answered, propping himself onto his elbow. "Sofia got back almost twenty minutes ago. Cisco and Philip got back ten minutes ago."

I cringed and climbed up to the window overlooking my driveway. "Shit. Do you think they heard us?"

"Yes!" A collective answer came from outside, below my window. I ducked down, laughing.

"They've been hanging around on the front porch," Miguel laughed. "They have beers. Do you want to go join or stay in bed?"

I grinned. "Join."

Drinks, laughter, Cisco talking non-stop about the campus, asking if I want to carpool, and me saying not a chance. May and Ben showed up after the new Master had arrived. They'd been camped out in the treeline outside the house he purchased in Point Grey. Mairi was there with Samuel. Demetrius arrived without the flare he was hoping for but brought two dozen vampires with him. Some May knew from previous hunts. She'd already emailed Ben with the information specs on the guy and his crew. Ben and May were flying out tomorrow for two weeks.

"Miguel, would you have a moment to speak in private?" Ben asked.

"Of course," Miguel answered. He held out his hand to me and brought me inside with him. Ben didn't question it, so neither did I. "What's up?"

"I would like to formally request permission to return to your territory after my holiday with May," Ben said, to my surprise. From what I had heard from Cisco and Sofia, Ben was a lone wolf. He lived in Caser's territory and joined his Pack for celebrations while in town but was gone to the wind and wild more often than not. "Perhaps you have time to discuss when we are finished here? Or may I formally request an audience with Pack upon my return?"

"You're welcome here, any time, Ben, you know that," Miguel replied.

"I would like to remain here, not as a visitor," Ben said, his voice deeper, almost shy. "It has been many moons since I've formally asked to join a Pack, but I would very much enjoy returning to my people, and this is where I'd like to be." Ben glanced at the door, sighing. "There is someone I'd like to put down roots for. She is one who asks no questions but would survive my life." Both Miguel and I smiled. May. "I have no wishes to challenge for an Alpha position but would request I am considered for a Hunter position. A guardian of my people would fit me just fine. This Pack could use us, Miguel. We have the power to bring them back to the true ways of Lycan. I would like to be part of that."

"Welcome home, Benedicto, first Hunter of the Noire Lune Pack." Miguel pulled Ben into his arms awkwardly. Ben was a hulk of a man but melted into that hug as if he hadn't had one in years.

"Thank you, Miguel, I won't let you down." Ben turned to me, tipping his head. "Ailis, I shall endeavor to protect you as my own blooded Pack."

"Philip is my second, guided by Cisco. Philip is in waiting and will rise to Lycaon when I step down," Miguel said. "Sofia has put out the call to our people in Mexico for Elders. Training and history are sorely missing here. They will never become a true Pack without purpose."

"If I may be so bold?" Ben asked.

"Please, Ben. Always speak freely with me. Lycaon title or not, we are family," Miguel answered.

"Bringing Elders will help the younger pups grow and give Pack a place to seek guidance and find courage, but I'd suggest bringing over a few Sentinels. Keep Demetrius in his place from day one."

"What's a Sentinel?" I asked.

"Similar to a spy, I suppose," Ben answered. "They answer to the Warrior of the Pack. Their sole job is to gather information and strike under the cover of darkness. They are the ghosts of Pack."

"Is it wise to invite so many people we don't know into our city?" I asked.

"They come on a visitor's permit, so to speak," Ben replied, and I relaxed a little, knowing we weren't just opening the door for anyone to move in. "There is a lineup for this Pack, knowing the new Lycaon is from the Los Luna Pack. Those coming will already know it will be similar to how Caser runs his territory. I doubt any who come will step too far out of line."

"Touch base with Sofia. She's holding lead Warrior until I step down," Miguel answered. "Caser gave her a list of Pack from Mexico, his recommendations of those seeking new territory, but there are a few names she will want to vet before extending an invite."

"Wait a minute," I interrupted. "You mentioned it would take years of training before you stepped down. Sofia is staying here the entire time? Is it fair to ask that of her?"

"I wasn't house hunting for myself, Lish. The moment Cisco asked to remain, I started looking for apartments for Sofia. They are a package deal and have been since day one. I won't separate them," Miguel replied. "Sofia formally requested to remain while Caser was here. Sofia and Cisco checked out a few apartments yesterday with Philip. She snagged a loft down in Blood Square, skipping the wait list thanks to Philip."

"This is good, Miguel. When I first arrived, I had little hope for this Pack. But tonight, while I watched over the transition of a new Master, it felt right."

"How the hell did you stay under their radar?" I asked.

"Oh, we didn't." Ben laughed. "Samuel brought lawn chairs, an icebox of drinks, holy water and food. He handed out a box of freshly blessed wooden stakes to make a show of it. The man is all flair for a guardian."

Ben pulled out his stake from his back pocket. Demetrius' name was carved into the side. "We made it known they were being watched. Pack, hunter, guardian, and wild witch, all watching as one collective. Two shifters showed up, and Samuel gave them drinks and a seat. Demetrius knew we were there and didn't appear to appreciate moving into a city he thought he'd have control over like his predecessor did. The only way this city stays safe is if we all find a way to work together, to hold each other accountable."

"I agree," Miguel said. "Go, enjoy your evening. We can speak formally tomorrow. Let us enjoy the night while we still can."

He tipped his head to both of us and reached for the door. "Thank you for this, Miguel. Having a place I belong again feeds my wolf."

We watched Ben step back out onto my front porch, and with one nod, cheers filled the night air. May feigned knowledge but smiled at the news. I wouldn't tell if she didn't. I curled into Miguel and listened as hunting stories were shared. Cisco retold the story of my first hunt, only this time I was much more fearless. May said she vomited on the first vampire she hunted, making her brother sick in the process. She'd apologized to the creature before staking him. She was seven at the time, so it didn't count. Sofia bragged about her apartment while Cisco counted down the days until he got the master bedroom back in the basement. Philip cried several times, not out of fear or sadness. Joy fell from his eyes for finally feeling what Pack was meant to be — family, safety, home. This time, no one ignored his cries. He was loved until laughter replaced the tears. Every fifteen minutes, Sofia's phone pinged with an update from the scouts she had running through the territory. Updates, she called them. Training, Cisco added, with my cat on his lap. Either way, I felt a little safer knowing Pack had their watchful eyes on the monsters. For once, I didn't have to do it alone.

My house was still full. My heart was even fuller. In the distance, wolves howled and answered by growls I didn't even want to know about. Miguel wasn't worried, so I wasn't going to let myself get worked up. Demetrius' name came up several times, but I didn't bother worrying about problems that weren't currently sitting on my lap. I let myself enjoy one night because nights of peace were far and few between for little witches who put their noses where they didn't belong. On this rare occasion of sitting outside when the moon was high, I'd relish every minute of it, surrounded by those fated to tear the hearts out of beasts who threatened my safety. I didn't know what tomorrow would bring, but I'd have a Pack of beasts at my back and a cat at my ankles. And in this day and age, it didn't really get any better than that. What more could a cursed witch ask for?

The next monsters who came for me would soon find out, payback's a witch and this witch had one hell of a memory.

Sign up for our newsletter and find out about all our romance book releases, eBook sales and promotions, sneak peeks and FREE romance books!

Want to see more from this author? Here's a taster for you to enjoy!

The Cursed: A Death Witch
L.A. Kennedy

Excerpt

I stared down at the third body of the night. Her blood soaked the cold concrete around her. There was no way I wouldn't be bringing a piece of her home with me. The sharp metallic scent of her blood hung in the air, mixing with the trash strewn about, making her body smell like the end of the day at the meat market. Death was never dignified, whether you were surrounded by your loved ones or tossed away like garbage. We all met our maker the same way, scared and alone.

Her wavy copper hair was styled in such a way as to reveal the startled look on her thin, tense face. It was the only part of her body that hadn't been ruined by the slaughter. Her pale skin was already graying from the cruel hand that had been dealt to her. Speckles of blood mixed with her freckles, and I held back the urge to clean them off with my hand. Her wide green eyes had seen her attacker, her fear forever frozen and staring back at me. The sparkle in her eyes was long gone, leaving a dead and empty gaze. It chilled me to the bone. The clover pin—which hadn't brought her any luck—attached to the collar of her once-white shirt, glinted under the flashes of police cruisers and unnecessary paramedics. She wasn't taking a ride in the bus tonight. Her chauffeur would come with a full-length zipper and handles.

That was the face of Rowan Sage, an earth witch, and it would haunt me until something worse took up her place in my memories. Given my chosen lifestyle, it wouldn't take long before I moved on from Rowan to something or someone new. Little by little, with each new scene I was called to, I created stains that hounded me while I slept and, at times, froze me during my waking hours. Some horrors never left, and until the sun swallowed the earth, there'd always be nights like this, reasons I slept with a gun and a Hellhound in training.

I crouched down, the movement wafting her last moments up to my nose. I swallowed my urge to gag and picked up her bag, standing and taking a few steps back, out of reach from the perfume of the dead. With gloved hands, I dug through her black bat-shaped purse. Nothing stood out as being reason enough to kill her in a dingy back alley. Handmade lip balm from the witches' market, a wallet with three cards and her level-one Coven membership, fifty bucks, house keys, and an uninvoked hex bag.

"Why you, of all people?" I whispered, scanning the victim once again. I took another look at the alley and wondered if there was any significance to the location. Aside from a fresh body, nothing stood out. Was it a case of the wrong place, wrong time? Or was she the target?

Level-one witches, especially earth witches, weren't high on hit lists these days. A couple decades ago, perhaps, but not today. I put her purse into a brown paper evidence bag, her identification in my hand, and jotted down her information for my report. I passed her driver's license and the brown bag to a nearby officer, who would tag it. After two decades and some change, her life was snuffed out. *What a waste.*

Her body had been discovered while I was at the second crime scene. I'd been called in by Mannix after the first body. He had sensed hell but hadn't been able to find traces of a demon or the energy left behind by another magic user. When I'd arrived, I hadn't seen any hints of hell or magic, either. Hope had called me to the scene, but curiosity kept me there once I came up empty of answers. Hope that such carnage was the work of the pits and not man. It was easier to sleep at night, thinking hell was responsible for all of humanity's problems. If we just kept the gates closed, all would be right in the world. *As if things would ever be so simple.* The truth was, mankind did worse to each other than any damned or cursed ever did. Demons didn't rob grocery stores, kill for a wallet with twenty bucks in it, or shoot up schoolyards. People did. But it didn't stop us from blaming the beasts, even in the face of evidence to the contrary. Of every case I'd been called into, where the guilty claimed they were possessed, only one had ever been able to use that as a defense. The fact is, we're more than capable of horror without hell needing to tinker with our morality. The best thing a demon could do to guarantee our demise was to sit back and watch us go to work on each other. We did all the heavy lifting for them.

Sure, hope had brought me to a dank alley, but I knew I'd leave without any of my own. Nights like these took it away and left me with the raw reality of the hell we all had created without the help of the pits. Some days, I really hated this world. But the alternative was a cage in hell, which wasn't much better.

I stepped back from the body and blurred my vision, seeing through my aura, a witch's sixth sense. Rowan's soul was long gone, but imprints of the night, those who had come and gone, still lingered. Magic in the air prickled my arms and pulled my attention in circles. My eyes roamed the backstreet, picking up hints of emotion and stains so deep and evil they'd take another few decades to fade. I scanned for the strongest imprints, like picking through a trash can for a missing diamond. Bits of magic and old taint floated in the breeze. It snaked along the ground and held onto the walls like chipped paint. The alley was a popular walkthrough, leaving too much of one thing and not enough of why I had been called to the new scene. I frowned when I didn't find what Mannix had been hoping for. I had come here for one reason and came up short. There were two reasons, if I was counting the memories I was making, that I didn't want.

"*Inretio*," I whispered, using my aura to send a net out into the alley to trap demonic energy. It was a new spell taught to me by my grandfather, Samuel. As a retired guardian, he was a walking, talking book of spells that I'd find nowhere else. The spell was still new enough that it felt uncomfortable to hold onto. It turned my hands cold and fingertips numb. I could feel every magic and emotion that had walked the alley for the last week, as though they were all here at once. As I suspected, I saw no hints of fresh black taint. The alley would look like spilled ink in water if a demon had been here recently. I would have been able to see his footsteps, as though his taint was burned into the ground. But I hadn't picked up any hellish happenings at the other two sites, either. With a wave of my hand, I dropped the spell to the ground, refocused my eyes and pulled my shields back into place. My soul breathed a sign of relief, cut off from the night's carnage.

"I'm ready." I motioned for Mannix, who had emptied the area of souls for me. I didn't need everyone clear of me to do the job, but the combined emotions of onlookers and police made my skin crawl when I was using aura magic.

"Please tell me you've got something, Ailis." He sounded as tired as I felt. Seven in the morning was a painful hour to be awake for those of us who hadn't yet been to bed.

"Like the other two scenes, there's something I can't quite put my finger on." I pursed my lips, thinking. I glanced around the scene once more, trying to piece it together. "Zero witnesses at all three scenes. It's not unusual in a city. It's just odd that three scenes didn't turn up a single set of eyes. None of us want to stumble into someone else's business if that business is ending lives, but it was one hell of a busy night downtown for there to be not a single onlooker. Someone had to see or hear something."

"We're canvasing and checking out the neighboring security tapes. See who came and went, but this alley is a void, like most of them. There's nothing down here of value, except the victim, to keep an eye on," he answered. "What are you thinking?"

"Besides there being eyes out there who likely saw this go down but are too scared to open their mouths, I'm thinking about what is missing from this scene," I replied.

"What do you mean, something is missing?"

"Whenever we're dealing with hell, it's common to feel hatred, pleasure, arousal, and absolute delight in the carnage they're causing. But this isn't hell, Mannix. I can feel the emotions I usually feel from a demon, but it's missing the actual hell part. There's no scent of the pits, no telltale demonic smells, no taint crawling over my skin, no fresh demonic energy. I can feel evil, but it wasn't caused by the pits. The energy is similar, but it isn't quite the same. There were souls attached to whoever did this."

"But I can feel it. I can feel hell," he replied. "I can smell hell. Why can't you?"

"You can feel and smell Rowan, as can I," I corrected him. "She's a level-one earth witch. I'm guessing what you're feeling and smelling is related to the circle she tried to set, and the lingering magic in the air as she pulled on the energy from hell." I led Mannix back to the body and pointed at the blood splatters on the ground. "These drops of blood are inconsistent with her wounds and the rest of the blood patterns. She was stabbed multiple times, and it sprayed as though the stabs were one after the other. I'd be surprised if the medical examiner came back with only one weapon used." I crouched down and lifted her left hand. "She has a fresh slice across her palm. It's too clean and shallow for it to be a defensive wound. I'd bet my cauldron there's a small blade kicking around somewhere, and it'll be hers." I stood and stepped back, walking in a circle around her. "I can feel the lingering power in the air. She set a circle, thinking it would help her. Whatever came for her, she thought her magic would save her. She had enough time to think she could protect herself. If this were a demon with her name on his list, a level-one wouldn't have time to scream, let alone try to set a circle."

"Unless she wasn't his target. If she was a bystander, she may have had time to set her circle and caught his attention when she pulled on energy," Mannix suggested. "We both know a powerful enough demon can take down a circle, especially one set by a level-one."

"True. But if a demon, powerful enough to take down a circle, did this, then where are the rest of the bodies?" I asked. "Mannix, we're downtown. Bealtaine festivals have been raging since noon. Between the festival and the after-parties, there are thousands of souls, ripe for the picking, all over the streets. People from all over the world are visiting for the celebrations. If this was a demon, we'd have found her sooner by simply following the trail of bodies he'd leave on the ground. Demons don't cherry-pick. They don't kill a few randoms and pack it in. They kill everything with a pulse until they're stopped, or they have what they come here for."

"Unless she owed a debt. Demons pop up all the time to collect souls and don't go on a killing spree. This, what happened to her, may have been a message to *her*, nothing more. I've been to plenty of scenes where demons took their sweet-assed time, carving chunks off of their victims, spending hours tormenting them before killing them."

"Three unrelated folks owing debts to the same demon in one night?" I asked. "The odds of that happening are astronomical. Demons don't save up their collections for a one-night grocery shop. They come the moment the soul is due for the taking."

"Fuck," Mannix groaned. The hope for simple answers faded, replaced with the frustration of the unknown. "I'm sorry I called you away from May Day," he said for the third time tonight. "I owe you."

"Don't worry about it. I'll be issuing an invoice for my consult," I replied. "I'm sorry I don't have the answers you were looking for."

"What are your thoughts?" He motioned at the body. "If you had to guess. I need to go back to my captain with something, anything. Empty-handed is not how I want to start my meeting with Holland. I don't get paid the big bucks to be behind the Eightball."

"Hate to say this, but you're not hunting a demon or magic user. My money is on humans doing all three murders," I answered. "A demon would have ravaged the soul completely. It would take days for that kind of torment to fade. Terrified souls stain the very air. We would have felt the residual energy like a slap across the face as soon as we stepped into this alley. But there's nothing here. It doesn't even smell like the pits. The only fresh odors are the trash cans, mossy earth magic, blood, and us. There are hints here and there from odors long past, but nothing recent enough to give me pause. Aside from the dead body, it feels like every other alley in the city."

"I'm not picking up any other unnatural, either," Mannix said, and I glared at the word he used. "What? That's the official name of a magic user. It's better than what some people call us."

"Metaphysical or magic user are the PC terms. Get with the times, witch," I replied. "But I agree. Every magic user I know would leave an imprint of their energy behind, and there's nothing fresh here, just like the first two bodies you found. I can pick up a little of the emotion left behind—hate, anger, arousal, but it's not strong enough to be hell. It's no stronger than a customer service line the day after a Black Friday sale."

Mannix opened his notepad and read his notes. "At the first scene, a young shifter, the only energy I felt was the victim. He was attacked from behind and stabbed in the heart. The coup de grâce was removing his head. The second scene, an elemental witch still in training, throat slit and stabbed in the heart. No residual energies outside of the victim's."

Mannix had written down the same thing I had, almost verbatim. "My point exactly. What demon does that? They don't stalk prey unless it is the one who called them, and the demon has no choice but to smoke them out, but they still leave a trail of bodies behind them while they are topside. Neither of the witches have knocked on hell's door even once. There is no debt they'd have. We'd smell the taint if that were the case. And the shifter, even if he somehow figured out how to do it, he didn't smell like he's been ringing a demon's doorbell."

"Shit," he groaned. "When I found nothing at the first scene, I hoped you would. I thought it may have been a demon I was unfamiliar with."

"Trust me, Mannix, you'd have known it was a demon even if they were unknown to you. For this, you need a bloodhound, not a witch. Track the smells, not the magic. It'll lead you to those responsible."

"He's not on shift for another week. His wife had twins a couple of weeks ago," Mannix replied.

"Tell Arlow I said congratulations." I smiled at the news. There were so few of Arlow's kind out there. Bloodhounds were naturally born, not cursed or infected. It had been the luck of the Gods when he had found another and married her. "Twin bloodhounds? Mercy, he's in for a fun few years. I went to high school with triplets. They were a nightmare for their parents until they outgrew puberty and could control their tracking impulses."

"Maybe he'll come out for a few hours," Mannix said.

"Bribe him with chocolate tarts from the bakery near Samuel's house. That's how I convinced him to track a troll when no one else would help me. His wife doesn't let him eat sugar," I answered. "It works every time."

"I'll give him a call," he replied. "Thanks for coming out. Send your invoice straight to me. I'll have accounting issue a direct deposit."

At the tape blocking off the scene, I pulled off my gloves and paper booties and tossed them into a biohazard bucket at the end of the alley. Mannix followed me to my car, jotting down a few more notes. I paused before opening my car door. Like spiders dancing down my spine, I felt eyes on me. Onlookers crowded the sidewalk and huddled in front of neighboring businesses. I motioned to the cameras above us.

"We're already on it, Ailis," Mannix said.

I leaned in. "Check these ones against the others. Look at the crowd and see if the same face pops up. You know what they say about the crazies."

"They like to watch," he replied. "I'll let you know what we find."

"Good luck. If you need me, you know where to find me." I got into my car, hoping he wouldn't need me for another crime scene.

I checked my phone and started my car. I missed a dozen text messages from Cisco, who had been at Samuel's Bealtaine celebration with me before I got the call from Mannix. He'd sent me photos of what I was missing out on. A pang of envy laced through me, but it was quickly silenced by a photo of all the cookies Cisco had smuggled out of the party in a Tupperware container. Miguel had texted me once he got home from Pack, saying to wake him when I arrived. That last message soothed my soul. From horror to home. Sometimes, love was enough to chase away the awfulness of the world. I sent him a text saying I was heading back to the house.

The drive was a blur of early morning traffic, but most were coming into the city while I was heading out. The radio played the same rhetoric from the Humans for Humans group as they did daily. Every turn of the dial had the hate group blaring. They were using the brutalization of three people as their soapbox today. The group had been around for years, and it didn't look like they'd be going away any time soon. They were one in a sea of organizations, all aimed at keeping the city clean of monsters. Fear breeds contempt, and contempt is deadly in the wrong hands. HFH members were usually on the news every night, stirring an already boiling pot. It was hard not to hate them with the same ferociousness they showed anyone who wasn't pure human.

I pulled into my vehicle-clogged driveway and smiled. Sofia, Ben, May, Cisco, Philip, and Miguel's vehicles were parked in perfect lines, each depending on who would be leaving first. I parked at the end, behind Cisco. If I was in the way, they'd move it. I grabbed my bag and stepped into the chilled morning air with the first smile of the day. It never got old, having a full house. On days I had my fill of people, I'd go to my office or bedroom, or Miguel and I would go for a walk. Those days were far and few, and they usually revolved around something evil that had come knocking or swallowing up one of my students. More times than not, being close to the others smoothed out the wrinkles of my sadness. I understood now why being a member of Pack was so important to them all, why they gathered in groups at every opportunity. When you fought a holy war every day and touched hell around every corner, having a family reminded you of why you kept going back out to do it again. Even though I only sprouted fur on weeks I didn't shave my legs, they still treated me like I was part of their family and welcomed me with the same care and love they had for each other.

When I opened my front door, I was bombarded with sounds that warmed me to my core. Inside, a chorus of laughter and chatter flowed from the kitchen. The smell of breakfast filled my nose, and my stomach growled instantly. I kicked off my shoes and headed straight for my shower. I smelled like dumpsters and death and half a bottle of perfume. It was not an agreeable scent. I reached the foot of my stairs before Miguel came from the kitchen with two cookies in his hand. He followed me up the stairs and into my bedroom. With the door closed, the emotions I had held in from seeing death up close and personal rolled from my eyes. I sat on the foot of my bed and tucked myself into his arms. Hugs, love and cookies—the trifecta of soul bandages.

"It was awful," I whispered around the tightness in my throat. "My heart hurts for the victim's families. One minute, their loved ones are here, and the next, Mannix is knocking on their doors. Dear god, they removed the head of the first victim. His family won't even be able to see him again while they say goodbye. The last victim, I lost count of how many times she had been stabbed."

Miguel hugged me a little tighter. "Death, whether expected or not, is painful. That it was done in such a horrid way is deplorable. I'm sorry you had to see that."

"It's the needless death that hurts me the most. I don't understand why we do this to each other," I answered. "Some days, I really hate the world we live in. Some of us are stronger than others, and we don't use that strength to protect each other. We conquer, we take, we kill. I don't get it."

"The world is filled with monsters, Lish. It always has been and always will be. I'm sorry you had to experience it up close," he replied.

"Why can't we just help each other?" I asked.

"I really wish it were that simple. In our world, Lish, most often, keeping your head down is how you stay alive."

I sighed. "I don't think I could ever just keep my head down. All too well, I know what it's like to be hunted. I couldn't just watch someone else go through that. I don't know how so many others can."

"I love you for your soft heart, but it's also why you're usually up shit creek and running for your life more often than anyone I know."

I shrugged. "We all need hobbies."

"Let's get you cleaned up," Miguel said, helping me to my feet. "You'll feel better once you can't smell it anymore. We'll get some food into you, and if you're up to it, we'll spend some time with people who care about you."

"I'm sorry. I must stink," I replied. "I sprayed myself with perfume before I came in."

"I've smelled a lot worse," he answered. "You don't have to hose yourself down with fruity scents before coming inside. This is your home. I am here whether you smell like you crawled through a gutter or daisies."

"You can still smell it under my body spray, can't you?" I asked, and he nodded.

"You smell like a dead body walking through the perfume department at the mall," he answered, making me smile. "I can also smell the donuts Mannix always bribes you with, coffee, and the ink you used to make your notes. Not much escapes the nose of a Lycan."

My clothes went into the hamper, and Miguel got my shower ready, climbing in with me. He washed the smell from my hair and body, gentle with every touch. He had this way of knowing exactly what touch I needed. Miguel knew my soul as well as I did. He wrapped his arms around me from behind and kissed my shoulder. He waited for me to respond before going any further. I pushed my back into him, hinting at my need. The memories of tonight would always be there, but I wanted to feel something good that would replace the heaviness in my heart.

Miguel turned me around to face him before pinning me against the shower wall with his hips. He moved my hand to meet his arm behind my back, locking it in place, holding my body open for him. He pressed his knee between my thighs, pushing my legs apart until I was straddling his thigh. Before I could say a word, his mouth was on mine, muffling my warning of being heard by a houseful of people. Miguel never cared, nor did his Pack. He lifted his knee between my legs, inching it up until my breath caught. I closed my mouth to keep my moans to myself.

Miguel leaned into my ear, licking my lobe. "Oh, Lish, you can try to keep quiet, but you'll scream for me today. I promise you that."

My knees buckled, and I jerked when my groin made contact. Miguel's knee kept me standing while I ground myself against him. He kissed my neck, and I bit my lip. He ran his free hand up and down my side, inching closer to the swell of my breast, teasing my nipple, before sliding his hand down to my hips, thighs and finally, my core. His hiss filled my ear. I was ready. I was waiting. Without warning, he dropped my trapped wrist and yanked me to his chest. He pushed his tongue into my mouth as he gripped my thighs and lifted me to his hips. I wrapped my arms and legs around him, bruising my lips on his. He shifted me on his hips, pulling himself back, and lowered me slowly onto his hardness.

Our groans filled the shower as he slid into me. Inch by inch, he entered me. My nails dug into his shoulders as I stretched around him. My mind and body filled with instant need. Miguel leaned me into the wall until my body accepted all of him. I squirmed against his stillness.

"Please," I said into his mouth.

"Please, what?" he asked, pulling from my kiss with a teasing grin, almost malicious in his intent to tease me. He held me tighter, keeping me from moving against his body. He controlled every movement I tried to make. "Say the words. I want to hear you."

"Fuck me," I said, my nails dragging up his back as I struggled to grind against him.

"Hold on, Lish," he said, and I pressed my chest into him, wrapping my arms tightly around his neck.

Miguel worked his hips slowly until he knew I was ready. His pace quickened, and my eyes rolled back. Leaning into me, holding my thighs, he lifted and pressed forward at once. Our rhythm echoed in the shower, skin against skin, moans, and my demands.

"Close," I groaned. "Please, don't stop."

My breaths came out as sharp gasps as the heat built in my stomach. Miguel pressed me into the wall, knowing I'd be lost to my orgasm soon and he'd have to keep me upright.

"Come for me," Miguel said, his pace quickening. "I want to feel you come."

I squeezed my eyes shut as his pace shifted into something frantic. He was as close as I was. His fingernails dug into my thighs, and his teeth bit into my shoulder. I finally screamed as my pleasure smashed down on us both. I worked my hips against his, matching his speed and intensity. Miguel's voice boomed through the bathroom. He drove himself as deep as he could go and pumped his orgasm to the surface. His heart pounded against my chest, but he didn't lose his rhythm until my orgasm had run its full course. He dragged every inch of pleasure from me until I was nothing more than one long and shaking moan.

Miguel grabbed onto the towel bar to keep himself from falling over. He helped me slide down his body to my feet, pressing himself against me to hold me standing. I wrapped my arms around him and settled into the afterglow. Our breathing calmed as we both slowly came back down to earth. He lifted my chin and kissed me softly.

"I love you," I said, tucking myself into his chest, his heart under my ear.

When our limbs could move without feeling like jelly, Miguel helped me out of the shower. I was past the point of exhaustion. My feet shuffled, and my legs felt like I had been running full speed for an hour. He skipped the usual conversation about his day and mine, knowing I'd have nothing to offer him with my head still in the clouds. Instead, he dried my hair, braided it, and helped me pull on my pajamas. Rather than heading straight to bed, I waited at my bedroom door for him.

"I just want to say good night first," I said, smiling.

"One cup of tea and into bed, or you'll be a zombie for class later." Miguel grabbed a pair of joggers from the foot of the bed and pulled them on before we hit the hallway.

I cringed at the thought of leaving the comfort of home today. "Thankfully, I only have evening class tonight. Ziggy is helping me show my students how to identify taint on objects and isn't willing to come until his shop closes."

"I really wish you'd stop playing with fire. Ziggtmoy is a demon."

"He's in recovery," I answered and chuckled to myself. "He's a card-carrying member of society, Miguel, who happens to have once been a demon."

"Recovery? He's literally wearing a person."

"So are you, wolf," I countered, and he rolled his eyes. "Don't throw stones. The same magic that keeps Ziggy in his meat suit keeps your wolf at bay."

"Apples to oranges," he replied. "I'm not a demon."

"But at one time, you all were considered demons," I reminded him. "When you die, you become a Hellhound. Your soul will live in hell. How many religions out there think Hellhounds are demons? All of them."

Miguel finally put his hands in the air, giving up on an argument neither of us would win. It wasn't a conversation we would see eye to eye on. Miguel, in human form and wolf, hunted demons. It was in his blood to hate them. I wasn't their biggest fan either. But any demon not wanting me dead and willing to help me in exchange for a slab of chocolate from the witch's market and not a chunk of my soul was worth programming into my phone. Ziggy had helped me more times than I could count and had never asked for a payment that came in the form of skinning my soul alive. Sure, he was a demon, and I'd never turn my back to him, but it was hard to be high and mighty when I smelled like a witchy teabag steeped in hell. I was as damned as they come.

We stepped into a full kitchen, and I grinned. The night washed away with a sigh and smiles as I was noticed. The conversation didn't stall. Cisco pushed out a chair, and I was invited into the group as though I had been there my entire life. May, the resident vampire hunter and partner of a Pack member, sat across from me, arguing with Cisco on the benefits of keeping a vampire hunt old school because technology failed more times than the reliable wooden stake. Cisco, on the other hand, thought differently. He was all about the latest tech. One glance around my house said he had upgraded every inch with top-of-the-line security. He had a thing for telling the lights to turn on and off while not moving a muscle. I had made fun of him for a week for it, but secretly, I loved not having to get out of bed to turn off my bedroom lights. I'd never admit it to him, though.

Breakfast came and went with me asleep on the couch. The noise in the background felt as warm as my blanket and as heavy as my cat. They whispered about the murders, speculating on motives while I let myself drop face-first into sleep. Unless the house caught fire or a demon walked through the door, I wasn't getting up for anything outside my alarm. Before the last voice faded, Miguel lifted me off the couch and carried me to bed, my cat in tow.

About the Author

L.A. Kennedy, beyond the story…

L.A. Kennedy is a Canadian born writer, living in the ever-growing city of Vancouver, Canada. Here, she spends her days getting lost in the beauty of reading and writing. L.A. Kennedy mainly writes fictional books. And can be found researching myth, folklore, and everything in between, with a special interest in edge-of-your-seat paranormal romance. L.A. Kennedy can be found behind a mountain of books, on any given Sunday.

L.A. Kennedy's writing credits include two hit series that mix mystery, horror, paranormal romance, fantasy, and intrigue.

L.A. Kennedy loves to hear from readers. You can find her contact information, website details and author profile page at https://www.firstforromance.com

ENTWINED PUBLISHING